"Scotland's complex history is as strong a character as the hero and heroine, and Joyce seamlessly merges the historical details of Robert the Bruce's rise to power with a captive/captor, forbidden love story. Highland history sings on the pages through Joyce's potent prose."
—*RT Book Reviews* on *A Rose in the Storm*

"As dangerous and intriguing as readers could desire. This is a tale reminiscent of genre classics, with its lush and fascinating historical details and sensuality."
—*RT Book Reviews* on *Surrender*

"First-rate...featuring multidimensional protagonists and sweeping drama...Joyce's tight plot and vivid cast combine for a romance that's just about perfect."
—*Publishers Weekly*, starred review, on *The Perfect Bride*

"Truly a stirring story with wonderfully etched characters...romance at its best."
—*Booklist* on *The Perfect Bride*

"Romance veteran Joyce brings her keen sense of humor and storytelling prowess to bear on her witty, fully formed characters."
—*Publishers Weekly* on *A Lady at Last*

"Sexual tension crackles... in this sizzling, action-packed adventure."
—*Library Journal* on *Dark Seduction*

BRENDA JOYCE

A Sword Upon the Rose

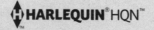

Recycling programs
for this product may
not exist in your area.

ISBN-13: 978-0-373-77885-0

A SWORD UPON THE ROSE

Printed in U.S.A.

For Rick Christen—
Because what happened in Vegas did not stay in Vegas,
Because second chances can really happen,
Because two is better than one,
Because I love you,
Always

A Sword
Upon the Rose

CHAPTER ONE

Brodie Castle, Scotland—December 1, 1307

FIRE RAGED EVERYWHERE, a blazing inferno. Men screamed in agony, horses whinnied in terror, and swords rang.

The smoke cleared. Horror overcame Alana.

A manor had been set afire, and before its walls, men fought with sword and pike, both on foot and from horseback. Some were English knights, mail-clad, others, bare-legged Highlanders. An English knight was stabbed through by a Highlander's blade; a huge destrier went down, impaled through the barrel, a Highlander leaping off....

Where was she?

Alana was confused. The ground tilted wildly beneath her feet. She thought she fell, and she clawed the ground, looking up.

Amidst the brutal fighting, she saw one man. The warrior was on foot, bloody sword in hand, his long dark hair whipping about his face, his leine riding his bare thighs, a fur flung back over his broad shoulders. He was shouting to the Highland warriors, urging them on—every man bloodied and desperate and savagely fighting for his life now.

The tides of the battle changed, some of the English soldiers fleeing, some of the knights deciding to gallop away in retreat. But the dark-haired Highlander did not cease, now engaged in fierce combat with an English knight. Their swords clashed viciously, time and again.

Alana tensed. What had she just heard?

Her gaze flew to the burning manor. A woman was screaming for help from inside. And did she hear children crying, as well?

Somehow Alana got to her feet. But the dark-haired Highlander was already at the burning manor door.

Smoke burned through the wood, and flames shot out of an adjacent window. He pushed his shoulder hard against the door, oblivious to the smoke, the heat and the flames....

Suddenly she was afraid for him. As suddenly he turned, and for one moment, she could see his hard, determined face. His blue eyes pierced hers.

And then he was rushing into the burning manor. A moment later he reappeared, carrying a small child. A woman and another child ran outside with him.

Relief overcame her. He had rescued the woman and her children—they would not die.

The roof crashed in. More flames shot into the sky. He covered the child with his body, now on the ground. Burning timbers fell around him.

Then he leaped up, racing away to some safer distance from the burning house where he returned the child to its weeping mother. He turned, his gaze searching the woods where Alana hid—as if to look for her.

As he did, a man with shaggy red hair, another Highlander from the same army, came up behind him, raising a dagger at the warrior's back.

"Behind you!" Alana screamed.

The dark-haired Highlander must have sensed danger, for he whirled as the dagger came down. He did not scream—he stiffened, the dagger penetrating his chest. And then his sword was cutting through the air, faster than her eyes could see.

The red-haired traitor fell to the ground, stabbed through his chest. The Highlander delivered another clearly fatal blow, and paused, towering over his victim.

He staggered and fell....

"Alana! Wake up! Yer frightening me!"

Alana gasped and tasted mud and snow. And for one more moment, she could not move, overwhelmed by the sight of the battle—the treachery—she had just witnessed.

The hair was raised on her skin, her nape prickling. She had the urge to retch.

"Alana! Alana! Quick! Before someone sees!" her grandmother cried.

Alana became aware of her surroundings now. She was lying in the snow, facedown. Her cheek was freezing, as were her hands, for her mittens were stiff and frozen. She did not know how long she had been lying there.

She fought for air, for composure, waiting for the nausea to pass. Her nape stopped prickling. Her stomach calmed.

She inhaled, but her relief was short-lived as she sat up with her grandmother's help. Dismay consumed her.

She was near the stream that ran just outside the castle walls in the spring. It had been a clear and cold winter day and she had gone outside the castle with some of the maids' children, who had wanted to play.

She must have frightened them when she collapsed; they must have rushed to find Alana's grandmother.

She stared at the stream. It was mostly frozen now, but patches of water where the ice was melting were visible. Dear God. The water…even now, it beckoned, dark and mysterious, offering up secrets no soul had any right to….

She hadn't had a vision in months. She had been praying she would never have one again. She jerked her gaze away from the dangerous water, releasing her grandmother and standing up.

Her grandmother stared, her lined face filled with worry. Eleanor quickly pulled Alana's wool mantle more securely about her. Alana saw now that they were not alone.

Duncan of Frendraught's son was standing behind her grandmother, his pale face twisted with fear and revulsion. "What did you see?" Godfrey demanded, blue eyes wide. He was wrapped in a heavy fur, and his booted feet were braced in a belligerent stance.

"I saw nothing," she lied quickly, lifting her chin. They lived in the same place, but they were not related, and although they were on the same side in the war that raged across the land, he was her enemy.

"She tripped and fell," Eleanor said firmly. Her tone was filled with an authority she did not have.

He sneered. "I'll ask you again—what did you see, Alana?" There was warning in his tone.

She trembled as she stood. "I saw your father, victorious in battle," she lied.

Their gazes locked. He stared, clearly trying to decide if she told the truth or not. "If you're lying to me, you will pay, witch," he spat. And then he strode away.

She sagged against Eleanor, relieved he was gone. What had she just seen?

"Why do you fight him? When he can strike you down if he wishes?" Eleanor cried.

Alana took her hand. "He goads me, Gran."

Her grandmother stared at her with worry. Eleanor Fitzhugh was a tiny woman, her eyes blue, her hair gray. But she was as determined as she was small. Her body had aged, but her wits had not. Alana did not want her to worry, but she always did. She was the mother Alana did not have, even though they were not actually related.

"He is rude and arrogant, but he is master here," Eleanor said, shaking her head. "And Godfrey will have a fit if we don't have his supper ready. But, Alana? You must not let your hatred show."

It was impossible, Alana thought. They had had this same conversation many, many times. She hated Godfrey not merely because he goaded her to no end, and not because he hated her, but because one day, he would be lord of Brodie Castle.

"I do try," she said.

"You must try harder," Eleanor returned. Though she was sixty and Alana just twenty, she put her arm around her, helping her back toward the castle's front gates, as if their ages were reversed. But Alana was weak-legged and still slightly queasy; the visions made her feel faint.

The huge wood gates were open, large enough to admit two wagons side by side at a time, or a dozen mounted knights, and the drawbridge was down. Godfrey had already vanished from her view. Unfortunately, he could not be easily avoided, not when Brodie was one of the Earl of Buchan's castles.

Brodie Castle had belonged to Alana's mother, Elisabeth le Latimer. It had been her dowry when she had married Sir Hubert Fitzhugh, Eleanor's son. Sir Hubert had died in battle without children, and Elisabeth had turned to Alexander Comyn, the Earl of Buchan's brother, for comfort. Alana had been the result.

Elisabeth had died in childbirth, and Lord Alexander Comyn had married Joan le Latimer, Elisabeth's cousin. Two years after Alana was born, Joan gave birth to a daughter, Alice, and a few years later, to another girl, Margaret.

Alana had met her father exactly once, by accident, when he was hunting in the woods, and his party had become lost. They had come to stay at Brodie Castle for the night. Alana had been five, but she would never forget the sight of her tall golden father in the hall's firelight—as he stared at her with similar surprise.

"Is that my daughter?"

"Yes, my lord," Eleanor had answered.

He had strode over to her, his stare unnerving. Alana had been frightened, uncertain of what he would say or do, and she had not been able to move. He had seemed so tall, unnaturally so, more like a king than a nobleman. And then he had knelt down beside her.

"You look exactly like your mother," he had said softly. "You have her dark hair and blue eyes…she was the most beautiful woman I had ever seen when we met, and to this day, I have yet to meet anyone as fair."

Alana was thrilled. Shyly, she had smiled. Somehow, Alana had known that was praise. And before leaving Brodie, he had told Eleanor to take good care of her. Alana had been in earshot, and she had heard. Her father cared about her!

But he had never come to Brodie again. She had expected another visit, and disappointment had become heartache. But the pain had dulled and died. She was just a bastard, and so be it.

When she was thirteen, she had been told he meant to arrange a marriage for her. Alana had been in disbelief. By that time, she had come to believe that her father did not even recall her very existence. And before she could become excited about the prospect of having a husband and a home of her own, she had learned that her dowry would be a manor in Aberdeenshire.

Eleanor told her she must be grateful, but as much as Alana wished to be grateful, she was disappointed. Brodie Castle had belonged to her mother. But an illegitimate daughter could not inherit such a stronghold, and as there had not been any other heirs, Brodie Castle had been awarded to the Earl of Buchan by King Edward of England, and in turn, he had given it to his loyal vassal, Duncan of Frendraught. Alana had been eight at the time. Foolishly, when her father revealed that he would give her a dowry, she had thought he would somehow—miraculously—return Brodie to her.

But he had not, and it did not matter in the end, for Alana remained unwed.

No one wanted to marry a "witch."

Eleanor held her arm as they hurried through the frozen and muddy courtyard. They passed long-haired cows, standing with their backs to the walls, their faces to the sun. A pair of maids was bringing in water from the well. A boy was carrying in firewood. They did not speak.

They stepped inside the great hall, which was warmer, two huge fires roaring there in two facing hearths. Godfrey and his men were seated at the trestle table before one hearth, and were in a heated discussion. Alana hoped they were arguing over her fabricated vision of his father being victorious in a battle. The idea gave her some small satisfaction, even when she knew it was petty of her.

Once they were safely in the kitchens, Eleanor pulled her aside.

"What did you see?" Eleanor asked carefully, keeping her tone low.

Alana glanced about the kitchens, where Cook and her maids were bustling to prepare supper. Venison and lamb were roasting on spits. She removed her fur-lined wool mantle, hanging it on a wall peg. "A terrible battle, and a stranger, a warrior, stabbed in the back by his own."

Eleanor started as their gazes locked. "Since when do you see strangers?"

She shook her head. "You know I have never had a vision about someone who was not familiar to me." It was true. Now, as she recalled her vision, she was shocked. Why had she seen some stranger in the midst of a battle with the English? The memory was causing her nape to prickle uncomfortably again.

Her stomach roiled—as if another vision was imminent. Yet there was no water to lure her into its depths....

"Are you certain you didn't know the man?"

Alana was certain, but she visualized him now, with his hard face and dark hair, his blue eyes. "He did seem familiar," she decided. "Yet, I don't think we have ever met. What could such a vision mean, Gran?" Would she now be cursed with seeing the future when it belonged to those she did not know? Wasn't it bad enough that she could foresee the future of her friends and family?

"I don't know, Alana," Eleanor said.

Suddenly the door to the kitchens burst open and Godfrey stood there, appearing furious. "Where is our meal?" he demanded, his hands on his hips.

Alana stared coldly at him. When he was in such a foul temper, there were always consequences to pay, and it was best to be meek—and to avoid him. His temper was so easily set off, and he was a cruel man—just as his father was.

"Your meal is to be served at once," Eleanor said easily.

"Good." Godfrey scowled.

"My lord, did the messenger that arrived at noon bring ill tidings?" Alana asked as politely as she could.

"He brought very ill tidings!" Godfrey swung his hard gaze to Alana. "Robert Bruce has sacked Inverness. He has burned it to the ground."

Alana froze. Inverness was a short distance to the south, within a day's march of Brodie!

For as long as she could recall, various families and clans of Scotland had been at war with England—and each other. But almost two years ago, Robert Bruce, who had a claim to the throne of Scotland, had murdered Red John Comyn, the Lord of Badenoch—her father's cousin. He had then seized the throne, and Scotland had been at war ever since.

Her mind raced frantically now, as a silence fell over everyone in the kitchens.

"Aye, you should all be afraid!" Godfrey cried.

"Bruce has been on the march all year, destroying everything and everyone that he can! If he comes here, he'll destroy Brodie—he'll destroy us all." He stormed out.

Alana glanced at the staff—everyone was white with fear.

She was afraid, too. When Bruce had first been crowned at Scone by a handful of bishops loyal to him, the coronation attended by his closest allies and friends, it had seemed impossible that he might actually be triumphant. How could he defeat the great power of England, and the great power of the Comyn family? And his army had been decimated at Methven that summer, by the mighty Aymer de Valence, who was now the Earl of Pembroke. Bruce and his ragtag, starving army had spent the rest of the summer of 1306 hiding from Aymer and the English army in the forests and the mountains, while retreating across Scotland on foot. They had finally found a safe haven with Angus Og MacDonald, the mighty chieftain of Kintyre. During the rest of that year, Angus Og and Christina MacRuari had given him men, arms, horses and ships.

Bruce had returned to Scotland last January with a terrible vengeance. He had spent the winter attempting to gain back his lands in Carrick, and when there was no outpouring of welcoming support from his old tenants, he had taken to the forests to terrorize the villagers and squires at will—until they sued him for peace, paying dearly in tribute for it. He had then gone to war upon all of Galloway, to exact revenge for the capture and execution of two of his brothers. He had met and defeated Aymer de Valence at Loudoun Hill.

And recently, he had turned his attention to the north of Scotland—to Buchan territory.

For the Earl of Buchan and the entire Comyn family was his oldest and worst enemy.

Bruce had taken a series of small strongholds since the fall, before attacking and destroying the Buchan fortresses at Inverlochy and Urquhart, in a quick sequence. And apparently, he continued to march up the Great Glen, for he had just taken and destroyed Inverness!

Was it now possible that Robert Bruce might be triumphant?

Would he even think of attacking Brodie Castle? Alana wondered with a shrinking sensation. Until now, the war had not concerned her—it had been a distant affair, the concern of her father and the family she had never been a part of.

Brodie was such a tiny stronghold! Why would Bruce bother?

What about the odd vision she had just had? Had she seen a battle in the war for Scotland's throne?

She hurried after Godfrey.

"Alana!" her grandmother called.

Alana ignored her, racing after Godfrey and catching up to him in the hall. "Where does Bruce go now?" she asked.

He glared at her. "He continues to march north, and he will surely descend upon Nairn or Elgin," Godfrey said furiously, referring to two of the greatest Comyn strongholds. "And Brodie lies betwixt them!"

Alana trembled. "Will he attack us?"

"I hope not! We are not fully provisioned," Godfrey said. "I have sent a messenger to my father, asking him for more men. Surely Duncan will send us soldiers. And I am hoping Buchan will send us men, as well. Meanwhile, I am rousing up every tenant and villager that I can, to bear arms in defense here if we must indeed defend the keep."

Alana stared. It was one thing to know that a terrible war raged throughout the land for Scotland's crown, it was another to be so close to the battlefront—to the path of destruction waged by the ruthless Robert Bruce.

Godfrey suddenly leaned over her, far too closely for comfort. He spoke and his breath feathered her face. "You should have a vision, Alana, a vision about Brodie and its future!"

She flushed. "You know as well as I do that I cannot see upon command."

"Truly? Or is it that you simply have no care for us here at Brodie?" He snorted in disbelief and strode to the table, where his men remained. "Bring more wine, Alana," he ordered, not looking back at her.

She watched him for another moment. No matter how she tried, she could not control how much she disliked him. And he was right—partly. She had no care for his welfare, none.

When she returned to the kitchens, where the lamb was now on a platter and about to be served, Eleanor took her hand. "What is it, Alana?"

"Bruce might attack, Gran."

For a moment, Eleanor was silent. Then, "At least you did not see Brodie Castle burning," she said.

There was finally some small relief in that truth. She had not seen Brodie aflame.

ALANA STRAIGHTENED, wiping perspiration out of her eyes in spite of the cold. She held a shovel, as did a dozen others, mostly young boys, old men and women her own age. They were helping to enlarge the ditch that surrounded the castle, in case they were attacked.

Her hands were frozen in spite of the mittens she wore. The sun was finally in descent and clouds were rushing in, indicating a coming snowfall. It had taken several hours to remove the frozen and crusted snow from the moat, and now, they were digging out frozen dirt. It was a task best suited to strong and grown men, but most of the adult men from the area had gone to war years ago; a handful remained to defend Brodie, should the need ever arise.

One of Godfrey's sergeants signaled them that they could go inside for the evening; they would finish on the morrow. Alana leaned on her shovel, exhausted.

Even as she did, images danced about in her mind's eye. She continued to recall the dark, powerful Highland warrior who had been commanding his small army as they battled English knights not far from the burning manor. How she wished he did not haunt her thoughts.

She did not even recognize the manor they fought for. She kept trying to remember if she had seen a banner, or the colors of a plaid. But nothing came to her. And she had not recognized the land, what little she had glimpsed of it. There was only one new detail—she had seen patches of snow about the ground.

So the battle had been in winter.

But what she truly wished to know was the identity of the Highland warrior—and the reason for her vision about him.

Alana followed the others inside. Although Godfrey was pacing in the hall, she went to one of the hearths there to warm her frozen hands. He whirled and stalked to her.

His expression was dark and so ugly. Then she saw the unrolled parchment in his hand. He waved it at her.

"You will be pleased to know that my father cannot spare a single man, and Brodie's defense falls to me." He threw the vellum at her.

Her heart thundered. "That hardly pleases me."

"Oh, come! We both know you covet Brodie Castle, that you think you have a claim to it, that you hate me because I will be lord and master here—over you!" He wasn't gloating. He was angry.

"This place belonged to my mother, so I do have a claim, but not unless something ill befalls you," she said carefully.

"And you pray for just such an ill fortune, do you not? I don't trust you, Alana!"

"I do not want Brodie to fall to Robert Bruce." She meant it. Her father might have forgotten her very existence, but he was her father, and she would be loyal to him in the end. "How can we defend Brodie?"

Godfrey looked at her oddly as he paced, his energy pent up. "I see no way to prevail if Bruce attacks us. We must hope his interest lies in Nairn, Elgin and Banf. The earl is on his way to Nairn as we speak, where my father is, to plan a defense of all the Buchan lands."

Godfrey was frightened beneath the anger. She almost felt sorry for him, for he was in a terrible position—he could hardly defend Brodie against Bruce without any men. "I heard that Bruce destroyed Inverlochy, Urquhart and Inverness. That he left few stones standing. Is that true?"

"It's true." His gaze was sharp. "I know what you

are asking. I don't know if he would burn Brodie to the ground. He is the devil. He destroys every castle he takes, so we cannot retake the ground and use it against him!"

She could not bear to see Brodie reduced to rubble and ashes, and she closed her eyes to ward off such terrible images. She felt faint.

She prayed she would not have a vision—that she would not see Brodie burned to the ground.

"You might want to know one other thing, Alana." His harsh voice broke into her thoughts and her eyes flew open. "Sir Alexander is on his way to Nairn, as well."

She froze.

"What is wrong, Alana?" Godfrey leered, but with anger. "You are white! But this is not the first time your father has been but a short distance from us—without his ever calling."

Her heart lurched, hard. This would not be the first time her father had been in the vicinity, although he had never come to Brodie except that one time when she was a small child. Did she foolishly hope she might see him again? And what would she gain if she did?

He had tried to arrange a marriage for her when she was thirteen, but his efforts had been short-lived. Since then, there had been no word. If he wished to see her, he would have simply sent for her. So either he had forgotten about her, or he simply did not care.

It hurt, when the hurt should have died ages ago.

"You are the bastard he does not want," Godfrey said.

She faced him, suddenly furious. "Does it please you, to be cruel?"

"It pleases me greatly. And, Alana? You are to go to Nairn, immediately."

Was this a cruel jest? She stared, trembling, trying to decide.

He slowly smiled. "My father demands you go to him now."

"Why would Duncan send for me?" she asked carefully, for she knew Godfrey might be toying with her.

"Why do you think? Witch!"

Alana was aghast. "What did you tell him?"

"Did you not see my father victorious in battle?"

She trembled. Duncan knew about her sight—everyone at Brodie did. "You told him about my vision," she said slowly, with growing dread.

"Aye, I did. And he wishes to speak with you." He bent down and retrieved the parchment. He then placed it in the fire, watching it begin to burn. "If I were you, I would begin to think about what I saw. He will want to know everything."

"I told you what I saw," she cried. Her mind raced frantically. She had lied about having a vision of Duncan. And she despised Duncan, feared him in a way that she did not fear Godfrey. What should she do? Duncan might beat her if he learned of her lie. He would surely punish her in some way.

"You are not pleased? Do you not wish to see Sir Alexander?" Godfrey asked.

Alana could not even think clearly. However, foolishly, she must admit that she did hope to see Sir Alexander again.

And now, she must hope Nairn was not attacked, not anytime soon.

"THIS IS MADNESS!" Eleanor cried. She was pale.

Alana smiled grimly. "I cannot refuse Duncan, Gran, and you know it. You also know he will be displeased if he learns I lied about my vision."

Eleanor sat down, stricken. The women were in the small tower chamber they shared, two narrow beds beneath one window, a small table between them. The only other piece of furniture in the chamber was a chest, in which they kept their belongings. Alana was folding an extra cote carefully, placing it with the other garments she meant to take with her.

"Well, perhaps some good will come of this." Eleanor was grim. "You will see your father again—and he might recall the fact of your existence!"

The stabbing of hurt was dull, like the taped tip of a knife's blade. Carefully, she said, "If Duncan had not summoned me, I would not be going."

"Do not play me, my girl. We both know you would be pleased to see your father again—and it would please me if he finally made good on his promise to see you wed properly."

"He cannot change how the world sees me." She smiled, not wanting to reveal that she did care about the opinion everyone held of her, a great deal.

"Of course he could—he is the great Sir Alexander, the earl's closest brother!"

Alana was suddenly overcome. "What would I do without you?"

Eleanor walked to the open chest and began removing garments from it. They were her clothes. "I am an old woman, Alana, and one day, you will have to get on without me. Which is why I wish for you to have a good husband at your side." She now removed a burlap sack from the chest, and began packing it. "I am going to Nairn with you."

Alana was surprised. "Gran," she began, instinctively protesting. Eleanor was agile and spry, and Nairn was but a half day's horseback ride from Brodie. Still, the woman could hardly ride—they would need a wagon or a litter. And the journey would be in the midst of winter, with snow threatening to fall. She should not come.

"Do not argue. I have not seen your father or Buchan in years. And you have never met Buchan. He has never met you. If your father has no care for your future, perhaps we can convince the earl to provide for you. You are his brother's daughter."

Alana did not want to jeopardize her grandmother's good health on a winter journey, even if it was a short one, and she had heard—everyone had heard—that Buchan was a cold and at times a ruthless man.

"He cannot change my infamy," Alana said.

"Of course he can. He is the most powerful man in the north of Scotland."

THEY LEFT THE next morning. The sun was high, but it had snowed the previous afternoon and night, and a fresh fall blanketed the road and the woods. The mountains surrounding them were white. Alana rode in a small wagon with her grandmother, driving the mule in the traces. Godfrey had not cared that Eleanor wished to accompany her, and had given them a single man as an escort. Connaught rode beside them, a mail tunic beneath his fur cloak.

The wagon and the snow made the going slow. In

the midafternoon, when they were but a short distance from the castle, Alana stiffened.

Something was wrong.

She did not need a vision to know it. She simply sensed danger, and as she did, she noticed a gray pall beyond the line of trees that lay ahead. She smelled smoke.

"There is a fire nearby," the soldier said sharply, abruptly drawing his mount to a halt.

Alana's nape prickled. The gray pall staining the blue sky was definitely smoke. She pulled hard on the reins, halting the mule. It snorted, long ears pricked, alarmed.

"Alana," Eleanor cried.

But Alana heard the horses whinnying in fright, saw the glow of a fire beyond the trees. And was she imagining it or did she hear men shouting in fear and agony?

Because the sounds of the horses and men were so familiar—exactly like the sounds in her last vision!

Her heart slammed. "Can you go ahead and see what is happening? Without being remarked?" she asked Connaught.

"Aye." He spurred his horse aggressively forward, galloping away.

Alana felt entirely exposed, sitting in the wagon with her grandmother, on the deserted and snowy road, no longer hidden by the surrounding woods.

Eleanor took her hand. "We should turn back."

She hesitated. "I am wondering if we are about to encounter the battle from my vision, Gran."

Eleanor's eyes widened as Connaught galloped back to them. "They have attacked the MacDuffs' home,

Boath Manor! They are burning it to the ground! And they carry Bruce's flag!"

Alana's tension increased. "Surely Bruce's army is not beyond those trees?" she cried.

"It is but a few dozen Highlanders, mistress. Still, they are warring with Duncan's men."

Her heart thundered. They were but minutes away from a terrible battle, a part of the great war for Scotland's throne.

"Turn the wagon, Mistress Alana," Connaught ordered. "We must go back before we are discovered."

She thought of the dark-haired Highlander who had been betrayed by one of his own men. If she was about to encounter him—and witness such treachery—she could not go back. She did not know why, but she was compelled to warn him.

Alana began to get down from the wagon. "Will you take Eleanor back to Brodie?"

"Alana," Eleanor gasped. "You cannot stay—we must turn around!"

"I have to see what is happening. But I will hide in the trees, I promise you." Before she had finished speaking, she could hear the men shouting, the horses neighing, more loudly. The battle had moved closer to them.

She turned, and she could see the fire on the other side of the trees far more clearly, bright and brilliant. "You'll never outrun them with a wagon. But damned if I will die to save an old woman and a witch." Suddenly Connaught was galloping away.

Alana choked, shocked that he would leave them there—two women alone and defenseless!

"Alana, if they are coming this way, you must hide! Forget me!" Eleanor's eyes were wide with fright.

Alana reached for the mule's bridle. "I am not forgetting you, Gran. Let's get you hidden."

"And what about you?" Eleanor demanded. "I am an old woman. My life is done. You are young. Your life is ahead of you!"

"Do not speak that way! Come." Alana led the mule and the wagon off the road, no easy task. The mule was balking and unruly, while the snow became deeper, until finally the wagon was stuck. But they were off the road, and not as obvious as they had been. In any case, she could not coax the mule any farther.

Alana glanced around and saw an outcropping of rocks. She could leave Eleanor in the wagon—or hide her in the cavern there.

Eleanor understood. "I'd rather stay here."

Alana nodded. "I will not be long." She covered her grandmother with a second fur.

Eleanor took her hand. "I am frightened for you. Why, Alana? Why won't you hide here with me?"

Briefly, Alana stared. What was wrong with her? Why did she wish to see if the battle just beyond the woods was the one from her vision? Why was she determined to warn the dark-haired Highlander of treachery? Perhaps sparing him any injury—and saving him from death?

For she had seen him stabbed, and she had seen him fall. She did not know if he would live, or if he would die.

"I am coming back. I am not leaving you here." She hugged her, hard.

Eleanor clasped her face. "Your mother was stubborn and brave, too."

Alana somehow smiled and hurried off.

She was too agitated to be cold, as she trudged through the snow back to the road. She headed toward the line of trees that lay ahead, and the sounds of the battle became louder as she approached it. The stench of smoke and fire increased. Filled with fear and dread, her pulse pounding, Alana reached the edge of the wood. She halted, grasping a birch to remain upright.

Her vision was before her, come to life!

The manor was aflame, and English knights and Highland warriors were in a savage battle before it. The snow was bloodred. Swords rang, horses screamed. And then a steed went down, the Highlander astride it leaping off....

Shaken, she felt her knees buckle. But she did not collapse. Frantically, she scanned the fighting men.

Her heart slammed.

A fur flung over his shoulders, bloody sword in hand, long dark hair loose, the Highlander was viciously fighting an English knight. Their huge swords clashed, shrieking, again and again, in the midst of the bloody, battling men.

He looked *exactly* as she had envisioned him.

Alana was stunned. What did this mean? To happen upon one of her visions this way?

Screams sounded from within the manor.

The Highlander heard them, too. He sheathed his sword and rushed to the door, which was burning. Flames shot from an adjacent window. He rammed his shoulder into the door.

And then he suddenly turned and looked at the woods—as if he was looking at her.

Alana stiffened.

For it almost felt as if their gazes had met, which was impossible.

Within a moment he had vanished inside the burning manor. Flames shot out from the walls near the door.

Alana did not think twice. She began to run out of the trees, toward the battling men—toward the manor.

He appeared in the doorway, a small boy in his arms. A woman and another child ran past him; he let them go first. As he ran out of the house, more of the flaming roof crashed down. He dived to the ground with the child, protecting the boy with his body.

Alana tripped, fell, got up.

He had risen, too, and was ushering the boy into his mother's arms. Then he whirled to face her.

This time, Alana knew she was entirely visible. This time, in spite of the warring men between them, she knew their eyes met.

For one moment, she paused, breathing hard as they stared at one another, in surprise, in shock.

And then she saw the man behind him. He was approaching rapidly, and was but a short distance away. His hair was shaggy and red.

Her heart seemed to stop. This man meant to betray his fellow Highlander, meant to murder him. "Behind you!" she screamed.

The Highlander whirled, sword in hand. Apparently he did not see any danger, for he faced her again. But the red-haired Scot held a dagger and his strides were unwavering....

Alana tried again. "Behind you! Danger!" As she cried out, he whirled, and his assailant swiftly stabbed him in the chest. Almost simultaneously, the Highlander thrust his sword through the traitor, delivering a fatal blow. Slowly, the other man keeled over.

The Highlander looked across the battle at her, staggered and fell. His blood stained the snow.

Alana heard herself cry out. She began to run toward him again. The English knights who remained mounted were galloping away. Those on foot who could flee were doing so. All that remained was the small, victorious Highland army, the wounded, the dying and the dead.

Alarm motivated her as never before. She had to swerve past bodies, and she tripped on a dead man's outstretched arm. Someone tried to grab her; she dodged his hand. And then she reached him.

She dropped to her knees in the snow, beside him. "You are hurt," she cried.

His blue gaze pierced hers, and he seized her wrist, hard. "Who are ye?"

She felt mesmerized by his hard blue eyes. They were filled with suspicion. "You're bleeding. Let me help." But his grip was brutal—she could not move.

"Ye wish to help?" he snarled. "Or do ye think to harm me?"

CHAPTER TWO

ALANA'S TENSION WAS impossible to bear. He would not release her wrist, and his stare was colder now. "Dughall," he said harshly, his gaze unwavering upon her face, "take the dagger from my chest."

"Aye, my lord." A tall blond Highlander knelt and ruthlessly yanked the blade from the flesh and tendon where it was embedded.

Alana cried out. The Highlander did not make a sound, although he paled and his grasp on her wrist eased as his blood spewed.

Alana jerked free and seized the hem of her skirts; she pushed a wad of it down hard on his wound. What had he been thinking?

"That was a fine way to remove the blade," she said tersely. But the enemy blade had missed his heart; she was relieved to see the wound was high up, almost in his shoulder.

He eyed her exposed knee as another man handed her a piece of linen. Alana quickly put it on his wound in place of her skirt. The wound continued to bleed. Dughall knelt, offering the warrior a flask. He took it with his right hand and drank.

Now on both knees in the frozen snow, she shivered—but not from the cold. She was terribly aware of the Highlander she was trying to help. His presence—his proximity—seemed overwhelming. "Your wound needs cleaning. It needs stitches."

His blue eyes were ice. "Why would ye help me—a stranger?"

She had no answer to give. She did not know why she was compelled to aid him. She did not know why she was worried. But he had clearly survived the attack—and she was relieved.

She had no explanation for her relief, either.

When she made no answer, his eyes darkened with suspicion. He struggled to stand. Instantly he reeled, as if he were a tree buffeted in the wind.

"What are you doing?" she gasped, left holding the bloody linen. She rushed to him to brace him to stand.

"Dughall, tell the men to raise our tents. We will spend the night here." He did not glance at her, shaking her off, his gaze on the burning manor. It was mostly rubble and smoldering ash now, although some timbers still burned. He appeared satisfied. "No one will use this place against us now."

Alana recalled what she had heard about Bruce— how his armies left no stones standing. So it was true.

He turned to Alana. "So yer an angel of mercy." He was mocking.

She flushed. He did not seem grateful for her aid. He seemed highly skeptical.

"I could not let you bleed."

He turned as if he hadn't heard her. "And, Dughall, get a needle and thread."

"Aye, Iain." Dughall raced off.

Her pulse was racing. *His name was Iain.* Why did that seem to matter to her? "I can see a simple knife wound will not kill you. You should sit back down, my lord."

"A true angel." He eyed her. "Why not, mistress? Why not let a stranger bleed to death?"

She did not know the answer herself!

"Why were ye in the woods? Did ye flee the manor when we attacked?" He spoke sharply.

"No." She hesitated, now thinking about the fact that Eleanor was hiding in the woods, and it would be dark in another hour. And he was fighting for Robert Bruce. He had been in battle with Duncan's men. It would be dangerous to reveal who she was, or where she had been going—or why. He was the enemy, even if she had been compelled to help him. "I was on my way to visit kin in Nairn." A version of the truth would surely do.

"Ye journey alone?" He was obviously doubtful. "And then ye rush *into* a battle, to aid a stranger?" His stare was unnerving.

She wet her lips. She could not blame him for being so suspicious. "I am not alone. My grandmother is in the woods, where I left our mule and the wagon. We heard the battle…." She stopped. Now what could she say?

"And ye decided to come closer? Ye'll have to tell a far better tale, my lady." But now, his gaze swept over her, from head to toe. "Who are ye? Whom do ye visit in Nairn?"

"I am not from the castle," she managed to say. Had he just looked at her as if she were in a brothel and awaiting his pleasure? "We are simple folk, farmers…."

She could barely speak. Men did not look at her with male interest—they were too frightened to ever do so.

For a moment he stared.

"My grandmother carries healing potions." That much was true. She could finally breathe, somewhat. "If you will allow it, we will clean the wound and put a healing salve on it, then stitch it closed. I must get her, my lord. She is old and it is cold out."

He turned. "Fergus, go into the woods and bring back an old woman and a wagon."

A Highlander with long blond hair rushed off to obey.

Alana hoped that was the end of the conversation, but it was not. He said, "Ye still cannot explain why ye rushed into the battle, mistress, when all other women would hide in the woods and pray."

She again had no answer to make.

His gaze narrow, he took her shoulder and guided her with him to the largest of the tents that had just been erected. He gestured and Alana preceded him inside.

It was warmer within. A boy was laying out furs and a pallet. From outside, she could smell meat roasting—a cook fire had been started. Alana hugged herself. She felt uncomfortable, and not just because of her lies. Twilight was near, and they were alone. He did remain the enemy, he was a warrior, and as such, was frightening.

Dughall stepped inside, carrying a small sack. "Do ye want me to sew it?"

Alana was alarmed. "My lord, the wound must be

cleaned first." He could so easily die of an infection if it were left dirty and unwashed.

His blue gaze upon her, he sank down on the pallet, shoving off the fur that had been loosely draped about his shoulders. For an instant, Alana stared at his broad shoulders, his huge biceps. The upper half of his leine was blood soaked. "Come, angel of mercy," he said.

Mockery remained in his tone. She looked aside and hurried to him. "Pressure must be kept on the wound." She tried to sound brisk. "Or you will certainly bleed to death."

"Give her a blade," he said to Dughall. To Alana, "Cut the leine off."

She nodded, taking the knife Dughall handed her. And then he seized her wrist another time. Alana froze, meeting his hard gaze once again.

"Try anything untoward and ye will suffer my wrath," he said.

She nodded. Did he truly think she might stab him now?

He released her. She quickly cut his leine down the front, to his belt, and pulled open the sides of his leine. She pretended not to notice the hard slabs of his chest, the dark hair there, or the small gold cross he wore. Then she uncovered his left shoulder completely.

The wound was bleeding again. Dughall handed her more linens, which she gratefully took and pressed to it. Iain inhaled in pain and their gazes collided.

"I am sorry.... I am trying not to hurt you." She avoided his gaze now, acutely aware of him.

"You have no calluses," he said.

She started, eyes wide, locking with his. What was he talking about?

"On yer hands." He was final—triumphant.

She finally realized what he meant. If she were a farmer, her hands would be callused. Alana could only stare. She had been caught in her first deception.

His smile was slow, dangerous. "Who are ye, lady? Dinna tell me yer a farmer's wife—falsehoods dinna sit well with me."

"We were summoned to Nairn," she managed to answer. "My grandmother carries healing potions."

"An answer that is no answer," he said.

She glanced at Dughall, her cheeks aflame. "Can you bring me warm water and soap?"

"Aye, my lady." He slipped from the tent.

"The truth," Iain said.

Alana felt mesmerized by his unwavering stare. "We do not know why we were summoned," she lied, feeling desperate. "But we believe my grandmother's potions are needed."

His blue gaze moved over her face now, feature by feature.

Did he believe her, when she was so deliberately lying? When she hated doing so, when she was a poor liar by nature? And Duncan of Frendraught was his enemy—would such a lie even protect her? "You should not speak. You should rest."

"Ye do not play these games well. Ye have no ready answers." He had become thoughtful.

She checked to see if his wound had stopped bleeding, and was relieved that it had. "Saving a life is no game."

He said, "Ye cannot or will not tell me who ye are. A spy would be prepared."

"I am no spy, my lord," Alana said tersely. He thought her a spy? She was horrified. "I am no one of any import."

He smiled coldly at her. "Ye have import, lady, or ye would not hide from me. And—" he paused for emphasis "—I am intrigued."

She was dismayed. She did not want his interest, not at all!

"A young woman, alone in the woods with her grandmother, not far from Nairn. A young woman who does not flee from a battle, but goes into it—and warns a stranger of treachery. How long do ye think it will take for me to learn yer name?"

If he wished to find out who she was, he would certainly be able to do so, quickly enough. She and her grandmother were well-known in these parts. But she would be long gone by then, or so she hoped.

"And you, my lord? You fly Bruce's flag. You command these men. You come from the Highlands. My guess, from your speech, is you come from the islands in the west."

"Unlike ye, lady, I have no secrets to keep. I am Iain of Islay."

"Iain is a common enough name." But Alana's heart lurched. She had heard gossip of one Iain of Islay—a warrior known as Iain the Fierce. The cousin of both Alasdair MacDonald, lord of the Isles, and his brother, Angus Og. He was renowned to be ruthless, bloodthirsty and undefeatable.

"Are ye frightened?"

Alana dragged her gaze to his as Dughall returned. "I hate war. I hate death. Of course I am frightened. Many men died today."

His gaze was on her face.

"Are you the cousin of Angus and Alasdair Mac-Donald?" she had to ask.

"So ye have heard of me," he said, but softly.

He *was* the savage Highlander known as Iain the Fierce, a warrior who never let his enemies live.

And she was in his camp, in the midst of a war for Scotland—as the enemy.

No, she was not just in his camp—she was in his tent.

She got to her feet, taking a step back and away from the pallet. "I have heard of you," she said.

He made a sound, perhaps of satisfaction. And then Eleanor hurried into the tent, shivering, Fergus with her, breaking the tension, the moment.

"Grandmother!" Alana hurried to her, relieved. "Are you cold? I am sorry I have been so long!" she cried, hugging her.

"I paused before the fire, Alana, so I have warmed up." Eleanor hugged her back while Alana flinched. Now Iain knew her name. Tomorrow, if he made enough inquiries, he would learn the truth—that she was Elisabeth le Latimer's bastard daughter, from Brodie Castle, and that her father was Sir Alexander. He might even learn that she was a witch.

She must leave his camp before he made any inquiries about her.

Iain was watching them closely. "Yer granddaughter has been kindly tending me, Grandmother," he said.

"Of course she has, for no one is as kind," Eleanor said. "May I help you, as well, my lord?"

"It is Iain, Grandmother." He glanced casually at Alana. "Iain MacDonald."

Eleanor went to him and knelt, responding as Alana had feared she would. "I am Lady Eleanor. Well, the wound is deep. You will need stitches. Alana, bring me the bowl of water."

Alana met Iain's amused gaze. He had just ferreted out her grandmother's name, as well, easily enough. When he asked about them, he would quickly learn that they were from Brodie Castle. It would not be difficult now.

They had to leave his camp as soon as possible.

Alana did as her grandmother instructed, then remained silent as Eleanor cleaned the wound. She did not look at Iain, but was aware that he was watching her. When Eleanor was done, she said, "Alana's hand is steadier than mine, and she makes a fine stitch. She will sew you up, my lord."

"It is Iain," he said. "I am no lord, just a fourth son."

Alana handed him the flask, absorbing that bit of information. Younger sons were either churchmen or soldiers of fortune. He had clearly chosen the latter. "I will need at least two men to hold you down."

He took a long drink from the flask. "Ye will need no one. Bring me the blade," he said.

He would struggle when she stuck a needle in his flesh, all men did. "My lord," she objected.

"Bring me the blade, Alana," he ordered.

She inhaled. It was so odd, unnerving, to have him call her by her name. Alana handed it to him.

She took up the needle, which was threaded. He would only make her efforts more difficult. It would be hard to remain steady if he struggled. How silly, to be so proud.

And Iain put the hilt of the dagger in his mouth. She carefully pricked the needle into his skin. He tensed, making a harsh sound, but he did not move.

Alana knew better than to look at him. Very swiftly, with determination, she put ten stitches into the wound, closing it completely. He did not move, or flinch, again. She knotted the thread, and Eleanor snipped it. Finally, she looked at him.

His eyes were closed, long, thick lashes fanning his skin. His face was white and covered with perspiration. For a moment, she thought he had fainted. And she hoped that was the case.

Eleanor began to apply a salve to the wound. His eyes flew open, gazing at her, not her grandmother. "Thank ye, Alana."

"Do not speak now," she told him. "Most men would be unconscious with such a wound. You should sleep."

He studied her, very closely. "Angel," he finally said.

Alana felt her heart flutter oddly. This time, she had not heard mockery in his tone. She lifted the flask to his lips—he drank. Then his eyes closed and his breathing deepened. He had fallen asleep instantly.

Suddenly exhausted, she rocked back on her heels. What had just happened?

He was the warrior from her last vision, yet he was a stranger, and now, there they were, together, in his tent, with her in attendance upon him! Why had she foreseen this battle—why had she foreseen him? And why was it so important to tend to his welfare? To prevent his death? He was a ruthless Highlander, renowned for his savagery in battle.

She could not tear her gaze away from him now. In sleep, his hard face relaxed, he was dark and handsome, but the MacDonald men were known for their dark hair, their blue eyes, their arresting features. And like any Highland warrior, he was powerfully built, his arms chiseled from years spent wielding sword and ax, his legs sculpted from the mountains he ran up and the horses he rode.

What kind of man was he? To suffer such a wound, as he had just done? To remain awake while she sewed him together? To lead his men so far from home in dangerous battle? To be known as Iain the Fierce?

Did he really leave no enemy alive? Hadn't she just seen him rescue a woman and her children from the burning manor—putting his own life at risk to do so?

She instinctively knew that she did not want him as her enemy, even if that was what they were. And while she had thus far been able to avoid telling him the truth about her family—her father—he would soon find out about her Comyn blood.

Would they be allowed to leave, once he had awoken?

Could they leave before he woke up?

Eleanor had finished applying the healing ointment, and was laying linen over the wound. She sank down onto her stool, facing Alana, her gaze searching. "I don't want to awaken him to bandage it. We can do so tomorrow."

"Tomorrow?" Alana gasped. "Maybe we should

leave now, before he awakens—before he finds out who my father is."

Eleanor took her hand. "We can hardly leave now, Alana. It is a short walk to Nairn, but it is dusk already and it will be too dark to travel soon."

She was right, they could not leave now. Alana looked at Iain. He was so soundly asleep now, his face softer, as if he were a little boy. But she was frightened. He was so suspicious of her.

"Alana—what has happened?" Eleanor whispered.

Alana turned to her, clutching her thin hands. "It was as I suspected, Gran! The battle for Boath Manor was the battle of my vision—and he is the stranger I saw being betrayed by his own man."

The two women stared at one another.

"I cannot comprehend this," Alana finally said, low.

Eleanor shook her head. "Nor can I. One day, we will know why you had such a vision…why you saw this man…. But it is useless to dwell on it now. There will be no answers tonight."

Alana realized that her grandmother was tired. She put her arm around her. "I am so sorry I let you come with me! You could be safely at Brodie Castle now, asleep in your own bed!"

"You did not have a choice, granddaughter." Eleanor smiled. "But what worries you so?"

Her grandmother knew her too well. "He is the enemy. He rides with Bruce. He was fighting Duncan's men," Alana whispered, worriedly. "What if he does not let us go? He is already suspicious of me." She did not add that she would never tell him about her visions.

"If he learns you are the Earl of Buchan's niece, we

will have to tell him everything, Alana, and pray he realizes that we have no value as hostages."

Alana hesitated. Buchan and Bruce were the worst of enemies—each wanted the other dead. Bruce would surely be pleased to have her in his control as a hostage, even if no ransom were forthcoming. She did not feel confident that Iain would blithely allow them to go on their way if he ever learned the truth. He seemed ambitious and terribly ruthless. They might explain that her uncle and her father had no care for her, that they would not ransom her, but he might not believe them. And even if he did, her instincts told her he was a complicated man—that his actions could not be predicted. He might think her a card to be kept up his sleeve.

She glanced at him again. He lay asleep, unmoving. He was so handsome, in such a powerful and masculine way.

Eleanor stood and put her arm around her. "Child, let's find a place to rest. It has been a long and trying day. My old bones are aching. And you should cease worrying. That will not solve anything, not tonight."

Alana nodded. She walked back to Iain and stared down at him for a moment, suddenly aware of being exhausted. How she wished she knew why he had been in her vision, and why she was now with him.

She bent and adjusted the furs, covering him up to his chin. As she did, she thought he stirred; she thought his dark lashes flickered. But he did not open his eyes.

"Child?" Eleanor called.

Alana turned and followed Eleanor from his tent.

THE SOUNDS OF the men taking down the camp awoke Alana.

She jerked upright. For one waking moment, she did not recognize the tent she shared with her grandmother, did not recall why she was there and not in her own bed.

And then all the events of the previous day came rushing back to her. The burning manor, the bloody battle, Iain of Islay…

Alana stared at the hides of the tent, stunned anew, and then looked down at Eleanor. Her grandmother remained soundly asleep.

She had hoped to be up and gone well before dawn. Now she remembered every detail of the previous day—mostly, she remembered just how suspicious of her Iain had been. She could not imagine what the new day would bring. But they had to get to Nairn, or suffer Duncan's wrath. And mostly, they had to escape this camp before Iain decided not to let them leave—before he learned she was a Comyn.

She prayed that he remained soundly asleep, which would not be unusual, considering he was afflicted with such a stab wound.

Alana slipped out from the furs she and Eleanor shared. A pitcher of water was on a small table in the tent, and Alana used some to wash her face and brush her teeth with one finger. She quickly loosened and braided her long dark hair. Then she paused to gently awaken her grandmother. "I am going outside."

As Eleanor got up, Alana lifted the tent's flap and stepped out. The sun was just rising, and it was a freezing cold December morning. She pulled her fur more tightly about her. They had overslept, for the sun was rising from the dark mists.

Her trepidation increased as she glanced at the camp, hoping their captor remained abed. A dozen men were standing about the cook fire, bread and ale in hand, while the rest of the Highlanders were packing up their tents and gear and saddling their horses.

Alana saw the lady of Boath Manor. Pale and blonde, she sat with her children on the fire's other side, the children busily eating bread and cheese. And Iain was with them.

She was in disbelief. He was up and about, as if he had not suffered a deep knife wound the previous day. And then she prayed that he would not ask about her identity another time, that he would thank her for all she had done and let her go on her way.

He had seen her. He was seated with the lady and her children, but now, he slowly rose to his full height, staring across the fire at her.

She no longer saw the woman and her children, or the other men. She hugged herself, unmoving.

His gaze unwavering upon her, he drained his mug, tossed a crust away and strode to her. "Good morn, Alana." He smiled carefully at her.

"Good morning," she managed to answer. His smile did not reach his searching eyes.

"Did ye pass a pleasing night?" he asked.

So he wished to make polite conversation? What tactic was this? "Fortunately, it was not too cold."

He glanced at the brightening skies. "It will be colder today."

He was probably right, as the skies were clear, which

meant it would not snow. She glanced at him from the corners of her eyes again. He did not seem like an injured man just then. Although his left arm was in a sling, he wore a long sword and a dagger. Beneath his fur, she saw his dark blue, black and red plaid, pinned with a gold brooch above his right shoulder. She was very aware that he was not bedridden, that he was powerful, masculine and very much the enemy.

"I did not expect to see you on your feet so soon."

"Did ye truly think I'd linger on a pallet in my tent?"

Was he amused? It was hard to tell. "Your wound must pain you."

"I care little about pain. It is always a good day when one awakens alive," he said. "Will ye break bread with me, mistress?"

"I am not hungry." She did not wish to share a breakfast with him. "We have been delayed as it is. We must get to our kin in Nairn."

He smiled. "Ah, aye. Ye have been summoned there, to heal someone, and ye cannot spare a moment to eat."

She knew she flushed. "It would be best to simply go on."

His brow lifted. "But ye had the time to attend my wound."

She could not help staring at him and their gazes locked.

"I will learn why ye nursed me, mistress, just as I will learn why ye truly go to Nairn," he said.

She had little doubt he would soon learn all that she hid from him and she was so tempted to blurt out the truth. Instead, she cried, "I do not even know, myself, why I wished so desperately to save you! I saw the terrible treachery, my lord, and I ran to your aid without thought!"

He started, his regard probing.

Her cheeks felt as if they were on fire. "That is the truth, my lord."

For one more moment he studied her. "Come eat."

She decided not to argue, aware that he had not forbidden her from leaving. Alana glanced toward their tent, but Eleanor had yet to come outside. She followed him closer to the campfire, took the bread he offered and quickly ate it. He continued to stare and it made her uncomfortable.

When she was done, she looked up and saw him flexing his left arm in the sling, wincing. He seemed pale beneath his days' growth of beard.

She knew her stitches would hold, if he undertook no abnormal activities. But men died from infected battle wounds more often than not. "Maybe I should look at your wound before I leave?" Alana heard herself say.

"So yer concern for a stranger in a time of war remains."

She did not want him to die, and she had already said as much—she would not say so again, especially when such desire was insensible.

He gestured. His tent had been taken down, so she followed him to a large wagon, one containing a catapult. He leaned against it, shaking his fur from his wounded shoulder. Their gazes danced together, his appraisal this time slow and steady.

She looked away, deciding that she preferred it when he looked at her with suspicion, not with interest. She pushed the plaid farther back over his shoulder.

She did not look up at him as she untied the sling, but she felt his gaze upon her face. She had the feeling he was scrutinizing her every feature as he had done the past night. It made her terribly uneasy.

She removed the sling, then pulled open the neckline of his tunic. Someone had secured the bandage. She lifted an edge, and was instantly relieved. "You are healing nicely."

"I have been well nursed," he said softly.

Aware of the heat in her cheeks, Alana tucked the linen back into the wrappings, and covered it with his tunic. She helped him put his arm back in the sling and tied it. But there was no avoiding contact—no avoiding the feeling of male muscle and bone. "I hope you will rest and heal for a few days, at least. I do not wish for my efforts to have been in vain."

"War waits fer no man."

She took a step back, to put some distance between them. "Surely you will rest for a few days."

"I am a soldier. I have no time to rest, mistress."

She was in disbelief. "Then you might die, for you can hardly wield a sword with such a wound."

He began to smile. "I will wield more than one sword today, my lady, I will wield two."

Alana gasped. "How can you raise a sword in your left hand? And you think to fight *today?*"

His smile vanished. "Why did ye come to help me yesterday? The truth, mistress." Warning filled his tone.

She froze. "I truly don't know. I have told you what I do know."

"That ye desperately wished to save a stranger—

with no previous thought?" He was dismissive. "Did ye shout a warning to me?"

She had no intention of telling him that she had visions, and that he had been in her most recent one. She would not tell him that she had foreseen the battle of yesterday, and the treachery committed by one of his men, so that she had, indeed, warned him, not once, but twice. "You could not hear anyone shout from the woods," she finally said.

"Aye, no man could hear a shout from the woods. But I saw ye standing there—and I heard ye scream at me, in warning. I heard ye as clear as can be—*two times*." His eyes blazed.

She wet her lips nervously. She had shouted at him to warn him against his assailant. But how had he heard her? It was impossible!

"Did ye try to warn me?" he demanded.

"Even if I did, you could not hear," she began.

He seized her arm. "I already told ye I heard ye! Confess! Did ye shout at me?"

Helplessly, she nodded. "Yes."

He shook her, once. "How can that be? How could I hear ye—and how could ye warn me of treachery *before* it happened?"

Alana cried out. "I don't know!"

"Ye shouted at me and there was nothing—then ye shouted again, and that bastard traitor stabbed me. Were ye privy to the plot?" His grip tightened.

"I was not privy to any plot!"

"Then ye must be a witch!" he cried furiously, releasing her.

She backed away, rubbing her arm. She had to lie. "I

am not a witch," she finally said, panting. "And I do not know why I shouted, everything is a blur in my mind!"

His look was scathing. Clearly, he did not believe her.

"Ye flush, perhaps with guilt," he snarled.

She started; wet her lips. "If I am guilty, it is of aiding the enemy."

"So ye admit that we are enemies." His smile was hard, triumphant.

She hugged her fur close now, entirely intimidated. "No."

"Do ye belong to Boath Manor or Nairn Castle? Or do ye belong somewhere else?"

Her mind raced. Should she give up her deception? And at least admit that she was from Brodie Castle? For then, perhaps, he would stop interrogating her.

"So ye still wish to deny me yer identity? Ye only pique my curiosity!"

She knew she must avoid revealing her relationship to the Comyn family, at least. God only knew what he would do to her if he knew she was Buchan's niece. "What does it matter, my lord? When you have survived this battle, and this last act of treachery? When I will leave—and we will never see one another again?"

His smile was hard. "And why would ye think we will never see one another again?"

She started, incapable of comprehending him.

"Treachery is like a serpent with many heads," he said abruptly. "Take one, and others appear, ready and able to strike."

What did he mean? "I do not know treachery as you do."

He made a harsh sound. "Ye knew of the treachery yesterday. Yer first shout is the proof."

Alana finally whispered, "I have tended your wound, my lord. I believe you are in my debt. Will you let us leave? We are expected in Nairn."

He slowly smiled at her, not pleasantly. "Are ye certain ye wish to play that card now, Alana?" He tilted up her chin. "That is a marker ye might wish to collect another time."

She flinched and he dropped his hand. "What do you intend?" she gasped, shaken.

"It is hardly safe for two women, one old, one young and fair, to travel about the country." His gaze was hooded now.

"Do you refuse to allow us to leave?"

"Ye have refused to answer my questions. Until ye do, aye, I refuse to allow ye to leave." His gaze hard, his tone final, he turned abruptly away from her.

From behind, Alana seized his arm, shocking them both. He whirled to face her, eyes wide, and she dropped her hand. Touching him had somehow been a mistake, she knew that, although she did not know why. She gave up. "I am from Brodie. I am the daughter of Elisabeth le Latimer," she said hoarsely.

His stare widened with surprise.

She could not withstand his intense interrogation, his cold badgering, his distrust—she could not. If she told him something of the truth, some part of it, he might lose interest in discovering the rest, and let them go.

"Elisabeth le Latimer," he slowly said. "Is her sister Alexander Comyn's wife?"

She swallowed. "Her cousin married Sir Alexander," she somehow said. She could not believe her father had so quickly entered the conversation. "My mother married Sir Hubert Fitzhugh, bringing him Brodie Castle, a part of her dowry."

He studied her with no expression, and then said, "I take it Sir Fitzhugh is not yer father?"

She flushed. "No. He died before I was born. I am Mistress le Latimer, my lord." She could barely breathe, and the conversation had become far too dangerous. "Duncan of Frendraught is my liege, and he has summoned us to Nairn." She tried to smile and knew she failed. "You will probably march on Nairn today or tomorrow or in the next week. I did not think it wise to reveal myself to you."

He was considering. "Duncan is lord of Brodie. Fitzhugh had no heirs?"

She shook her head. "Duncan became lord of Brodie when I was eight."

"Why would he summon ye in a dangerous time of war? Surely there are others in Nairn with healing potions."

She did not wish to lie again. "Duncan has no care for me. He never has. We did have an escort, a single guard, but he fled, abandoning us."

His gaze darkened. "Ye did not answer, mistress."

She hugged herself. "Have I not said enough?"

"I cannot imagine what could be so urgent that he would summon ye to Nairn now. But clearly, it is a wartime matter."

She was grim. How right he was.

"Ye have no husband."

Taken by surprise, she stared. But she had introduced herself as Mistress le Latimer. "No."

"Why not?"

She tensed.

Just then, Eleanor stepped up to them. "Alana, are you ill? You're pale this morning."

Alana took her hand. "Lord Iain said we could leave, if we told him the truth. I told him we are from Brodie, and I am Elisabeth le Latimer's daughter." She knew her grandmother would never volunteer information dangerous to her survival. She faced Iain. "I have no husband because I have no significant dowry."

He barely glanced at Eleanor. "Really? As comely as ye be, ye hardly need much of a dowry to wed some young knight."

Alana shook her head. He knew that something was amiss, of course he did. "I am a bastard, my lord, and my tainted birth has further limited my prospects."

His gaze narrowed as they stared at one another.

Eleanor put her arm around her. "My lord, you owe my granddaughter a great debt. But you discomfort her instead. We must be allowed to go on to Nairn."

He never even looked at Eleanor. "Who is yer father, mistress?"

Alana stared at him, aware of moisture gathering in her eyes. She was ready to admit defeat and tell him all, but Eleanor said, "We do not know. Elisabeth never said, and she died in her childbed."

Alana closed her eyes, relieved. A silence fell as Eleanor hugged her close.

Iain turned, now impatient. "Fergus! Ye will escort both women, but not to Nairn."

Alana gasped. "We had an agreement! I have told you the truth!"

"Did ye?"

"You let me believe you would allow us to go on our way if I told you who I am."

"Bruce's army is near Nairn. Choose another destination, or I will choose it for ye." He strode past her.

Alana was furious. She ran after him and reached for his arm, jerking him back. He whirled, incredulous. "I have done my part. How can you do this?"

He shrugged his arm free. "I dinna ken what part ye play, but ye cannot go on to Nairn. I will not put ye in harm's way. Make some other choice or ye can return to Brodie." He was final.

"You do not care about me," Alana finally said, but she felt as if she were asking a question. "Why would you care where we go? Or if we are at Nairn when it is attacked?"

For a moment, he did not answer. Then, for the second time that morning, he tilted up her chin. "Ye said so yerself—I owe ye a great debt," he said softly.

She began to tremble. What was he doing? Were his eyes dark and smoldering?

"Then let us go to Nairn," she said.

He made a harsh, disbelieving sound. Then he lowered his mouth to hers.

Alana went still, shocked, as his mouth claimed hers—in a hard, demanding, aggressive kiss.

And when he stepped back, her heart was thundering, her skin aflame and her knees buckling.

He gave her a look that could not be mistaken before he strode away, calling to his men.

Alana stared after him. What had just happened?

Iain did not trust her—but he had kissed her. She had never been kissed before. Men did not desire her, they feared her.

Except for Iain of Islay—who did not know she was a witch.

She became aware of Eleanor, for her grandmother had approached. Still stunned and breathless, Alana dared to face her.

There was no censure in her grandmother's eyes. Alana saw speculation, instead.

"Will you speak?" she asked. "Will you berate me?"

"I have no desire to berate you, but later, we should talk about the Highlander. We must get to Nairn, and we must do so before it is attacked."

Alana was finally jerked back to some sensibility. "He is sending us back to Brodie."

"If your father and uncle were not on their way, I would wish to return to Brodie. We must get to Nairn, Alana," Eleanor said. "I can make up a potion for Fergus, one to make him ill."

Alana nodded grimly, as they had no choice but to poison Iain's soldier. She gazed across the land. His men were all mounted now. The camp had been entirely dismantled, with no sign of it ever having existed. A dozen wagons were filled with their tents and war equipment. Beyond the army, the manor was a pile of rubble, except for one lone chimney that was still standing.

Their wagon and the mule had been brought forward, and Mistress MacDuff was beside it, with her two children in the back. Fergus held the mule's bridle, and that of his warhorse.

Only Iain remained afoot, his long hair streaming about his fur-clad shoulders. It was as if she could still feel his lips on hers.

His squire led a big dark horse over to him. Iain leaped astride easily enough, gathering up his reins. And for one moment, the land was silent, except for the snorting of horses, the creak of leather, the jangle of bridles. Iain's gaze was on her.

Alana stared back. He had been hostile and suspicious since meeting her, but he had kissed her with unimaginable passion. She did not know what to think.

He turned to face his men, standing in his stirrups, and he lifted his hand. "A Donald!" he roared.

A hundred men roared back at him, a reverberating Highland war cry. And then the army was galloping away from the burned ruins of Boath Manor.

Beside the mule and the wagon, Alana held her grandmother's hand, staring after Iain until he was gone and only snowy mountains remained.

CHAPTER THREE

"NAIRN," ELEANOR SAID.

Alana trembled, seated beside her grandmother in the front seat of the wagon, Mary MacDuff and her children huddled under wool blankets in the back. The dark stone castle rose out of a promontory on a hill above the town, the skies blue and sunny above it. Snow was clinging to the rocky hillside, and the deep blue waters of the Moray Firth were visible behind it.

It had taken them a few hours to travel the short distance from the MacDuffs' burned manor to Nairn. Poor Fergus had been left in the woods not far from last night's camp, retching up his breakfast. In a few hours he would be well enough to go on his way.

From the towers, shouts rang out.

Alana tensed. She had been to the town of Nairn many times, as it was a bustling port and she enjoyed the market there. But she had never been within the castle, which had always seemed threatening.

It had been garrisoned with royal English troops for years because the great barons of north Scotland were at war with England more often than not. Edward I had taken Nairn and provisioned it for his use, and now, English archers loyal to his son were upon its walls, staring down their bows at them.

Of course, they would not fire upon a wagon with

women and children, not unless ordered to do so. Duncan had been given command of Nairn two years ago, by the Earl of Buchan. She wondered if the earl had arrived; she wondered if Sir Alexander was within.

She wondered if Iain of Islay would be amongst those attacking Nairn, if that is what Bruce did.

"They have seen us," Eleanor said.

Alana smiled grimly and lifted the mule's reins, clucking to him. Her tension felt impossible to bear. It had been difficult enough forgetting her every encounter with Iain, especially that shocking kiss. She felt fortunate to have escaped him, and she was determined not to dwell on their strange meeting or even stranger parting. No matter what he had said, it was unlikely that she would ever cross paths with him again.

She had more urgent matters to consider. She would soon meet her powerful uncle, and see her father for the second time in her life.

The journey up the road to the castle's front gates seemed endless now. The hill was steep, the road rutted and frozen. The going was slow, made the worse by anticipation and dread. She wished she knew if the earl and her father had already arrived at Nairn, if they were within, and preparing to receive her.

When they finally reached the very top of the road, and were but a shout away from the watchtowers, a group of English soldiers galloped out of the barbican to meet them. Alana halted the mule, her heart skipping as the knights thundered up to them.

The knights formed a tight circle around them. They were clad in full armor, but each man had his visor up. Alana saw a dozen hard faces, the elderly ones lined, the young ones boyish and pale, and a dozen pairs of hard, cold eyes.

A middle-aged knight with a gray beard and chilly blue eyes rode up to her. "Identify yourself."

"I am Alana le Latimer and this is my grandmother, Lady Fitzhugh," she said quickly.

"Sir Duncan has been expecting you," the elderly knight said. "I am Sir Roger, Duncan's sergeant at arms. You're a day late. What has kept you?" He was harsh.

Alana somehow smiled. "There was a battle at Boath Manor. We were put out to hide, and then we wished to aid the mistress and her children. So we had to wait until Bruce's men were gone. They did not leave until dawn."

The knight nodded, glancing at Mary and her children in the back of the cart. "I will escort you to Sir Duncan. He is impatient to speak with you."

Alana did not look at her grandmother as they drove the mule into the keep. Because of Mary's presence, they had not discussed the impending interview with Duncan. But Alana had spent the past few hours considering it.

Duncan of Frendraught would want to know about her encounter with Iain of Islay. She could not tell him that she had succored his enemy. He would be enraged. He might even accuse her of treachery. It seemed better to insist that the battle at Boath Manor had delayed them, and that they had spent the night in hiding.

Iain might be the enemy, but just then, she preferred him as her ally against Duncan. She was acutely aware that how she felt was inappropriate, but Duncan was even more intimidating than his son. He had absolute control over her, and Alana despised him even more greatly than she did Godfrey.

In the courtyard, Sir Roger helped her and Eleanor from the wagon. Mary slid down by herself, then got her two children out. Alana went to her.

She had hardly had a word with her, but she smiled kindly. The woman had no belongings, no home, and her husband was at war, fighting in Buchan's army. "I will insist that Duncan give you a chamber. But what will you do next?"

Mary was very fair and though she was in her late twenties, her eyes were filled with fatigue, her face lined with worry. "I will try to get word to my husband, and when this war is over, we will rebuild our home."

Alana took her hand. "You are welcome at Brodie Castle, Mary, until your home is rebuilt."

Mary's eyes widened. "How could I accept such charity?"

"I am certain we could find a place for you in the household, until you are settled at Boath Manor again."

Tears of gratitude filled her eyes.

Sir Roger was waiting impatiently, and Alana turned away. She and Eleanor followed him up the steps and through the great hall's pair of wooden doors.

Duncan of Frendraught was awaiting them. He stood in the center of the hall, hands on his bulky hips, scowling. Like Godfrey, he was blond, blue-eyed and arrogant. Unlike Godfrey, he had spent most of his life fighting for the Comyn family, and was a hardened soldier. He had been awarded command of Elgin last year, as well as several manors and an estate.

He strode toward her, clad in a dark blue cote, the sleeves tight and fitted, a short brown surcote over it.

Rings glinted on his thick hands. He wore his sword, a sign of the war that raged so close by. "What has kept you, mistress?"

"There was a battle at Boath Manor," she said, unsmiling. "We had to hide in the woods, even through the night, as the army camped there."

"You spent the night in the woods with your grandmother? I am amazed you did not freeze to death." He reached up and toyed with a tendril of her hair.

She pushed his hand away.

Duncan smiled mockingly. "Perhaps you should have allowed a maid to attend you before meeting me, Alana." He reached out again and tucked the tendril behind her ear, his fingers lingering upon her skin.

She flinched, furious. Duncan had been toying with her since she was twelve—when he had tried to touch her breasts and thighs in a most lecherous manner. For several years, only her quick wit—and the threat to curse him—had left her unharmed. When she was fifteen, he had assaulted her after a night of heavy drinking. Alana had crashed a pot upon his head, and ever since, he had kept some distance, but his behavior remained rude and suggestive.

"Still afraid of a man's touch?" He laughed.

"Afraid? I am not afraid, I loathe your touch."

"Only because you are as cold-blooded as your mother was not."

Alana wanted to strike him. But he had referred to her mother as a whore so often that the insult had lost much of its significance. She could control her rage—she had had years of practice doing so. "Perhaps." She shrugged. "I did not come here to trade old barbs with you."

"No, you came because I commanded it." His stare had turned to ice.

"Yes, I came upon command, for you are my liege." She looked at her feet and curtsied. Now they had an uneasy truce. She knew he disliked her as much as she did him.

"As your liege, I will tell you I am tired of your lies. So do not claim you spent the night on the road in the midst of winter. Lady Eleanor would be dead," he snapped.

She lifted her chin and stared. How she felt like taunting him—and telling him that she had succored Iain of Islay. "We spent the night in an abandoned farmhouse, down the road from the manor."

He eyed her with suspicion. "If I ever learn that you have lied, Alana, you will pay dearly."

She smiled coldly, even as dread formed. "What else could have possibly kept us?"

"I intend to find out!" He turned his back to her and called to a serving maid. Then he faced her anew. "We heard about the battle," he then said to her. "I had sent a small force south, and Iain of Islay defeated my men at Boath Manor. Did you see the fighting?"

"When we heard the battle, we hid in the woods until it was safe to escape to the farmhouse, where we spent the night, waiting for the army to leave." She would repeat this story until the end of time, if need be.

"You forget, I know you well, I have known you since you were six or seven." Duncan had become her guardian when she was six, which was when he had also become castellan—not lord—of Brodie. "You remain as curious as a wild little cat. You did not care to see who was fighting?"

"This war means little to me."

"Yet it means everything to Buchan—your uncle."

Alana shrugged.

"So you never saw Iain of Islay—Iain the Fierce?" The question seemed rhetorical, as he began to reflectively pace. Head down, hands clasped, he said, "He is a cousin to Angus Og, Bruce's best friend in this war, and Angus has given him an army of savage Highlanders. They have murdered and raped their way across the mountains, burning down both home and field alike."

Alana trembled. She did not believe it.

He stared. "And how is it that I now have your interest and attention?"

Iain had turned Boath Manor into a pile of ash-strewn rubble. But no one had been murdered or raped—not that she knew of. In fact, she had seen him risk his life to rescue Mistress MacDuff and her two children.

"He sounds frightening," she said.

"He does not take prisoners, and he leaves no enemy alive."

Alana bit her lip. She was the enemy and she was very much alive. But of course, she was a woman.

"How is it, Alana, that he or his watch did not remark you?"

Alana shook her head. "I told you—we hid in the woods until we thought we could go back down the road to the old farmhouse." And there had been an abandoned farmhouse on the road, one partly burned, but hopefully, inhabitable. They had just never paused there.

"Then you are very fortunate. I am fortunate that

you were not captured." He eyed her with continued skepticism. "How fares Godfrey? Brodie?"

She felt chilled, and she rubbed her arms. "When we left, the castle stood, unharmed. Do you think it will be attacked?"

"Bruce's army has made camp to the south of us. He could strike Nairn, Elgin or Brodie, or any number of smaller castles and manors." He gave her a dark and long look. "We do not know where he will strike next, Alana." He walked over to her and laid his hand upon her shoulder.

Alana trembled. Did he expect her to predict where Bruce would next attack? She pulled away from his odious touch.

Eleanor asked, "Has the Earl of Buchan arrived, my lord?"

"He is expected at any time. Why do you ask, Eleanor?" He was mocking.

"I have not seen the earl in a great many years and I am curious." Eleanor smiled pleasantly.

"Curious? Come, old woman, we know one another too well. You seek something from the mighty earl—everyone does."

"And do you truly care?" Eleanor asked.

Duncan stared at Alana now, his blue gaze unwavering. "If you think to place Alana under Buchan's protection, then yes, I care. She is *my* ward."

Alana was stunned and dismayed at once. "You have no care for me," she began.

"Shut up," Duncan said. He now approached tiny Eleanor. "She has always been your sole concern. Will you not appeal to her great-uncle, on her behalf?"

Eleanor still smiled. "You know me well, Sir Duncan. Alana needs a husband."

"Alana could be valuable to me, old woman. I need her."

Alana inhaled. "I have never been valuable to you! Not in the dozen years I have been under your protection at Brodie Castle!"

He approached, smiling coldly. "But we have never been in such danger. The earldom is under attack!"

A terrible silence fell. He suddenly found her valuable because of her sight. "What do you want of me?" she asked. But she knew. This was not about the lie she had told his son. He wished to know about Bruce's plans—he wished for her to foresee them!

He slowly smiled. He touched her chin with his stout finger. She recoiled inwardly, but did not move. "You begin to please me, at last.... Tell me what you saw the other day."

She stepped back, and his hand fell away. "I saw a battle, that is all." Images from her vision—from the battle at Boath Manor—flashed. They competed with every memory she now had of Iain, and of her last glimpse of the manor, burned to the snowy ground.

"No. Godfrey says you saw me triumphant in battle."

Alana did not dare glance at Eleanor. Her mind raced. She did not want to have any value to Duncan. It had been bad enough being his ward for most of her life, when he mostly ignored her and occasionally lusted for her. If she let him believe she had had a vision about him in battle, he would certainly think her a valuable asset. He might even think her valuable if she told him that she had foreseen the battle at Boath Manor. She could do neither, then.

But she did not want to anger him, either—not if she could avoid it. She decided to try to hedge.

"I saw a battle, and there was both victory and defeat. I cannot be certain you were the victor. It was a confusing sight."

His face mottled with anger. "That is not what Godfrey claimed. He wrote me and said you saw *me* triumphant, Alana." Warning was in his tone. "So think again and do not lie to me."

"Men were fighting, and I saw Bruce's flag." She hesitated. "I think you were there. I do not know anything else."

"You think I was present? You do not know anything else? You told Godfrey I was victorious!"

"The vision was not clear."

He was disbelieving. "The vision was not clear? Or you will not tell me about it?"

Eleanor stepped forward. "We are sorry, my lord, truly sorry."

Alana now regretted ever lying to Godfrey in the first place, and all for spite. But if she had not lied, she would not have been on the road near Boath Manor. Clearly, she had been meant to be on that road, although she still did not know why.

She thought of Iain, of his kiss and knew she must not allow her thoughts to go further.

"Buchan will not be pleased to hear of such a confusing vision," he spat. He strode to the table and picked up a mug and drained it. Then he slammed it down. It was a moment before he faced her. "I am not pleased. I need details, Alana."

Dismay flooded her. "Why will you tell my uncle about this small, confusing vision?"

"Why do you think I brought you here? I wish for you to help us! To help me! If your uncle doesn't know about your visions, then I will be the first to tell him." Duncan whirled and waved at a maid. "Wine, wench, bring me wine!"

Alana turned away. Did the Earl of Buchan even know that she had the sight?

Would her father have even bothered to mention that his bastard daughter was a witch? She simply did not know.

And what would happen when Buchan arrived? When her father arrived? Duncan now, suddenly, considered her valuable. Until now neither her father nor Buchan had thought about her. Was it possible that would change?

Would her uncle—her father—value her because she was a witch?

She felt no excitement. Instead, Alana wanted to cry.

Eleanor put her arm around her. "My lord, we are both fatigued from such an unusual journey. Could we retire?"

"I am not done with you." Duncan turned his regard on Alana. "If you hid in the woods near Iain of Islay's army...*did you see him?*"

Alana did not know what to say.

"Tell me the truth, Alana. Had you been in the woods, you would have stolen forth to witness the battle—I have no doubt! Well? Surely you would notice him!"

Alana wet her lips, shaken. "Why would you ask?"

"I was told Iain was wounded. There was a great

deal of blood. Did you see him bleeding out? If I am very fortunate, he is dead!"

"There was blood everywhere! There were wounded men and the dead!"

Duncan stared angrily. "I think you enjoy lying to me. Well, you will not enjoy it when Nairn falls to those bloodthirsty Highlanders."

Alana shivered and pulled her wool mantle closer.

"Is he such a terrible enemy, my lord?" her grandmother asked.

Duncan faced her. "Before he was given this army, he was but one more mad Highlander eager to slit our throats in the night. He preyed upon our ships on the western seas. Upon our merchants on the high roads. But that has changed. Bruce has come into the habit of having him advance first in every fray, to secure a path for Bruce's larger army. He has not been defeated since his cousin provisioned him." He turned his stare upon Alana, and she glimpsed dread and fear in his eyes. "If he takes Nairn, none of us will survive."

Alana finally spoke, but thickly, "Is a peace possible?"

"No." Duncan was vehement. "Bruce intends to be king—just as he intends to destroy the earldom of Buchan."

And it seemed as if he was succeeding. The greater ramifications of the war began to sink in. Buchan destroyed, Brodie lost, her uncle and father hanged as traitors...

"If Nairn is attacked—if any of my castles are attacked—I will instruct my archers to place all their attention upon any man who resembles Iain of Islay." Duncan was final.

Alana was aghast. Duncan hoped to assassinate Iain? Eleanor quickly put her arm around her. "We should go up," her grandmother murmured.

But Duncan walked over to her and rudely clasped her shoulder. His grip was hard, and Alana was forced to meet his gaze, as she could hardly get free.

"Buchan will be here tomorrow," he said. "By tomorrow, I expect you to have the answers you did not have today."

"I have told you everything."

"Have you?"

"I cannot tell you what I do not know."

"Then try harder, Alana, to know what you must. Unless you wish to displease me another time, and displease your mighty uncle, as well." Duncan released her and turned his back on them.

Alana looked at her grandmother and, as one, they hurried from the hall. Outside, they paused, clasping hands. "He is threatening me!" she cried.

Eleanor was as shaken. "We must be careful, Alana, truly careful, now."

"Yes, because suddenly I am valuable to them! But I am to please my uncle? How will I do that?" Alana cried. She lowered her voice. "Lying to Duncan is one thing. I do not think it wise to lie to the Earl of Buchan."

"You must not lie to your uncle—but you will not please him if he ever learns you care about Iain of Islay," Eleanor said in a terse whisper.

Alana flinched. "He is a stranger, Gran, that is all, and I doubt I will see him again."

Eleanor gave her a pitying look.

"It is the Earl of Buchan," Eleanor said, hurrying into the small tower chamber they shared.

It was the next afternoon. Alana took one look at her grandmother's grim countenance and worried eyes and she rushed to the room's single window. The shutters were closed to ward off the cold but she opened them and looked outside.

It was another sunny day, with bright blue skies, the countryside patched with snow. A huge army was below the castle, a sea of tents being formed. And dozens of knights were riding up the road at a rapid trot, the earl's banner waving above them. A black bear and gold lion were rampant atop a field of red, against a black, red and gold shield.

She gripped the stone ledge of the window. Buchan would be amongst the first knights, wouldn't he? She did not have a clue as to which rider he was.

And was Sir Alexander with him?

Would she finally see her father again, after all of these years? She was so afraid of what their reunion would be like!

Eleanor put her arm around her. "Whatever you do, be polite, and do not displease him," she said.

Alana felt ill. "He will soon ask me about my vision—and it is a lie. I could not sleep at all last night. Every tale I have ever heard about the earl recurred to me. I do not know what to do."

"Then maybe it is time for the truth," Eleanor said, low. "Without revealing your feelings."

Alana jerked, shocked by the suggestion. Was she saying that Alana should reveal her true vision about the battle at Boath Manor—about Iain of Islay? For if she did, Buchan would value her not as his niece, but as his witch.

Both women turned back to the window and watched until the knights had ridden beneath the tower gates, and could be seen no more. Alana gripped her hands in front of her. She knew she would be summoned downstairs soon. She was frightened. "Is Buchan as ruthless as is claimed?" Alana whispered.

Eleanor gave her a reassuring smile. "When I knew him as young man, he wasn't ruthless at all," Eleanor said. "Infamy is never kind."

Alana did not answer. Her uncle was infamous now. All of Scotland, and perhaps all of England, knew of the Earl of Buchan and his ruthless rage. For his young wife, Isabella of Fife, the Countess of Buchan, had betrayed him by crowning Bruce two years earlier at Scone. It was even said that she had been Bruce's lover, and Bruce had gone to great lengths to keep her safe with his queen and daughter. But all the women of Bruce's court had been captured by the English that summer. And now, Isabella was kept in a cage at Berwick, a spectacle for all the world to gawk at and scorn.

The mighty Earl of Buchan did not care; in fact, he wanted her dead.

A knock sounded on their door. Alana jumped as Eleanor opened it. Sir Roger nodded at them. "The earl wishes to see Mistress Alana," he said.

Alana's anxiety spiraled uncomfortably. "Come with me," she said to Eleanor, taking her hand.

The two women followed Sir Roger down the narrow stairwell. Hard male voices could be heard from within the great hall. One was Duncan's. The other had to belong to the great Earl of Buchan.

They had reached the threshold. Alana faltered and stared.

There was no mistaking the Earl of Buchan, and not because he was well dressed in the fashion of the French and English courts, his rings gold, the hilt of his sword bejeweled. Middle-aged and gray of hair, he emanated power and an air of command. He instantly turned to stare at them.

"Lady Fitzhugh and Mistress le Latimer," Sir Roger said, but informally.

Buchan stood alone with Duncan, not far from one hearth. Her father was not with them.

Buchan smiled. "So you are my niece."

Alana nodded and curtsied. "My lord."

Buchan paced over to her, his gaze filled with speculation. "I remember your mother, Mistress Alana. You so resemble her." He spoke firmly, but not unpleasantly.

Alana did not know what to say.

"She was very beautiful. And you are from Brodie Castle? The place that was once your mother's?"

Alana nodded, her gaze glued to his. He did not seem ruthless. He seemed kind. "Brodie was my mother's dowry, my lord."

"Yes. I recall that. But the circumstances of your birth prevented you from having a claim. Duncan tells me you are twenty, and unwed."

She so hoped the subject of witchcraft would not arise. "I am not wed."

"So my brother has forgotten you," he said flatly.

Oddly, she felt that she must defend Sir Alexander. "He tried to arrange a marriage, some time ago." She dared ask, "My father is not with you?"

"He is on his way," Buchan said. "But no marriage was arranged."

She felt certain she knew where he led. "No."

"Because no man wishes to wed a woman who can see the future?"

She flinched. "No man wishes to marry a woman like myself."

"What do you mean, Mistress Alana? Speak plainly."

She felt her cheeks heat with shame. "I have the sight," she whispered. "I am thought to be a witch."

He studied her in silence then. "So it is true," he finally said. "You can foretell the future."

"Sometimes, my lord."

"Sometimes? So you have visions, sometimes? At will, Alana?"

"No, they are never at will." She hesitated, feeling desperate. "I wish I had no visions, my lord, but they began when I was a small child."

"How do you know that they are visions? Do they always come to pass?" he asked.

She bit her lip. "Yes, they always come to pass."

"Give me an example, Alana."

She did not dare glance at Eleanor. "Our kitchen maid was with child. I saw her in her childbed, the babe born alive, the poor maid dead. There was so much blood."

"And did the maid die in childbirth?"

"Yes—exactly as I saw it." She hugged herself. Poor Peg had died giving birth six months ago, but Alana had known she would die for months before that.

"And now? Now you have seen battles from this war?" he asked thoughtfully.

She froze, and then she glanced at Eleanor.

"From time to time," Eleanor said.

"I didn't ask you, Lady Fitzhugh," Buchan said, but mildly.

"I have had one vision of the war," she breathed, and actually, that was the truth.

"Ah, yes, Duncan tells me you saw a battle, and you first thought he was victorious, then had no thoughts at all. What did you see?"

It was hard to breathe, impossible really. The earl's stare was relentless. Eleanor's advice echoed in her mind—do not displease him. "The vision was not clear," she said. She dared a quick glance at Duncan—he was scowling.

But he was hardly as intimidating as her uncle.

"That will not do." His stance was more aggressive now. "Did you or did you not see my knight in battle?" He did not raise his tone, but it remained firm, unyielding.

Duncan might beat her, but she would survive. Eleanor was right—she must not displease Buchan. She took a deep breath. "I must confess, my lord, to you."

"Confess what?"

She fought despair. "I do have visions, but I did not have a vision of Duncan in battle. I lied."

Buchan's eyes widened. Duncan turned red, and his eyes popped.

"You lied?" Buchan asked with disbelief. "Explain yourself, mistress."

She hugged herself, trembling. "Godfrey goaded me, as he always does, I lied to spite him. I did not have a vision of Duncan in battle."

A terrible silence fell.

Alana looked nervously back and forth between the two men. Duncan was enraged, but the earl was somehow far more frightening. She felt how his thoughts raced. She wished he would not stare.

"You will pay for this," Duncan snarled.

Buchan lifted his hand. "Enough. Lies do not sit well with me, mistress."

"And that is why I did not wish to lie to you." She looked at her uncle, needing courage to do so. "Six days ago, I saw the battle for Boath Manor—I saw the manor in flames, I saw Highlanders fighting the English, and I saw their dark-haired leader rescue a woman and her two children from the inferno." She was hoarse with fear.

Buchan's eyes were wider. "The battle for Boath Manor was the day before yesterday."

"Yes, it was, we came upon it—and it was exactly as I had seen."

Duncan charged forward. "So you lied again? You saw Iain of Islay?"

"Yes," Alana said, afraid he might strike her.

Buchan gestured at Duncan, clearly meaning for him to stand back. "Now we are getting somewhere. Boath Manor is done. How often do you have these visions, Alana?"

"It varies."

"That will not do," Buchan said. He gave her a sidelong look and began to pace, slowly, his expression still thoughtful.

Eleanor hurried to her side and put her arm around her. She dared to glance at Duncan, who glared at her with raw hatred.

Buchan returned to stand before her. "You know I am pleased with you," he said, smiling.

She was incredulous.

"How can we encourage your visions?"

"I cannot summon them," she tried.

Duncan interjected, "Water, my lord. She has visions when she looks into water."

Buchan seemed pleased. "Find a large glass bowl and fill it with water, and place it beside her bed," he told Duncan. "You, Alana, will spend your days and nights staring into it."

Alana felt ill. "I never look at water. I avoid looking into water, my lord!"

"Not anymore. You do wish to be useful to me? To your family?"

What could she do? She nodded.

"Good." Buchan tilted up her chin. "Then you must have these visions—you must seek them out—and I must know the future of my earldom."

He was asking for the moon and the stars, but she nodded, the feel of his blunt fingers under her chin disturbing. Worse, moisture seemed to gather in her eyes.

"You may retire," he said. He walked away from her, to the table. Relieved, Alana realized the interview was over.

But as he sat down, he glanced at her. "And, Alana? I am not a patient man." He smiled.

She managed to nod, her heart thundering. His meaning was clear. She must have a vision about the earldom—soon.

ALANA STOOD BESIDE her bed as one of Buchan's knights carried a large glass bowl of water inside. It was placed on the chamber's single small table, between the two beds. She realized she was looking at the bowl of water, and she jerked her gaze aside. Then she saw Duncan standing in the doorway, red-faced.

Eleanor immediately stepped between him and Alana. "My lord?"

He looked at her with contempt. "You are to vacate this chamber, old woman. Buchan has ordered it."

"What?" Alana cried, aghast. "Surely you have misunderstood!"

"There is no misunderstanding." He shoved past Eleanor, almost knocking her down. Alana reached out quickly to steady her. "His lordship wishes for you to spend your time without distraction—just you and the water."

Alana was in disbelief. "Where will she go?"

"There is a chamber above you. She'll have to share it with the maids."

"It is hard enough for my grandmother to get up and down the stairs to this chamber. She cannot go up another flight!"

Duncan stepped over to her and leaned close. "You lying little bitch!"

Alana flinched. His fist was clenched and she dreaded a blow.

"Don't worry. I am not stupid. I can't hit you, though you deserve a beating. Buchan has great expectations, Alana. I would not disappoint him if I were you."

His breath was foul. Alana stepped back. "I wish to see my uncle." She would beg him to allow Eleanor to stay with her.

Duncan laughed. "You are to stay here until you

are summoned." He turned, nodding Eleanor toward the door.

"What?" Alana cried.

"You heard me, Alana—you will not leave this room until you are summoned." He was savagely satisfied.

"Am I to be imprisoned here?" Alana was in disbelief. She could feel the glass bowl of water behind her—as if the water had a life of its own.

It beckoned.

"Come, old woman," Duncan ordered.

Alana seized her grandmother's hand. "Gran!"

"I will be fine, Alana. And so will you."

She was to be locked in her room with water. How could she be fine? Her visions were never pleasant ones. She had spent her life avoiding them—avoiding water. Dear God!

"You will help him, if you can see the future of Buchan," Eleanor said. "And then maybe he will help us."

Somehow, Alana nodded. Duncan snorted and took her grandmother's arm, guiding her rudely from the room. He did not look back as the knight who had brought the glass bowl to her room closed her door. Stunned, Alana sank down on the bed closest to the door.

Behind her, she felt the bowl of water, a forbidding and omniscient presence.

She heard two pairs of steps departing. She stood and went to the door, taking up the latch. As she did, she heard a movement outside. The knight remained in the hall.

Tears arose and flooded her eyes. She walked back

to the bed and sat down on its end. She folded her hands in her lap. She did not turn her gaze to the glass bowl.

Was she a prisoner? How could that be? Perhaps the knight was there to protect her, but from what, she could not say.

She wiped the moisture from her lids. There were secrets in the room now, and they felt heavy. They felt dark. She refused to look up.

She recalled Iain of Islay, as he was about to break down the door of the burning manor, as he turned and gazed across the battle at her. She closed her eyes in despair.

This was not the time of think of Iain. She must think about her uncle, her father, her Comyn relations—and the earldom. She must have the courage to seek a vision, instead of dreading one.

Slowly, Alana turned around until she could see the glass bowl of water.

It seemed to stare back at her, cool and clear.

Her heart was rioting in her breast.

The water was still. Silent.

Alana stared, the bowl blurring, but not from any vision. She could not see through her tears.

"Good morning, Mistress Alana," Buchan said the next morning, his smile pleasant.

Alana stood on the threshold of the great hall, a knight with her. She had been summoned by her uncle, and the knight had retrieved her from her chamber and escorted her downstairs.

Alana managed to reply. "Good morning." But she was filled with trepidation. She had not slept at all last night. And she had not had a single vision, either.

Buchan gestured her inside. Several knights sat with him at the table, as did Duncan, staring hatefully at her. Her grandmother was not present.

Alana walked to the table, and took the seat indicated by Buchan. "Did you pass a pleasant night?" he asked.

Would he be angry when she revealed that she had not had a vision? Or would he be reasonable? This far, he had not been ruthless or unkind, although she could not decide if she was being kept a prisoner. "I am unaccustomed to sleeping alone. My grandmother has shared my chamber since I was born. I did not sleep well, my lord."

"I am sorry to hear it."

"Will I be allowed to see my grandmother today?"

"Of course." He gestured at the knight who had escorted her down. "Please ask Lady Fitzhugh to come down for the breakfast."

Alana bit her lip. "Thank you, my lord."

"You're welcome. Did you see the future, Alana?"

She did not move, hands in her lap. It was a moment before she spoke. "No, my lord, I did not."

"Then I am not pleased." His smile was gone, his stare uncomfortably piercing.

She flinched. "I tried, my lord. My visions frighten me and I dread them, but I tried."

"Trying will not help me and it will not help the earldom," Buchan said. "We do not have time on our side. Bruce is but a day's march away. There will be a battle soon. You must try harder, Alana, to see the future for me."

"I understand," she said.

"Do you? Did you look at the water? Reflect upon it? Pray?"

"Yes, my lord, I did."

He studied her closely. "Your father has never spoken of you. I had heard years ago about his affair with your mother, and that a daughter had been conceived. But I had truly forgotten your existence, until Duncan brought you here. Would it inspire you if I told you I am eager to help you now that you have my protection?"

Alana somehow smiled, stiff with tension. She was no fool. If she pleased him and had a vision as he wished, he would be helpful to her—he would find her a husband. "I am already inspired, my lord," she said, when the opposite was true.

"You should be married, with a manor of your own."

"No man will have me."

"They will if I say so," Buchan said.

Alana could not look away.

"Do you wish for a husband? A home of your own? Children?"

She could only recall Godfrey's bullying and Duncan's arrogance and advances—and Iain's courage in the battle for Boath Manor. She suddenly looked at him. "Brodie Castle is my home."

"Of course it is. Clearly, you are attached. You do know it would not be out of the question to return it to you."

Alana gasped.

"Would that please you?" he asked.

She knew she was being played and manipulated. But dear God, it would be a dream come true, to have Brodie returned to her. It would be just.

"I see you would wish, very much, to be the lady of Brodie," he said softly.

Oh, God, she thought, *if only I could have a vision—one that will please him!* "Yes," she whispered. "Yes, it would please me so much." From the corner of her eye, she saw Duncan, who was in shock.

But he did not need Brodie! He had two manors and an estate!

Buchan leaned close. "Bruce murdered my cousin," he said to her, more softly. "He stole the throne, and even my wife. And now he rapes and plunders Buchan lands. He has destroyed Inverlochy, Urquhart and Inverness."

Unable to look away, she trembled.

"Will he march on Nairn? Will he march on Elgin, on Banf? Will we defeat him? Will I?"

He was asking for so much! "It is hard enough," she said, low, "seeking out a vision, much less requiring a specific one to occur."

He patted her hand. "But you are a Comyn. You are your father's daughter as much as your mother's. As a Comyn, you must do your duty to me and mine."

"I want to do my duty," she cried. And it was true. Never mind that she had not been raised as a Comyn, or that the entire Comyn family had never considered her one of them, now she wanted nothing more than to have the vision he wished for.

"Good." He picked up his knife and fork and began to eat.

Alana did not move. Although she had never given any thought to her future, not as a man's wife, not as a child's mother, tears arose. Was it possible that she might one day have a husband, children—a family?

"You are not eating," Buchan said.

Alana was jerked out of her hopes and dreams. She smiled at him, and picked up her utensils. Dutifully, she began to eat.

CHAPTER FOUR

THE MEN WERE leaving the table. Alana made no move to get up, as Eleanor had joined them, but they had had no chance to speak privately yet. "My lord?" she called to Buchan's back.

In the doorway, the earl turned.

"Dare I ask you about my father?" She trembled as she spoke. She had not heard Sir Alexander mentioned, not even once.

Buchan returned to her. "Your father was on his way here, Alana, but I sent him a missive ordering him to remain in the south—to hold the line against Bruce if Bruce marches north toward Nairn or Elgin."

Her mind raced. Didn't Iain always lead Bruce's army? Would Iain's army clash with her father's?

"You seem dismayed," Buchan said.

She forced a smile. "I was hoping to see him. It has been many years."

"I am sure you will see Sir Alexander, in time. I will let you know when he is on his way to Nairn." Buchan turned to go.

"My lord? Could I visit with my grandmother, just for a bit?"

He glanced at her. "You may have a few minutes, Alana, but then I wish for you to return to your chamber and seek out a vision for me." He left with Duncan and the other men.

Alana stared after him. So that was how it was to be? She would now spend her days closeted in her chamber with a bowl of water? And would she only be allowed a brief moment with her grandmother—her best friend, her closest confidante?

And her father was not on his way to Nairn.

Eleanor took her hand. "Alana?"

She stole a quick glance at the door, but the men were gone. Only a single knight remained—the English knight who had been outside her door since the previous day. Clearly, Sir John was now her guard. "I am fine—but I have not had a vision."

Eleanor squeezed her hand. "I have been so worried about you! He is keeping you locked up with that glass of water.... Shame on him, to use and abuse you so!"

"Gran! Hush! We must not speak ill of the earl!" Alana shot a glance at Sir John, who was listening to their every word. She flushed, as he did not try to conceal his interest. Although it was not quite true, she said, "I do not feel exactly like a captive, Gran. I think he believes that solitude will aid me in my quest for a vision. I so want to help. He is my uncle." She pulled her grandmother toward the hearth, farther from Sir John.

She realized she was defending her uncle—and that she wanted to defend him. Was it not inexplicable? Yet he had treated her far better than anyone in the Comyn family had ever done. She did not need a guard—she would obey him if he merely asked. Surely, she was not a prisoner.

"I do not recognize the earl anymore," Eleanor said.

"The young man I once liked has grown up into a ruthlessly ambitious man."

"He has been kind to me," Alana began.

"Oh, child! He is tossing you crumbs, and you devour them as if they are an entire loaf! The earl is using you for his own ends. He does not care that you are his niece."

How her grandmother's words hurt—and how they rang true. Alana refused to listen to her now. "He has suggested he will return Brodie Castle to me if I please him with a vision."

Eleanor cried out. She finally said, "And what if your vision is not what he expects? What if the future is not to his liking?"

She could not have a vision that he did not like. Fate could not be so cruel. "Gran, I must see a good future for the earldom!"

Her grandmother said, very low, "Perhaps you should create the vision he seeks."

Alana started, her heart lurching. Speaking as low, she whispered, "I do not want to lie to him. He is my uncle."

"Do not be deceived. He does not care about any blood ties!"

Alana tensed. "I am not sure of that."

"Please, Alana, be wary of him." Eleanor took her hand. "I know how much you yearn for affection from that family. I know how you hope for it. But you must keep your wits about you—now more so than ever."

Eleanor was the wisest person Alana knew, and she sensed she was right—though she wished that wasn't so.

"Mistress Alana." The knight came forward. "The

earl has told me you are allowed five minutes and that time is over. You must return to your chamber."

"Already?"

"You will be allowed to walk in the afternoon—and to sup with his lordship this evening," Sir John said.

Alana suddenly realized the extent of her confinement. "Gran—are you well cared for?" she asked quickly as the knight took her arm.

Eleanor nodded. "I am fine, Alana. But it is you we must worry about. I am praying for you. The sooner you have a vision pleasing to the earl, the sooner we will be able to go home."

With dismay, Alana comprehended her meaning exactly. She sent her grandmother a last smile, and went with Sir John up the stairs.

SEVERAL DAYS PASSED, each day exactly like the one before it. In the morning Alana was summoned to the hall for the breakfast, and there, Buchan asked how she had passed the night. He would then ask if she had had a vision. But there were no visions in the glass bowl of clear water, and with trepidation she would tell him that she had no prophecies to make. He would smile politely, but his displeasure was obvious.

Eleanor was always present for the breakfast, and they would briefly speak before Alana was taken back to her room. There she would stare at the water and pray for a vision of the earldom's future—one pleasing to Buchan.

Each afternoon she strolled about the courtyard with her grandmother and Sir John. In the evening, she supped with the earl and his men.

And at night, in the glow of the bedchamber's firelight, she stared at the glass of water, desperately awaiting a vision. None came. There was only a growing sense of despair.

And would she ever be allowed to go home? Brodie Castle was her home, even if it belonged to Duncan, and even if, one day, it would be Godfrey's. She had been at Nairn almost a week, and the four walls of her chamber were beginning to feel like a jail cell.

It was dusk now, and Alana entered the great hall, Sir John behind her. To her shock, only her grandmother was present. Eleanor hurried toward her. "There is rampant gossip about the castle this afternoon!" she cried.

Alana seized her arm. "What has happened, pray tell?"

"Your father defends Lochindorb Castle—from Iain of Islay!"

Alana froze.

She had thought about the dark Highlander who fought for Robert Bruce. He had been impossible to forget, and not simply because of her vision about him. His dark, powerful image haunted her. So did his inexplicable kiss.

She did not want to recall the brief time she had spent in his camp. She did not want to be interested in him, not even remotely, not in any way. But she had wondered how he fared. She even worried about Duncan's plan to assassinate him should he attack Nairn. And she did fear that her father and Iain might cross paths in this war, with Sir Alexander left in the south to defend them. And now, it seemed as if the worst had happened.

"Where is Lochindorb?" Alana asked.

Eleanor looked at Sir John, who came forward. "It is two days to the south, if one rides without interruption," he said.

"Is it true?" Alana asked him. "Is my father at Lochindorb—defending it from Iain of Islay?"

Buchan stormed into the hall, followed by a dozen knights, everyone in full armor. Obviously he had heard her question, for he snapped, "It *was* true. Lochindorb has fallen." His eyes were burning with barely repressed anger.

Alana could not quite breathe. "My father?" she managed to ask.

"I do not know where he is, but the keep fell two days ago. The battle did not last an entire morning!" Buchan cried. He began to pace in a frenzy, head down, as he clearly deliberated the next course of action.

Alana stared at him. Her uncle wasn't just angry— he was uneasy and anxious. Was he afraid that Sir Alexander was hurt? She prayed her father had survived his encounter with Iain. "Can we send a man for news of Sir Alexander?"

He stared at her, as if in disbelief. "I cannot worry about my brother now, when I must defend my land from Bruce!"

Her heart sank. Didn't he care about his brother? Or was he only afraid of losing this war to Bruce? Everyone was dressed for battle. Clearly, her uncle was leaving to take his army to war.

"His army has turned north," Duncan said grimly. "They have left Lochindorb standing, perhaps because it is so small, and Iain of Islay leads them once again."

They were marching north. They were marching north and Iain was leading them.

Her heart had turned over, but not with dread. Oddly, she was not afraid.

She had always assumed they would never meet again. Now she had the strongest feeling that the reverse was true—that they would meet again—and soon.

Buchan turned. "This would be an excellent time for a vision," he said harshly.

"I want to help," she whispered. "I truly do!"

"Good!" It was a shout. Buchan turned and seized a pitcher from the table and thrust it under her nose. "Then help! Do your duty! Prove your loyalty! Are you a witch or not?"

Alana flinched. She could not stand to look into her uncle's cold, hard eyes. She looked into the pitcher, but was blinded by her tears. It was not that his words were hurtful, which they were, it was that his tone was so cruel.

The pitcher vanished, replaced upon the table, and she heard Buchan and Duncan heatedly discussing the defense of Nairn and Elgin—they did not know which castle would be attacked first. Buchan wanted to know where his damned spies were. Alana closed her eyes tightly, the tears burning.

Lochindorb had fallen—to Iain. Her father had been in the battle, and now, Buchan did not know where he was, or even if he lived. He desperately needed her help, and she desperately wished to give it!

She glanced at her uncle, who remained in a furious and frantic conversation with Duncan. Neither man looked her way.

He had just shouted at her—almost as if he despised her.

Impulsively Alana lifted her skirts and ran from the hall. As she did, she glimpsed her grandmother's startled expression. She did not care, and no one shouted at her to stop, to return.

Twilight had fallen over the hills surrounding the castle, and the courtyard was filled with long, dark shadows. Alana tripped as she ran. No one called after her still.

Because no one cared what she did—no one cared for her at all.

She sank down on the ground, curling up, and cried.

She cried because Buchan was using her, and she had known it from the beginning, even if she had tried to believe otherwise. She cried because she had yet to see her father, who might be hurt or, dear God, dead. She cried because neither her uncle nor her father gave a damn. And she cried because Iain of Islay was the enemy, yet he was the only man who had ever looked at her with interest.

Realizing that she was mired in self-pity, she choked back her tears. Crying would not solve anything. A brief stay at Nairn would not change a lifetime spent being shunned by the Comyn family. Alana wiped her eyes.

I am a fool, she thought.

Why not lie to Buchan and give him the prophecy he wished for? She might be given Brodie—and if not, at least she would be able to go home.

Alana slowly stood up, filled with desperation. Was she truly considering more deception? Lying to her uncle felt so immoral. How could she live with such a choice?

There was a well in the center of the courtyard.

She tensed, staring at the dark shape of the wood fence surrounding it. A bucket hung upon a rope pulley above it. A ladder lay against the fence. There was a full moon in the dark night sky.

Alana slowly walked over to the well, her heart now thundering. The stockade fence was chest high. She reached it and clutched its top.

The wild pounding of her heart increased. She began to feel tipsy, faint. Her stomach began to churn. *I am going to have a vision,* she thought, but there was no relief. Instead she felt dread—horror.

From where she stood, if she wished to, she could stare down into the well and into its black depths.

But Alana didn't look down. She did not have to.

For she could feel the water below her. It was so heavy, and like a huge weight attached to her limbs, it began pulling her inexorably down.

Alana moaned and looked down into the darkness.

Flames blazed from its black depths. The fire shot up at her face.

She was scorched, but she did not move—she could not move. In the flames, she saw the terrified faces of men, women and children, their eyes white, mouths wide. For one moment, there was no sound.

And then she heard their screams.

They were being burned alive....

She did not want to see any more and she closed her eyes as she fell. Vaguely, she felt the dirt and rocks under her face, her hands. But now she saw the men, women and children running from the fires—entire villages aflame. Houses, shops, barns were blazing... crops were burning...forests were an inferno! Horses and cattle ran from the fires, frantic, a stampede....

Then suddenly, the fires were gone. The sky was blue, marred only by passing white clouds. A Highland army appeared, astride. Bruce's yellow banner with its red dragon waved above them.

The army was galloping now across the countryside, the forests black, the hills scorched and barren, roadside farms gutted, villages burned to the ground, a castle reduced to rubble, one tower partly standing.

Women and children cowered in the woods, watching the passing army, clad in rags, gaunt from starvation, sobbing in fear and anguish....

And when the army was gone, there was a banner upon the road. Trampled into shreds, she knew whose red, black and gold banner it was.

"Mistress Alana!"

Alana clawed the cold dirt and rough stones beneath her hands, still consumed by the horrific images. She heard Sir John call urgently to her again. But all she saw was the devastation and carnage left by Bruce's army, the starving women and children.... She got onto all fours, retching.

"Alana?" This time it was her grandmother, her hands on her back.

Alana had never been as ill, and she thought she would vomit again. She had never shaken as violently, nor could she stop. The tears flowed.

She had never witnessed such death and destruction, such merciless savagery, before.

Dear, dear God. She had just foreseen the annihilation of the earldom and its people.

"Mistress Alana?" It was Sir John. "If you have had a vision, you must go in and tell the earl!"

Alana closed her eyes, fighting the nausea, which

refused to recede. Her head continued to spin. Surely, this vision was a warning, not a prophecy. Buchan was the most powerful earl in the north of Scotland! How could he be so thoroughly destroyed?

"You are shaking as if with fever," Eleanor cried, helping her to sit up.

Alana heard her. But the grotesque images of terror, fire, blood and death would not go away. She could still see those frightened men, women and children in vivid detail!

But she somehow forced herself to see past their terrified faces until Eleanor's worried countenance came into view.

"Alana?" she cried, aghast, for she knew the vision had not been a good one.

Alana could not yet speak. She could hardly think. She only knew that they must never let such destruction come to pass. "Sir John! Could you get her some water, please?" Eleanor cried.

Sir John whirled and lowered the bucket into the well. As he did, Alana leaned heavily upon Eleanor who sat with her on the ground. A moment later he returned with a ladle of water. Alana used it to wipe her mouth, and then took a long draught.

Sir John knelt. "I am sorry, mistress, but I must take you inside. I am under orders."

Alana wanted to protest, she wanted to delay. She did not want to face her uncle now! But when she finally looked at the knight he was ashen.

"Alana! What did you see?" Eleanor cried.

Alana met her gaze, finally somewhat lucid, but not yet coherent. What was she to do?

Should she lie? When lying to her uncle was so abhorrent? *Could* she lie, after such a horrific and devastating experience?

"We must go in, Lady Fitzhugh." Sir John was firm. He helped both women up, avoiding all eye contact now.

Alana shrugged free, aware that she frightened him now and he did not want to touch her. "I am fine," she said, a complete lie. She continued to tremble uncontrollably. She still felt faint and ill.

Alana went inside with Eleanor, Sir John following.

Buchan turned as they came inside. He took one look at her and his eyes widened. "What has happened?" he demanded, hurrying toward them.

"I found Mistress Alana on the ground, crying and screaming. She then became ill," Sir John said gravely. "I think she had a vision."

"Is it true?" Buchan demanded.

Alana somehow nodded. "Yes." Her mind raced, but uselessly. She did not know what to do next, or what she would say when asked.

"What did you see!" he cried.

Alana stared at her uncle. How could she deceive him? If she told him of some pleasant future for the earldom, and her vision came to pass, she would never forgive herself. Should he not be warned? This vision must never come true! "Niece!" Buchan grasped her shoulder and shook her.

"I saw our villages being burned to the ground, our villagers being murdered," she whispered, feeling ill yet again. "I saw Highlanders murdering the innocent people of Buchan…. I saw the land, scorched and destroyed, from one end to the other, no village, no farm, no castle left standing."

Buchan's eyes were wide. He stared speechlessly. "How do you know it was Buchan land you saw burned and destroyed?"

Tears fell. "Bruce's flag flew above—yours lay in shreds in the ashes."

He roared in rage. "This is the vision you give me?"

Alana meant to speak, but his hand flew across her face so swiftly that she could not utter a word. Pain exploded and she was knocked off her feet.

"This is your vision after all I have promised you?" he roared again.

His fist was raised. Beneath him on the floor, she cringed. "Maybe it is a warning!" she cried.

He struck her again, even harder, across the same side of her face.

She choked on the blazing pain.

"Stop! Stop it, John, stop it!" Eleanor screamed at him.

But Buchan did not hear. "I asked for a vision of victory, Alana! Instead, you tell me Buchan will be destroyed? Damn you! Damn you to hell!"

"I cannot help what I saw," she sobbed. "Please! You must make certain I am wrong!"

Buchan seemed about to kick her. Instead, he caught himself and stood over her, panting from his exertions, the hall so silent, only his heavy breathing was audible.

Alana curled up, trying not to cry, her face on fire. Eleanor scooted to her and knelt, taking her in her arms. Alana clung to her grandmother.

"We have a war to attend," Buchan finally said harshly. "We will ride out now, as planned."

Alana dared look at him over her tiny grandmother's arm and cringed.

He was staring furiously at her.

Duncan stepped forward. "What about her?" He nodded at Alana contemptuously.

Buchan was now striding across the hall, past Alana and Eleanor. He did not look at them again. "Take her and the old woman back to the tower. Lock them both up until I decide what to do with them."

THEY WERE THE Earl of Buchan's prisoners now.

Alana stood at the window of her small tower room, which she now again shared with her grandmother.

Three days had passed, and she had not been allowed to leave the chamber. Neither had Eleanor.

Meals were brought to them. A maid came to attend the fire, bringing kindling for them. She also changed their chamber pot. Both women had taken up sewing to pass the time.

There was no news. No news of Buchan, no news of Bruce and his army, no news of her father—if he had lived, or if he had died. Alana prayed for him.

Now she stared outside at the deserted and snowy hillside, lightly holding the sill. She had had an odd feeling all day—of expectation. She wasn't exactly afraid. But something of great import would soon happen, something with grave consequences. She was certain.

"Are you watching for someone?" Eleanor asked. She came to stand beside her. "The road has been deserted all day."

"If only a messenger would come, and at least bring us news of the war…and my father," Alana said. She should not be wondering about Iain just then, but he remained on her mind. But then, he might lead the attack on Nairn when it came—if it came.

She sighed and turned away from the window. She heard the bolt being lifted upon the door. A maid stepped inside, holding a dinner tray.

Alana knew Mairi well now, and she started, for the young blonde girl's eyes were wide and her freckled cheeks were flushed. "Mairi?" Alana asked warily.

Breathlessly the maid set down their dinner of bread, cheese and wine. "Buchan is returning. The watch has seen his knights on the south road!"

Alana seized her arm. Was this the news she had been awaiting? "Do you know what has happened? Did he battle with Bruce's army? Was he victorious?" Had her uncle chased the mighty Bruce away?

"I have heard that Bruce is marching on us!" Mairi cried, ashen.

Alana glanced at Eleanor, who was pale. Bruce was on the march—Nairn would soon be attacked.

This could not be the event she had sensed coming. She had not felt fear or dread. But she was afraid now—Bruce meant to attack Nairn! "Is Buchan returning to defend us?" Was there time to escape? Would they and the other innocent residents of the castle be allowed to flee?

"I dinna ken," Mairi cried. "I ken what the watch has seen—Buchan is returning. Lady! Have ye ever been in a siege?"

Alana touched her arm. "No, Mairi, fortunately, I have not."

"They will rape and murder us." Tears welled in Mairi's eyes.

Alana inhaled. "We do not know that."

Mairi looked at her as if she was mad.

Alana stiffened. She was not a simple maid, like Mairi was—she was Buchan's niece. And Bruce was on the march, his ambition to destroy her uncle and his earldom.

Their rivalry went back generations, to the time when Bruce's grandfather had unsuccessfully sought the throne against John Balliol. But it was worse than that. Two years ago, Bruce had murdered Buchan's cousin, Red John Comyn, the Lord of Badenoch. Buchan had sworn revenge, and the enmity between the families had, impossibly, increased.

If Bruce took Nairn, what would happen to Buchan, to her father, if he was present—to her? They were his worst, most hated and most despised enemies.

"Can you come back and tell us what is happening? Please?" Alana implored. The maid usually did not come back till the morning. "You could pretend we need more firewood!"

"I'll try." Tears in her eyes, little Mairi fled.

Alana had no faith in her. But she could not be left in ignorance now, and if Buchan were returning, she wished to speak with him! Never mind that she now feared him impossibly. He had to release her and Eleanor, so they could flee this battle.

She rushed to the open door—only to be barred in the doorway by Sir John. "You know you cannot leave," he said sternly.

"Will we be attacked?"

"That is what everyone in the castle is speaking of, mistress."

She trembled. "Will my uncle stay and defend us? Why else would he return?"

"I have received no orders yet. But the earl will be here within the hour." He turned to leave.

She gripped his arm, preventing him from closing the door. Startled, he flinched and met her gaze. "Is my father with him? Please, Sir John, I do not know if my father is even alive!"

He shook her off. "I do not know!"

"And who leads Bruce's forces?"

He shook his head, about to close the door.

"Wait!" she cried, pushing between him and the door. "Will my grandmother and I remain imprisoned if we are attacked? I must speak with my uncle immediately! He must release us!"

His answer was to scowl and shut the door in her face. Alana stared at the wood, her nose practically touching it, flinching when she heard the bolt being thrown.

Eleanor approached. "If Nairn falls, perhaps we will be set free."

Alana stared at her. Would Iain free them? "Either that, or we will become the prisoners of our worst enemy."

THE ATTACK BEGAN at dawn.

Alana had not slept well. She had been unable to stop her racing thoughts as she worried over whether or not the castle would be attacked, and what might happen to her and her grandmother, trapped as they were in the tower. If Iain were leading the attack, and he was aware of her presence in the tower, she was certain he would not allow them to be hurt. But he would not know that she and Eleanor were present. If the castle were taken, enemy soldiers would overrun every inch of it. Buchan's soldiers would be killed. Alana was afraid of her own fate and that of the other women who were present.

As for what might happen should Bruce ever learn of her identity, she could only pray he would consider her a worthless and unwanted bastard—though she felt certain that would not be the case.

Mairi had not come back. Sir John had refused to open the door to speak with her, no matter how often she shouted at him. She had finally given up banging on the door, as his answer remained absolute silence.

She could not see the south road from her window, only the north road, which was rarely used as it went to the sea. She could only assume that Buchan had returned, perhaps with Duncan, and perhaps with her father, and that he meant to defend the castle.

Alana fell asleep in her grandmother's arms, fighting tears of rising hysteria.

The siege engines awoke her.

She heard a boom from the front gates, the sound shocking. Instantly awake, she could hear the sounds of battle from outside—screaming horses, shouting men, whistling missiles.

"Gran! We are under attack!" Alana cried, seizing her mantle. She ran to the window and pushed open the shutters.

"Alana, stand back!" Eleanor screamed.

But Alana could not move. Hail after hail of arrows flew at the castle walls, along with flaming missiles.

She flinched but did not move. Bruce's army was arranged across the ridge below the tower where she stood. The barbican was on the south side, and she had not expected such a sight.

But his soldiers snaked around the walls to the west, and she felt certain his men ringed the castle entirely. He had hundreds of archers in the first rows of his army, foot soldiers with shields and pikes behind them. She espied several groups of mounted knights, and then, a small army of mounted Highlanders.

She stared across the archers and foot soldiers at the Highland army atop the ridge. Were those Iain's men?

More arrows flew toward the north wall, and the tower where she stood. Catapults had been set up at intervals, and fiery rock bombs were whizzing at the ramparts. She ducked and stepped away from the open window, her heart slamming.

The siege engine in the south sounded again, a huge banging sound, almost like an explosion. Would they soon break the front gates down?

She ran back to the window.

"Alana!" Eleanor seized her from behind.

Alana ignored her, just as she ignored more whizzing arrows. They sounded like rocks and gravel, peppering the walls around the tower. But the missiles screamed, exploding as they hit the walls, far too close for comfort. She seized the sill and dared to look down, directly below her.

Because the north road was the fastest way to the docks and the wharves, there was a gate below, through which the castle's supplies and provisions came.

A battering ram was being slowly pushed toward the north gate.

She held her breath as the machine came closer and closer and then she tensed as an explosion sounded. Before she could take a breath, a burning bomb landed on the wall outside her window. Fire and sparks shot at her as Alana leaped away from the opening, slamming the shutter closed.

Eleanor pulled her away from the window, ashen. "Are you burned?"

Alana touched her cheek, where a spark had burned her. "I'll be fine."

Eleanor ran to the table, seized the pitcher and returned. She wet her sleeve and laid the cool cloth on her tiny burn.

"Will Nairn fall?" Alana asked. She trembled with fear. It was one thing to calmly speculate about its fall—and being freed—when all was as it should be, another to do so when under attack.

"We cannot remain here, like this!" Eleanor cried.

Her grandmother was the calmest, wisest and most courageous woman Alana knew. But she was frightened now.

Alana silently agreed. She ran to the door and banged on it. "Sir John! You must let us out! We cannot remain here, trapped like rabbits in a cage, a wolf at the door! We need to know what is happening and we can help defend the castle." She banged on the door again, furiously, desperately.

There was no answer. Alana pulled on the door handle, but the door remained bolted from outside. She turned, wide-eyed. "He is gone."

Eleanor was pale. They stared at each other, shocked.

"They have left us here?" Alana finally gasped.

"He must be helping defend the keep," Eleanor said slowly.

"And if we are overrun? Who will defend us?" Alana cried. Her mind raced as she rushed back to the window and opened the shutter. Iain was surely a part of this attack, but she had yet to see him. How could she get word to him?

"Alana! Do not go near the window!" Eleanor begged.

Alana ignored her. Enemy soldiers had thrown ladders up against the walls to the left of the siege engine. She saw from their dress that they were Highlanders, but Buchan's archers were on the ramparts, firing down at them. Thank God, she thought, with a flooding of relief. Finally someone was on the north walls, above them, defending them.

She saw one of the Highlanders struck by multiple arrows in his chest and arms. Screaming, he fell from the ladder to a certain death.

But another Highlander was aggressively scaling the wall. If he was not shot, he would soon climb over the ramparts.

Alana whirled. "The Highlanders are coming. Should I pen a message for Iain?"

"We must do something," Eleanor cried, quickly sitting at the table. She took parchment and a quill from the drawer and began to write.

Alana remained huddled in the corner, not far from the window. She did not know how she would get the message to Iain, and it was becoming harder to think.

The battering ram exploded against the north gate another time, so loudly, so powerfully, that Alana felt the floor shift beneath her feet. She jumped.

And then a face appeared outside her window.

It was inches away. Alana gasped, for one moment shocked, as the man stared into the chamber. Their gazes locked.

And then she realized that his eyes were wide and

lifeless eyes, his face contorted in pain and death. And then he vanished.

She ran to the window and leaned out. A ladder was beneath her, and the Highlander was falling like a leaf twisting in the wind. She looked away as he hit the ground below her.

Alana gripped the ledge of the windowsill, stunned. No one else was attempting to scale that ladder. She inhaled. Was she brave enough to attempt to go down?

She was afraid of falling, of being shot—and of leaving Eleanor alone.

Eleanor had come to stand beside her. "It is too dangerous!"

And then, from the corner of her eye, Alana saw Iain.

She whirled. She would never mistake him on his black charger, sword raised, long hair flying in the wind. He was galloping from the west, toward the north gate. He paused, his horse rearing, and she knew he was shouting at his men. More Highlanders were on more ladders now, and more men were pushing the battering ram.

Arrows hailed down upon them now.

It was Iain. And they meant to assassinate him.

Alana seized the windowsill and screamed at him. "Iain, beware." He was too close to the walls, too close to Buchan's archers! Yet she also knew he would never hear her, not in the din of battle.

The words were barely out of her mouth when a hail of arrows flew from the ramparts directly at him.

He must have sensed the danger, for he held up his shield. Dozens of arrows struck the metal and leather there, bouncing uselessly away. Others landed in the ground around him and his horse.

Alana cried out as another barrage of arrows flew at him. She held her breath as they struck his shield, the horse's breastplate and the ground.

This time he whirled the stallion and galloped back to the safety of the rest of the army.

Alana felt her knees buckle with relief. At least he knew he was a target. At least now, he would be prepared.

Another explosion sounded, and wood cracked. The stones beneath her feet reverberated so strongly that she lost her balance.

Alana caught the sill and leaned out of the window again. The north gate was directly below the tower where she stood, and all she could see was that the men were pulling back the ram, clearly preparing for another assault.

The hail of arrows and missiles from Bruce's army had ceased. The fire from the ramparts had decreased dramatically, to an occasional arrow, and an isolated oil pot. A dozen Highland soldiers were climbing the castle walls, and now, they were undeterred. She watched a dozen Highlanders climbing over the ramparts. She watched them assault Buchan's archers, wrestling them off the walls and to their deaths.

The floor shook as the north gate exploded. Alana cried out, as did Eleanor, some rock from the ceiling above falling. Alana ran to her grandmother to protect her with her body. "Nairn is falling," she said.

THE BATTLE WAS OVER. Alana had watched Iain ride triumphantly into the north gate with a dozen of his mounted men, his banner flying. That had been several hours ago. Since then, the countryside had come alive with tents and cook fires. She could see and hear Bruce's men celebrating outside—singing and dancing, drinking and feasting, laughter. Bruce's banner flew high in the dusky sky, above the sea of tents, brightly yellow and red.

He had captured Nairn. What would happen next? Had Buchan been captured? What of her father? And Duncan?

And what would happen now?

Alana did not want to worry Eleanor, but she kept thinking about the fact that Bruce was in the habit of razing every castle he took. Lochindorb had been an exception. She was frightened, because if they meant to burn Nairn down, would they find both women first?

As of yet, no one had come to the door, and in a way, she was grateful—for she also remained frightened of enemy soldiers who might happen upon them. She did not know what to expect when they were finally discovered.

Alana kept returning to the door, to place her ear upon it, to strain to hear. There were no celebratory sounds inside. Whatever was happening downstairs, they could not hear. For all she knew, no one was downstairs—everyone had been rounded up and taken away through the south gate.

It was so terribly quiet upstairs, it was unnerving.

"Sometimes no news is the best news," Eleanor whispered.

Alana did not know how to reply. At times she was tempted to bang on the door and shout until her voice was raw, but then her fear held her back. Her mind always returned to the possibility of being raped and murdered, before veering to being identified and imprisoned far more significantly than now.

How could Buchan have left them like this? She refused to believe her father would have consented to such cruelty and neglect.

Alana returned to the bed and sat down beside her grandmother. "Are you hungry?" she asked softly.

"I am fine, Alana."

She had to be ravenous, as they had not eaten all day. But Alana did not say so. She smiled and squeezed her hand.

And then she heard the bolt outside the door being freed.

Alana tensed, as did Eleanor, both of them staring, half in horror, as the door swung open.

A huge Highlander with a gray beard stood there. "Who are ye?" he demanded. "And what do ye do in this chamber, locked inside of it?"

"We were imprisoned by the Earl of Buchan," she said quickly. She stood up. "We must speak with Iain of Islay." She hesitated. "Tell him it is Alana."

His eyes widened. "I'll tell him." He shut the door, bolted it and left.

Alana turned to her wide-eyed grandmother, trembling. "I will convince him to free us."

Eleanor stood, but stiffly. "Have a care, Alana, he answers to Bruce."

Alana stared. "He doesn't know anything yet."

"Make sure he never does."

Alana felt a terrible dismay. But Eleanor was right. Bruce was somewhere at Nairn—she could never be honest with Iain about her Comyn blood now.

Alana turned to stare at the locked door. Iain owed her a vast debt—he had said so. Surely he would free them. Surely she could convince him to do so.

But what if Buchan were below, and the truth came out?

She inhaled. Even if Buchan did not reveal her identity, most of the castle's inhabitants knew she was Buchan's niece. Even if Iain decided to free them, she was in peril, until she was safely gone from Nairn.

Footsteps sounded outside, heavy and male, with the jangle of spurs. She glanced at Eleanor, who smiled reassuringly. Alana felt her heart slam as the bolt was thrown and the door opened.

Iain stood there with the graying Highlander, his blue eyes wide with shock.

Alana smiled. "My lord." She trembled, hoping to be deferential. But her heart raced, and she could not deny a moment of joy.

He strode to her, unsmiling, his eyes hard, and touched her chin. He tilted it up. "By God! Who did this to ye?"

She tensed. There was a terrible bruise on the right side of her face, and her lip was swollen from where it had been split. But she was fortunate that her uncle had missed her eye. And the bruises were healing. They were bluish-green now, not darkly purple.

She hesitated. "I fell, my lord."

He dropped his hand from her chin. His stare intensified, and she flinched, but she could not look away. "Why will ye protect the man who did this?"

She did not know how to respond. "Because it doesn't matter," she finally said.

"It matters," he said with warning. "And ye were burned in the battle!"

Alana started. Iain almost sounded as if he cared.

"A small missile almost came through the window," she began.

"And ye were here, locked inside, for the entire battle?"

"We have been in this chamber, yes, for the entire battle."

He gave her one last incredulous look, and turned to Eleanor. "Lady Fitzhugh, are ye unharmed?"

"I have not been hurt," Eleanor assured him. "But I am weary."

"Do ye wish to take to yer bed? I will have a meal sent up," Iain said.

"I am afraid these old bones need some rest," Eleanor said.

Alana went to her. Eleanor seemed unusually frail, so suddenly.

Iain turned his attention to Alana. His stare was so direct that she became nervous. "Why did the Earl of Buchan imprison ye?"

"I displeased him."

His stare sharpened.

"Can we not leave it there?" she asked, smiling slightly. "Please? My grandmother and I are exhausted, frightened and hungry. We can tell stories another day."

"Did ye tell Buchan ye nursed my wound? Is that why he was displeased?"

It would be so easy to take that tangent, which he had offered her. "No."

It was a moment before he spoke, as he considered her words. "So it was Buchan who struck ye?"

She started in alarm. "I did not say that!"

"Ye dinna need to." His eyes were dark with anger. "Did he strike ye, Alana?"

Alana was grim. Then she reminded herself that it didn't matter if he knew Buchan had hit her, as long as he did not know why. "Yes. Where is the earl?" she asked carefully.

"He fled, coward that he is."

Alana glanced at Eleanor, surprised. "Did Duncan also escape?"

"Aye. They escaped together."

She trembled. Nairn had fallen, her uncle and Duncan had escaped—perhaps with her father—but she had been left behind. She did not know what to think, except that now, these lords would not be downstairs to reveal her identity to Iain and to Robert Bruce.

"Ye seem dismayed."

"Duncan is my guardian—I am pleased."

His gaze narrowed. "They ride for Elgin, to defend it from us next."

So they would attack Elgin next. She stared at him and finally sat down. He was right. She was dismayed. She had been left behind, because no one cared about her fate. She should not care, or even feel hurt, but she did.

And then she looked up and saw Iain gazing far too closely at her again. She managed a small smile. "I see that you are unscathed."

He continued to stare, then turned to Eleanor. "Do ye wish for a different chamber? I can try to arrange it, although these halls are full tonight."

"Do not bother, my lord," Eleanor said. "If you bring me some repast, I will be fine."

He nodded and his expression softened slightly as he glanced at Alana. "The castle maids are preparing a feast for the king. Will ye come downstairs?"

Alana stiffened. She could not go down and dine. She did not dare meet Bruce, or attract his attention, in any way. She could not risk discovery. She realized he was staring. "I am the enemy, my lord."

"Alana is exhausted, my lord," Eleanor said carefully. "We have feared for our lives this day."

Iain gave her grandmother a sharp glance; clearly sensing something was amiss. "Ye have my protection tonight. Tomorrow, ye will return to Brodie. Tomorrow, I will fight yer liege, and God willing, kill him and Buchan. Tonight, we will not think of the war and we will not be enemies. Tonight, we will enjoy the king's feast."

Alana bit her lip, her heart racing. It was not wise to mingle with the enemy. "Will you tell Bruce who I am? That I am from Brodie?"

His stare narrowed. "Do ye fear the king?"

She nodded. "Very much."

He reached out and slid his fingers along her cheek. "Then ye will not meet him," he said.

CHAPTER FIVE

IAIN CLASPED HER ELBOW, guiding her down the corridor. Alana was acutely aware of his touch, of his presence and his proximity.

But even so, she remained afraid. She should have refused his offer to dine. It was too late now.

His step also slowed. "What is wrong?" Iain asked softly.

She smiled nervously. "I am weary, that is all."

His brow lifted. "Are ye still frightened?" he asked. "Did I not promise to protect ye—even from the king?"

He sensed her unease, she thought. "Yes."

"Maybe one day ye will tell me the truth—and why ye fear the king so much."

He clasped her hand and pulled her forward, toward the open doors of the hall.

"I am the king's enemy," she said.

He gave her a glance, indicating that he knew, very well, that there was far more to her fear than such a simple explanation. He was astute. How long could she deceive him, when she did not even want to?

It was so hard not to stare at him. Without the fur he habitually wore, she could see the hard, muscular outline of his shoulders, his chest and torso through his clothes. He was a tall, powerfully built man. He had to be three times her size, and all male muscle. And he still held her hand. Her mouth was dry.

He smiled slightly, as if he knew how discomfited— and interested—she was. "Come. Ye must be hungry, as am I."

She tried to smile at him and wondered if she succeeded. As she did, she glanced past him and into the great hall.

A great feast was taking place within it. Alana looked past everyone there, a huge crowd of knights, nobles, women and Highland men, and she instantly saw Robert Bruce.

She had seen his likeness once or twice, and even if she had not, she would have instantly known which man was Scotland's king.

He was simply impossible to mistake. He was a giant among men, although taller men were present. He was handsome and powerfully built, although others were more so. And he was superbly dressed. A red doublet over a blue surcote, red hose sheathing his powerful legs above his black boots. A red-and-gold mantle swung about his shoulders. He wore gold rings, a gold chain, a gold cross.

But mostly, he had an air of power and authority— and the presence of a warrior and a king.

It occurred to her then that she might deceive Iain through evasion, with female manipulations, and the attraction they shared. But Bruce would not be so easily fooled.

However, the hall was so crowded that there was no room left to sit or stand. It would be so easy to enter it and go unremarked. Yet Alana remained uneasy.

She ducked her head, averting her face from all

those they passed, as they walked inside the great hall. Alana tried to make herself even smaller than she was, shrinking against his side. If he noticed her behavior, he did not remark it. Fortunately the crowd was mostly inebriated. A few men shouted a greeting to him. Iain did not pause. He led her to one of the many makeshift tables that had been erected in the room.

Alana was clinging to his hand. She glanced carefully at the table, standing somewhat behind Iain. Every possible seat was taken. It crossed her mind that they might have to leave—and she would not mind, this was simply too stressful—when Iain tapped a man on the shoulder and a place was instantly vacated for her. Inhaling, Alana slid onto the bench, Iain standing behind her.

A quick look around the table told her that she was surrounded by strangers, all of them English knights in Bruce's service, from his lands in Carrick and Annandale. Alana flung a glance over her shoulder, past Iain. Bruce was surrounded by a large group of enthralled admirers, mostly noblemen in jewels and knights wearing their swords, as well as several very beautiful women. He was engrossed with his friends, and she was relieved.

Iain laid a hand on her shoulder and bent over her. "Perhaps ye will enjoy the evening now." His chest pressed upon her shoulder and his arm against her breast, while his breath feathered her nape.

Alana felt her mind go blank. At the same time, her heart raced.

Then, before she could wonder at what he was he doing, Iain shoved his way onto the bench next to her. There was no room to accommodate him, yet he pushed between her and the man next to her, forcing a place to be made. His large, powerful body wedged against hers, from shoulder to hip and hip to knee. He smiled at her, then handed her a mug of wine. "Drink and ye will feel better," he said.

Alana was shocked. Did he mean to seduce her? He had deliberately pressed his body against hers a moment ago, she was certain. She seized her mug and drank. It was so hard to think clearly!

He handed her a slab of bread with a piece of cheese upon it. Their gazes collided as he did. Alana was certain her cheeks flamed, and she hurriedly looked away.

"I am glad ye were not more scathed from this battle."

She set the bread and cheese down, untouched. Her pounding pulse made eating impossible. His tone was so soft, so intimate. "You were once—so recently—suspicious of me."

"Ye were once—so recently—suspiciously spying from the wood." He smiled and ate.

Alana looked away, somewhat breathless, and took a bite of the cheese. His smiles were making him seem like a different man—as if he were not Bruce's ruthless warrior. "I wasn't spying."

He was piling up a plate with roasted game and warm bread. "Even if ye were, that was then, and this is now." He set the huge plate down in front of her. "Ye need yer strength, Alana. Eat."

He began preparing another plate. Alana stared at the food, unable to fathom his words. Did he still think she had been spying? If so, why had he kissed her at Boath Manor, and why was he so kind to her now?

Iain began to devour his food, without pause, fast

and furiously. Alana lifted her knife and stabbed a piece of venison. She had no appetite. They would be finished dining, soon. And then what?

Something was changing between them. It was almost as if they were friends, and upon the brink of becoming lovers.

If he asked her to bed, should she accept?

He was the enemy, and she only had to look over her shoulder at Robert Bruce to know so. And she was keeping so many secrets from him. He did not know she was Buchan's niece—or that she was a witch.

Her mind raced, her thoughts jumbled up with conflicting worries and strange yearnings—Iain, Bruce, her identity, her visions, Iain's kiss....

"Why won't ye eat?" Iain asked flatly.

Still acutely aware of how they sat next to one another, Alana managed a tight smile. "Why will you let us return to Brodie tomorrow?" she asked softly, so no one could overhear.

He shoved his plate away, pouring more wine into his mug from the pitcher. He took a sip and turned to face her. "Is there a reason ye should be kept a prisoner? Ye keep telling me yer no spy."

"Of course not!" She flushed. "And I was not a spy. It is just that...today you are kind."

His face tightened. "Ye were beaten and imprisoned. I think ye have suffered enough unkindness today."

"They say you are ruthless!" she exclaimed, shoving her own, very full, plate away.

He looked down at his plate. "Are we on the battlefield? Are ye a soldier—a knight?"

She somehow shook her head.

He faced her and said, abruptly, "Ye will not eat?"

She took a breath. "I cannot."

He leaped to his feet, and pulled her to stand, as well. His blue eyes were as dark as storm clouds. "Then we are done here."

Her heart thundered as he grasped her arm and guided her through the crowd. His strides were rushed, and Alana almost ran to keep up.

Once in the hall outside, they were alone, the sounds of laughter and conversation dull and distant. Iain halted, still holding her arm. "I did not expect to meet again, so soon after the battle at Boath Manor." His hand climbed to her face. He caressed her cheek and moved a long tendril of hair aside. It had been caught on her breast.

She shivered. "What did you think?"

"I thought," he said, his stare far too direct, "that I'd visit ye at Brodie Castle."

Her mind was dazed. There was no doubt as to his meaning—as to why he would have come to Brodie to see her. "That might have been difficult."

"I doubt it would be difficult, Alana." He leaned over her, bracing the corner of the hall with both hands, locking her between his arms. "And if I had come... would ye let me in?"

Inches separated his chest from hers. "Yes," she heard herself whisper.

Triumph flared in his eyes, and he wrapped her in his arms, kissing her.

Alana had thought their one previous kiss hard and demanding, but it was nothing like the kiss now. His mouth opened hers, forcefully, instantly, and his tongue swept deep, filling her. She found herself against the wall, off her feet and holding on to his shoulders. He kissed her again, and again, and again, until she could not stand the intensity of her desire, until she began to pant and whimper. Her body had become hot and swollen, explosive. She had never felt so desperate to be with a man.

He pulled away. "Ye can check on yer gran later."

She realized she was not being given any choice in the matter of going to his bed—not that she even knew if she could, or would, deny him. But his arm was a vise about her waist now as he pulled her downstairs.

"Where are we going?" she managed to ask.

He rushed her down a steep stairwell. "Every room is full. Do ye wish for company?" His smile was brief. "I want ye to myself."

They had reached the ground floor, which was rough and dank, with only a few torches lit on the walls. "We are in the cellars?"

"We are in the cellars." He pulled her into his arms. "Alana. Dinna deny me."

In his arms, the shock dissipated. "I don't know," she managed to say.

His answer was to catch her face in his hands and kiss her again, as hard and passionately as before.

Desire exploded within her, and it was mindless, insane. She seized his shoulders, finally kissing him back.

He groaned, as their teeth caught, as their tongues met and mated. Then he pulled away, breathing hard, looking around. He pulled off his plaid, making a pallet on the stone floor, behind a pile of sacks of wheat. Before Alana could move, he had divested her of her mantle, which was fur-lined, and added that to the pallet he had just made. Kneeling, he looked up.

Her belly was hollow; she felt faint. She would worry about what she was doing tomorrow! Alana held out her hand.

He took it, rising, and guided her back into his arms, and as one, they sank onto the cloaks. Slowly, Iain came down on top of her, hooking the skirt of his leine in his belt. He smiled at her, but it belied the blaze in his eyes.

"Are ye a virgin?" he asked.

She nodded, trying not to glance at his erect manhood and then giving up. He was massively proud.

And his eyes blazed, clearly triumphant. "Do ye like what ye see? Are ye pleased with me?" he whispered roughly.

And he found her mouth. But this time, his lips were like feathers, gentle, plying and teasing.

Alana closed her eyes as pleasure washed over her. She was incapable of answering.

He feathered kisses down her neck and along the edge of her bodice, while pulling up her skirts. And then one of his strong knees moved between her thighs, opening them.

Alana cried out, her eyes flying open, as she seized his strong shoulders. Something ballooned in her heart. It was huge, buoyant—it felt like love.

"I need ye, Alana," Iain said hoarsely. His expression strained, Iain seized her bodice and ripped open all her garments at once. He gathered her up, and she felt his penis against her, rock-hard and slick. Their gazes met.

The pleasure surging between them was stunning. Alana gasped and moved her calves over his back.

"Ye have amazed me as no other," he murmured, and then he kissed her, thrusting his tongue deep.

Alana held him harder, clawing at him now, kissing him back.

He broke the kiss, panting, and rose up over her. Their eyes locked. And then he surged into her, crying out, grunting.

Alana cried out, as well. The pain was brief. Instead, pleasure blinded her.

She threw her legs higher around his waist. He slowed his rhythm, and their gazes met again. And the moment they did, she could no longer bear it. The pleasure became ecstasy.

He PULLED HER into his arms. "Have I hurt ye?"

Alana labored to breathe. Her mind began to clear. They had just made love—explosively, mindlessly. "No." Her heart was racing wildly, but it still held that huge, buoyant feeling, as well.

Still keeping one arm around her, he reached down and pulled off each boot in turn. Then he leaned over her to kiss one of her taut, still aching nipples. "I owe ye a gown." He now reached between them and removed his belts. The sheathed swords hit the stone floors loudly.

Alana realized he had torn her clothing open from collarbone to navel. She began to blush. A torch was on the wall, somewhere behind them, and she lay in the light while he remained in shadows.

He laid his hand on her ribs, beneath her breasts. "Ye dinna have to hide from me. I have never seen as beautiful a woman."

Her heart thundered. Desire returned, instantaneous.

Alana took his hand and moved it over her breast. "You do not have to flatter me."

"I do." He removed her hand and kissed her breasts. "I will," he said, nuzzling her. "Ye have amazed me from the moment we met, with yer beauty, yer courage, yer kindness."

She lay back, letting the pleasure grow and spread. "I am a simple woman, Iain," she said.

"There's nothing simple about ye—yer deep like the oceans, so deep, I wonder about ye all the time." He nuzzled her ear.

She thought about the secrets she kept, and hated them.

"I want ye again, Alana, I always will." His kisses went lower, down her ribs.

Her pleasure became a restless yearning; she moaned.

His fingers floated over her thighs, her sex. "And I'm fiercely pleased ye were a virgin—that I am yer first man."

She could not speak as he stroked her.

Within moments, he moved over her and into her once again, eyes ablaze.

ALANA AWOKE AND realized she had fallen asleep. She lay in Iain's arms, upon his cloak and hers, in the dark cellars below the castle. Recalling their lovemaking, she was stunned.

What had she done?

He remained asleep, breathing deeply, his arms

about her. Alana was afraid to move, but she finally inhaled.

Oh, God, she had let him make love to her—twice—and it had been glorious. He was her worst enemy, truly, but she was insanely attracted to him, in every way, and she had not thought once about denying him. Their passion had been beyond anything she had imagined possible. In fact, being in his arms felt right, not wrong! And now, love felt like it was filling every possible space inside her chest.

So why did she feel like crying?

She stared up at his face as he slept, her chin on his chest, some torchlight playing upon them. She did not have regrets, she could not have regrets. But dear God, Iain did not even know the first thing about her.

She could not imagine how he would react to the news that she was Buchan's niece, or worse, that she was a witch.

He would certainly be angry to learn that she was a Comyn—that she was a part of the family that was his king's worst enemy. Bruce meant to destroy the Comyns. His efforts probably included her. Would he be able to forgive her that deception?

She trembled, hoping the day would never come when Iain knew she was Sir Alexander's daughter, but such a secret would have to come out, sooner or later. And she was frightened.

But it was so much worse than that, because they were surely not the first lovers to have opposing loyalties in a war. What would he think and do when he learned she was a witch? Wouldn't he react like all other men when he learned of her sight? He would be horrified and repulsed; he would not want to share his bed with her then! He would probably end their relationship the instant he learned the truth!

Alana felt moisture rising up in her eyes. If only they could continue on this way, as if she were an insignificant and ordinary woman!

But that was impossible, wasn't it? It was one thing to deceive the enemy, another, her lover. Surely she had to confess the extent of her deceptions. Didn't she?

Because she could never walk away from Iain of Islay now to keep her secrets safe. She knew this was a beginning, if she could manage her deceptions.

"Yer awake and ye did not awaken me?"

She jerked and met his teasing blue gaze. "You were sleeping so soundly." She touched his chin, a gentle caress.

He smiled and pulled her beneath him. "I am not sleeping now."

He was stiff and hard and Alana went still, her pulse soaring. "Iain," she began, knowing they must speak.

"Shhh," he said, nuzzling her neck. "Whatever ye wish to say, it can wait."

Iain wrapped her in his powerful arms and began kissing her, his lips feathery and teasing. Desire surged within her and she began to kiss him back. His grasp tightened on her and his kiss deepened. Alana tried to capture his tongue with her own; he used his powerful thighs to spread her legs wide. Alana moaned.

Iain moved slowly into her, with restraint, inch by inch. Alana clawed at his back. "Hurry. You are teasing me."

"Aye," he murmured, and then he thrust hard.

Alana gasped, consumed with growing pleasure, and now, they moved swiftly, hard, as one. Alana shattered, crying out again and again, Iain grunting his own pleasure.

And then they lay very still, breathing hard, in one another's arms.

"We must get up," Iain said softly, his mouth against her ear. "Even though I wish to stay with ye this way fer all the day."

Alana's pulse was still racing somewhat. "You could never spend an entire day in bed," she whispered, amused at the thought.

He released her, sitting up. "With ye, I think I could."

They smiled at one another. She did not try to sit up. He moved away to pick up his clothes, and she became aware of dawn's light, creeping into the tiny window slits high above them, in the ceiling, where the castle's ground floor was. She glanced up.

A new day was coming. Pale light was trying to filter within.

Some of her satisfaction dulled. Worry crept over her.

She heard Iain stand, and begin to dress. She finally sat up, reaching for her cloak, to cover her nudity. She was somber now. Every thought she had just had returned, full force. How could she continue to deceive him?

Now dressed in his leine and boots, Iain went to the wall, took a torch down, and brought it back to them. He set it down in a pocket in the stone floor. He glanced at her with some speculation.

They were both in the light now, and her heart lurched. She could not continue to deceive him. But after last night, how could she tell the truth? She could not bear to lose him.

He handed her torn clothing to her. "Ye do not look like a woman who is well pleased. What is amiss, Alana?"

She slid on her chemise, then the cote and surcote. "You know how pleased I am."

"Do I?"

Alana held her bodice together. "I am so very pleased.... But what do we do now?"

He squatted beside her. "I make certain ye get upstairs with no one the wiser, and then I make certain ye get to Brodie, where ye will be safe from this war. I will send ye there with an escort." His gaze was searching.

Did he feel about her, the way she did about him? Was it possible? "Do you care, Iain? Do you care if I am safe?"

"I care," he said roughly, rising to his full height. "But I also care about the secrets ye and yer grandmother keep."

She froze, and she felt all the blood draining from her face. "Secrets?" If ever there was an opening, he had just given her one.

But how could she tell him she was Buchan's niece? That she was a Comyn? She did not want to destroy what was happening between them. And even if they survived that revelation, they would not survive the fact that she had the sight. She felt certain of that.

So if he cared as much about her, he cared about a lie.

Alana did not know what to do.

"I care, Iain. I also care about you, and...a war divides us. I am afraid!"

He stared searchingly at her, for a long, terrible moment. "The war only divides us if we let it," he said
grimly. He bent and put on his first belt, in which was
sheathed a small dagger. Then he put on his sword belt.

Alana stood, wrapping the cloak about her so no
one would be able to tell that her clothing had been
ripped off of her.

He finished buckling the belt and touched her elbow.
"Do ye have another gown?"

She nodded, wanting to ask him how they would
navigate this war, and when she would see him again.
"When do I go back to Brodie?" she asked instead as
they started for the stairs.

"Ye will leave today, Alana, this morning, if I do
not mistake my guess." He took her arm and sent her
ahead of him, up the narrow winding stairwell.

"I leave today?" she said, shocked.

"I ride north, Alana," he said.

"And when will we see one another again?" She
could barely believe she was being so bold, but she
had to know.

He smiled slightly. "Do ye miss me, already?" He
sobered. "I dinna ken. I will come to Brodie, even if
for an hour, when I can."

He would come to Brodie for an hour when he could.
Alana was afraid she would not see Iain again, that the
war would truly come between them, and that their
love was over after a single night. "I already miss you,"
she whispered.

He gave her a serious and sideways look. They had
reached the ground floor, but none of the men and
maids coming and going paid them any attention. Iain
urged her up the next set of stairs.

Alana hurried, reaching the landing where the tower chamber was. She thought of Eleanor for the first time since supper the night before. "Gran must be frantic."

"She kens ye were with me." He took her elbow and halted her.

Alana faced him, her heart slamming. "Now you are the one who is not pleased."

"Ye belong to Brodie Castle. Duncan is yer liege. Yer guardian. I'll kill Duncan when I can—mayhap today." His demeanor of the past few hours was gone. He was a ruthless warrior once more.

She felt ill. Duncan was rude and overbearing, he had assaulted her, molested her and insulted her, for most of her life, but he was her guardian and he was a human being.

His stare intensified. "Who are ye loyal to, Alana?"

She froze. "What?"

"Ye heard me. I go to war against yer guardian. I go to war against yer liege, the Earl of Buchan. Who are ye loyal to?"

She was dismayed. She did not know what to say, or how to say it! "Iain!"

"Ye cannot answer, or ye will not answer?"

She flinched. How could she choose now? It was too soon! "I don't know what to say! I want to be loyal to you!" But could she be loyal to him? They were lovers, and she would gladly give him her loyalty—but she could not abandon her family, either—the family he still did not know about. "I despise Duncan," she said. "Brodie was my mother's dowry, but now, it is his. Iain, I *want* to be loyal to you."

He took two steps to stand in front of her, and he tilted up her chin. For a long moment, he stared, considering her words. "Wanting to be loyal is not enough. Ye will have to choose sides, and soon," he said flatly, and his face was hard. "Everyone must choose sides in a war."

"I don't want to choose sides!" she cried. "Why can't we just go on this way?"

His eyes widened. "Get dressed and gather up yer things. Make certain Lady Fitzhugh is ready to travel. We'll speak once more before ye go." His face still hard and uncompromising, he turned and strode away.

Alana sagged against her door. How could he demand that she choose sides now? After a single night?

But didn't she know which side she *wanted* to choose?

Behind her, the tower room door opened. "Alana?"

Wiping her cheeks, Alana turned to face her grandmother. "I hope I have not worried you!"

For one moment, Eleanor stared. "Why are you crying? Has he hurt you already?"

She trembled, wanting to let the tears flow freely. But she did not. "You will not scold me for what I have done?"

"He is a proud, brave soldier, Alana, who has helped us not once, but twice, in our time of need. So no, I will not scold you. You are a grown woman, and you know who you are."

Alana hugged her. "I may be falling in love, Gran," she whispered.

Her grandmother clasped her face as if she were a tiny child. "That is what I feared the most," she said.

As THEY PACKED up their few belongings, Alana could barely believe how her life had changed in the past twenty-four hours. She had been Buchan's prisoner, and now she was going home—but only after spending the night with the enemy. It seemed impossible, like a tall tale, but her memories were real.

There were such huge feelings swelling in her heart. She wanted to thrill, but instead she felt dark despair. Iain seemed to care about her, but he wanted her loyalty, and she was not free to give it to him, because she was Sir Alexander's daughter. He already questioned her loyalty. He would question it even more once she told him of her paternity.

And didn't she question it, too?

But she could not continue to deceive him, not after the intimacy they had shared. She knew that, especially now, in the light of a new morning. Guilt weighed her down. But she was so afraid he would be angry. She was afraid that he would feel betrayed. She was afraid he might not care about her after all, not once he learned she was the niece of his king's worst enemy.

But what if they could get past her deception? What if, eventually, he could forgive her—and accept her for who she was?

Alana was blinded by sudden tears. She knew that they had no future. He would never accept her for who she was, because she was a witch.

Alana hugged her clothing to her chest. "Gran? What am I to do?"

Eleanor knotted her satchel. "You are speaking of your affair with Iain?"

"I hate deceiving him. It isn't right. But he won't be pleased when he learns that Buchan is my uncle."

"You haven't told him who you are?" Eleanor gasped.

"I have been afraid to do so!"

Eleanor stared, shocked, and Alana was ashamed. "There was no time," she finally whispered. "Do you think he will reject me when he learns of my father?"

"I don't know, Alana," Eleanor said, a bit briskly. "I had assumed you had told him before sharing his bed."

Alana hugged herself. "You disapprove."

"I do. I am sorry, Alana, but you are more honorable than that! If you truly love him, you will find the courage to tell him what you must. True love cannot withstand lies, Alana, but that you must know."

"And if he loses all interest?"

"Then he does not love you, and it is better you find out now."

"What about my powers, Gran? Why do we even bother to speak of his reaction to the news I am a Comyn by birth? I am such a fool. We both know he will be repulsed when he learns I am a witch."

"Do we? I stopped predicting male behavior a long time ago, Alana, especially when love and lust are involved." She smiled. As she did, a knock sounded on their door. As Eleanor turned toward it she said to Alana, "Everyone has been told to leave Nairn by midmorning. We have tarried, I expect."

Alana pulled on her fur-lined mantle as her grandmother opened the door.

A lean, freckled Highland lad of about fifteen appeared in the doorway, his hand on the hilt of his sword. He wore a mail tunic beneath his dark blue plaid. "Ye must go out now, ladies, and it is an order. Why do ye take so long to pack yer things?"

"I was helping my granddaughter to dress," Eleanor said with a reprimand in her tone. "And to gather up our belongings."

"Ye can gather up yer things, but only if ye can do so in the next five minutes. The king has already left Nairn, and Iain the Fierce is impatient to do so."

Alana wondered at the urgency. She now recalled that Iain had said they would speak once again before she left, and she was determined to do so. "We are ready," Alana said. As they left the chamber, she asked, "What is your name, lad?"

He glanced at her, his blue eyes bright, his freckles brighter. "Donald, my lady."

"It is Mistress le Latimer," she said. They hurried downstairs, no one coming up the steps now, the castle feeling eerily deserted. "Are we the last to leave?"

"I dinna ken, mistress," Donald said. "But I think so."

Alana glanced into the empty hall as they passed. Dread began. Why empty the castle—if not to destroy it? "Do you know why Iain is in such a rush to depart?" she asked as they approached the open front door.

"Everyone knows. They march on Elgin. Bruce has gone on ahead, but to wait for Iain." He smiled slyly and said, "The Earl of Buchan has gone into hiding there. Rotten coward."

Alana inhaled, glancing at her grandmother. Was her father with Buchan? Was her loyalty to be tested immediately?

They stepped outside, into the bright, early morning sun. At that moment, images flashed in her mind—of the countryside blackened and burned, castles reduced to rubble, villages burned into ash.

Alana blinked and saw the dirty gray snow of the

courtyard, the castle's gray walls, the soldiers leaving. She was relieved. The images had not been a vision, just memories of the horrific vision she had had.

As they went down the front steps, Alana saw that the castle's remaining inhabitants, mostly kitchen maids, serving boys and cooks, were filing out through the front gates. A dozen Highland warriors were mounted and stood sentinel by the entry tower, watching them as they left. A handful of soldiers were loading two wagons with the last of the army's equipment, draft horses in the traces. Otherwise, the usually busy courtyard was deserted.

Alana did not have to ask to know that no one, not even a pig or a cow, was left within the castle's walls. Dread consumed her.

"Go on," Donald said.

But she did not move. "Is Buchan alone at Elgin?"

Donald started. "I dinna ken yer meaning, lady."

"How many armies does he have?" she asked. She wanted to know if Sir Alexander was at Elgin—and about to be attacked. "He has many brothers, one was at Lochindorb, and he has a fine army."

"I know nuthin' of Buchan's brothers but I was at Lochindorb," Donald said, grinning. "We chased them cowards right away."

Alana shivered and rubbed her arms. She would have to wait until she got home to learn of her father, she realized. Donald gestured at the entry tower, and they hurried after the others who were leaving. She wondered if they were the very last ones to depart. She glanced wildly around, but did not see Iain within.

She felt a surging of panic. He had said they would speak before she left, and it felt very important to see him again before she returned home and he marched upon Elgin Castle. Maybe she would have enough time to tell him the truth.

They reached the main entry tower, atop the south road, and went through it. Across the hillside and filing down the single road, which led to Aberdeen and Dundee, she saw an exodus of men, women and children.

Alana instantly realized that the population was not just from the castle, but from the surrounding farms and the nearby village. And all the country's livestock had been released. Cows, pigs and goats, as well as a few horses, grazed at random about the hills and alongside the road.

Then she saw what the soldiers were doing—wood was being piled up at intervals, along the castle walls.

Alana seized Eleanor. "They are going to burn the castle down." They began to run away from the entry tower and its front gates. Alana's heart exploded in fear. Disbelief warred with dismay.

How could he burn Nairn to the ground? How?

But wasn't that what her uncle had said about Iain? About Bruce? That he burned enemy strongholds down, leaving no stone standing?

But she would never believe the rest of what Buchan had said—never.

And why were the villagers being sent away? Why were all the farm animals loose?

"I am taking ye to Brodie," Donald now said. He pointed to where a soldier held a saddled horse and a mule, the latter animal harnessed to their wagon.

Alana hesitated, but Donald was already helping Eleanor up into the wagon's single seat. Frantically, she scanned the countryside, and as she did, gallop-ing hoofbeats sounded. She whirled and saw Iain ap-proach, astride his dark horse, coming from the far side of the castle. He halted before her, his mount rearing. He jerked its reins hard to settle it.

Their gazes locked.

He seemed grim—yet the heat between them re-mained, she felt certain. "Iain?"

"I wish ye Godspeed, Alana," he said.

She shook her head. It was hard to speak. "I wish you Godspeed, too, Iain."

He studied her. "Are those tears fer me?"

"For you…for me…for them." She pointed to the men, women and children walking down the road, away from the castle.

He looked at them, not speaking.

"What are you doing, Iain?" she begged. But she knew, and the knowledge was making her ill.

"Nairn burns today, Alana," he said harshly.

Was he avoiding her eyes? "How can you burn Nairn Castle down?" she cried. "And what of the village, the farms?"

"Do ye wish for Buchan to return here and use it against me?"

She hugged herself. "No."

"I dinna think so." He gathered up his reins.

She did not want her uncle to use Nairn Castle against Iain. But some of the women who were leav-ing the castle were crying. Their children were pale and afraid. She could only imagine how the villagers felt at being forced to leave their homes.

She turned back to Iain, and caught him watching the exodus, too. "Will you spare the village, at least?"

His face was hard. "Dinna interfere, Alana."

She could not help herself. "Have you even thought about the suffering you cause? I know you are not the savage Highlander of legend! Look at them, Iain! Look at the men, women and children whom you are sending into exile! How will they eat? Where will they sleep?"

"Ye think to interfere in this war?" He was incredulous, flushing. "They will build new homes. They will make new lives. In a new village, on new farms."

"Yes, I suppose they will, just as Mistress MacDuff must build a new manor," she said, trembling. She realized her fists were clenched at her sides. "Is this what you did at Inverlochy? Urquhart? Inverness?"

"So ye choose sides against me."

"How can you say such a thing? After last night?"

"How can ye condemn me after last night?"

She continued to shake. She must not criticize him—not when she loved him. "I do not believe you are pleased to do this."

"I am a soldier, Alana, the king's man. Nairn will burn—the castle, the village and its farms."

"Why?" she cried. "Why?"

"Tomorrow, no one will support Buchan against us, not ever again."

She felt tears upon her lashes now. "No. They will not support Buchan tomorrow."

She turned toward the wagon, blinded by pain, not tears. How her heart hurt her now. He did not care about the innocent lives he was endangering. He did not care about the swath of destruction he was deliberately inflicting upon the countryside. Did the truth even matter now?

Because she could not love such a ruthless man.

He must have leaped down from his stallion, because he seized her shoulder from behind, turning her back to face him. "So this is yer farewell? Ye walk away in anger? Ye said ye cared about me!"

His eyes were so fierce that they were frightening. Alana did not know how to answer. Her heart screamed that she did care, but she could see past him, and the men, women and children leaving Nairn were tragic—and his responsibility!

His eyes blazed. "Very well. We ride to Elgin. Donald will take ye back to Brodie. Just go."

Her heart turned over, hard. They must not part like this, in contention, in anger! But she could only say, "God keep you safe, Iain. I will pray for you."

He stared, unsmiling. "If I come to Brodie, will ye see me?"

Alana hesitated. She suddenly did not know what she would do. The war already divided them, as did her lies. It would be best to stay away.

"So ye have chosen sides after all." He seized her by the waist and lifted her effortlessly onto the wagon.

No, she thought desperately, *I am on your side!* But she did not speak—because she knew she must not say so.

"Ye should be safe at Brodie." He turned away.

Alana fumbled for the reins, the pain inside her chest terrible now. His back to her, Iain leaped astride his charger. Without another glance at her, he galloped back up the hill, toward the castle. She had lifted the reins without knowing it, and the mule began to go down the road, Donald trotting beside them on his horse.

Eleanor patted her hand.

Alana did not look at her, lost in misery and grief. She heard the fires blazing behind them, but she would not look back at Nairn burning. She would not.

CHAPTER SIX

BRODIE CASTLE SEEMED so small, so insignificant, with the country in the throes of such a great war over the fate of Scotland.

Alana lifted the reins and halted the mule. "We are home," she said.

It was but a few hours later. She had halted the wagon inside Brodie's narrow courtyard, its red stone walls rising around them. They seemed lower than they had been. She did not see any watch atop them. And she did not recall the courtyard being so small, or so oddly barren. But she could not help comparing Brodie to Nairn, which was huge in comparison. Its bailey never seemed quiet—it was always a hive of activity, with soldiers, women and children coming and going.

Her heart lurched with dread and she closed her eyes, but all she saw was Iain's hard face, his flashing eyes, and his men piling up wood against the castle's walls, as Nairn's residents and its farmers and villagers left the countryside in an exodus.

How could he be indifferent to the suffering he was causing the innocent?

He had rescued Mistress MacDuff and her two children from Boath Manor as it burned!

The mule shook its head with impatience, pulling on the reins, and she opened her eyes, setting the wagon's brake. She must not dwell on what was happening at Nairn, for she was one small woman in the midst of this war—she could not affect it.

But her chest ached. For surely it was over with Iain now. His behavior as a warrior was hardly unusual but for her it was the cause of so much distress and so much disappointment. She could not blithely accept it, no matter how heartbroken she was.

A stable boy was running toward them. Alana recognized the young lad and she summoned a smile. She did not feel as pleased as she had thought she would upon coming home, either. She felt almost indifferent. "It feels as if an entire lifetime has passed since we left here not long ago," Alana said.

"Yes, it does. You are distraught, still," Eleanor said, clasping her shoulder.

"I am sad." Alana slid from the wagon, then helped her grandmother down. It was snowing, so it was not that cold, and the ground was partially thawed underfoot. Donald had left them a half an hour ago, as he could hardly venture close to Brodie without becoming in danger of being captured. Gratefully, Alana handed over the reins to the boy while patting the mule's neck. As she turned toward the steps leading up to the hall, the door there opened and Godfrey stepped out.

She tensed, so wishing to avoid a confrontation now. "Good afternoon."

He had not bothered to don a fur cloak, and he gave her an ugly look, his hands fisted on his hips. "So you have returned." His cheeks were flushed, a sign of his ill temper.

Alana lifted her chin, instinctively defiant. She was exhausted in every possible way—how she wished she could stop thinking—and she wanted nothing more than to escape Godfrey and steal off to her chamber. She had been at Nairn for eight entire days, and she was almost certain Godfrey had received at least one communication from his father, if not several. Duncan would have told him about her bald lie. "We are very tired, Godfrey. We have endured a great deal, including the battle for Nairn."

"And did you endure the battle? How could that be? When you enraged your uncle with your true vision, so that he imprisoned you?"

She sighed. "How that must please you," she said.

"You boldly lied to me over an important matter, because you lust for Brodie still, and it is to be mine! You have finally gotten your just deserts, so I suppose I am pleased." He came down the steps to confront her. "Nairn is in ashes!" he snapped, hands on his hips. But he was pale. "I received word just hours ago. Does that please you, Alana?"

Duncan must have sent a messenger after they had left Nairn, Alana thought. A messenger would travel more swiftly than two women in a cart. And of course Buchan would leave spies in the woods to remark Nairn's terrible fate.

"They were burning it when we left. No, it hardly pleases me. I am sorry." She did not want to recall her vision, in all its horrific detail, but she continued to do so. And she did not want to remember the piles of wood stacked against the castle walls, or the exodus of men, women and children, or Iain's cold expression when they had argued about what he meant to do.

He had burned that fine castle to the ground. It was

done. There had been no change of heart. "And the village? The farms?"

"It is all burned to ash," Godfrey cried. "And God only knows if Brodie Castle will be next!"

She paled. Iain would never burn Brodie down—would he? It was her home!

"At least you care about Brodie," Godfrey said grimly.

"Of course I care about Brodie." She turned to Eleanor. "Let's go inside."

As Alana helped her grandmother in, Godfrey followed them. "How is it that you were freed? Did Bruce's men free you when they took the castle?"

She was belligerent. "Your father hardly freed us. I am certain he did not care if we died in that attack. So yes, Bruce's soldiers freed us."

Godfrey stared and Alana wondered if he was sorry she was freed. Eleanor sat down in one of the chairs before the hearth, and said, "Buchan and Duncan fled Nairn when it was to fall, leaving us behind. They left us locked in the tower during the battle, Godfrey, two women alone to defend themselves."

"My father has told me everything," Godfrey said harshly, "in the last missive he sent. You told him the earldom will be destroyed. Of course he locked you in the tower!"

"It is what I saw," Alana said. "I never wanted such a horrible vision!"

"Really?" Godfrey flushed. "You see the destruction of Buchan's earldom, and you tell him the truth! You see Iain of Islay in battle, and you lie!"

"You goad me like no other," Alana said. "Yes, my

vision was of a different battle entirely, and I saw Iain of Islay in it, not your father."

Godfrey shook his head. "Why did Iain of Islay let you go? Why did he not keep you as hostages? Or did his men let you go unbeknownst to him?"

Eleanor spoke now. "Why would he keep us, Godfrey? He doesn't know Alana is Buchan's niece, or that she has the sight."

There was a moment of silence, as Godfrey stared at her. Alana's heart skipped. Godfrey was surprised that Iain did not know she was a Comyn, and perhaps, that she was a witch. If he ever learned that she wished to keep such secrets, he would deliberately reveal them— she had no doubt.

Alana inhaled. "Actually, I truly regret allowing myself to be goaded into lying to you. I have paid for what I have done."

His eyes widened. "You blame me for your lie?"

She did, but she somehow shook her head. "It was petty of me. And it was also foolish."

He eyed her with suspicion. "Is that an apology, Alana?"

She hesitated. She actually was sorry, on this single count, anyway. "If you had been at the battle of Nairn, you might understand. It was terrible and terrifying. But even worse was how ruthlessly they destroyed Nairn afterward." She fought the compulsion to cry. Brodie must never come to such a fate!

"I think we should have some wine," Eleanor said. She nodded at a maid, who went to the table to get the pitcher and mugs for them.

"I am not thirsty," Alana said. She did not wish to drink wine with Godfrey.

"I am," Godfrey said. As the maid brought mugs to the women, he went to the table and poured his own mug. Then he turned to face them. "I do not know how I can ever defend Brodie when I have so few men and arms."

Alana took a sip of wine. He was worrying about Brodie, too. "I am praying that Brodie is too small and too insignificant and will be forgotten in the war."

"No place is forgotten in war—and no one," Godfrey said.

"I hope you are wrong. And I do not know who we could beg for aid from, should we be attacked." She wondered if she would one day beg Iain not to attack her home. She did not think he would heed her then, as he had not listened to her pleas for mercy at Nairn.

Godfrey approached. "You could beg for aid from your father."

Alana was shocked by the suggestion. She slowly stood. "I do not even know if he is alive! I have had no word since I heard he was defending Lochindorb."

"He escaped with most of his men. They withdrew before the fighting became heavy, which was wise, as he would have surely lost the battle to Iain of Islay." Godfrey was grim. "He is at Elgin with my father and the earl."

She felt stunned. And then she was flooded with relief, as if she had lost Iain that day, but that now something precious had been returned to her.

"You are so loyal to him, when he has never openly acknowledged you," Godfrey said.

"He is my father—and that will never change." But her heart cracked at his words.

"If you wish to write to him, I can send your missive with my own to Duncan."

Alana stared, suddenly confused and slightly suspicious. "So you wish for me to write him?"

"One day, we may need his help." Godfrey was blunt.

How she hoped he was wrong. But he was right, and for the first time in her life, she saw him in a new light—as a young man who wasn't entirely a fool, and who was wise enough to plan ahead in the event that Brodie was attacked. "I will write him." She turned. "Gran? I am going upstairs to rest. Will you come?"

"I am enjoying the fire, Alana. I will be up a bit later," Eleanor said.

Alana realized her grandmother wished to speak with Godfrey alone. As she left, he said, "I will send parchment and ink, Alana. My messenger rides in the morning."

He was insisting she write to Sir Alexander, she thought, a flutter in her heart. She left the room, and unable to help herself, she paused in the hall. She didn't intend to spy, but she knew they meant to discuss her, and she wanted to know what they were saying.

"Perhaps it is time to make amends, Godfrey. Fighting with Alana doesn't help you, your father or any of us. It does not help Brodie. Not in a time of war," Eleanor said.

"Tell her that!" he exclaimed. "She played me for a fool—she humiliated me in front of the earl and my father."

"She is truly sorry. Surely you can see that."

"I don't trust her," he said flatly. "And, Eleanor? She enjoys lying to me."

Eleanor sighed. "But you treat her shamefully—as you know. You bully her constantly. I think it wise to end the bickering. I intend to tell Alana as much."

There was silence. Alana turned around and walked back to the threshold of the room.

Godfrey looked at her. "She would love to see me stabbed in the back, because she thinks that one day, she can claim Brodie as her own."

Eleanor did not see Alana, who stood facing her back. "You are wrong. Alana wishes ill will on no one."

Alana hardly wished for Godfrey to be stabbed in the back, but she did yearn for his downfall, because she coveted Brodie.

"Then she will have to prove it—with a good vision. And she will pay dearly if she deceives us another time." Godfrey faced Eleanor and smiled. "Mostly, I am hoping she is as loyal to Brodie as she claims."

Alana had heard enough. She picked up the hem of her skirts and rushed away. Eleanor was brokering a truce. Her grandmother was right: this was no time for petty differences, ancient grudges and old grievances.

She went up to the chamber she shared with Eleanor and sat down at the small table between the beds. Sir Alexander's handsome, golden image came to her mind's eye, his features blurred and indistinct. The parchment and ink had yet to arrive, and she tried to think of what she would say to her father, when she hadn't seen him in fifteen years.

A shudder racked her. Pain bubbled up in her chest.

Sir Alexander's image was followed by Iain's dark one.

Nairn was rubble now.

She wiped tears from her eyes. Crying would not

solve anything—it would not change Iain into a different man.

She could not believe that, a few hours ago, she had been deliriously happy—she had even thought herself in love. Now she did not know what to think. Could she love a man who burned down farms and villages upon command?

Her heart hurt terribly, but it refused to tell her that she did not love Iain of Islay. And for one brief moment, she allowed herself to think about the night they had spent together.

More tears arose. Alana finally closed her eyes, afraid that she was in love with a ruthless warrior, one who had no honor, who did not think twice about destroying the lives of the innocent.

There was only one thing she was truly certain of— she was loyal to Brodie, and it must not suffer the same fate as Nairn.

"Mistress?" A soft voice spoke from the open doorway. "I have brought ye a quill, ink and parchment."

Alana turned and smiled. "Thank you," she said.

NEWS OF ELGIN'S attack came the next afternoon. It was snowing furiously when the messenger arrived.

Alana was mending a chemise, seated in a chair before the hearth. Eleanor sat beside her, embroidering. Godfrey was drinking wine at the table while throwing dice with one of his men, when one of his soldiers led a boy of fourteen or fifteen inside. Snow clung to his wool cloak and dusted his red hair.

Godfrey leaped to his feet, Alana ceased sewing, and Eleanor set her embroidery down. They all stared at the boy.

"What news do you have?" Godfrey cried.

"I come from Duncan, my lord. Elgin has been attacked and the Earl of Buchan is determined to defend it," he said.

For a moment, a silence fell as they all continued to stare at him.

Then Alana leaped up, pouring a mug of wine, which she handed to the boy. He smiled gratefully at her.

"When did Bruce attack?" Godfrey demanded, his expression twisted with dismay.

"Yesterday at dawn, my lord," the boy said.

"How was it when you left?"

The boy shook his head. "Bruce had seven hundred men combined, far more than the earl and yer father. But only a small army attacked—the rest of his men were waiting in the woods." He finally sipped the wine.

Alana's heart lurched with dread. She knew who was leading that small army. But Elgin could not fall. It could not suffer the same fates as Inverness, Inverlochy, Urquhart and Nairn. For if it did, Brodie could be next.

She closed her eyes to ward off a recollection of her last terrible vision, to no avail. All she could see was Scotland, blackened and burned, with Bruce's flag waving above the ashes and rubble.

She shook herself free of the recollection. "Is Sir Alexander Comyn with the Earl of Buchan still?" she asked.

"Aye, mistress. Sir Alexander defends Elgin with Duncan and the earl."

Her father was with Buchan and Duncan, defending

Elgin from Robert Bruce—battling Iain once again. Alana fought for air. She felt dizzy.

She wondered if her father would ever receive the letter she had sent to him that morning. It had been so awkward to write, but in the end, she had expressed her concern for his welfare and told him she prayed for him. She had also mentioned that they feared for their own safety at Brodie, where they had no actual defenses.

"And how did the first attack go?" Godfrey asked.

"When I left, there was no sign that Iain of Islay would succeed. His men were being turned back from the walls."

Alana was relieved. She wished to ask about Iain, but was afraid to, and besides, thus far, he was in command. She looked at Godfrey. "Perhaps my grandmother is right, and we share a common cause."

He gave her a disdainful glance. "Maybe you should take up a bowl of water, Alana. Maybe you can tell us Elgin's fate before the next messenger arrives!"

Alana started. So he knew what Buchan had done to her. "If I have a vision, you will be the first to know. And I will tell you the truth." She meant it. "We cannot afford to be enemies."

"No, we cannot," Godfrey replied, but reluctantly.

A PALL SETTLED over the castle as they awaited news of Elgin's fate. The days passed with agonizing slowness. Alana avoided Godfrey, amazed that she now intended to forge a truce between them, as fragile as it was. Because they so disliked one another, it was better to keep her distance—for Brodie's sake. At times she slipped outside for a lonely walk along the castle walls, her only company a gray wolf watching her from the forest, but mostly she kept to the small chamber she shared with Eleanor. There, her gaze was continually drawn to a pitcher of water left for drinking, as if it dared her to look within.

She did not. She was too afraid she might see Elgin in rubble and ashes.

And she wondered about her father. Had Sir Alexander received her letter? What had his reaction been to such a missive, sent from the illegitimate daughter he had abandoned and forgotten? Would he even bother to reply? And she also wondered, against her will, how Iain fared in the battle for Elgin Castle.

There was no word for four days, but then another messenger arrived, shaking the snow from his fur, as they assembled in the hall to greet him. "My lord! Bruce and his army have been turned back! They have fled Elgin," he cried, beaming.

Godfrey was so exultant he danced a Highland jig. "Finally, the tides of war favor us!"

Alana stared in shock at the messenger as Godfrey skipped about the hearth in the hall, gloating. Bruce had retreated. He had been defeated.

Stunned, she took a seat at the table as the messenger shed his cloak. Relief finally began. Elgin remained intact!

"How is my father?" Godfrey demanded. He handed the young soldier wine. "How is the Earl of Buchan?" He glanced at Alana. "And his brother, Sir Alexander?"

"They are all well, my lord," the boy said, smiling.

Her father was well. "Please, come sit and eat," Alana said, her heart leaping. As he slid onto the bench, not far from her, she stood and indicated that a maid should bring him refreshments. "Do you have a message for me, by any chance? From Sir Alexander?" she asked.

He started. "No, my lady, I have no messages for anyone."

Her heart sank. She reminded herself that she did not even know if Sir Alexander had received her letter in the midst of such a furious battle.

"How great were Bruce's losses?" Godfrey asked, taking a seat facing the young messenger. "Did we rout him at long last?"

"He lost thirty men, my lord, and we lost half that." The second messenger was a blond Englishman in a fur-lined cloak. "It was no rout, merely a hard-fought battle that seemed evenly matched. Bruce withdrew quite suddenly. The siege lasted but an entire day and a night."

Godfrey scowled as Alana wondered why Bruce had chosen to retreat, rather than fight a protracted siege. She did not want to think of Iain, but of course she did. He was always there in her mind—her heart.

"Bruce hardly suffered any losses, his army remains strong!" Godfrey said.

"Aye, my lord, and he is well fed by most of the villages here now." He tore some bread in half and dunked it in the wine.

She looked at Godfrey. "Why would Bruce retreat, when he so outnumbered Buchan and Duncan?"

"I don't know. It worries me—maybe it is a trap." Godfrey was grim.

Alana did not like the sound of that. She realized how impossible her position was—to be against Bruce, to pray for his defeat, yet to fear that defeat too because she did not want Iain captured, wounded or killed.

"Are the villages in Buchan supporting him now?" She thought of how he had destroyed Nairn—Iain had claimed the villagers there would never dare support Buchan against Bruce again. She believed him.

"The damned traitor is growing in popularity," Godfrey said.

The maid returned, setting down a trencher of bread, smoked fish and goat cheese. The lad began to eat hungrily.

Alana sat back down. She no longer felt as relieved about their victory at Elgin. And what of Iain? Where was he now? Should she ask openly about him? Godfrey knew he had freed her, and she could claim that was her reason for concern.

Godfrey watched the young man. "What is Bruce's position now? Where will he strike next?"

"When I left Elgin, Buchan was thinking that the war will wait until the spring." The boy shoved his plate aside. "My lord, I have one more bit of news. Bruce has taken the manor at Concarn."

Godfrey leaped up. "Concarn Manor belongs to my father!"

The boy glanced worriedly at Godfrey. "I am sorry. Bruce's army rests there now."

Godfrey turned red and fell into an amazed and distressed silence, staring into his wine.

Alana said, "What of Iain of Islay?"

Godfrey whirled to stare at her.

"Bruce has sent him to Aberdeen," the boy said. "He plunders the country he passes through, warning everyone not to oppose Bruce."

Dismay overwhelmed her. Iain was not hurt, apparently, but he was destroying Aberdeenshire as he had destroyed Nairn.

"You seem distressed," Godfrey snapped. "Why do you ask about the goddamned Highlander?"

This was a good time to flee. She got up. "He freed me and Eleanor, Godfrey, when he did not have to do so. He might be the enemy, but I owe him some gratitude." She turned. "Thank you for bringing us so much news," she said to the boy. "I am going to retire for the night."

Godfrey jumped to his feet and went to quickly stand in front of her. "You should pen another letter, Alana, in case Sir Alexander did not receive the first one. They have taken Concarn—and it is smaller and less significant than Brodie."

Alana realized what he meant. Protecting Brodie meant more to her than protecting her own pride. "Very well. I'll do so immediately."

"Good," Godfrey said. He seemed about to touch her shoulder, but then he thought better of it and paced over to the fireplace to stare into the flames.

Eleanor had arisen. "I will go with you." She took her arm and they left the room, her grandmother speaking softly. "It is all good news, Alana."

Alana nodded as they went toward the stairs. "Yes, for now, it is all good news." But was it? The shock over Bruce's withdrawal was fading, as was her relief that her father remained unharmed. Bruce was at Concarn—was Iain really raping the countryside, demanding loyalty from those he terrorized?

As they reached the stairs, a young Highland lad

with long red hair, in a tattered plaid and fur, darted out of the shadows. "Mistress Alana!" He seized her wrist.

Alana was so startled she jumped. Incredulous, she faced a boy of twelve or thirteen, staring into his bright blue eyes. "Who are you?" She had never seen the boy about Brodie before. And was that plaid dark blue with black and red stripes?

"Shh!" He glanced at Eleanor. "Is she yer gran?" he whispered.

Alana nodded. She reached for his plaid, to bring an end closer, as it was dark in the hallway. How would this lad know that Eleanor was her grandmother?

"Iain has commanded me to bring ye to him," he said.

Her heart slammed. He wore the MacDonald colors, of course he did. She dropped the wool. Alana was so stunned, it was a moment before she could speak. "Iain sent you here?"

"He returns to Concarn, lady. But we must hurry. If I am caught they might whip me!"

Eleanor seized Alana's arm, her eyes wide. "You cannot go."

Shocked, Alana briefly met her wide, worried gaze. Images flashed—of Nairn aflame, and then of her in Iain's arms.

Iain was sending for her.

Oh, God, what should she do?

She realized that she had not instantly ruled out the possibility of going to him. Instead, she was torn.

They had parted in anger and disappointment. After the night they had shared, it was a terrible and painful way to part. It still caused so much heartache.

She hadn't thought he would still wish to be with her.

She was weighed down by her deception, as well. Not a day went by that she did not wish that she had told him the truth, and that they had gotten past the facts of her birth and her visions. It was so foolish to wish that he would love her for who she really was, and even though she knew that, she did.

It was too dangerous to go to him at Concarn— when he was with Robert Bruce. Wasn't it?

And what of Brodie and its defenses? She thought of Godfrey. She still disliked him, but they shared one overriding ambition—to keep Brodie safe.

Before she could speak, the lad said boldly, "He said to tell ye he misses ye—and he will not take no for an answer."

She gasped. Tears moistened her eyes. Oh, how skilled he was at wielding that final thrust! "How far is Concarn?"

"Alana!" Eleanor exclaimed. "Robert Bruce is at Concarn! You cannot go into his keeping!"

"A short day's ride—we will be there by nightfall," the boy said quickly.

She should not go. She must not go. Bruce was there. He could take her hostage.

She looked at Eleanor. "I have to see him again."

Eleanor blanched. "Very well—but not now, not at Concarn!"

Her mind raced. Iain would never let Bruce hurt her, she was certain. "Iain will protect me," she said.

"You think Iain will lie to his king for you?"

Alana stared at her grandmother, not quite seeing her. Was she mad? What if she was wrong? Iain was as ruthless as claimed; she had seen it, herself. But her heart was clamoring at her now.

The war only divides us if we let it.

"I have two horses hidden in the forest. I have furs and blankets. We must go!" the boy cried in a whisper.

She looked at Eleanor. "Tell Godfrey I have gone to see my father."

"Alana, please, do not go," Eleanor said, ashen.

"I have to go to him, Gran. I love him."

Eleanor closed her eyes briefly in despair. "Then God help you, Alana."

BY THE TIME they reached Concarn, the snow had stopped falling, and the gray skies were clearing.

It had taken them much longer than a long afternoon and a few hours of the evening to reach the small village in northeast Aberdeenshire. The new snow made the going difficult, delaying them. They had been forced to stop around midnight, when the winds came up, the snow blinding, and they had spent the night in a stable behind a farmhouse.

"We are here." The boy smiled at her widely.

Alana managed to smile back at the young boy, whose name she had learned was Ranald. And then she stared at the army camped below them.

They were on a small hillock astride their horses, a sea of tents below them. The village was to the left, several stone walled pastures between it and the manor house. Snow covered the tents, the fields and the woods. It covered the rooftops in the village, the manor, its barns and sheds. And Bruce's flag waved above the camp, yellow and red and shockingly bright.

Alana stared at Robert Bruce's flag. A pang of fear pierced her.

The boy clucked to his horse, kicking it, and Alana

did the same. She had had a day and a half to consider what she was doing, and to question her decision to go to Iain in the enemy's camp. But once upon the road, she had no doubts. She knew she must see him again. There might not be another chance, the future was that uncertain.

She had not had to worry about her paternity while at Brodie. She had not had to worry about her deception. Now she had to worry very much about the secrets she kept from Iain.

She was torn. He deserved the truth—all of it. It did not feel right continuing to deceive him, yet deceive him she must, for her own safety. Even if she wished to tell Iain about her father and her uncle, she could not do so now.

There was some relief in having a valid excuse for not confessing her deception to Iain. She no longer had to worry about his reaction when she told him Sir Alexander was her father. Not just then. It gave their relationship a reprieve.

And if their relationship survived this meeting, when the time was right, she would tell him about Sir Alexander—and that she had the sight. But that time was not now.

Ranald paused to ask a soldier where Iain was. Alana sat her mount, aware of being remarked by the closest soldiers. Her heart was thundering. It crossed her mind that if Bruce walked by, which was unlikely, he would glance at her, as well. An attractive young woman was not a common sight in a war camp.

Alana pulled her hood down lower over her forehead. She must be careful to avoid all the soldiers, she thought, and she must especially make certain to avoid coming into contact with Robert Bruce.

They were directed to a larger tent not far from the manor. Instantly she saw his banner flying atop the tent, streaking the sky. Her tension spiraled. The fluttering in her chest increased. They slowly made their way through the other tents.

When they were close enough to dismount, the flap door of his tent opened and Iain stepped out.

She trembled. He had not bothered to don a fur or any cloak—he was clad in his leine, which swirled about his bare thighs. He wore two swords and a dagger. Huge rowels flanked the spurs on his leather boots. His long hair was loose, rioting about his shoulders. She had forgotten how powerful his presence was, how masculine and handsome he was.

His gaze instantly found her.

He strode toward them, his strides hard and filled with purpose. He reached them and seized her mount's bridle. "Well done," he said to Ranald. But his piercing blue gaze never left her face.

Her heart slammed wildly. All doubt vanished. Alana was so happy to see him. She was so relieved he was well. And it no longer mattered that he was ruthless; not then.

"I am sorry that the snow delayed us," Ranald said, halting his horse.

Iain finally glanced at him. "I worried ye'd come to some harm."

"I would not let harm befall yer lady," Ranald said, sliding from his horse.

Iain smiled briefly. His gaze locked with Alana's

again, and then he clasped her by the waist, his hands large and strong, and pulled her from the mare.

He did not release her, and she remained in his powerful embrace.

His stare unwavering and heated upon hers, he said, "Tend to the horses and get yerself food and rest, lad. Ye did well."

Ranald grinned a bit slyly, taking both horses and leading them away.

"I could not decide if ye'd come," Iain said, unsmiling and terse.

How her heart pounded. "There was no decision to make."

"Then I am pleased ye still care for this savage."

Alana found her hands creeping to his shoulders, her knees weak, her body on fire. She was agonizingly aware of him—his heat, his strength, his scent. "No matter what happens in this war, I will always care."

His eyes darkened. "Ye berated me at Nairn. Ye strongly disapproved."

"I did not approve—I can never approve," she answered. She opened her hands and spread her fingers across his hard, broad shoulders.

"I dinna want to speak of the war now," he said roughly.

How she now recognized his tone, his need. It was hard to breathe with her heart racing so swiftly. Now she recognized her own need, too.

Alana reached up and took his face in her hands, aware that no lady would ever do as she was doing. But she could not stop herself. She did not care who saw them, or what they thought. She kissed him.

He stiffened in surprise. Alana's blood was rushing

so violently in her veins that she felt faint. Holding his nape, she forced his mouth open, thrusting her tongue past his. And she kissed him even harder, with all the passion exploding inside of her.

Suddenly he reversed their roles, locking her in his embrace, and breaking the kiss. His eyes were heated, but wide with surprise.

It was a moment before she could speak. "I missed you, too," she said. And it was the truth.

He suddenly swept her into his arms and carried her into his tent, using his shoulder to shove the flap door in. He strode to his pallet and laid her down, coming down on top of her in one fluid movement. Straddling her, he slid his arms behind her back. "If ye had refused to come, I would have come to ye at Brodie."

She thrilled. Alana reached for the outermost buckle of his two belts, yanking on it. It came apart and fell from him, his sheathed swords sliding to the bed around them.

He caught her hand, jerking it aside as he came down on top of her, kissing her. Alana cried out, pulling at his leine, as their mouths mated furiously. His tongue deep within her, he unbuckled his second belt and flung it away. Alana jerked up his leine and he pulled on her skirts. Hot and hard, he surged into her.

And within moments, they were both crying out, Alana blinded by both pleasure and joy.

And then she was drifting back to the earth, aware of being in his arms, beneath him on the small pallet. He shifted to his side, taking her with him, and he laughed, the sound male and satisfied. "So ye have missed me, truly."

She snuggled her cheek against the slab of his chest.

"Is it not obvious?" She kissed his chest. "How shameful we are."

"I am not ashamed." He kissed her forehead. "There are hours left until we sup…" He slid his hand over her bare backside; her skirts gathered about her waist.

Alana could not think about anything other than making love now. She sat up, untying her girdle. The gleam in his eyes intensified as he watched. She tossed it aside.

Then she slowly removed her blue surcote. As slowly, she removed her long-sleeved lavender cote. Clad only in her linen chemise, she undid her braid and shook out her long, heavy waist-length hair and smiled.

He growled and pulled her down beneath him, ripping the chemise in two.

"YE WILL MEET King Robert," Iain said. "Bruce is here."

Alana lay nestled under the wool blankets and a fur cover on his pallet; he was standing and fully dressed. She had never been as sated, and she had never wanted to avoid contemplation and reason more. But his words instantly caused alarm.

"Surely I have not exhausted ye so that ye cannot get out of bed?" he teased, grinning.

"But you have," she said softly, her smile brief. She did not want to meet Bruce, not now, not ever. She slowly sat up, holding the fur that had covered them over her chest.

His smile faded. "What is amiss, Alana?" He pulled a stool close to the pallet and sat down upon it.

She hesitated. She had such a good rationale to continue to deceive him. Yet her heart raged against the deception. How could she continue to deceive him when she loved him so much?

And Alana knew if she dared to think, she would beat a hasty retreat. So she shut off all internal debate. "Iain."

"What passes, Alana?" he asked quietly, unsmiling. "Why are ye so sad, so suddenly? So grim? Did I not please ye tonight? Or is something else the matter?"

"Of course you pleased me," she answered. She knew she must tell him the truth—and not debate her decision. She could barely breathe or move, much less speak.

"Ye look as frightened as a deer caught in the archer's sight."

"I am frightened," she breathed.

"Then ye must be very worried about yer loyalties," he said grimly. "Is that it? Do ye worry about yer loyalty to Brodie—to Buchan—over me?"

She hugged herself. "I am not thinking about my loyalties now."

But he pressed on. "Do ye still think of the burning of Nairn? Ye were angry with me."

She tensed. "I do, but that is not what we must discuss."

But his gaze was narrowed. It was a moment before he spoke. "If ye cannot be loyal to me, ye must be honest."

She stared. This was an opening—one she must take. "I care so much about you, do you know that?"

His eyes widened with alarm. "I also care about ye, Alana," he said carefully. He stood up.

"I fear for your welfare when you are in battle, yet at the same time, I do not want Bruce to succeed."

"That is very honest—and a very difficult course to take."

"It is very difficult. But there is more." Holding the fur covers, Alana also stood. "I don't want to lose you, Iain."

"What is this dance, Alana? Why would ye lose me? We can be lovers, even if we are on opposite sides of the war. What do ye truly fear telling me?"

She felt tears arise. "I have been lying to you."

His eyes shot wide. "How?"

"My mother is Elisabeth le Latimer—but I do know who my father is. I have been afraid, terrified, to tell you."

He stared at her, surprised. "Who is yer father, Alana?"

She pursed her mouth while her heart exploded in her chest. "Please, forgive me. Sir Alexander...Comyn."

For one moment, he simply stared, his expression frozen. Then shock filled his eyes.

CHAPTER SEVEN

ALANA WIPED THE tears from her cheeks. "Will you say something?"

"Yer the Earl of Buchan's niece?" he asked, stunned.

Somehow Alana nodded. "I am sorry," she whispered.

"Sorry?" He began to tremble. His cheeks were turning red. "Yer the niece of the king's worst enemy, and yer sorry?"

"Very."

"Yer Buchan's niece, and yer sharing my bed!" he exclaimed.

He was now horrified. She was naked except for the fur, so she turned and found her clothing. Her back to Iain, she shrugged on her torn chemise, as quickly as she could. She had not even reached for her cote when he seized her arm from behind.

She cried out. "You're hurting me!" His grip was brutal.

He whipped her around to face him, his eyes now blazing with the kind of fury she had prayed she would not see. "So Buchan sent ye to spy on me!"

"No!" she gasped. "Iain, how could you think such a thing?"

He shook her and she choked on a sob. "Easily! He

sent ye to Boath Manor, did he not? And then he sent ye to Nairn—he left ye in the tower, for me to find!"

"No!" she screamed.

"Aye," he shouted, shaking her. "Did he strike ye because ye refused to spy, at first? Or did he beat ye to mark ye, so ye could play upon my sympathies more easily? Have ye played me for a fool, Alana?"

Her arm was throbbing in pain. But that was nothing like the pain erupting in her breast. "Iain, dear God, I have hated deceiving you—I have feared just such a reaction!"

He flung her away, so hard she fell onto the pallet. "Damn ye!"

Alana cowered as he turned and smashed the stool he had been sitting on with one blow from his fist. She had feared he would be angry, but she had never expected this!

She was terrified that Iain would never forgive her and that he might even hurt her.

The tent flap blew open, two Highlanders charging inside, swords raised. Alana cringed even more.

Iain looked almost blindly at them.

The men gaped at him and then at Alana.

Realizing she was more naked than clothed in the thigh-length cotton shift, Alana grabbed the fur cover and put it around her body again. She was sick, enough so to retch. Surely Iain would realize she was not a spy.

"Ye can lower yer swords and leave," Iain said harshly. He was shaking as wildly as she was.

"Aye, Iain." Both men glanced curiously at Alana again before ducking out of the tent.

As Iain turned, Alana flinched with fear. "Don't hurt me," she said.

He stared, breathing hard. "We hang spies," he finally said. "We hang traitors."

She cried out. "I am not a spy. I am your mistress! I have not betrayed you!"

He laughed at her without mirth. "My mistress?" He shook his head. "Get dressed."

Alana did not move. "Iain, please, listen to me."

He walked away from her instead, took up the pitcher of wine and drank directly from it. "Get dressed, Alana." He finally glanced at her, his expression hard with anger.

She slowly slid from the bed, their stares locked. She felt like a trapped, hunted animal. "What do you intend? To drag me before Bruce? When you have not even heard me out?"

"He needs to know."

"Will he really hang me?" she cried. "Would you allow it?"

"He is my king!" he shouted at her, flinging the pitcher across the tent.

She hugged the fur close to her body. "This cannot be happening. I came here because I love you. Surely you know that."

"Dinna speak to me of love, Alana—not ever again!" he warned. "Only a fool would come here, or a spy. And yer no fool."

Tears arose. She was going to lose him forever—and she would soon become Bruce's prisoner—unless she could reason with him! "I am not a spy. How could I be? I met Buchan for the very first time at Nairn. He did not even know I had tended you at Boath Manor. Iain, please believe me."

"I cannot believe such a story. I will not. I am not a fool, to be played as ye have done."

"You are not a fool! You are one of the wisest men I know! Iain! I am telling you the truth—I happened upon you at Boath Manor, it was coincidence!"

"And ye just decided out of the goodness of yer heart to tend to my wounds?" He sneered. "I was suspicious, Alana—and I was right!"

"No." How could she tell him about her visions now? "You are wrong."

His gaze ice-cold, he walked over to her. She stiffened as he demanded, "Why did he hit you, Alana?"

She froze. Fear curdled within her. "I displeased him."

"Because ye did not wish to spy?" He was scathing. "Or did yer uncle try to bed ye, as I first thought?"

The tears returned. "He did not try to bed me. I displeased him. I gave him news he did not wish to hear."

"What news?" he demanded, towering over her.

Her heart thundered. How could she tell him about her visions now? And the one thing she could not do was tell him another lie.

"Ye cannot answer me!"

She cringed, expecting a blow. "Buchan wished to use me, yes!" she cried. "But not as a spy! At first I could not aid him, and when I could, he was furious with me."

"If not as a spy, then what? As a whore? As my whore?" he roared.

"No," she sobbed. "I cannot say!" She dared look up through her tears.

He was so furious—enraged. Alana thought he meant to strike her. But he did not. His hands shaking, he fisted them and put them to his sides. "Ye should have stayed at Brodie," he finally said, panting. "But now I ken why ye fear Bruce so much."

"Please, don't take me to him."

"He is my king, damn it."

Alana gasped. "I hoped when I came here that if you ever found out about my father, about my family, you would protect me from Bruce."

"Ye hoped wrong!"

Alana stared in disbelief. "No."

He paced across the tent and shoved through the door. As he left, the flap slammed closed.

Alana began to shake all over again. Holding her knees, she buried her face there and wept.

ALANA WAS DRESSED and sitting on the pallet, when Iain returned. No more than an hour had gone by since he had left in a whirlwind of rage and suspicion.

She stiffened, her hands clasped tightly in her lap. He paused, holding the tent flap open, his face taut with anguish and anger. "Get up. Get yer fur."

She was not quite able to move. "We need to speak."

"There is nothing left to say. Bruce has summoned ye."

She staggered to her feet. "You turned me in?"

He stared grimly at her. "He doesn't know yet. But he has summoned us to the hall."

Alana was breathing hard. "You haven't told him about me?"

"I told him about ye, Alana, days ago, when I sent Ranald to fetch ye." His mouth was turned down. "He found it curious that ye cared for me when I was wounded in Boath Manor and that Buchan locked ye up." He made a harsh, mocking sound. "I made light of the matter, but the king sensed yer treachery, even then. Let us go."

Alana's mind raced. Iain hadn't told Robert Bruce about her, not yet—but Bruce had summoned her to his hall. "Iain, I cannot go. I cannot meet Bruce. You cannot tell him who I am. I am not a spy, but he might hold me as a hostage! Neither Buchan nor my father would care. No ransom would ever be paid!"

"He is my king, and he has summoned us." Iain caught her wrist.

Alana inhaled in pain. Her wrist was black-and-blue from his brutal grasp earlier, and she tried to pull away. He saw the state of her arm and let her go. And because she had not picked up her fur cloak, he did, and he threw it at her. Then he nodded for her to go.

Alana covered her shoulders with the fur, preceding Iain outside. She was about to meet Bruce, to whom Iain would falsely reveal her as a spy. She stumbled, incapable of walking normally.

He caught her arm. "Mayhap ye should have thought about the price ye would pay if ye were caught." He guided her firmly forward. It was frigidly cold out, the skies blue and cloudless, and ground frozen underfoot. Ahead, smoke curled from the manor's chimney.

"It never occurred to me, not even a single time, that you would think me a spy for my uncle." Alana felt bitter. More tears moistened her eyes. "I was afraid you would be angry at being deceived, and that you might feel betrayed, but I never dreamed you would accuse me of such ruthless treachery."

"And I never dreamed I'd be bedding Buchan's

niece." But he glanced at her, his expression filled with pain.

"If only I had told you the truth when we first met! You would not think me a spy now!" Alana cried. She was so agitated that she stumbled again.

Iain caught her, putting his arm around her, and half dragged her to the manor's heavy front door. He shoved it open and pushed her within, following.

She felt as if she were living a nightmare now. It was as if she were walking to her fate—her death— her legs moving, when she wished for them to stop. How could Iain do this?

The front door opened directly into the hall. It was dark and smoky inside. The hall's slanted ceilings were timbered. Stag and boar heads were mounted upon one wall. A fire roared in its single hearth. Six makeshift tables had been set up, and each was entirely occupied. Alana's gaze slammed over everyone present, and she finally saw the King of Scotland.

Robert Bruce sat at the head of one table, speaking to his men. But the moment they entered he turned and saw them. He smiled, his gaze slamming onto Alana.

Iain clasped her shoulder and propelled her forward, toward him. But he was not as forceful as he had been earlier. Alana trembled as they went to meet him. She did not know how her legs functioned properly.

She glanced up at Iain. "Please protect me," she whispered.

Briefly, their gazes met. He instantly looked away.

Bruce was dressed in a red doublet and brown hose. Gold trimmed the doublet, as it did his fur-lined mantle. A large gold cross dangled from a chain about his throat. His blue eyes were piercing as they paused before him. Alana averted her eyes, not wanting to meet his gaze, as she curtsied.

"So this is the beautiful Mistress le Latimer," Bruce said. "No wonder you could not live without her. How beautiful you are, mistress."

Alana looked up at him. She could not speak to say thank-you, and did not think it mattered.

Bruce looked sharply at her and then at Iain. "What passes, Iain? Have I happened upon a lovers' quarrel?"

"It is more than a lovers' quarrel," Iain said tersely.

Alana flinched, filled with dread. She gazed pleadingly at him.

"I have just learned she is Buchan's niece," Iain said.

Alana cried out, as Bruce's eyes went wide.

"Her father is Sir Alexander Comyn," Iain continued brusquely.

"Well, well, the enemy is in your bed," Bruce said as if amused. He smiled slightly and turned thoughtfully away from them.

Alana seized Iain's hand. He gave her an angry look and shook it off. "She claims she is no spy," he said.

"Really?" Bruce faced them again. Now, he stared at Alana.

"Your Grace, may I speak?" Alana managed to ask.

"Please do," he said, almost benignly.

"I am not a spy. I care deeply for Iain, and I have dreaded this day, when my conscience would force me to tell him about my father."

Bruce studied her for a moment and looked at Iain. "She is so beautiful, it is almost impossible to deny her, is it not?"

"Yes," Iain said, flushing.

"Mistress, why would we believe, even for a moment, that your father and your uncle did not send you to bed one of my best commanders?"

She had to look at Bruce—into his eyes—and she trembled with fear. "Everyone knows my father abandoned me before I was even born, that he has no care for me, and that my grandmother raised me. I met Buchan for the first time, my lord, at Nairn, a week ago! Is that not reason enough to believe me?"

"No, it is not. Your father may have abandoned you before birth, but he or Buchan could have solicited you last week or the week before."

Alana felt helpless.

Iain said, "She confessed her identity to me, Yer Grace, freely, of her own will."

Bruce started. "A point in her favor," he said.

"Why would I confess if I were a spy sent by Buchan or Sir Alexander?" she asked. She gave Iain a grateful glance.

He looked away grimly.

"You might have confessed because you knew you were in jeopardy of discovery," Bruce said. "In such a circumstance, such a confession is usual." He leaned close. "No one plays these games of politics and intrigue as well as I do, my dear. I know every nook and cranny of the maze."

She recoiled.

He straightened. "Buchan did strike you and lock you up—how can I not think it a trap meant to lure Iain into your fold? Unless, of course, you can explain why he would beat and imprison his own niece."

Alana stared grimly. In that moment, she knew that, unless Bruce meant to hang her, she would not reveal she was a witch. Iain felt betrayed already. She could not imagine his reaction to the other piece about her.

"She will not say why she was beaten and locked up," Iain said harshly.

"It doesn't matter," Bruce said suddenly. He laid his hand on Alana's shoulder. "Even if she is a spy, I am prepared to forgive her."

Alana cried out. What trick was this?

Iain seemed as stunned. "Yer Grace?"

"As long as she proves how much she cares about you. It will be a test." Bruce did not smile now. His stare was like daggers.

"I do care," she whispered. "What do you wish of me?"

"You will become my spy," he said. "And you will spy on your father and Buchan for me, all in the name of love."

Alana stared at him in horror.

"Well, mistress?" Bruce finally smiled. "How difficult could it be?"

She finally cried, "I know nothing of spying!"

"You seem clever—I am sure you will learn," Robert Bruce said.

ALANA WAS SEATED at the table on Iain's left side. Strangers filled the rest of the benches, some of them northern Englishmen, others Scots from the Lowlands. Iain was the only Highlander present. Bruce sat at the table's head.

Supper was being served, and everyone was eating and talking at once. Except for Alana, as she had no appetite.

She stared at her plate, a piece of fish resting there,

aware of Iain, who was in conversation with Bruce, and acting as if he did not even know her. Pain knifed through her heart.

Had he ever loved her?

She had never dreamed he would feel so betrayed by her deception, or that he would believe her a spy. She had believed he would be angry but he would forgive her. And she had hoped he would protect her from Robert Bruce.

He had not.

"Has anyone else fallen ill since we attacked Elgin?" Iain was asking.

"No. The five men who became sick are almost well," Bruce said. He leaned back in his chair, his glance straying to Alana. Their eyes met and she realized she had been staring; she flushed and looked away.

"When those men fell ill, I truly feared a plague of some kind," Bruce said. He was grim. "But no one else has become ill."

"I think ye made the right decision to retreat," Iain said. "If ye had been right, and it was the plague, our entire army could have died by the next night. Ye could have been captured, Yer Grace, with no one to defend ye."

So that was why they had retreated, Alana thought, staring at her plate. The fish had been smoked whole, probably in the fall, and its lifeless eyes stared up at her. She picked up her utensils and removed its head from its body. God, she was ready to weep.

Bruce had commanded her to spy upon her father and her uncle. What was she to do?

Horror accompanied her heartbreak. He wished for her to prove her love for Iain? She was more than ready to do so, but not by spying upon her family! She could not imagine betraying them that way.

"I have decided to wait until next week to march," Bruce said. "It is pleasant enough here. If no one else becomes ill, we can be satisfied that no new and strange plague has befallen us."

Alana slowly cut a piece of white meat from the fish. As she ate it, she did not know what she would do. She could not let their love end this way. She had to prove herself to Iain. But she could not spy on her father and the Earl of Buchan. Could she?

If anything, shouldn't she tell them that Bruce would march next week?

A buxom maid was refilling Bruce's mug with wine. She turned to Iain, her smile coy, trying to catch his eye as she poured for him. Iain nodded at her, unsmiling.

Dismay pierced through her. Iain hadn't noticed the maid's interest, but for how long? Alana stared as the pretty redhead brushed her breast against his arm as she straightened and moved away from the table.

But Iain continued to stare into his mug, as if deeply in thought. She glanced at Bruce and stiffened—he was watching her closely. He knew she was distraught at being ordered to spy, and now, dismayed by the other woman. He turned to Iain and Alana heard him say something about Nairn.

She briefly closed her eyes. She could not wait to get back to the tent and crawl into the pallet and bury herself under the covers—and cry. Then she realized she did not know where she would be sleeping that night. But she doubted it would be in Iain's tent.

"There were no surprises," Iain was saying. But then he glanced at her.

She met his regard, but he instantly averted his gaze. She realized they were talking about Nairn, and Iain had just thought of finding her in the tower, as a prisoner, which had been a surprise. She looked away, but she could not help listening. And if they did not want her to hear, they would have sent her away.

"I have not forgotten how easily we took Nairn—and your part in such a triumph," Bruce was saying. "And yes, there were really no important surprises, other than that of Mistress Alana."

"I have brave men, men I trust," Iain said, clearly refusing to look at her. "And Buchan and Duncan fled like the cowards they are. They were easy to rout, Yer Grace, and I look forward to doing so again."

"Your men are my best soldiers. I am hoping your cousin Angus will give us another army soon."

"I am happy to speak with him on yer behalf," Iain said.

"And I may have you do so, soon." Bruce glanced at Alana, and their eyes caught. She realized she could not help herself from staring at the two men.

"And we have spoken in the past of your reward for serving me," Bruce said, finally moving his gaze back to Iain. "Since Nairn, I have had some time to think upon the kinds of lands I wish to grant you. When this war is done, Iain, you will rebuild Nairn and it will be yours. You have earned Nairn."

Iain stared, wide-eyed. Alana stared openly now, too.

"Thank ye, Yer Grace," Iain said harshly. He was clearly stunned, but pleased.

Of course he was pleased. Alana would be pleased

for him, too—it would be a great and important stronghold, once rebuilt—but Nairn was Buchan territory.

If Bruce won the war, Iain would be the lord of Nairn. He would probably also be the lord of Brodie, which had been under Nairn's control for decades. She did not know what to think.

"And that will not be all, Iain, you deserve more than just Nairn," Bruce said, cutting into her thoughts. "You need a wife—an heiress with great, significant lands."

Alana stared at Bruce, incredulous, and he stared back at her.

Of course Iain would marry an heiress one day. He fought for Bruce for gain, not sentiment…all men wished to marry heiresses, especially younger sons. But she felt even more ill than before.

The king smiled at her. "Have you no appetite, Mistress Alana? Or does the fish displease you?"

Her fists clenched in her lap. She hated Robert Bruce! "I have no appetite, Your Grace."

He studied her. "Surely you expect Iain to marry one day."

She flushed. "I have not thought about it."

"Do you know where your father is now, mistress?"

Alana had been rigid, but now, she was impossibly so. "No, Your Grace." How adeptly and swiftly he had changed the subject! Was his talk of a wife for Iain a trap, to lure her into a state of dismay, so she could not think clearly? Because she was dismayed, whether rightly or wrongly so!

He glanced at Iain. "It is ironic, actually, but Mistress Alana's sister is an heiress—one I have thought about for a long time."

Alana froze.

"Do you not have a sister, Mistress Alana? A half sister?" Bruce asked.

Iain turned to her.

She could barely speak. "I have two half sisters…."

"I am speaking of Buchan's heir, Lady Alice Comyn," Bruce said.

Alana choked and shot a glance at Iain. My God, what was this?

"You do know that Buchan has no other direct heirs. If he is to die, Lady Alice inherits the earldom."

Alana realized she was clawing the wood table with her short, chipped fingernails. She glanced from Bruce to Iain wildly. She had not realized that Alice was next in line to inherit Buchan's earldom!

"I have plans for the earldom when I defeat Buchan," Bruce said. His tone had hardened, and his eyes were dark with lust now—bloodlust. "I will carve it up and give away the pieces to my best, most loyal men."

Iain was staring at her. He turned to Bruce slowly, his eyes as dark, as wide, as before. "Whoever marries Alice will have a legitimate claim to her lands."

"Yes," Bruce said. He suddenly drained his wine and stared at Alana. "So tell me, mistress, where do you think your father is?"

"I last heard of him when he was at Elgin, defending it from you."

"That is no answer. You have appeared to care about Sir Alexander, even if you do not know him because he abandoned you. Do you not ask after him?"

She managed to nod, aware that he wished to inflict even more pain on her. He had succeeded. "All of the time!"

"Good, then continue to do so. I wish to know where he is, and soon. I may approach him with an offer for Alice."

Alana was suddenly sick to her stomach, violently so.

"Buchan, however, remains at Elgin. I have spies there." Bruce stood. "He is seeking more allies, mistress. He needs more friends to fight against me if he even thinks to win. He knows it and he has summoned the Earl of Ross and Sir Reginald Cheyne, amongst others. You will tell me who his new friends are."

"How will I do that?" Alana gasped. She was still trying to comprehend what Bruce had been saying. Had he suggested he might marry her sister to Iain? Did he mean to contact her father about such an alliance?

"I am certain a clever woman like yourself will find many ways to prove her devotion to her lover," Bruce said.

Alana stared, aghast. She realized all the men had risen to their feet, out of respect for their king. She alone remained seated. Slowly, she got up.

"I look forward to your answers, mistress. And, Alana? Once you become my friend, you will be well rewarded, too." With that, he turned and strode from the hall.

Alana held on to the table, her knees buckling. Iain seized her elbow.

At first, she thought he meant to offer her his support. But when she looked at him, his face was hard, and he averted his eyes.

Alana looked away.

ALANA COULD NOT keep up with Iain. His strides were rapid, but that was not the reason why. She was beyond shock, and she felt ill—so much so that she could not move swiftly. She stumbled time and again.

He did not slow to help her, and he kept his grasp upon her arm. It was dark out now as they crossed the frozen yard. Alana wanted to know where they were going—they seemed to be heading to his tent. She did not believe she would sleep there, but at least he had not left her locked in the cellars in the manor.

Not that anything mattered now. All she could really comprehend was that she was commanded to spy upon her very own father, and that Iain might be awarded her sister in marriage.

When they reached his tent, she was losing the last of her composure. How she needed to cry in despair, in fury. But she fought the rising flood. She must not cry in front of him.

He pushed open the tent's flap door, finally releasing her arm. She went inside ahead of him, stumbling again.

She heard the flap door drop closed. Oh, God. How could he be so cold, so cruel? And could Bruce really intend to marry him to her sister—one of the greatest heiresses in the land? Men married for power all of the time, but she could not bear the notion. Alice already had everything.

He was behind her, lighting candles. She was acutely aware of him, of her pain, and that the tent was too small for them both. The interior became dimly illuminated. His shadow danced upon the hide wall. Alana fought her tears, the heartache. The pallet they had so recently shared was beside her. She refused to look at it.

As he lit the last candle, she slowly turned. "Would

you consider marrying my sister?" she heard herself ask with a huge catch in her throat.

His expression was hard, strained. "She may be the greatest heiress in the north of Scotland. Aye."

She inhaled. Had he ever cared about her? "How could you even think of doing such a thing?"

"Do ye think I left my home and went to war for a few trinkets and some gold?"

Of course not, she thought, but she did not say so. "She is my sister." When he did not answer, she cried, "If you don't care, why did you defend me to Bruce?"

"I dinna defend ye." Warning was in his tone. He began to toss hides on the floor, one on top of the other.

"You told him I had confessed my identity—that was a defense," Alana said hoarsely.

He straightened and whirled to face her. "It was no defense! I merely spoke the truth!"

His every word was a pointed barb—now he implied that she had not spoken the truth. "I wanted to tell you the truth at Boath Manor."

"But ye dinna tell the truth. Ye lied! I was suspicious of ye when we first met—just as I am suspicious now." He picked up a piece of rope.

She trembled wildly. "Iain, I know you feel betrayed, and it is clouding how you are thinking. So do not think. Look into your heart! Please!"

He walked over to her, taking her wrists.

"What are you doing?"

He tied her wrists in front of her, never once looking into her eyes. "Do ye think I trust ye?"

"I will not try to escape!"

He ignored her, knotting the rope and releasing her wrists.

"How can you do this?" She choked. She was so close to tears. "I thought you cared about me! This is not the behavior of a lover!"

"I dinna care!" he said harshly, his eyes blazing. "The woman I cared about doesn't exist."

"I do exist!" she cried, agonized. "Look at me! I am Alana le Latimer!"

"Aye, yer Buchan's niece!" he cried back.

"So you will tie me up, keep me prisoner, force me to spy and marry my sister?"

He stepped back from her. "You're Bruce's prisoner, Alana, not mine." He was as breathless as she was. "I am to guard ye, and well, until ye return to Brodie to spy for us. So aye, I will tie ye up while I sleep."

Alana began to shake. "I trusted you," she heard herself say.

"That was unwise." He now flung the fur from his shoulders onto the pile of hides.

"I trusted you to protect me." Tears finally blinded her. "I have trusted one person my entire life—Gran. And then, I trusted you!"

He flinched, his back to her. Then he stalked to the small table where a new stool had been placed and sat down, his back to her. He poured wine. His hand shook as he did so. "No, Alana—I trusted ye."

Tears fell. She could not stop them. His back was so rigid with anger. Alana walked to him and laid her bound wrists on his shoulder. She was so afraid of what was happening to them. "I never meant to betray you," she whispered.

He sat as still as a statue—for several harshly drawn breaths. "Stand back, Alana," he warned.

She trembled. "I cannot lose you, Iain."

"It's too late." And then he whirled, knocking over the stool, crushing her in his arms. His mouth claimed hers, hard and hurtfully.

He growled and increased the viselike pressure of his arms. He was rough, and she knew he wanted to cause pain. Fear warred with desire. Surely passion could bring them back together, she thought. Desperation arose.

As he kissed her, Alana gasped and he deepened the kiss deliberately. She tasted blood. Her hands were between them, and she brought them up against his chest. It crossed her mind that even if she protested, he would not heed her. He was so angry.

He walked her back a step and pushed her down onto the pallet, very abruptly.

His kiss was bruising and he was angry, but she loved him. She did not know if he meant to punish her, and even if he did, she would bear it. For surely sex would turn into lovemaking. Surely passion would bring them together again. She was desperate—she would do anything to get past his anger, to regain his love.

And she did not think she could resist him, anyway. Not when she loved him so. "Iain. I love you," she said.

He broke the kiss to look at her, his eyes blazing. "This isn't love."

Tears arose once more. "Yes, it is," she answered. Before she could protest further or plead with him he came down on top of her, kissing her again. He was determined to take her as coldly and as cruelly as possible, she thought. But she understood. Alana kissed him back, but not with passion. "I love you," she whispered again.

He grunted in satisfaction. Now, their tongues entwined. Alana kissed him again, desire beginning in spite of his cruelty. She would always love him, want him, she thought. Desire flamed. Their mouths fused, she moved her bound wrists lower, brushing up against his manhood, and finding the hem of his leine. She tugged it upward, while hooking her ankles over his calves.

He inhaled harshly, found her skirts and moved them up past her waist, breaking the breathless kiss as he did so. In the dull candlelight, their gazes met.

His eyes blazed with lust—and anguish. "Would you untie me?" she managed to ask. She wanted to wrap him in her arms. She had never meant to hurt him this way.

His answer was to kiss her, hard, shoving one thigh between her legs.

Alana forgot about her wrists. He was hard and male between her legs, dulling the fear, the desperation, causing more urgency. He rocked against her and Alana heard herself moan.

And then he pushed deeply within her.

Alana lay still, unable to hold him, caught between grief and desire. He wanted to use her, and she knew it. As he began to increase his rhythm, Alana raised her bound wrists to touch his jaw. "Iain," she whispered.

He trembled. "Ye betrayed me."

"No." She reached up with both hands and touched his cheek.

He kissed her now, deeply, otherwise unmoving. Deliberately Alana kissed him back. More desire surged. She welcomed it. Iain rose up over her, and she gasped. This time, he watched her as he moved deeply inside her.

She wanted to tell him again that she loved him, but now, she could not speak. She cried out, blinded by the growing pleasure. *She would always need him.* They pushed hard at each other, and harder, endlessly, until Alana felt the tide of ecstasy. It broke. Washed over her. Again and again.

She wept helplessly in his arms.

She drifted in contentment, unable to think. Cool air wafted over her.

Alana's eyes flew open. Iain had left their bed.

She turned onto her side and levered herself to sit up.

Iain was reaching for his fur cloak. He put it on as he straightened. And not looking at her, he began snuffing out each candle.

Dismay began. What had just happened? She was stunned by their lovemaking. Except—it had not been lovemaking. And she was still tied up like a prisoner. Fear arose, clawing at her. "Iain."

He snuffed out the last candle. The interior of the tent became dark. He did not answer her, and she could just make out his big body settling onto the pallet of hides across the tent from her.

Pain erupted in her breast. Alana lay back down, hugging her pillow tightly. It was a long time before she fell asleep.

CHAPTER EIGHT

THICK CLOUDS COVERED the sky, making it gray. It would snow before nightfall, Alana thought, which was still hours away. She fought the urge to weep.

She was astride a small brown mare, a soldier on each side of her. Iain rode ahead of them, leading the way, Ranald beside him. They had ridden out of Concarn shortly after sunrise, and it was now midday. Alana suspected that they would arrive at Brodie shortly.

They were riding though the snow-covered forest on a well-used deer trail, most of the snow underfoot packed hard from the riders who used it. Alana held on to her saddle. She was so distraught that she felt faint, enough so to fall off of her horse.

She was sick in her heart. The passion she and Iain had shared last night had not changed anything. If anything, it had put an even greater distance between them. For it had been tainted with her fear, her desperation and his distrust. Even though she had found release in his arms, she felt used and abused, like a woman taken merely for the man's pleasure, only to be cast aside the next day.

For hadn't she been cast aside? He had awoken her that morning without a word, slitting the rope on her wrists, causing her to awaken in alarm, and then he had left the tent abruptly, before their eyes could even meet. A few moments later Ranald had come to get her, telling her that they were riding for Brodie now.

Tears crept into her eyes. If passion could not bring them together, then what would?

Iain suddenly raised his hand and halted. "Brodie," he said.

He turned in his saddle and looked over his shoulder at her, his expression cast from stone. "Ranald will be going with ye. Ye will put him in the stables and disguise him as one of the village children."

Alana somehow nodded. Dear God, was he going to send her on her way without a private word?

"Do ye think ye can bring me information when Mistress Alana sends it?" he asked the boy, his tone softening.

Ranald nodded eagerly. "Aye, my lord, 'tis an easy ride to Concarn."

He smiled at him. "We will not be at Concarn for long. When ye hear an owl hooting at noon, ye will come out to the woods here to meet me, or my man. But only if 'tis at noon, Ranald."

The boy nodded.

Iain slid off his stallion, handing the reins to Ranald. He stared at Alana. "I have instructions to give ye."

She trembled, so sickened by the tension between them and what seemed to be his indifference. And now he would instruct her on how to spy? She started to dismount but he seized her bridle. "Ye can stay astride, as the orders are brief." He led her horse aside from the rest of their group.

She did not want to stay astride. She wanted to dismount—and leap into his arms and demand he cease this nonsense. A man could not care for a woman one day and despise her the next! "I cannot part this way," she said tersely.

He halted her horse by a small brook that was mostly frozen. Her mare lowered its head to sniff at it and find a place to drink. Iain looked up at her. "How many soldiers does Duncan have at Brodie? How many archers?"

"That is what you ask me? You ask me about Brodie's defenses?" she cried. Holding the saddle, she flung one leg over it and hurriedly dismounted. "You do not ask me if I am happy, or sad or hurt?"

He quickly caught her before she fell. For one moment, his hands held her waist, and then he released her. "I told ye to stay astride," he said darkly.

She stared up at him. "What happened last night?"

He flinched. "If I hurt ye, I am sorry."

She could barely breathe. "You have broken my heart, Iain."

"No. That is impossible."

"You did not protect me from Bruce—and last night, you used me as if I were some common serving wench!"

"Ye seduced me, Alana," he warned. "Ye came to me!"

"No. I did not seduce you. You thought to punish me, I think, by taking me as if I were some harlot—and not the woman you love."

"I did not take ye aside to discuss last night!"

She inhaled, shocked and taken aback.

He flushed.

A terrible silence fell. She finally said, "I know you are very angry—that you feel betrayed. But my only betrayal was to avoid telling you about my father, because I was falling in love with you. I am not a spy." She hesitated. "One day, you will believe me." She thought of her sister Alice. "I only hope that when that day comes, it is not too late."

For a moment, he was silent, his gaze unwavering. "We must speak of Brodie, Alana."

She wet her lips. "Why do you ask about Brodie's defenses?"

"One day I will command Nairn. Brodie will be significant to me, then."

"How?" she cried. "It is a tiny place!"

"I will provision it well, and use it as my first line of defense for Nairn," he said.

She instantly understood his strategy, which did not bode well for her home. "Brodie is *my* home. It belonged to my *mother*. By right, it should be mine—not Duncan's, not his son's."

"Is that a warning?"

"Will you attack Brodie?"

"I am asking the questions, Alana. How many men does Duncan keep there?"

She hugged herself. He coveted Brodie now. She imagined Alice as his wife, as the mistress of Brodie. She could not bear to think of Alice in her home. "I cannot say, because I do not know."

"Ye do not know, or ye do not wish to tell me?" he asked skeptically. "Ye spy for us now, Alana. Ye must tell me everything ye can about Brodie's defenses."

"Iain, do not make me do this! Brodie is my home! Surely you can understand that. And we are lovers, still."

"I dinna know what we are, Alana." He tugged on

her mare's reins, leading it forward and looping the reins about the saddle. Their interview was over. He wished for her to mount.

She stared at him as he held her horse, her vision blurred. Impatiently, he turned and looked at her.

"What will you do when you find out that I am not a spy? That my only sin was that of fear?"

His eyes widened.

"Will you still hate me?" she asked.

He breathed hard. "I dinna hate ye, Alana. But I dinna trust ye."

She was so dismayed. She lifted her skirts out of the snow and walked over to him. He took her by the waist and lifted her effortlessly onto the mare. Alana picked up her reins.

"Make certain ye have the answers I seek in two days. Send Ranald to the woods here at noon."

She would never tell him the precise nature of Brodie's defenses, she thought. He would have to discover that himself. "Even though I am Sir Alexander's daughter, I love you, Iain." She nudged the mare with her heels, to go over to Ranald and out of the forest. Brodie sat atop the adjacent hill. "God keep you, Iain. God keep you safe in this war. I could not bear it if anything happened to you."

"Wait." He stepped up to her and seized the mare's bridle. His gaze wasn't angry now; it was searching. "I will always care that yer a Comyn," he said harshly. "Always. For even if ye truly love me, ye will care for yer family and it will always strain yer loyalty."

She gasped for breath. "What are you saying?"

He stared deeply into her eyes, as he had not done since learning her identity. He finally said, "If ye did not come to me at Concarn to spy, if ye came because ye truly love me, then mayhap I could forgive yer deception."

Iain released her bridle. "Go." He hit her mare on the rump.

The mare picked up a trot, hurrying toward the castle, Ranald urging his mount to join her.

Alana turned and stared over her shoulder at Iain. There was hope. It wasn't over yet.

ALANA WASN'T CERTAIN of the reception she would get from Godfrey, and now she recalled asking Eleanor to invent the excuse for her absence that she had gone to speak with Sir Alexander. She had no wish to undo the fragile truce she had developed with Godfrey. She intended to be careful to maintain it, and not expose her deception, especially if Iain had some interest in acquiring Brodie.

The watch had identified them, and they were now passing through the castle gates. Alana stared across the courtyard, immediately alert. Several soldiers in English mail were leaving the stables. Her gaze veered to the front door of the great hall. She expected to see Godfrey come out to demand where she had been.

But the front door remained closed. Alana watched the soldiers head for the hall as they crossed the courtyard, still astride. "We have company," she said to Ranald softly. "I have never seen those soldiers before."

"I can find out who they are," Ranald said with a grin.

Alana halted her mount and slid off, as did Ranald. The head stableman appeared from within, greeting her with a smile. "Mistress Alana." He beamed. "Let

me take that poor, tired mare from ye." The groom—
Seamus MacKinnon—eyed Ranald curiously.

Alana clasped the boy's shoulder. "Thank you, Seamus. This is young Ranald, from Tor, and I have told
his mother he can work here in our stables for a while.
She has eight and she cannot feed them all."

"Eight, eh?" Seamus lifted bushy gray brows. "Yer
welcome here, boy, but only if ye do as I say, when I
say."

"He's a good lad," she said. She glanced past him
into the stables, which were full. Her alarm increased.
"Seamus, do we have visitors?"

"Aye, we do. The Earl of Buchan is in residence, my
lady, with his brother."

Alana stiffened. *Her father was at Brodie.* For one
moment, she was paralyzed with disbelief.

"Are ye ill, mistress?" Seamus asked gruffly.

"I am surprised, that is all."

"I had better feed and bed down these horses. Boy?
Let's go."

Alana smiled at Ranald and watched him hurry off
with Seamus, knowing he was in good and kind hands.
Then her heart turned over hard.

She did not know what to expect when she went inside. The past twenty-four hours had been the worst of
her life. She did not know if she could withstand any
more conflict, or much more disappointment. And her
uncle was with her father. She now feared the Earl of
Buchan.

She left the stables resolutely. As she went up the
front steps to the hall, Godfrey finally stepped outside,
his expression grim.

Alana clutched her cloak tightly to her body. "Hello. What has happened?"

He remained unsmiling. "Did you find your father, Alana?" His eyes darkened.

So he was suspicious of her, and rightly so. "I should have told you what I meant to do, and I am sorry, but leaving to find him seemed like a good idea," she said as evenly as possible. "But he wasn't at Elgin—I had just missed him."

Godfrey stared suspiciously and said, "He wasn't at Elgin because he is here, with the earl."

She pretended to be surprised. "Buchan isn't flying his flag."

"He's at war! His presence here is a secret," Godfrey snapped.

"Godfrey, what is wrong?"

"You should have stayed here so we could greet Buchan together. He was angry that you had left! He took it out on me—as if I can control you!" Godfrey exclaimed.

"I am sorry."

"I am fortunate he did not send me to toil in the moat with the commoners and the foot soldiers," Godfrey said. Then he came down the steps in a hurry and took her wrist. He lowered his voice. "They have been writing letters and sending messengers all over Scotland! They are worried about Bruce—they do not think Elgin will withstand a real attack. If Elgin falls, with Lochindorb gone in the south, we are surrounded."

Alana trembled, thinking of what she had heard—that Bruce would march next week. But she did not know where he would go. And what of Iain's new interest in Brodie? She no longer knew if she cared who won the war for Scotland's crown, but she knew she must fight for Brodie, even against Iain, especially if he was awarded her sister. "Will we be given more soldiers?" she asked.

"No. My father remains at Elgin. We haven't been given more men. No one cares about Brodie except for you and I." He suddenly rubbed his face with his hand and cursed.

He was right, she thought. "I am sorry I wasn't here when they arrived."

He looked at her. "Buchan is angry. You had better give him a good vision, Alana."

Inwardly she cringed. "I haven't had any other visions."

"Maybe you should make one up—one that will get us defenses!" He took her arm. "They're in the hall. They know you have returned." His gaze turned searching.

Alana began to shake. "My father...how is he?"

"He is well, Alana. He asked about you."

"He did?"

"You cannot avoid this meeting, and isn't this what you have been hoping for?" Godfrey pulled her toward the door. "He isn't at all like Buchan," he said, low.

Alana could not ask him what he meant, because at that moment she saw her father. He was seated with Buchan before the fire, but now, he looked over his shoulder at her. And eyes wide, he got to his feet.

She faltered.

Godfrey pulled her inside and shut the door behind them. "My lords," he said. "Mistress Alana has returned."

He was exactly as she remembered, Alana thought,

her heart suddenly racing. He was tall, golden-haired, handsome. He looked more like a god from Greek mythology than a man, never mind the fine clothing he wore.

No wonder her mother had loved him.

The Earl of Buchan had risen and he strolled around both chairs and toward her. "We have been waiting for you to return, Alana," he said.

She flinched and met his cool gaze. He was displeased with her. Her pulse pounded more swiftly. "I am sorry, my lord," she said. "I had no intent to keep you waiting." She slowly pulled off her fur-lined cloak.

"You are a brave woman, to venture off alone as you have," Buchan remarked. He paused before her and lifted her chin. "So Iain of Islay took Nairn—and freed you."

She flushed, wondering if he had somehow learned the truth about her and her relationship with Iain. Fear stabbed through her. In that moment, she knew that her uncle would ruthlessly destroy her if he ever learned that she had betrayed him and his cause by sleeping with his enemy. "He did not know I was your niece, my lord," she managed to tell him. "Nor did he know about my ability to see."

"Then you were fortunate. He would have never freed you had he guessed your value." Buchan released her chin and gestured at Sir Alexander. "I believe you know your own father, mistress."

Alana was free now to gaze upon Sir Alexander, who smiled and came forward. "My own daughter," he said softly.

He seemed pleased to see her, but she could not smile back. Instead, as he took her hand, she stiffened. She had been waiting for this moment for fifteen years, she thought, incapable of drawing an even breath. She had been hoping for a reunion, but now that he was there, she was at a loss. Now, she did not know what to say, or how to feel. She did not know if she was thrilled to see him or dismayed. "My lord," she said, inclining her head.

"I remember when we met, so many years ago, when you were a little girl." Alana looked up. His smile faded. He studied her for a moment. "Even then, I thought that you looked just like your mother."

"We met when I was five," she heard herself say hoarsely. "I have not forgotten." Hurt stabbed through her chest.

He appeared kind; as if he cared. But he had not come to see her in fifteen years! He could not be kind or caring, could he? If he had cared, he would have come not once, but many times.

"I have not forgotten, either," he said softly. "My brother told me how you have grown up into a beautiful woman." He inhaled. "Your mother was one of the most beautiful women I had ever seen. You resemble her exactly."

Were his eyes tearing? Why was he close to crying now?

She wanted to ask him if had loved Elisabeth, or if he had merely used her to sate his own lust. She wanted to ask him if he would have married Elisabeth had she survived childbirth, or if he would have married Joan, anyway. She wanted to know what he had felt when he had learned that his lover was with child. And mostly she wanted to ask why? Why had she been abandoned, dismissed and forgotten?

But she could not ask him any of these things.

Instead, Alana curtsied. "I have heard that my mother was very beautiful. I doubt I resemble her that much."

He smiled. "What a perfectly modest reply."

"Thank you, my lord," she said politely.

"Your mother was modest, too. And she was clever. Strong."

There was no doubt in Alana's mind that he had felt fondly toward Elisabeth. At least he had cared about her mother.

"Lady Fitzhugh tells me you are all of those things," Sir Alexander said. "You must be fatigued, Alana. And hungry. Shall we sit together?"

Did he now wish to speak with her? Spend time with her? "Thank you, my lord." Her head was spinning. The Earl of Buchan had returned to his seat at the table's head, and Alana took a place on the bench. She did not look at the earl as she did so. Sir Alexander sat down across from her. He signaled a maid for food, and poured Alana wine.

Godfrey took the seat next to Alana. Oddly, she felt comforted by his presence now. She gave him a grateful glance.

"I was very pleased when my brother told me we would come to Brodie," Sir Alexander said, handing her the mug.

"You could have come at any time, my lord," she said carefully.

His eyes widened. Before he could respond, Eleanor hurried into the hall, and he appeared relieved. "Lady Fitzhugh, you can cease worrying. Alana is back."

"I can see that!" Eleanor sat down beside Alana,

patting her hand. But her gaze was sharp, piercing. "Alana, dear, are you all right?"

"I am fine, Gran." Alana hugged her briefly. Then she studied her father, aware that he was staring. What excuse did he have for not calling upon her even once in the past decade and a half? She wondered. Would he offer an explanation, an excuse? Did she dare ask him directly? "How long will you be in residence?" she finally asked.

"We will probably take our leave on the morrow," Sir Alexander said. "We are gathering up our allies in this war. We do not have a great deal of time to linger."

Alana tensed. She instantly did not want to hear any more—if she did not know anything, she could not spy on anyone for Bruce, much less her uncle and her father.

"Our spies tell us Bruce will march soon," the earl said. "We do not yet know where, although we have our suspicions. We must prepare our defenses and rout him once and for all."

Alana wondered yet again if she should somehow reveal that Bruce would march next week. But she said nothing.

"Alana, you are never to place yourself in danger again," Buchan said abruptly.

Alana started, facing him with dread.

"You are Duncan's ward. When he is away, you are to obey Godfrey in all matters." He looked directly at Godfrey. "It is your duty to keep her safe. Should ill befall her, I will hold you responsible."

Godfrey paled. "Aye, my lord."

Alana's heart sank. She knew why Buchan so suddenly cared about her welfare. He wished to make use of any new visions of the war that she might have.

"Godfrey says there have been no new visions, not a single one," Buchan said, confirming her suspicions.

She glanced at Sir Alexander. His stare was sharp now. She turned back to her uncle, even more dismayed. Did her father also wish for her to have visions to aid them in the war? "There have been no new visions," she said. She stared down at the table, thinking about the image forever engraved in her mind of the earldom in ruins, with Bruce's flag flying high in the skies. "I would be pleased if I never had a vision again."

"I wish to be notified the instant you have a vision, good or bad. And I do not care if it is about the war or a damned cow!" Buchan faced Godfrey, eyes dark and flashing. "Every vision she has is to be recorded—every single one."

Godfrey nodded, ashen.

"You will send me the record, immediately."

"Yes, my lord," Godfrey said.

Buchan faced Alana. "And you will do your duty as my niece—as your father's daughter."

Alana did not glance at Sir Alexander now. She stared at her uncle. He was angry, but he was also afraid. She knew that now. He was afraid he was losing this war to Robert Bruce.

And she did not think she cared who won, or who lost. She thought about the fact that somehow, she was directly involved in this damned war, when she only cared to safeguard her home.

Then she revised her thoughts. She still cared about Iain. She cared whether he lived or died, whether he suffered defeat or triumphed.

"I wish to do my duty, my lord," she said. But she did not know if her words were heartfelt and sincere. How could she be loyal to her family, to Brodie and to Iain? It was impossible.

"Good." Buchan seemed satisfied as wine was poured for everyone. A platter of bread and cheese was placed before Alana, followed by a plate of oatcakes.

Alana could barely eat, but she tore off a piece of bread.

"Tell me about Iain of Islay," Buchan said.

Alana almost choked on the bread she was chewing. When she had swallowed, she said, "I beg your pardon?"

"He freed you from the tower. You were released from Nairn the next day. I have spies, Alana, surely you know that?" But he sat back in his chair, toying with his mug of wine.

She could not breathe properly. Did he have spies within Nairn? What if someone had seen them together in the cellars? Or afterward—outside her chamber door—or when they were saying farewell with heat, disappointment and anger?

Had their behavior been remarked?

If it had, she would be a prisoner once again, she was certain. She found her voice. "Yes, we were found in the tower, and allowed to go home the next day. What is it you wish to know, my lord?"

"Everything. Why did he release you?"

"I do not think there was a reason for him to keep us. As I said, he did not know of my Comyn connections, or my visions. He wanted to know why we were imprisoned, and I would not say, except that I had displeased you."

"And he allowed such an answer?"

She hesitated. "He wasn't pleased. But I could not tell him who I was, or about my abilities."

"That was shrewd, Alana, and wise. Had you told him the truth, you would be his prisoner now. Iain of Islay is ruthless. You must have displeased him with your answers."

She shrugged helplessly. "I think he had greater matters on his mind, such as burning Nairn to the ground."

"Your beauty probably affected his judgment," Buchan mused.

"I wouldn't know," she said quickly.

"Do you blush?"

She knew her cheeks were heated. "My lord, I approached him the next morning. I begged him to spare the castle, and if not that, the village and the farms."

Buchan's eyes widened.

"He was angry, he did not heed me, as you know. So…I do not think my appearance moved him."

Buchan sat back and sipped his wine. "Bruce would lose a great commander if he lost Iain—possibly his best commander."

Sir Alexander said to his brother, "Your archers failed to strike him even a single time."

"Do not remind me, but there are other ways to rid oneself of an enemy," Buchan said. "And I am not talking about poison."

Alana seized her wine and gulped it.

"The Earl of Ross paid dearly for his peace with Bruce," Sir Alexander said. "Could we bribe Iain?"

"Ross wasn't bribed. Bruce was going to destroy him on the battlefield. Ross had no choice but to pay

Bruce for a truce, and to go over to his side. And now he wavers because his loyalty is with us."

"Iain of Islay is no earl—he is a soldier of fortune," Sir Alexander said.

"You do not know that he is loyal to his cousin Angus Og, who is more of a father to him than his oldest brother. I am not certain gold would move him to betray his cousin and his liege. I have no desire to empty my chests of gold and have Iain then betray us. But...Iain has no land, no titles and no wife."

Alana sat up straighter, realizing where Buchan would lead.

"He is here in the north. Obviously he wishes for lands here," Sir Alexander mused.

"Bruce has offered him Nairn," Buchan said. Alana gasped. He glanced at her. "I do have spies, my dear." He turned back to his brother. "So we need to offer him lands, titles, a wife."

Alana looked at her lap, filled with dread. First Bruce wished to offer him an heiress, and now Buchan did.

"I thought about this last night," Buchan was telling Sir Alexander. "I have no daughters to offer and no other available nieces, not since William's daughter married Alexander MacDonald, betraying us all. You have two daughters, Alex, both of them heiresses, both of them pretty and pleasing."

Alana flinched. Buchan would offer her sisters? Was this truly happening?

"Alice is your heir," Sir Alexander shot tersely. He was clearly angry—he did not want Alice offered to Iain.

"Yes, she is my heir...because my damned wife lives

when she should have been hanged for her treachery."
Buchan now slammed his empty mug down. "Hanged,
her body dragged through the city, her head cut off and
placed on a pike. Wine!"

Alana stole a look at him—he was enraged. She
had never before thought about the fact that he could
not remarry while his wife remained alive, and his
wife, Isabella, was King Edward of England's prisoner.
Her sentence for her treason—for crowning Bruce at
Scone—was to live out the rest of her years in a cage,
like an animal, for all to gawk at and insult.

"How long can a woman live in a cage?" Sir Alexander asked angrily. "If you are fortunate, she will fall ill
and die and you will remarry and have heirs. I cannot
approve of Alice being wed to a MacDonald savage."

"I am fifty!" Buchan exclaimed. "As if you wish
for me to have an heir of my own! Have no fear, Alex.
Alice is far too valuable to pawn off to a Highland savage just to peel him away from Bruce. One day, little
brother, if you outlive me, you will be the power behind Buchan, with your daughter its countess, wed to
some powerful courtier."

Alana dared to regard both men now. They were
staring darkly at one another, as if antagonists, not
brothers.

Did her father covet the power of Buchan?

He no longer seemed amiable and gentle.

"I wish to offer Margaret to Iain of Islay. She has
Tarredale as a dowry. I can even add to it—perhaps I'll
give him command of Nairn, once she is with child,
and we can be sure of his loyalty. I think the offer a
good one. Don't you, little brother?"

Sir Alexander sat back, his expression grim and

unhappy. He did not wish to marry even his second daughter to Iain, but clearly, he would not have a choice. "Will I have a day or two to think about it?"

"Think about it all that you want," Buchan said. He suddenly stood. "I am done here. I am going to finish my letters. I imagine father and daughter wish to become reacquainted." He walked around the table and laid his hand on Alana's back.

She flinched as he did so, looking up.

"I am sorry my men did not free you from the tower, as they were ordered to do. They were cowards, fleeing instead, and they have been punished for their cowardice."

Alana did not know if she believed Buchan—if he had ordered her and Eleanor's release before he had fled Nairn—but she forced a smile. "Thank you, my lord."

Buchan walked away. As he did Godfrey gave her a concerned look. He also stood. "I am going to speak with the sergeant of the watch, Alana. If you need me, I will be in the watchtower."

She felt oddly grateful to him, as if they were friends. "I am going up to rest shortly," she said.

He nodded, glanced at Sir Alexander and left.

"Alana, do you wish for me to stay?" Eleanor asked with obvious concern.

"I will be up shortly, Gran," Alana said, squeezing her hand.

Eleanor looked at Sir Alexander. "You owe her a great deal," she said sharply, and then she left.

They were alone in the great hall.

For one moment, Sir Alexander stared into his mug,

which he clasped with both hands. Then he looked up at her and smiled.

Alana hesitated nervously. "You do not wish to marry my half sister Margaret to Iain of Islay," she said.

"I have hardly said that."

"It seems obvious."

"You have met him. He is a savage and barbaric Highlander. Your sisters have spent half of their childhood at the French court, when we were allies of the French king, and some of the past year at the English court, to please King Edward when he came to the throne. I do not think Margaret will be happy married to a Highlander, especially if he takes her to Islay to live."

She felt so hurt. Did he know that when he spoke of Margaret's happiness, it was like a knife stabbing through her? What of her happiness? He clearly cared about her sisters, and as clearly, he did not care about her. "But they can live at Tarredale and at Nairn."

Sir Alexander stared closely at her. "Are you about to cry?"

She was choking on tears. She shook her head and managed to find composure. "What is she like?"

"Margaret?" He seemed surprised. "She is fifteen and very sweet. She is blonde and very pretty—but not as pretty as you."

Alana rubbed her forearms. "But what is she like? What pleases her? Is she well liked?"

"She is skilled with the needle, and she loves to embroider and sew. She plays the harp beautifully. She has the voice of an angel. She never argues, and is fond of poetry. Everyone likes Margaret."

Alana looked at her hands, clasped in her lap. She

could not imagine Iain with a wife who played the harp beautifully, who liked poetry, and never argued. "And Alice?"

"Alice is dark-haired, although not as dark-haired as you. She is pretty, and very clever and very strong. She will make a fine countess one day."

She could not stand it. He was so proud of Margaret and Alice—or so it seemed. "Does Alice like poetry? Does she sing? Does she voice her opinions?"

"She has a poor singing voice, she dislikes poetry and she is always ready to tell me what she thinks."

Iain might like Alice—he might like her very much!

"You and Alice are very much alike," Sir Alexander mused.

They were alike? Alice was a great heiress. Alice had grown up with both of her parents—in the lap of luxury, of privilege. She had spent half her childhood at the French court! She would be the countess of Buchan one day!

And she had never been molested by an older man—never been sexually assaulted by her own guardian. She had never been struck by her uncle.

Nor had she ever been jeered at by her peers, or insulted and mocked for being a witch.

Alike? They were nothing alike!

"I would like it if you met your sisters one day," Sir Alexander said suddenly.

Alana slowly looked up into his blue eyes—the same bright shade as her own. *Why?* She almost asked. She wanted to scream at him, to demand why he had abandoned her. Why didn't he love her the way he loved his other daughters?

Instead, very quietly, she asked, "Do they know about me?"

"No."

She looked away.

"Alana." He reached across the table and pulled her arm forward, taking her hand. "There is nothing I regret more than your mother's death."

Alana felt moisture arise in her eyes. She must not cry now. She willed the tears away. "Why?"

"I loved her." He smiled. "I fell in love with her at first sight."

Alana pulled her hand away and stared at him.

"You seem doubtful."

"She was a widow for over a year when you met. If you loved her, why didn't you marry her?"

His smile faded. "My father had already decided upon my betrothal to Joan. I knew of his wishes, and that I would one day wed her. But we could not ignore how we felt about one another. We never meant to fall in love, but we did."

Alana did not know if she wanted to know more. And she hadn't realized he had all but been promised to Joan at the time. She could only hope he had really loved her mother. And she desperately wanted to know what had happened when he had learned of Elisabeth's pregnancy.

"Joan knows about you," he said. "She has known about you from the time Elisabeth began showing."

Alana stared in surprise.

"She was not pleased. Her father was furious, and so was my father, the earl." He rubbed his face then. "I had to confess that the child was mine, but there were rumors—we were not discreet." He stopped. "I wanted to be with your mother, but it was not to be."

She trembled. He had not been able to defy his father, the earl, she thought. Had he even tried?

"I wish Elisabeth had lived, not for my sake, but for yours—to take proper care of you. Thank God for Lady Fitzhugh."

Alana began to understand. There had been no question of his breaking his impending union off with Joan.

"I wish I could have given you a different life," he said, looking at the table.

"But you could not." As she spoke, she thought about the intervening years. His father had died years ago. He could have come forward since then, to claim her and give her a better life.

"I hope you will one day understand."

"I do understand," she said, proudly lifting her chin. His duty had been to his other family, not to her. He had cared about his other family, not her. He had not had the will to defy his father, or now, his brother. "If Iain of Islay accepts, will you agree to his marriage to Margaret?" She did not even have to ask—of course he would, even if he did not like it. He would obey his brother, the way he had once obeyed his father.

"Yes," he said. "I know you are upset, and you need a husband of your own. If you please my brother, it will be arranged. He has told me as much."

Her stomach churned. "Yes, I must give him a pleasing vision, and he will even return Brodie to me."

Sir Alexander reached out and laid his hand on her shoulder. "It is important that you please the earl. It is important that we all please him," he said.

Alana pulled away and stared. "So you fear him?"

"He is our liege lord. We are bound to obey him. And, Alana, he can give you the life you deserve."

Alana studied him. It was very hard to stand still, to keep her expression impassive. "So I must please him, and he will reward me for doing so."

"Yes. You must seek out these visions. You must do your best."

Alana somehow nodded. More hurt stabbed through her. "I will try, Sir Alexander."

WHEN ALANA REACHED her chamber, Eleanor gave her one look and pulled her into her arms. "I am not going to cry," Alana whispered, her face against her chest.

"Oh, my poor dear," Eleanor said.

Alana pulled away, wiping her eyes with the hem of her sleeve. She sat down on her bed. "My father wishes for me to have a vision. Is that why he is here? Of course it is!" she cried.

Eleanor sat down beside her. "Alana, I do not want to ever speak ill of him."

"He loves my sisters! That much is clear! But he has never cared enough to come to see me, except now, when Buchan needs a vision from me." She swiped at more tears.

"If it helps at all, I agree with you—but not complctcly. I think Sir Alexander would love you, too, if he were allowed to."

Alana turned to her. "What does that mean?"

Eleanor sighed. "Joan hated Elisabeth. How could she not? They were cousins, and Elisabeth took her betrothed as her lover."

"So my mother was the harlot Duncan has always accused her of being?"

"I did not say that." Eleanor put her arm around her. "You know as well as I do that life is complicated. Your mother loved my son. She grieved for a long time when he died. When she met your father, he was such a handsome and dashing young knight. He made her smile for the first time in a year...." Eleanor smiled at the memory.

Alana sighed. How could she judge her mother now? But she very much wanted to judge her father. "Buchan is going to offer my sister to Iain."

"What happened at Concarn, Alana?"

"I told Iain the truth about my father. Iain and Bruce think I was sent to spy upon them."

Eleanor paled.

"I love him, but I do not think he loves me right now." She stood and walked over to the window. The shutter was closed and she pulled it open. A pigeon was standing on the ledge outside the window, drinking from the small pool of water that had gathered there from melting snow. It flew off.

Alana watched it for a moment as it vanished into the darkening sky, and then she glanced at the bright silvery puddle.

Eleanor said, "Maybe that is for the best."

But she sounded far away, when she was seated so close by, upon the bed. Alana realized the tiny puddle was mesmerizing her. She must look away. Instead, the silver within the water intensified in brightness, becoming blinding. She felt light-headed and dizzy; she felt faint.

Silver beckoned, a bright, frightening light. Alana had never seen such a bright white light before.

The light shimmered like a cloud floating in space.

She saw the outlines of a stone chamber, dully lit by torches and candles. She saw that four people were standing there. It took her a moment to realize that all four figures were women, and it took her another moment to realize that something terrible was about to happen.

One of the women sobbed. Three of them held one another, as if to stand upright. The fourth stood alone. Her dark hair was long and oddly familiar.

Alana realized she was staring at herself.

And then one of the women dashed to the bed and screamed.

A man lay there, the sheets blood soaked. His face was ghostly white. His blue eyes were wide and sightless. His hair was blond....

It was Sir Alexander.

"Alana!"

Alana began to vomit, clawing the stone beneath her fingernails. All she could see was her father, lying dead upon that bed, as the floor spun crazily around her.

CHAPTER NINE

ALANA PAUSED ON the threshold of the great hall the following day, clasping a wool mantle tightly to her chest.

Everyone had gathered for the breakfast. Buchan was eating with a hearty appetite, as was Godfrey. Her father was sitting back, not eating, clearly absorbed in thought.

Alana stared at him, trembling.

What did her vision of the night before mean? Was her father going to die—and would she be present when he did?

She had not slept at all last night, worried as she was about her father. She might be distrustful of him and his intentions, and she was hurt to the quick by his favoritism, but she had no wish for him to die.

As she had done when she had had her vision of the destruction of the Buchan earldom, she prayed this vision was a false one, too.

And if it was not? What was she going to do?

Her father saw her and smiled.

Buchan saw her, too. There was no turning back. Alana started forward with Eleanor, her insides churning. She wanted to do her duty, of course she did. The problem was, she no longer knew what that duty was, or to whom it was owed.

Alana sat down next to Godfrey, across from Sir

Alexander. As she greeted everyone, all she could see was her father lying dead on that bed, the sheets soaked with his blood.

"Good morn, Alana." Sir Alexander was cheerful.

Alana somehow smiled. "Good morning."

"You are not eating," Buchan told his brother. "If my scouts come early enough today, we will ride out immediately."

Sir Alexander stabbed a piece of duck. "My appetite has suddenly improved." He smiled at Alana, but it quickly faded. "Do you not feel well today?"

Alana realized she could not smile back. In that moment, she understood why her mother had been charmed. His smile made him a beautiful man, and he had the ability to seem so concerned and caring. "I am fine."

She began to eat some bread with cheese, realizing she had hardly eaten in days. She stole a glance at Buchan. She had no intention of suffering his wrath another time. She was not going to bring him a vision he did not like.

"Are you all right this morning?" Godfrey asked, low.

She glanced quickly at him. Was he beginning to know her well, after all these years, so that he could see she was distressed? Or had he always known her well—and she had not wanted to see it? "I did not sleep well. You frightened me when you spoke of Elgin falling, and Brodie being surrounded. What happens here at Brodie when my uncle leaves?" she asked him.

"He is leaving us with twenty more men," Godfrey said.

Twenty extra men would not hold Iain back should he ever wish to take Brodie.

"I cannot spare more," Buchan said, having been listening to them. "I received a message from Mowbray last night. He wants to find Bruce, chase him from his lair and rout him, once and for all."

Alana laid her bread down. "Is that even possible?"

"It's possible if we can surprise him," Buchan said. "Did I not tell you the news? King Edward is sending us an army."

"So the fighting will not wait till the spring," Alana said.

"And that dismays you?" Buchan asked sharply. "Do you not wish for the goddamned mad King Robert to be captured and killed once and for all? Do you not wish for peace here in the north of Scotland?"

"Of course I do." She also knew she feared for Iain, should there be an ambush.

"If we can peel Iain of Islay away from Bruce first, so much the better," Sir Alexander said.

"I sent a scout to Concarn last night, with a privy message for him," Buchan said. He burped and pushed his plate aside.

Alana quickly stared at her plate, certain her cheeks were heating. Did her uncle's message concern a marriage offer to her sister Margaret? What else could it contain?

"You did not tell me," Sir Alexander said tersely. He pushed his food aside, uneaten.

"I was not aware that I must tell you of my actions," Buchan said.

"Are you making an offer of marriage in a letter?"

"Of course not." Buchan was contemptuous. "We

need to have a privy meeting, Alex, without Bruce knowing, so I can offer him Margaret and her lands."

Sir Alexander rubbed his unshaven jaw grimly.

"Do not look so unhappy. If we can convince Iain to betray Bruce, to fight with us, I think we can end this war once and for all."

Would Iain ever betray Bruce? Alana did not think so, but she had seen how he coveted land and power. She was his mistress, but he was interested in a marriage to Alice. Alana was not naive. Men changed sides in war, they changed their politics all of the time, motivated by self-interest.

Maybe Eleanor was right. Maybe it was better this way—with Iain no longer caring for her. Perhaps she must stop caring about him now, as well. Otherwise she would never survive his marriage to one of her sisters.

Alana shot a glance at Sir Alexander and realized he was still staring, and very closely. He said to Buchan, "This talk of marriage is distressing for Alana."

"Is it?" Buchan said. "Then she must give us a vision or two so I can reward her appropriately with a husband of her own." He smiled at Godfrey.

Godfrey started, as did Alana.

"You want Brodie back, and you do have a claim," Buchan said. "Godfrey is meant to inherit here. Would that not be a good union, should you manage to please me, Alana?"

Alana gaped. She was shocked by the suggestion that she would marry Godfrey—her nemesis from childhood, and her recent, sudden ally. She glanced at him and he looked back, his cheeks pink, his eyes as stunned as hers must be.

"That is a very good suggestion," Sir Alexander said.

Alana breathed hard. In that moment, she saw the future, but it was not a vision. She would be Godfrey's wife, and Iain would be lord of Nairn and liege lord of Brodie—and married to one of her sisters.

"Alana? Surely you are pleased," Sir Alexander said.

Alana knew she was red. She turned to her uncle. "Thank you, my lord," she said.

But she had not even finished speaking when a bell sounded, shrilly, in warning. Every man at the table leaped up, reaching for their swords.

Alana leaped up, too. She seized Eleanor, wondering if they were under attack. Two soldiers in mail burst inside. A Highlander was in shackles between them.

They dragged him forward. "My lord, we found him in the woods, speaking with a boy, your messenger dead at their feet. The boy escaped."

Alana inhaled. The Highlander was familiar—she recognized him from Iain's tented camp at Concarn. He had been beaten and his nose was broken, blood spilling from it. His gray eyes met hers. Clearly he recognized her. But he looked away and did not speak.

Alana also looked away, horrified. Iain had sent this Highlander to meet with Ranald. But he had been caught while Ranald had escaped....

"He killed my messenger?" Buchan shouted.

One of the soldiers handed him a rolled parchment. "Your seal, my lord. We found it on this dog."

"Take him outside and when you come back make certain you can tell me exactly where Iain of Islay is, and where Bruce is."

Alana began to shake. They were going to beat the information out of the Highlander. And then, she suspected they would kill him. What about Ranald? Was he hiding in the woods? "I thought Bruce was at Con-carn," she managed to say.

Everyone turned to look at her as if she were mad—which she was, for daring to speak.

"There is more, my lord," the soldier said. "The boy was from the stables here."

Buchan's eyes widened. "A boy was placed here to spy?"

Alana cringed.

"Find that damned boy, as well. And hurry," Buchan spat.

The soldiers left, dragging the Highlander with them.

Alana's mind raced. How could she stop the soldiers from killing that Highlander? She prayed Ranald had fled far into the woods, and that he would not attempt to return to Brodie! Not only would he be in danger if he returned, but her deceit might be revealed, as well.

"Come with me, Alex," Buchan ordered. The two men walked swiftly out.

Alana sat back down, shaking. At least Buchan's message to Iain, asking for a secret meeting, had been intercepted. But that seemed like her smallest worry now. For if he meant to marry an heiress, he would.

Godfrey was at the door, about to leave, but he turned and looked at her. "What is wrong with you, Alana?" He started back toward her. "You look ill."

She hated having to lie to him. "Did we have a spy here, in our midst?"

"I don't know. But I am going to speak to Seamus and find out where that boy came from." About to go, he suddenly paused. "This damned war could end, sooner than later, if we can turn Iain."

She wet her lips. "I do not know if he will betray Bruce."

"Because you met him once? Because he freed you from the tower?"

"He burned Nairn to the ground, Godfrey.... He is ruthless."

"If he is ruthless, he might very well accept Margaret and her lands, and betray Bruce." His stare was searching. "I know you well. There is more you are not telling me. But I cannot decide why you truly do not want your sister wed, especially if Buchan will allow you to wed, too."

She trembled. "You heard him," she whispered.

"Is the idea of a union betwixt us so repulsive?"

Tears finally came. "No. Once, maybe, but not anymore. But, Godfrey, I do not love you."

"Love has nothing to do with marriage," he said.

ALANA HUDDLED IN her fur on the steps outside the hall later that day.

It was snowing. The Earl of Buchan was mounting his dark steed. His best knights were already mounted and awaiting his command to leave. Alana stood with Godfrey and Eleanor, relieved that they were leaving, yet frightened for her father's safety, too.

Sir Alexander had not yet mounted. He led his gray warhorse over to her and smiled. "We have had such a short time to get to know one another," he said.

Alana realized that, as much as she needed Buchan gone, she was going to miss her father. She hurried down the steps. "It was a very short time," she said hoarsely. She did not point out that they did not know one another even now—that a few days could not make up for a missed lifetime.

"You seem sad," he said, clasping her shoulder.

"This war frightens me. Please stay safe."

"I will do my best. And, Alana? When the time is right, I will send for you."

Alana reeled in shock. "For me?"

"It is time you met Alice and Margaret." He hugged her briefly, surprising her even more. Then he turned and mounted gracefully.

Alana felt ill. She did not want him to die—she wanted to meet her sisters, and get to know her father.

She knew now she did not want to betray her father, even though she was forced to spy by Bruce, even though she remained worried for Iain. She did not want to betray Sir Alexander because he was her father.

But she had to know what was transpiring—because of her feelings for Iain and because she feared for his safety.

"Father."

He halted his horse abruptly, his eyes wide.

She hadn't meant to address him in such an intimate manner—it had just slipped out. "Did you learn where Bruce is?"

"Yes, we did. And that is why my brother is in a rush. We will surprise him with an attack—on Christmas Day."

Alana gasped. Christmas was eight days away!

"If you are worried, don't be. Our army has grown and we will have the element of surprise on our side."

She fought for air. "Where is he?" she whispered.

"He is at Slioch, Alana." Sir Alexander's gaze narrowed. "Why do you ask? Is this about your sister?"

She stiffened. She had not been thinking of Buchan's interest in marrying her sister to Iain until her father had brought the subject up. Had Buchan sent another message to Iain? She imagined so.

"Alana," he continued, "when you meet Margaret, you will come to love her. Your jealousy will pass. I am certain. She has not a single enemy in this world—everyone likes her."

She could barely assimilate his words. So everyone adored pretty Margaret! She almost told him she was not jealous, but she remained silent, because he was right. But she could not dwell on her sister now.

Buchan and her father rode to war—and they would ambush Bruce at Slioch Mountain in eight more days, when they would be the most unsuspecting.

She had to warn them.

Alana hugged herself, watching as the two men led the cavalcade of knights from the courtyard and through the entry tower.

It began to snow more heavily.

When they were finally gone, the castle gates outside the entry tower were shut and barred. Alana sank down on the bottommost step.

Godfrey walked down to stand beside her. "Why do you care if Margaret marries Iain?" he demanded. "You should be pleased if we can buy off that barbarian! You want this war to end as much as I do!"

She finally looked up. "I do want this war to end."

"What do you know that I do not?"

"Nothing."

"No, Alana, you are hiding something, and you are upset—extremely so. I know you are jealous of your sisters, but I also know that is not the reason for your distress." He grimaced. "We aren't enemies now. We have come to terms, or so I thought.... I am your friend, if you wish to confide in me."

Alana hugged her knees. She hated lying to Godfrey. She wished she could confide in him, but obviously, she could not.

He turned grimly and walked across the courtyard, then climbed the stairs to the watchtower.

Alana watched him until he had disappeared inside. She stood and met Eleanor's disapproving gaze. "You are going to warn them, aren't you?"

"I have to."

"Alana! If Buchan ever finds out that you are betraying him, he will not care that you are his niece, he will take your head."

Alana could not speak. She hurried past her grandmother, knowing she was speaking literally and that she was right.

ALANA SAT UP in her bed, then slid from it. The small bedchamber was cast in darkness, except for the remains of a fire, which burned in the grate. Eleanor also sat up and lit a taper.

Alana was grim, stepping into her boots. She picked up her fur cloak, not looking at her grandmother.

"Alana, don't do this," Eleanor said. "You cannot possibly get to Slioch Mountain! You cannot possibly traverse the northwest of this land in the winter, in the snow, even with Seamus's son to help you!"

"I do not have time to argue," Alana said.

Eleanor stepped from the bed and seized her wrist. "You put yourself in terrible jeopardy, if you are caught, whether leaving this castle, or while on the road, or afterward!"

Alana finally faced her. "Gran, I cannot stand by and let Iain be ambushed. He could die!"

"If the attack is not a surprise, your father could die," Eleanor shot back.

Alana had already thought of that. "I am in a terrible position. But if I have to choose, I choose Iain." She put on her fur cloak and started from the room.

"He doesn't want you," Eleanor said.

Alana faltered, then pushed open the door. "I will be back as soon as I can. I love you, Gran." She stepped outside and closed the door, her heart slamming.

It was silent in the corridor, the entire castle asleep. Alana crept down the hall, now worried that Godfrey might awaken and find her stealing out.

It was a windy night, and boughs scraped the castle walls, making her start, while shutters shook. A rat even raced across the stairwell, almost causing her to cry out. Eventually she reached the hall below. It was empty, as she had expected. If they had more soldiers, it would not be.

Alana hurried through it, feeling some guilt. She paused before the front door, glancing back, almost expecting to see Godfrey standing there, his look one of accusation and hurt.

There was no avoiding it. He would learn she was gone in the morning, and she would have to invent an excuse for her absence yet again before she returned to Brodie.

It was still snowing when she crossed the courtyard. Seamus met her in the stables, holding her horse for her. A satchel was tied to the saddle. Another horse was also saddled, and one of his sons held the reins. "I wish ye'd behave like other ladies," he said.

She touched his cheek. "I am not like other ladies, but you already know that. I will be back soon. And, Seamus? Thank you."

He shook his head, clearly unhappy. But Alana knew he would not ask her why she was leaving Brodie a second time. He had been the stableman when her mother was Brodie's mistress, and he was as loyal as a Scot could be. When she had told him she had a trip to make, he had offered one of his sons as a guide. Ranald had not returned and Seamus clearly did not suspect Alana of knowingly bringing a spy from Bruce's camp into their midst, as he was still willing to help her. Craig was one of Brodie's few soldiers, but just then, she needed him more than Brodie did.

They mounted up and set off.

ALANA WONDERED IF she would freeze to death, now that they were almost at their destination.

It had snowed for two entire days, on the one hand keeping the temperatures more reasonable, but on the other slowing them down considerably. They had only paused to rest for a few hours every night, taking shelter in passing farmhouses. Time was not on their side.

They were on the third day of their journey, and its last leg. They had reached Loch Maree, which was partially frozen, Slioch Mountain looming on its northwestern side. The snow had stopped the previous night, and the temperature had dropped. Alana's fingers and toes were frozen beneath her gloves and boots. So was her nose. The moisture from her eyes was solidified on her cheeks.

"We will be there in hours, Alana," Craig said, smiling. His nose was bright red, and ice clung to his beard. But he did not seem otherwise affected by the cold. "Do ye wish to stop? There is no one on the road. I can make a fire, to warm ye up a bit."

She shook her head. Bruce had to learn of the attack immediately. She shivered, her teeth chattering in a spasm that was occurring with more and more frequency. She caught Craig looking at her without his usual smile, very alarmed by her condition.

She tried to speak. "I am f-f-f-fine."

"We should stop and make a fire. Ye need to eat."

"N-n-n-no."

They were on the banks of the loch now, approaching from the southeast. Alana tried to see the topmost ridges of the mountain. Not only did it seem impossible to see all the way up it, she saw no sign of Bruce or his men.

Suddenly she was frightened. What if Bruce wasn't at Slioch? Had he moved? Or could Sir Alexander have been mistaken?

Buchan had spies close to Bruce, close to Iain. What if they knew of her treachery? What if Sir Alexander had sent her to Slioch on purpose, knowing Bruce was not there?

Alana felt dizzy. She was clinging to her saddle, a beautiful waterfall on her right. Ice clung to the rocks as the water poured over it.

Craig rode ahead of her, and Alana looked back at the waterfall. The water danced over the rocks, brightly white, almost silver…she stared down into the lake. The water there was dark and blue, silent, deep, beckoning....

No! She thought in panic. She knew what was within those dark, secretive depths....

She saw Iain smiling at her. She wanted to ask him if he had forgiven her, but before she could speak, Buchan appeared behind him, enraged, a sword in hand. In horror, Alana realized her uncle was about to murder Iain.

She screamed as the sword came down, and then she hit the snow, falling through it, deeper and deeper, until she saw only white before complete darkness.

THE BURNING PAIN awoke Alana. Her fingers, her toes and her nose were on fire. Tears of agony blinded her.

"It will pass," someone said.

She began to shiver violently, helplessly. Someone held her feet and rubbed them, someone else held her hands, thawing them.

"Add more wood to the fire!"

She was in so much pain it took her a moment to realize that it was Iain ordering the fire stoked.

Her heart lurched wildly. She had left Brodie with Craig three days ago! She had almost frozen to death... but she had found Iain, at last!

"Drink this, Alana," Iain said.

She opened her eyes and saw him staring grimly at her. He was forcing a mug to her lips.

She tried to smile at him, but was too frozen to do so. And then she remembered that she had had another vision—a terrible one.

"Drink, Alana," he ordered.

Alana took a sip. The wine was warm and spiced. Its heat crept through her.

He put the mug down, picked up her hands and rubbed them gently. "Ye will not die from the cold today," he said tersely. "But ye might have died, had ye spent another few hours in the snow."

Her stomach churned. "Iain," she tried to say. Her lips were blistered from the cold and it hurt to speak.

He held her hands against his chest. "I will shout at ye for being ten times the fool another day."

Did he care? "Iain," she said, through her cracked lips. She was in his tent, she saw. A fire was in the center, but holes in the hide allowed the smoke to escape.

"I am here, Alana. Do not speak, yer lips are bleeding." He turned and a woman appeared, blonde and freckled, in a long leine and a fur cloak. She dabbed a salve on Alana's mouth and nose.

What day was it? Bruce was going to be attacked! "No. Iain. Please." She struggled to sit up.

He instantly put his arm around her and helped her. Alana put her hands on his chest and whimpered, for her fingers hurt terribly—but not as much as before. He wrapped her hands in his.

For one moment, she closed her eyes and laid her cheek on his chest. The pain was passing. The cold had burned her extremities. She would look later to see if she had lost a finger or a toe.

Alana realized she was nestled in Iain's arms, and that he had his chin on top of her head as he held her hands. He had forgiven her, she thought. Either that or he cared so much about her that what he thought was her betrayal no longer mattered.

"Impatient, headstrong wench," he said.

She looked up at him. "I have come…to warn you."

His gaze narrowed. He handed her the warm wine again. She took another sip. And another one.

He set it down and Alana took a breath. "Buchan plans to attack you at Slioch on Christmas Day."

His eyes widened. "Christmas is but four days away!"

So she had not been unconscious for long. Craig must have brought her here very recently, before departing back to Brodie.

"Are you sure, Alana?"

"I have risked my life to warn you…. Yes, I am certain."

His eyes wide, he stood. "I will be back. Meg will take care of ye until I return." He left the tent immediately.

Alana lay back on the pallet, closing her eyes. She had done it. She had warned Iain. Now she must pray that there was enough time to move the army or mount a proper defense.

She immediately thought of her father, praying she had not put him in jeopardy. She did not want to think about her vision of his death just then.

"Do ye wish for more wine, my lady?"

Alana glanced at the servant, and felt wary. Who was this? She was Alana's own age, a pretty blonde with a small nose and vivid blue eyes. She had seen women at Bruce's other camp at Concarn, but they had been camp followers—the kind of loose and impoverished women that were always present among an army. Alana did not like the fact that this woman was so pretty and so unworn. She did not like the fact that she was tending Alana on Iain's behest.

"Yes, please," Alana said, struggling to sit up. She used her hands and cried out as she did so.

The woman hurried to her. "Try not to use yer hands, my lady. Do they feel better? They have been terribly burned. I was hoping to bandage them, but Iain told me to wait. My name is Meg."

Alana was now sitting, and she allowed the other woman to help her sip the wine. "Are you his lover?"

Meg looked at her, flushing.

Alana looked away instantly.

"So ye love him," Meg said. "To ride across the Highlands to warn him of an attack."

She slowly glanced up. "Yes, I love him. How did you meet?"

"I am the Macleod's youngest daughter." She shrugged. "My husband fought for Iain and died a few months ago." She stared closely now. "Ye must be very beautiful, when yer not frozen and blue. Are ye a lady?"

"No." She hesitated. She did not think Meg a spy, but she decided not to reveal her identity, although it would probably come out soon enough. As they stared at one another, the tent flap opened, and Robert Bruce strode inside. Iain followed him in.

Alana started, as Bruce pulled up a stool and sat down beside her. She began to flush. "Your Grace."

He picked up her hand and looked at her fingers, then laid it in her lap. He tilted up her chin, forcing their gazes to meet. His blue eyes were kind. "Send the other woman away," he said.

Iain asked Meg to leave the tent, and she did.

"Is it true?" Robert Bruce asked.

Alana nodded. "Yes, Your Grace."

He studied her, his gaze lingering on her cracked lips. "You have risked your life to warn us of this attack."

She nodded again. "I did not expect it to be so cold, or Slioch to be so far."

"I am very pleased with you, Alana," Robert Bruce said.

Alana felt her eyes widen impossibly. She looked past Bruce at Iain. She wanted to ask him if he now realized that she loved him—if she had proved herself.

"You will be rewarded for your courage and your loyalty," Bruce said flatly. He stood. "We will march at dawn. Make certain we leave our best scouts here and that Buchan is remarked before he ever reaches Loch Maree's shores."

"Aye, Your Grace."

Bruce turned back to her. "I am sorry for what you have suffered—and amazed, still. Now I can truly call you my friend, Mistress Alana."

Alana stared after him as he left, stunned. Then Iain knelt beside her.

"I have a great deal to do between now and the dawn. But ye must rest so ye can travel."

Alana was alarmed. "Iain, I cannot bear even the thought of the journey home." She was afraid she might die this time. And she did not know what she would say to Godfrey about her absence.

He smiled slightly at her. "Yer not going home. We

will speak about it later. For now ye must rest, and thank God ye have all yer fingers and toes."

She smiled at him, her heart dancing wildly. "I am forgiven? You trust me?"

"Yer forgiven," he said. He stood. "Meg will attend ye."

She felt her smile fade. "I don't want her here."

"Worry not, Alana. She means nothing to me." Then he turned and left.

CHAPTER TEN

THEY HAD RIDDEN down Slioch Mountain at sunrise, on a well-used but icy road that went down the ridge's back side, and continued south through Macleod land. They had not paused, and by the afternoon they were traveling through the great forests of Glen Carron. It was close to sunset now. They had reached the northern shores of Lochalsh, and a camp was rapidly being erected.

Alana slowly dismounted, as exhausted as she was cold. She hadn't realized an entire army could move so swiftly, and endure such a determined pace for so long.

"My lady?" Meg took her reins, having dismounted, as well. The two women had ridden side by side; Meg had been ordered to attend Alana, never mind that Alana would have preferred the other woman to remain far behind.

Alana was taking off her mittens. She rubbed her frozen fingers together, aware of the small prickling of pain. Her toes tingled hurtfully, too.

"It is not unusual, after such frostbite, to have some discomfort."

She whirled and saw Iain sliding from his huge black charger, his fur barely drawn over his shoulders. She had seen him several times during their journey. He had made a point of riding over to her to ask after her welfare. "I think I am fine," she said, although she was not sure. "It doesn't hurt the way it did yesterday."

"I am sorry ye had to ride like this, today."

Alana met his gaze. It was openly concerned, and she could not doubt that he still cared for her. Meg took their horses away. "How long will we stay here?"

"'Tis a good place for us to rest. MacDonald kin control these lands. We will stay a few days, as the men have ridden hard since we left Concarn."

There was more relief. Her legs ached from so much riding in the past few days, and her back hurt, too. She was not a warrior, accustomed to such exertion.

Iain took her hands in his and glanced at them. Instead of releasing her palms, he gripped them tightly, smiling at her. "I've seen worse. Ye'll be fine."

She moved closer to him, her skirts brushing his thighs. "I could not bear it when you were angry with me."

His gaze darkened, but not with anger. How she recognized the slow burning gleam. "I am still angry.... Ye could have died, crossing the northwest Highlands in the winter!"

She pulled her hands free of his and placed them on his chest. "I could not sit idly by, allowing you to be ambushed, not when I had learned of my uncle's plans."

"So ye have chosen sides." He covered her hands with his, holding them against his chest.

Alana tensed. "I chose you, Iain, over my father, but I do not want anything ill to befall him." She prayed yet again that her vision of her father's death had been wrong.

"Ye almost sound as if ye know he will be in jeopardy."

They should not have secrets between them, not now, Alana thought. How she wished to tell him about her visions. But she did not dare, not now, not yet.

"I haven't had a chance to speak with you. Sir Alexander came to Brodie with Buchan. I finally met him a second time, after all of these years." Her breath caught with some lingering pain. She looked away.

He tilted up her chin. "And he has hurt ye again?"

So many thoughts went through her mind, and she could not speak. She thought of her mother, who had loved him, and now she could understand why. She thought of her sisters, whom Sir Alexander loved, so much so he did not want either of his daughters to marry Iain. And then there was her life.

She could not imagine how her sisters must feel, knowing they were so well loved. At least she had Eleanor.

"Your tent is ready," she said.

He glanced behind them. His tent had been erected, his banner flapping in the breeze above it. "What did he say, Alana, to distress ye so? What did he do?"

She tried to pull away, but he still clasped her hands. She gave up and said, "I am growing cold, standing here like this."

"So ye will not speak of him?"

Alana had the urge to cry. "Maybe," she whispered, "another time."

He studied her closely. "Bruce wishes to speak with me. Why dinna ye rest, and we will sup together in a few more hours."

Alana felt as if she had been given a reprieve. But when he released her hands, she clung to him. She had risked her life to warn Iain of the ambush because she loved him. She let his wrists go and slid her hands up his broad, hard chest. "Will you come in with me?" she asked.

"I will come to ye later," he said.

Alana shook her head as she whispered, "No, come now. I have missed you and I need you."

His eyes blazed. Before he could think of his king again, she took his hand and tugged him with her into the tent. She saw Meg within, unrolling the rug to cover the snowy ground. His stool, small table and pallet had already been set up. "Leave us, please," Alana said.

Meg's eyes widened. She looked between Alana and Iain, and at their clasped hands. Then she hurried past them and left.

"What do ye plan, wench?" Iain said softly.

Alana's heart was slamming uncontrollably in her chest. She dropped his hand and tossed her two furs onto the pallet, making the bed for them. As she straightened, Iain seized her from behind.

He locked her in his embrace and kissed the side of her neck. "Temptress."

Alana wriggled against him, spooning against his huge, hard arousal. "I think *you* have missed *me*." One of his sheathed swords bumped her calf.

He pushed her down onto the pallet, coming down on top of her. "I think ye have quickly learned how to entice a man." He kissed her neck again, slowly lifting her skirts and running his hands over her bottom.

Alana gasped when his fingers touched her. He laughed at her whimper of pleasure and wrapped her in his arms and thrust deep. "Iain!" Alana gasped.

"Ye tempt me as no other," he gasped back.

They surged hard against one another for a few moments, and then Iain flipped her over. Alana wrapped her legs around his waist and cried out in a shocking release. He grunted in satisfaction, moved harder, and gasped in his own climax.

Alana held on to him, hard. Tears arose. She had missed him so much. She kissed his shoulder. She had never been as grateful that they were no longer at odds. She must never allow anything to come between them again!

He kissed her cheek. "Are ye crying?" He sounded surprised.

"No." She caressed his broad, strong back. Then, "Yes. Just a little."

He held her in his arms, and his embrace tightened. "Dinna cry," he whispered.

"I am so grateful," she whispered back, "that we are no longer at odds."

His gaze was searching. He released her slowly, sitting up. "Bruce is waiting. I'll be back as soon as I can."

Alana sat up, adjusting her clothes as she did so. She nodded. "Hurry."

He smiled at her, eyes darkening. "Impossible wench." Alana felt her smile fade after he left. She took up one of the furs, wrapped it around herself and hugged her knees to her chest.

She was deeply in love. Iain had forgiven her, that much was clear, and they were lovers again. But now what?

She had been successful in warning him of the Christmas Day ambush. When she had learned of Buchan's plans, she hadn't had to think twice about what she must do. She could never let Iain be surprised and attacked, she had had to warn him—to protect him.

She now realized the extent of what she had done. For all intents and purposes she had spied on her uncle and her father, even if that had not been her deliberate intention. She had purposefully betrayed them. She had revealed their war plans to their enemy.

Buchan would imprison her as a traitor if he ever found out. Or he might do far worse. He would be within his rights to hang or behead her for treason, if he so chose. Having seen his temper, and knowing how he felt about his own wife, she thought he might choose to execute her.

Had she chosen sides in this war without even realizing it? She had wanted to protect Iain, not betray her own family! But now the betrayal was done. And having betrayed Buchan, how could she ever return to Brodie?

Dismay flooded her. Brodie was her home. It had belonged to her mother! She tried to think of a plausible excuse for leaving Brodie, but her mind was blank. The best she could come up with was that she had decided it was time to meet her sisters. Would Godfrey believe that? Would Duncan? Would Buchan?

She could probably convince Godfrey of almost anything. As she thought of her sisters, there was more dismay.

Bruce was possibly planning a marriage for Iain to Alice, while Buchan hoped for a marriage to Margaret. She did not think Iain would ever betray Bruce. But if Buchan was defeated, as she was certain he would be, Alice was ripe for the plucking. How would she stop him from marrying such a great heiress—her own sister?

The answer was simple. She could not force Iain

to heel. He was a powerful and ambitious man. When the day came where Buchan was defeated, and he was presented with Alice as a bride, he would accept her if he wished to do so—there would be no stopping him.

Alana covered her face with her hands, her elbows on her knees. Her visions thus far had always come true. Buchan would be defeated; Bruce would reign supreme as King of Scotland. And her father was going to die....

What of her last vision? She would have to warn Iain that Buchan was going to try to kill him. At least she hadn't seen the final blow, or his head being severed from his body!

Alana did not know what to do. She was just a bastard daughter who had been forgotten, a warrior's mistress who could be cast aside at any time, and a witch most people feared. She could not depend on her father or her family, she knew that, and as much as it pained her, she really could not depend on Iain, either. Where did that leave her?

She would have to take care of herself when the time came, when Buchan disowned her, when Bruce became Scotland's one true king....

And all she had was Brodie. It was all she had ever had.

She sat up straight. Brodie would be hers. Bruce was very pleased with her now.

Alana stood abruptly. She had risked everything to warn Iain—and Bruce—of the ambush. She must collect her reward from Robert Bruce.

Alana stepped to the tent flap and opened it slightly, peering outside.

Meg rushed over. "Are ye hungry, my lady?"

Alana gazed past her. Some campfires were lit, cook pots hanging over them. Bruce's tent was in the camp's precise midpoint, surrounded by a sea of hide tents, his yellow-and-red banner flying above it in the gathering dusk. "I must speak with the king," she said.

Meg started. "He is with his commanders, my lady. Ye cannot interrupt."

No, she could hardly interrupt. And then she saw a group of men leaving Bruce's tent. Iain was with them. She trembled with nervous anticipation.

He saw her and quickened his stride. Alana waited for him to cross the camp, not moving until he had reached her. "Is something amiss?" he asked immediately.

"Iain, when can I speak with the king—about my reward?"

It was a moment before he spoke. "Ye wish to press him for Brodie?"

She had a flashing image of herself as mistress of Brodie—receiving Alice and Iain there. "Yes."

"Let us go. Bruce is in a cheerful mood. If he will see ye now, this would be a good time." He took her arm.

Alana glanced at him as they walked toward Bruce's tent. "You approve?"

He smiled slightly. "Brodie belonged to yer mother. I approve."

Alana faltered. His smile was warm and she realized he genuinely wished for her to have Brodie.

"Why are ye surprised, Alana?"

"Sometimes," she said carefully, "I feel as if you truly care for me."

He gave her a quick, odd look.

Two soldiers stood guard outside Bruce's tent. They moved aside for Iain without hesitation. Becoming terribly nervous, Alana waited outside as Iain went in. She ignored the two soldiers, who glanced curiously at her with some guarded male appraisal. She was accustomed to being regarded with fascination and fear, but no one in Bruce's camp knew of her abilities. She was being looked at as an ordinary woman.

It was so pleasant.

Iain opened the flap and gestured. Alana summoned up her courage, and hurried inside.

Bruce sat with two other knights at a small table, drinking wine. He smiled widely at her. "I always have time for a beautiful woman, Mistress Alana," he said.

Alana curtsied. "Thank you, Your Grace."

He gestured for her to take a seat; the table was flanked with two benches, as well as his chair and a stool. Alana took the stool. Iain stood behind her, and Bruce handed her a cup of wine. "This is Gilbert Hay and Sir Robert Boyd," he told her. "Two of my most loyal friends."

Alana nodded at the men. Their stares were direct and very intent. But then, they knew she was Buchan's niece.

"Are you feeling better today?" Bruce asked. "We worried about you, mistress, having to travel in the cold after your recent ordeal."

"It seemed warmer today," Alana said.

"It is always warmer when one travels south," Bruce said. He drained his wine and set the mug down. "Iain tells me you have come to request your reward."

Alana was grateful Iain had spoken so forthrightly. "Will it displease you, Your Grace, that I am so bold?"

"Nothing you do right now could displease me, mistress. You are high in my favor. Speak your mind."

There would never be a better moment, she thought. "Brodie is all I have left of my mother and the great le Latimer family," she said. "Your Grace, my father abandoned me before I was born. He was betrothed to Joan le Latimer even as he pursued and won my mother. He told me himself, recently, that he loved my mother, but could not go against his father, and did not even think of doing so. His wife, Joan, knew of me from the beginning, and because she had no kindness in her heart, I was abandoned, forgotten.... I was raised as a commoner by Lady Fitzhugh, and given over to Duncan of Frendraught as his ward. I have had nothing from my father my entire life, and I have had nothing of my mother's or her family's, either. But I covet Brodie. I covet Brodie with my entire being, my entire heart. Had my father cast off Joan and married my mother, Brodie would be mine." Bruce was listening intently—everyone was—and his expression was hard to read. "Duncan has many estates. Godfrey will inherit all of them, as he is an only son. I am asking you for Brodie Castle."

Bruce poured a cup of wine and stood. He held it up. "I do not think you are asking for too much. It is a small stronghold with little significance, except as an outpost for Elgin and Nairn, once they are rebuilt. And I have given Nairn to Iain. So aye, Mistress Alana, I will give you Brodie, for your courage and loyalty, because you are our true friend." He saluted her with his cup and drank.

Alana began to shake uncontrollably. He would give her Brodie, just like that?

Brodie was going to be hers!

Iain still stood behind her, and he said, "We should take Brodie before we march on Elgin and Banf. It is undermanned, and if Godfrey thinks to resist, it would fall in hours."

Alana jerked to glance up at him. Was it possible she would be in command of Brodie so soon? Well before this war ended?

"You are so eager to install your mistress there?" Bruce asked, but he was smiling, clearly amused. Then his smile faded. He looked at Alana. "You will have to swear your allegiance to us, mistress. You will have to make an oath of fealty."

Alana stiffened. Hadn't she already proven her loyalty? "I betrayed the Earl of Buchan, my uncle."

"Aye, you did, but a man's pledge is of even greater significance than a single act. Are you unable to swear your fealty to us?"

Alana had already chosen Iain over her own father, and the choice had been oddly easy to make. But acting out of fear for Iain's life was one thing. She would betray her father and her uncle a dozen times over to keep Iain safe—she knew that. But to make an oath of fealty to King Robert was a pledge that screamed louder than any action ever could. It meant she was declaring her loyalty to Bruce, vowing it before God, for all the world to see. It meant she was walking away from her Comyn family, once and for all. There would be no turning back from such a pledge.

"Alana?" Iain said. He clasped her shoulder.

"I hate my uncle," she said, her tone sounding choked to her own ears. "But I do not hate my father, and I do not even know my sisters."

"So you will not swear fealty to me?" Bruce wasn't smiling now.

Tears flooded her eyes. Alana knew she did not have any other options. She shook her head, stood and dropped to her knees, bowing her head. "I will take the oath now."

"Good." Bruce spoke from above her. She then felt his sword's blade upon her right shoulder. "Uncover your head, mistress. Do you carry weapons?"

Alana removed her hood, so she was bareheaded, and shook her head, as she did not carry even the tiniest knife.

"Speak as I speak," Bruce commanded.

Alana nodded, still bowing her head. Her tears fell freely onto her hands. She hoped no one could see.

"I, Mistress le Latimer, daughter of Elisabeth le Latimer, bastard of Sir Alexander Comyn, do swear before God, that I will be faithful to my lord, King Robert Bruce of Scotland, now and in the future, and that I will never do him harm, never cause deceit, and will faithfully obey in all things, all commands of King Robert Bruce of Scotland, may God strike me down otherwise."

Alana inhaled. "I, Mistress le Latimer, daughter of Elisabeth le Latimer, bastard of Sir Alexander Comyn, do swear before God, that I will be faithful to my lord, King Robert Bruce of Scotland, now and in the future, and that I will never do him harm, never cause deceit, and will faithfully obey in all things, all commands of King Robert Bruce of Scotland, may God strike me down otherwise." She felt his sword upon her other shoulder.

"You may rise," Bruce said.

Alana began to get up, but Iain lifted her effortlessly to her feet. She blinked back her tears rapidly as their eyes met. He smiled encouragingly at her.

"Mistress le Latimer, of Brodie Castle," Bruce said, raising his cup.

Gilbert Hay, Sir Robert Boyd and Iain all raised their mugs, smiling. Alana looked at the circle of men and felt faint. Was this truly happening?

"Will you not drink?" Bruce asked pleasantly.

Alana looked at him. Did she dare? "Your Grace? May I ask one more thing?"

Bruce started, surprised. "You wish for more than Brodie Castle?"

Alana felt Iain grasp her shoulder. She ignored him. "I wish for what all women wish for, my lord—a husband."

She felt Iain's hand tighten on her. Bruce relaxed, appearing thoughtful. Iain dropped his hand and walked around her to look at her, his stare hard and surprised.

But she refused to look at him. She stared at Bruce, instead.

"Of course you wish for a husband," he said. "All women do. And you are young and beautiful. How old are you, mistress?"

"Twenty."

"And you have no children?"

"None, Your Grace."

"Hmm. Brodie would have to be your dowry…. I will have to think on this, but I am not opposed to finding a husband for you."

She inhaled. "Give me Iain of Islay," she said.

Iain stiffened. Alana saw his reaction from the corner of her eye; he was taken by complete surprise.

As was Robert Bruce. "You wish to marry my best commander in the north?" he asked, incredulous.

"Yes, I do. I know he covets far greater lands, and a great heiress—one greater than myself. But you have given him Nairn and he will have Brodie. And I am certain he will conquer other estates in this war." She did not dare look at Iain now. She was shaking.

Bruce started to laugh. "She has more courage than most men, combined!"

"Yes, she does," Iain said tersely.

"Your mistress wishes to marry you!" Bruce kept laughing.

Alana flushed. Boyd and Hay were as entertained, their smiles wide. Now, she glanced at Iain. He gave her a dark, disbelieving look.

"Mistress Alana, Iain has fought very hard for us," Bruce said. His smile faded. "No matter how much you please him, he would not be pleased with such a small dowry. I have promised him great lands and titles for his service to me."

Her cheeks felt like they were on fire. Alana glanced at Iain. His gaze was unwavering upon her.

"However, I will give a great deal of thought to finding you a proper husband—a strong knight, perhaps, from the south, who is seeking a name here in the north. And you will have Brodie when we choose to take it from Duncan of Frendraught."

Alana trembled with disappointment. She hadn't planned to ask for Iain as a husband, and now she wished she had thought it through. Her cheeks still burned. "Thank you, Your Grace," she said, low.

He waved dismissively at her and sat back down. Alana began to turn away when Iain took her arm, quite forcefully, and pulled her with him from the tent. Just before they stepped outside, Alana stole a glance at him. His profile was hard and tight.

She had been about to ask him if he was angry with her. She gulped down the words. She had to hurry to keep up with him as they hurried through the maze of tents, past several small cook fires. His grip did not ease.

Iain pulled open his tent door, guiding Alana in and stepping in behind her. Meg sat at the small table there on his stool. When they came in, she jumped up, spilling her wine as she did so.

Iain released Alana. "Leave us," he said.

Meg picked up her plaid, flung it about her shoulders and scurried out.

Alana tensed, facing Iain.

He took her furs from her and flung them aside, seizing her shoulders. "So ye want Brodie—and ye want me," he said harshly.

"Iain," she began, intending to try to explain herself and defuse the situation.

But he did not allow her to speak. He pulled her into his arms, kissing her heatedly, tongue to tongue, and then he was pushing her down on the pallet.

ALANA BRAIDED HER hair, glancing into a small looking glass on the table when she was done.

She was amazed by her own appearance. Her skin glowed like pearls, her cheeks were tinged with a pretty flush and her eyes sparkled. For the first time in her life, as she regarded herself, she understood why she was considered a beautiful woman.

She glanced across Iain's tent at his pallet, which

was vacant. They had made love several times last night, and she had then fallen asleep in his arms. Exhausted, she had slept well past sunrise, and when she had awoken, Iain had been gone.

Alana walked over to the tent flap and opened it. She stood still and stared out at Bruce's camp.

Because the army was not marching, his soldiers were seated around the various campfires, eating and drinking. A group of men were heading off into the woods on foot, with bows upon their shoulders. She hoped there would be venison that night.

She scanned the camp. Last night, they had not spoken, not even once, about what had happened in Bruce's tent or about anything else.

She remained in some disbelief. King Robert had given her Brodie in exchange for her fealty...even if he had refused to give her Iain.

She had taken sides in this war now.

"So yer awake."

Alana almost jumped out of her skin, not having heard Iain approach from the back side of the tent. She smiled, but nervously. Would they discuss what she had done? Would they speak of her having asked for him in marriage? Would they discuss his eventual marriage to someone else?

His gaze moved slowly over her. "Ye slept well," he said. "After we finished lovemaking, ye did not move once the entire night."

She blushed. "I do not think I have ever slept as deeply." She hesitated. "Are you angry with me?"

"Why would I be angry?" He touched her cheek and winked, lewdly. "Ye ken I am very pleased today."

She blushed again. "You know that is not what I meant."

"I am not angry, Alana."

She did not know if she truly wished to raise the subject of their relationship—and future—now.

"And ye? Are ye pleased? When we take Brodie, ye will be her mistress again."

"I am pleased," she answered. "When will we take Brodie, Iain?"

"Ye lust for power as much as I do."

She did not smile back. "No. I lust for my own power, and for what is mine, by birthright."

"Yer father is a fool, to be led by the nose by his wife, to have abandoned ye. He could have three fine daughters. Instead, he has two."

She started, hurt by his words, because they were the painful truth. "He is weak, Iain."

"'Tis the same to me." He shrugged. Then, "Bruce is moving his army to the west tomorrow. I am taking my men east."

"To Brodie?"

"Aye, Alana, to Brodie."

She found it hard to breathe. "I must come with you. Iain, Godfrey is in command, he is my friend.... Surely I can convince him to surrender to you."

"He will hardly think to surrender, if he learns ye have betrayed his father and Buchan, and that in surrendering, Brodie will become yers."

Alana was aghast. "Surely you are not planning on leaving me here, while you go back to Brodie!"

"War is no place for a woman, even one as bold as ye. I will send ye into the care of my brother, on Islay. Ye will go tomorrow. And I will march for Brodie at dawn. I hope to attack Brodie before anyone ever learns of yer treachery."

Alana was shocked. "I am not going to your brother, and I am not going to Islay! I have to come with you. I cannot allow you to attack and destroy my home!"

"Brodie has no defenses. I can take the castle easily enough. And Alana—ye have no power to allow me anything."

She flinched. "Of course I have no authority to tell you what to do, and what not to do. I can help, Iain. I can persuade Godfrey to surrender without a fight. Why destroy Brodie if you do not have to?"

"Alana. I need to know about Godfrey—and Lady Fitzhugh."

Alana froze. Her grandmother was at Brodie—and she could be held hostage and used against them.

"Would yer friend, Godfrey, hurt yer grandmother?" Iain asked harshly. "He is Duncan's son."

Alana seized his arm to remain standing. "No. Godfrey would not hurt her."

"Then why are ye as white as a corpse?"

"Duncan would use her against us—so would my uncle." She began to shake. "Iain, you cannot attack Brodie while my grandmother is there." Once Buchan learned of her treachery, he would strike at Alana in any way that he could—even if it meant using an old woman to hurt her.

"If Duncan remains in the north, defending Buchan lands, and Buchan is also in the north, we can take Brodie before either man thinks to order Godfrey to hold Lady Fitzhugh."

Alana felt sick. She did not want her grandmother placed in any jeopardy, not now, not ever, even if it meant giving up her dream of recovering Brodie. "Maybe we should leave Brodie for now."

"Is that what ye truly want?"

"I do not want Eleanor hurt!" Tears arose. "When my uncle learns of my betrayal, he will hurt her to hurt me. I have no doubt. He is ruthless and savage, but you know that—you saw what he did to me!"

He pulled her close. In his arms, Alana trembled wildly. "Ye love her greatly, as ye should."

"I love her more than anyone in this entire world, and she is all that I have."

His gaze moved slowly over her features. "Ye have me."

She shook her head. "No. I do not."

"Aye. Truly." He pushed some hair out of her eyes. "If we move swiftly, there is every chance we can take Brodie before the word of yer homage to Bruce is out. And then ye'll have Brodie and yer grandmother will be safe."

"And what if we get to Brodie, and the news is already known to them?"

"Then, Alana, yer grandmother will be in great jeopardy."

They had to take Brodie immediately. "Then your best chance to take Brodie is to have me speak with Godfrey. Please. Do not send me to Islay." She touched his face. "Please, Iain."

He was grim. "Ye have learned how to play me too well."

She had won. Alana felt faint with relief.

CHAPTER ELEVEN

Brodie Castle—January, 1308

ALANA'S HEART SURGED as they crested the ridge, finally reaching its flat topmost plateau. Brodie Castle sat on the adjacent hill. It was such a welcome sight.

Iain raised his hand, halting the dozen warriors who accompanied them. The rest of his army was hidden in the forest below them.

He glanced at her and she smiled at him, her heart racing. Once Godfrey surrendered, she would be mistress of Brodie. She would have her home back.

It remained incredible. But she had paid dearly for Brodie. She was now committed to Robert Bruce and his triumph, and not because of the act of homage she had had to perform. Bruce had to conquer Scotland. He had to defeat Buchan. Otherwise she would be taken from Brodie the moment Buchan could attack it and seize her.

She had arrived at Bruce's camp on Slioch Mountain just ten fateful days ago. How her life had changed, as she had not even dreamed it would. And while she was Iain's lover, and she shared his tent as well as his bed, they had never discussed the appeal she had made to Bruce, or his eventual marriage to another woman one day.

She would survive, because Brodie was hers now.

"The snow has melted," Iain said, breaking the silence of the afternoon.

A January thaw was not uncommon. Patches of snow covered the tops of the ridge they rode upon, and the adjacent terrain, but the ground was mostly mud otherwise. Alana knew what he was thinking—she knew him so well now. It was far easier to attack one's enemy in the snow than in the mud. "You will not have to attack. I will make certain of it."

He smiled at her. "Ye have the determination of a queen."

"That is high praise, indeed."

"Ye have changed, Alana, since we first met. Ye were a young, untried girl then. I sometimes see that girl, but mostly, I see a proud, headstrong woman."

"So much has happened. I hope the changes you have seen are pleasing to you."

"Ye are pleasing to me." He was final. "We have four hours till dusk. Let us go."

Alana nodded, her nerves high. So much depended upon her efforts to persuade Godfrey now. Iain lifted his hand and they started down the steep western side of the ridge, traversing it upon a deer path. It was rocky, partly frozen and partly mud, and the going was slow and difficult.

It took an hour to reach the glen below, and another half an hour to begin the small ascent to Brodie's front gates, which were barred and closed. The walls seemed empty, too. But when they were almost within calling distance of Brodie's watchtower, her bells began to ring.

"Yer watch is poor," Iain observed. The bells tolled

loudly and shrilly now. "The watch should have re-marked us well before this."

Godfrey's soldiers appeared on the castle walls. Iain continued on, Alana beside him, two dozen Highland-ers behind them.

And then they were close enough for her to see God-frey take up a place on the walls, amidst his men. His fair hair was unmistakable. Iain signaled his men to halt.

"I should ride forward, alone," Alana said, remov-ing her hood. She wanted Godfrey to recognize her.

"Ye will do no such thing," Iain returned.

"His archers will try to strike you," Alana said sharply with fear.

"Is he that much of a fool?" Iain asked. "I am ap-proaching his gates with a handful of men. He does not know my army lies in wait in the forest. And I am bringing ye with me. He cannot be so stupid, Alana, as to fire the first shot without asking my business, first."

Godfrey wasn't a fool, and he was committed to Brodie. He would probably want to speak with Iain before taking any aggressive action that might have terrible consequences for him.

She glanced behind them. Iain's banner was flying in the wind, but so was a white flag of truce. She was surprised. She hadn't realized he would raise such a flag.

Iain spurred his stallion forward and Alana followed him on her red mare. She heard the strings of numer-ous bows being pulled taut against ready arrows, the sound sharp and high, like a violin striking the wrong note. She looked up at the archers on the walls. Every man there was aiming their arrows down at them.

And behind them, steel screamed as all of Iain's men drew their swords.

"Do ye not see our white flag?" Iain demanded loudly, halting his horse. But he was angry, and the charger whirled nervously.

"Identify yourself!" Godfrey cried, leaning over the wall. His face was white.

"I am Iain of Islay, and yer father's ward, Alana le Latimer, is with me. Have yer archers stand down!" Iain ordered. Lower, he said, "Stay behind me. He may be a fool after all."

Alana ignored him. Godfrey was stunned and he seemed stricken, even indecisive, and she spurred her mare forward, past Iain. "Godfrey! We must speak!"

"Alana?" Godfrey cried, peering down at her, turning whiter.

Iain rode up to her and seized her reins, giving her a furious look. Then, to Godfrey, "Come down and parley with us. Bring three of yer knights if ye must."

Godfrey was incredulous. Alana knew he had not heard of her treachery—and he could not comprehend why she was with Iain. He could not imagine what they wanted, either. In that moment, she felt sorry for him, and ashamed of what she must do.

"I am not leaving Brodie," Godfrey finally said. He turned to his soldiers and archers. "No one is to fire, unless I give the command."

The bows groaned as the tension in each weapon was released. The archers replaced their arrows in their quivers. Alana took a deep breath, hoping to never look up at so many archers ready to shoot at her again.

Iain signaled his men, and steel rang again as they sheathed their weapons.

"Alana," Godfrey cried. "Are you all right?"

This time, she glanced at Iain for permission. He nodded, and she moved a few strides closer to the wall. "I am fine, Godfrey, considering the circumstance I find myself in."

Godfrey stared down at her, his face taut. "You vanished from Brodie! We feared you were abducted! And then we realized you had taken a horse and ridden away with one of Seamus's sons. Why, Alana?" His blue gaze veered wildly to Iain. "Seamus claims he does not know your affairs! He is so loyal to you!"

She trembled. "You will find out soon enough. I am with Iain now, Godfrey."

He stared blankly at her, clearly not understanding.

"I love him," she said. "And I am sorry."

He cried out, shocked. "What are you speaking about? You cannot love him! You do not even know him! He freed you from the tower at Nairn—you could not have spoken with him more than a time or two. He was there but a day, not even!"

Alana did not glance at Iain. Oddly, as much as she loved Iain, she felt ashamed now. She had violated her family's trust. "Does it matter? Godfrey, I am here to help. Robert Bruce gave Iain Nairn."

Godfrey was shaking. "Nairn? Nairn is in ashes! And yes, it matters, Alana!"

She was holding her reins so tightly now that her mare tossed its head in protest. She relaxed her grasp. "Godfrey! King Robert has decided to take Brodie after all. I begged Iain to let me come and speak with you! I do not want to see you or the men here hurt. Please, Godfrey, he will attack and take Brodie by force, unless you surrender."

Godfrey gaped at her.

He was shocked, more so than she had predicted. She looked at Iain. "I need to speak with him privately."

His eyes widened. "Ye will not go in there by yerself! He will never let ye leave, and then I will not be able to attack!"

"He will not hurt me, Iain." She faced Godfrey. "Godfrey? Can I come inside to speak with you—as your friend? I do not want anyone to die today!"

Godfrey's face was a mask of shock, anguish and anger. He nodded.

Iain seized her shoulder. "No. Godfrey!" he shouted. "I command Nairn, and I will command Brodie, too. I will not allow Alana to go inside. Surrender Brodie and avoid great bloodshed today. Otherwise, I will attack."

Alana did not know what to do. She felt certain if she could speak privately with Godfrey, as difficult as it would be, she could convince him to surrender.

Godfrey was shaking. "You are with *him* now? Is it true?"

Alana wet her lips and nodded. "We are lovers," she said.

Godfrey turned red. "God! So did you ride off into the night to be with him? Is that what happened, Alana? You chose your lover over me? Over Brodie? Over your *family?*"

"I still care about Brodie the way that you do," she began.

"Liar!" Godfrey shouted. "You rode off to be with him after, what? One night at Nairn?" He was furious.

Alana was not going to discuss her relationship with Iain. "You know how I feel about Brodie," she cried.

"Do I? I thought I did! I thought I knew you! The

woman I knew would never hand Brodie over to the enemy!"

Iain wasn't her enemy, yet she did not dare say so. Nor did she dare tell him the truth—that the moment he surrendered, Brodie would be hers.

"Godfrey!" Iain shouted. "I am losing my patience, and my men will attack at dawn if ye do not surrender."

Godfrey looked wildly at Iain, with panic and fear.

"Godfrey!" Alana said. "I am begging you! Iain will attack and he will destroy Brodie if he has to. You know that is his way. He will have Brodie, even in ashes, just as he now has Nairn. So please. Surrender to him."

Godfrey looked at his archers and suddenly every bow was drawn again, the dozens of arrows pointing at her. Alana froze as she heard Iain's men unsheath their swords.

"Don't fight," Alana cried. "You are my friend! I do not want you to die!"

A terrible silence fell. The only sound to be heard was the horses blowing, their bits jangling, their saddles creaking.

Iain broke it. "My army is in the woods. I am three hundred strong. Ye have thirty-five men."

Godfrey gave Alana a disbelieving look. She winced. He straightened and stepped back from the crenellations. He did not look at Alana now. His voice rough, he said, "Open the gates."

ALANA RUSHED INSIDE Brodie's great hall behind Iain and forty or fifty of his men. It was several hours later. Iain's army now surrounded the castle, while his men were occupying the walls.

Godfrey was sitting at the table there, his hands clasped upon it, staring in a strange, almost horrified manner at the hall's threshold. A handful of serving maids stood behind him, each one ashen and afraid. As Alana entered, she finally saw Eleanor, who came rushing toward her from the shadows.

Alana hugged her grandmother hard. "I have been so worried about you," Eleanor said.

Alana smiled through tears of relief. "I am fine."

Eleanor took a good look at her. Clearly, her grandmother could see that she was pleased and well.

Iain had paused before Godfrey, who did not stand up. "Ye have done the right thing, Godfrey." He flung his fur cloak aside, one hand on the hilt of his sword, his posture commanding and aggressive.

Godfrey made a derisive sound. "So you will not take me prisoner?" He was mocking and angry. Now he finally looked past Iain at Alana.

"When yer ransom is paid, ye will be released." Iain also turned to look at her.

Alana's cheeks were hot. There was no avoiding what must happen next. She slowly approached Godfrey. "Iain? I must speak with Godfrey. Alone."

Iain's gaze narrowed. "Ye may speak with him as much as ye like. But he is very angry now, and he will be under guard until his ransom is paid."

"You will not let me speak with him alone?" Alana was incredulous.

Godfrey spat, "So that is the lover you have chosen?"

Alana trembled as Iain gave him a warning look. "Ye can hold yer tongue and speak pleasantly and remain here, with yer guard, or ye can be put in the dungeons with the rest of yer men."

Alana was not going to allow Godfrey to be put in the dungeons! They had not even discussed his capture. And what of all of Brodie's men? She was expecting them to pledge their allegiance to her—not to become prisoners of war or worse.

"Who is yer sergeant of arms?" Iain demanded.

Godfrey folded his arms. "Roger de Foret."

Iain turned and ordered his soldiers to bring him de Foret. "I am going to inspect our defenses," he said. "Angus, guard Godfrey. If he gives ye trouble of any kind, send him below."

Angus was a middle-aged Highlander who was taller than Iain, his face rudely scarred, his gray beard so long that it reached his chest. He looked as if he had been at war his entire life. "Is that necessary, Iain?" Alana asked.

"He is the enemy, Alana." He signaled a handful of the men in the room to join him, and he left.

"Are you pleased with yourself? Does betrayal suit you?" Godfrey asked.

Alana jerked. "I do not expect you to understand."

"You have stabbed me in the back. You have stabbed your father and Buchan in the back. My God, Buchan will kill you for this."

Alana trembled as Eleanor put her arm around her. Her grandmother did not speak, and she knew Eleanor agreed with Godfrey on his last point. But then, so did Alana.

"Why, Alana? Why? And do not tell me that you love that Highlander! No one forsakes their entire family for love!" Godfrey cried.

Alana sank down on the bench not far from him. "I do love him. I have never loved a man before." She had forsaken her family for love, she thought, Godfrey's word having a chilling effect. Yet Iain would one day be with another woman.

Godfrey began shaking his head. "I thought you were amenable to marriage to me. God, I am a fool!"

Alana shivered, rubbing her arms, wondering suddenly if she was the fool. "We are friends now. It is not the same."

"Not the same as lovers?" He stood abruptly, causing her to leap up, as well. Angus drew his sword.

Godfrey raised his hands high, indicating he meant no harm. "And will you marry him, Alana? Is that it? You will marry him and become mistress here?"

Tears arose. "I will not marry him, that much has been made clear...but I am mistress here."

Godfrey dropped his hands. "What?"

"I am sorry," she whispered.

"What?" he roared.

Angus seized his arm.

"Bruce has given me my home," she said. "The home that was my mother's. It is to be my dowry.... I am mistress of Brodie now."

"Bitch!" He screamed. "You have gone over to Bruce? Bitch!"

Angus began to drag him away. "Ye'll sleep below tonight, my English lord."

Godfrey struggled uselessly against the larger man. "I am not English, you savage ass! What did you do, Alana? And why? Why?" He was screaming, tears running down his face.

"Bruce will be king," she gasped, and she realized

she was crying, too. "Please, Angus, unhand him, we are only talking!"

"Iain said he is to go to the dungeons if he causes trouble," Angus spat.

"He is not causing me harm," Alana said. Godfrey laughed again, without mirth.

"And what will your lover think when he learns the truth about you?"

He meant to tell Iain about her sight? A weight dropped within Alana's chest. "Godfrey!" She rushed to him. "There is no reason to say anything!"

"No reason? You have stabbed me in the back! You have stolen Brodie from me!"

"Don't do this," she begged. "We are friends."

"Friends? Friends do not betray one another! Friends do not steal from one another!"

"Brodie was stolen from me!" Alana cried. "From me!"

Iain stepped back into the hall, saying, "The whole castle can hear ye screaming at one another." He was dark. He looked back and forth between them, with suspicion.

Alana stared silently at Godfrey, begging him with her eyes to keep her secret.

His gaze filled with tears, Godfrey stared back. Then he turned to Iain. "Do you not want to know the truth about her?"

Iain glanced at Alana. She felt her gaze becoming moist, and she turned away, sinking back down onto the bench. Eleanor sat beside her and took her hand.

"What is he speaking of, Alana?" Iain asked, very quietly.

Alana made a helpless gesture. "There is something," she began. She choked. How could she tell him? Images flashed in her mind, of times when he had looked at her with warmth, with affection, with lust or with admiration…and too many images then followed, rapidly, of other men, staring at her with horror, in fear, repulsed.

"She is a witch," Godfrey said.

Iain started, glancing at Godfrey.

"Your lover is a witch. Everyone knows. Ask anyone."

Iain seemed amused. He turned to Alana, who trembled, sick with desperation, her gaze glued to his. His amusement vanished. Puzzled, he said, "Alana? What does he speak of?"

She hugged herself. "He is telling you the truth."

"What?"

"I have the sight, Iain. I am a witch."

He stared at her for a long moment. Then he said, "Everyone leave us."

AN ETERNITY SEEMED to go by then, as everyone left the hall, Angus pulling Godfrey with him, Eleanor shooting Alana a worried glance, as she, too, got up and left. When they were all gone, Alana remained seated on the bench at the table, alone. Iain stood before her, his stance braced, one hand on the hilt of one sword. The only sound to be heard in the chamber was the hiss and crackle of the fire and Alana's heavy breathing.

"I dinna understand," Iain finally said.

How calm he sounded. Alana bit her lip, fighting tears. She had dreaded this day since meeting him. "I can see," she whispered.

"If ye were not so frightened, I'd think this a jest."

She shook her head.

"What do ye mean, exactly, that ye have the sight?" His knuckles turned white.

"I have visions…of the future…sometimes."

He made a disparaging sound, his gaze fixated upon her. "No one can see the future."

"I can."

Another silence fell. A log fell in the fire, popping and hissing. "Ye only think ye can see, Alana." He was firm. "'Tis impossible."

He did not want to believe her. She was almost relieved. She was so tempted to let him continue to think as he was doing—but they were at Brodie, and everyone knew of her visions. "My father gave me a small dowry when I was fifteen. But everyone here in Buchan knows the truth, and the real reason I am not wed is because of my power," she said hoarsely. "No one would have me, not even with my dower lands."

He continued to stare, his eyes wide and hard, his expression becoming aggrieved. "I dinna believe ye," he finally said. "No one can *see*."

She shrugged helplessly. "I have had visions since I was a child of five or six."

Another terrible silence passed, in which neither moved. "What have you seen?" he finally asked.

She rubbed her cold arms. "I saw you, Iain, before we ever met, in battle at Boath Manor."

"What?" he exclaimed.

"I saw every detail of the battle days before it happened. I saw your Highlanders battling Duncan's soldiers, I saw the manor burning, I saw you rescue

Mistress MacDuff and her children. I even saw that red-haired Highlander try to stab you in the back."

"I dinna believe ye," he said again, but with less certainty.

She could drop the subject, she thought, but the doubt was there, in his eyes, along with confusion and a determination to ferret out the truth. "When Eleanor and I were on our way to Nairn and we came upon the battle, I knew what was going to happen. So yes, I did shout at you in warning."

"I heard ye," he said, his mouth turned down. "But why did ye rush to me when I was stabbed? Why?"

"I don't know why. I had to help you. I was terrified you were hurt, or that you would die!" She started to cry into her hands.

"Do not cry now," he warned. He started to pace, wildly, with confusion and growing anger. Alana fought her sobs, but it was impossible. Her heart was breaking. He whirled to face her, seizing her wrists, and removing her hands from her face. "Yer tears will not move me, Alana," he warned. "Why did ye help me? Why? Was there more to yer vision?"

"I don't know why I helped you! It was as if I loved you already, I was that frightened for you!" she cried.

He shook her once and released her. "Ye couldn't have loved me then. Were ye looking for me? Were ye sent to look for me?"

He was so suspicious, again! "My uncle sent for me, but no one knew of that vision except for Eleanor."

He absorbed that. Then, "What other powers do ye have?"

She stiffened. "None."

"I dinna believe ye! God—or the devil—gave ye but one power?" His blue eyes were wild now. "Have ye cast a spell on me?"

She gasped. "Of course not!"

"Because I have been bewitched, from the time we first met! Did ye cast a spell on Godfrey? He is smitten with ye! On Bruce? Who so easily gave ye Brodie, who so quickly allowed me to march on it?"

Alana staggered to her feet, reaching for him. He swiped her hands away. "Iain, I cannot cast spells! My only power is the sight!"

He stared at her for many moments. "Ye need to go to yer chamber, Alana," he finally said. "I'll send for ye when I am ready to speak with ye again."

"Nothing has changed!"

He sent her a dark look. "Everything has changed."

ALANA WENT INTO Eleanor's arms as Angus shut the door upon them. She closed her eyes tightly and fought the incessant tears. She had expected Iain's anger, but she had not expected him to think that she had used witchcraft on him.

"It will be all right, Alana," Eleanor said.

"Will it? He is furious, and he has sent me away! He thinks I cast a spell on him, to make him want me! And have we been locked up again? Are we Iain's prisoners?"

Eleanor stroked her hair. "You had to tell him. He was going to find out. And it is who you truly are."

"But I didn't tell him, because I have been a coward." She wiped her eyes and stood, thinking of how Iain had told her she was brave. Now he knew that truth, too! "Godfrey told him—to spite me—and I do not blame him." Her heart sank with more dismay. Poor Godfrey. Had he come to truly care about her? "I have hurt everyone."

"You never meant to hurt anyone. You found love when you have been treated like a leper your entire life. You had Brodie returned to you, when it should have never been taken away. You have done nothing wrong, Alana."

Alana did not believe her. She felt as if she had betrayed everyone, and for what purpose? For the sake of having Brodie returned to her? To spend a few nights in her lover's arms?

She walked to the door and tested it. To her surprise, it was not bolted, and when she opened it, no guard stood there.

She sighed in relief. At least Iain was not keeping her prisoner…yet.

"I eavesdropped on you," Eleanor said, patting the place beside her on the bed. Alana returned and sat down at her side, and they held hands. "He is shocked, as he should be. And he is angry. But the shock and the anger will pass."

"He is filled with suspicion again. He is filled with doubt, when it was so hard to win his trust. And he sent me away." She trembled, a knife stabbing through her heart.

"I heard an angry, shocked man in the hall tonight, a man trying to sort through his own confusion, a man trying to comprehend you. A man who wanted to understand."

"What are you saying, Gran?"

"Was he horrified? Frightened of you?"

She was afraid to have any hope, but she had not seen horror or fear on Iain's face. "No."

"You must give him some time, to realize what you truly are—a wonderful woman with a power that is at times a gift, and at other times, a curse."

Her grandmother was the wisest person she had ever met. "Gran, do you think he might come to accept me as I am?"

"I think he is different from other men, Alana."

Iain was different. The fourth and youngest son of a Highland lord, he was intelligent, shrewd and ambitious. He was powerful, and not just as a soldier. He was ruthless, but he could be kind. He was, truly, exceptional.

Alana shook herself free of her fanciful thoughts, her fanciful hope. "Even if he could accept me, he will marry someone else. I asked Bruce for Iain as a husband, and I was refused. Bruce has made it clear that Iain will have a great heiress for his loyalty, and Iain has been as clear that he expects as much."

"There are worse fates than being a beloved mistress." Eleanor smiled and touched her hair.

"I am not beloved now, Gran."

"Are you certain?"

Did her grandmother think that Iain loved her? Alana was unable to speak, when a knock sounded on the door. "Enter," her grandmother said.

The door was pushed open. Iain stood there on the threshold, staring at Alana, unsmiling and grim.

Her heart surged and she slowly stood up.

"Lady Fitzhugh, would you leave us?" Iain asked. But it was not a question, even if his tone was polite.

Eleanor hugged Alana once, and said to Iain, "She is precious to me—and to you, I suspect." With that thinly veiled warning, she left.

Iain closed the door but did not step any farther into the room. "So ye have had visions since ye were a child," he said quietly.

Her gaze riveted to his, she nodded. "Yes."

"Visions, not dreams?"

"Visions," she said hoarsely. Would they now calmly discuss her ability to see?

"What kind of visions? How often do ye have them?"

Dismay began. Was this an effort on his part to comprehend her—or to avail himself of her power? "I have never had a vision that is pleasing. I only foresee tragedy, bloodshed and death."

He flinched.

"They happen when I least expect it," she continued, "and when I am fully awake, and always, when I have glanced into a body of water."

"When ye look into water?"

"I could look into a puddle of water, or a lake, and suddenly I am dizzy and faint, and then I am inside my own vision, as if it is really happening." She wrung her hands. "I am always sick afterwards. Why do you ask me this, Iain?"

"We have been sleeping together since December, and suddenly I learn you are a witch, with the power of sight. I am not to ask questions?"

She could not decide what he truly wished to gain. She shrugged, indicating he could ask what he wished.

"How often do ye see the future? Once a month? Once a year?"

"It varies. A few times a year, perhaps."

"And do the visions always come true?"

She nodded without hesitation. "Yes, Iain—always."

He stared now, silently, still standing by the closed door.

He finally said, "Ye said ye saw the battle for Boath Manor a few days before it happened. Is it always that way? Do yer visions come true so swiftly?"

"No. It might be weeks or even months before my vision is reality." She thought of the visions she had so recently had, of the destruction of Buchan's earldom, of her father's death, of Iain about to be slain by her uncle.... "It has never been more than a few months," she whispered.

He was grim, wary even, but he no longer seemed angry. He was thoughtful. She knew Iain well now. He was trying to understand her abilities. If he also meant to use her in this war, it was not clear.

Until he spoke next. "What other visions have ye had, Alana, of the war—of me?"

She hugged herself, dismayed. "Is this why you have sought me out? To ask me about the war?"

He shot her a puzzled glance. "If ye have seen the future of the war, I must know."

"That is why my uncle locked me up, Iain, the first time. He wanted me to have visions for him. That is why he summoned me to Nairn. And when he learned I cannot whistle a tune and sing a tale of the future upon command, he locked me in the tower—with a large clear bowl of water. I was not to be released until I had a vision." She knew she sounded bitter. "I cannot see when someone asks me to! I cannot summon up a vision like one orders a maid to the kitchen!"

"I am not surprised yer uncle wanted a vision from ye," Iain said. "What happened?"

"Do you condone what he did?" she cried, standing. "Will you lock me up with a bowl of water, until I have a vision for you?"

"Have I locked ye up?"

She was shaking wildly. "I don't know. I feel like a prisoner!"

His eyes flashed. "There was no guard outside, and ye damn well ken, just as ye ken the door was unlocked."

She shook her head fiercely. "I have been shunned my entire life because of my visions. Shunned, outcast—feared! And then, with this damned war, my uncle suddenly cares for me! And my father visits, as suddenly, when I have not seen him since I was five! Suddenly, I am important to them! Suddenly, I am a beloved niece, a beloved daughter!"

"So ye feel sorry for yerself?"

She realized she was mired in self-pity. But she nodded. "Right now, I feel very sorry for myself!" she cried, fists clenched. "For a while, with you, I was an ordinary woman!"

His mouth curled slightly. He shifted off of the door. "Alana, even without the power, yer no ordinary woman."

"You took me as a lover, because I was ordinary! No man has ever wanted me, until you."

His gaze narrowed. "Then they are all fools."

What did that mean? Was it possible that he did not fear her now?

He looked away from her for the first time, staring at his booted feet. "Buchan and Sir Alexander would want ye close. It makes sense. They'd be the fools otherwise. And if they thought to manipulate ye by their sudden affection, it was up to ye, Alana, to realize the ploy."

He did not understand how hurtful that was.

He glanced sidelong at her. "What happened at Nairn? Did ye have a vision, as Buchan wished? Is that why he beat ye? To make certain ye'd see for him?"

"I had a vision, finally," she whispered. "But it was not the vision Buchan wanted, and he was furious with me—enough so to beat me and lock me up."

"What did ye see?"

She sat down. Iain wanted to know about her visions, just as Buchan and Sir Alexander had. In a way, it hurt, but not as badly, because she wanted to help him if she could, to keep him safe. Yet she did not want to be used by him, not now, not ever.

"I have seen Buchan defeated, his earldom in rubble and ashes, destroyed, Bruce's flag flying high in the sky." She looked up. "Bruce wins. My uncle is destroyed."

Iain's eyes were wide. He suddenly came and sat down beside her on the bed. "My God," he said. "And ye told all of this to yer uncle?"

She nodded, wiping a stray tear from her cheek, looking at her lap. "I was praying he would take such information and defend the earldom.... He was furious instead, and he beat me and locked me up."

Iain laid his hand on her shoulder. "I am sorry for that, Alana."

Their shoulders, arms and hips touched as they sat side by side on the small bed. And for one moment, the sensation of his large, powerful male body against hers was acute and so familiar to her.

"When will Bruce triumph over Buchan?"

"I don't know," she said. "It seemed to be springtime… there was a little melting snow left on the ground." She studied him carefully now. He was elated. She could feel his thoughts racing. Then he realized her close regard, and he glanced at her, smiling slightly.

She was in disbelief. "You don't fear me, at all?"

He stood, towering over her. "Should I fear ye, Alana?"

"No!"

His gaze was narrow now. "If this is the only power ye have, then I do not fear ye."

He had asked her if she could cast spells, worried she had bewitched him, and even Bruce. "I cannot cast spells, Iain. I am not that kind of witch."

He studied her. "And what of yer other visions?"

"There have only been two," she said. "I saw my father dead. He is going to die, Iain."

He absorbed that. "I ken ye care for Sir Alexander, even now, although I cannot comprehend why. And the other vision?"

"You must be on guard. Buchan will come up behind you, his sword raised—he will be a moment away from killing you."

After a pause, he asked, "Does he succeed?"

"I don't know," she whispered.

Iain finally turned away from her, his expression thoughtful. Alana knew he was done—that he meant to leave the room. She wanted to call him back, but she did not know what she would then say. She wanted to ask him to come to her later, to sleep with her, as they had been doing every night. But she was afraid he would refuse.

Mostly, she wanted to know what the truth really meant to him. But she was terrified of that answer.

"It must be difficult, Alana, to have such a power," Iain suddenly said. "But it is useful—very useful." And he left.

CHAPTER TWELVE

"ALANA, YOU ARE EXHAUSTED," Eleanor said. "Why don't I have a maid bring you supper? There is no need for you to go downstairs tonight."

Alana was curled up in her bed, dozing. Several hours had to have passed since her conversation with Iain, as it was dark outside now behind the closed shutters. She had fallen asleep, but her grandmother's light touch had awoken her.

She did not know if she wanted to go downstairs. In spite of how uncertain the future was, she had been so happy until the past few hours. And before falling asleep, her mind had gone around in circles, for she could not decide how Iain felt about her ability to see—or how he felt about her.

The only thing she was certain of was that he was no longer angry.

"I am tired," she finally admitted.

"It is a man's feast downstairs, anyway. They are carousing below as if they have taken Balvenie."

Alana could not smile. Balvenie was the seat of Buchan's earldom. She had never been to the castle, even though it was within a day's easy riding. She had always wanted to see it; it was renowned to be very grand. Now she would never have the opportunity. "How long do you think it will be before my father and my uncle find out about Brodie—about me?"

Eleanor's smile faded. "Bad news travels as swiftly as any raven."

Alana flopped onto her back, staring up at the stone ceiling. "I wish things were different. I wish there had been other choices to make." But that would have meant living in a peaceful land, when Scotland was always racked by war, pitting family against friend.

"I know you better than I knew my own son, and I know you hated betraying your father. Alana? We both know he hardly deserved such loyalty from you."

Alana did not answer, well aware that Eleanor did not care about her betrayal of the earl, but was as torn as Alana over the betrayal of her father. Giving her a solemn look, Eleanor left, not bothering to close the door.

She quickly shut off her recollections of her uncle. But she had to wonder how her father would react when he received the news that she was mistress of Brodie now—and that she had paid homage to Robert Bruce.

If he had loved her a little, he probably would not love her now, Alana thought, staring into the torch-lit hallway. She could hear the sounds of the revelry coming from the hall below. Brodie had fallen without a fight, so the soldiers were celebrating. How pleased Iain must be, as well. He had not lost a single man.

She knew what it was like downstairs. The men were eating their fill and then some, while drinking beyond reason. Every young maid in the castle, if unmarried or widowed, would be in attendance, seeking to ensnare a handsome and victorious soldier. Meg would be downstairs.

She would be pouring him wine, flattering him, brushing against his shoulder. She might even be sharing his supper with him. She wondered if Meg would return to his bed. Why wouldn't she?

How the notion hurt, like a knife stabbing through her breast.

Alana turned onto her side, away from the open door. She did not want to contemplate his affair with someone else. She turned her thoughts to Godfrey. Guilt consumed her. So did shame.

She did not know if he had been put in the dungeons, or if he was under guard in his own chamber. As difficult as it would be, she must visit him tomorrow, and make certain he was being properly cared for. She should also try to push Iain to make a ransom demand as soon as possible so Godfrey could be freed.

She heard footsteps outside in the hall—booted and male. Alana flipped over instantly.

Iain paused in the doorway, leaning one shoulder against it.

Her breath caught—as did their stares.

He had been drinking, she saw, for his expression was relaxed and benign. He did not seem angry, not at all. He wasn't wearing his swords or his plaid, and he held a mug of wine in his hand. His blue gaze was direct.

He slowly looked away, his dark, thick lashes fanning his face.

She sat up, her heart slamming. Had she just seen the smoldering look that she thought she had? Tension made her spine rigid. "What are you doing?"

"I told Lady Fitzhugh to find another chamber," he said, launching his body away from the wall.

He meant to sleep with her now? After all that he knew? No man wanted a witch in his bed!

"Why do ye look so surprised?" He half turned, never taking his heated gaze from her, and kicked the door closed.

"I did not expect you to want me."

He approached, his stride uncharacteristically indolent. "Why would that change?" He set the mug down on the table and reached for her.

Alana was pushed down onto the bed as he moved on top of her. "I am a witch," she gasped.

"Aye, and ye may have bewitched me." His knees were hard between her thighs. "Ye can confess, Alana," he murmured. "Even if ye put a spell on me, I am staying with ye tonight. Confess…. Ye cast a spell, and that is why I lust for ye the way that I do…that is why I am so fond of ye." He suddenly held her shoulders down, his gaze brilliant upon hers.

Her pulse exploded, urgency racking her body. Iain still desired her—the only man to ever do so! And he cared, he had just said so. "I cannot cast spells. I vow it!"

"Liar." He kissed her. "Witch." He kissed her again, now reaching for her skirts. "How can I be so hard, so often, unless there is a spell?"

She wanted to answer. She wanted to refute him—debate—but it was impossible, because he was driving into her. Alana held on to his shoulders, arching back in sheer pleasure, her heart thundering.

Iain desired her still. No proof could be greater.

He lifted her and held her close, increasing the pressure, until Alana had to close her eyes and climax. She wept as she did so, clawing his back. And she almost told him that she loved him. Somehow, she retained enough sanity to hold back.

He nipped her neck and pounded into her, finding his own release. She was floating in satiation—in disbelief—when he cried out, collapsing on top of her.

She stroked his back, relief swelling. Then she wrapped her arms around him and held him tight.

What did it truly mean that he had come to her now, after her terrible confession?

He rolled off her, out of her embrace, and to his side. "Beautiful witch," he said softly. He flung his arm up over his head and fell instantly asleep. And then she slowly sat up, staring at him.

His words hadn't been mean or cruel; she knew that. His tone had been tender. But Iain had never made love to her just once in the course of an evening, much less so quickly. He was both selfish and selfless in bed, with the kind of stamina a woman would expect from a young Highland warrior.

Dismay began. If he was genuinely tired, if his odd behavior had nothing to do with the truth about her visions, then why wasn't she in his arms? She always slept in his arms.

Alana slowly lay back down, not quite touching him, although the bed was small, making it difficult to keep a finger or two's length between them. The dismay turned into heartache. Something was wrong, she sensed it.

Did he still wonder if she had cast some kind of spell upon him?

Hadn't he said that everything had changed?

Grimly, she pulled the covers up and closed her

eyes. Too late, she realized she wanted—needed—far more than lust and desire from Iain.

"WHAT DO YOU WANT, Alana?"

Alana was stiff with tension as she faced Godfrey from the threshold of his chamber. He had not been sent to the dungeons, for which she was grateful, and had been placed under guard in his own chamber instead.

She had not asked for permission to see him. When she had awoken that morning, after a restless night, Iain had been gone. She hadn't fallen asleep until the early morning, and that must have been when he had silently left.

It was easier to simply make an attempt to visit Godfrey on her own than seek Iain out and face him after the night they had shared. She did not know what to expect from him when they finally came face-to-face.

Angus had not questioned her appearance outside Godfrey's door, and now he stood watchfully by her side. Alana smiled tightly at Godfrey. "I have come to make certain you are all right. May I come inside?"

"Do I look all right?" Godfrey demanded. In fact, he was red-eyed, and clad only in a long-sleeved tunic, his hose and boots. His clothing was rumpled, his short pale hair disheveled. He seemed to have passed as miserable a night as she had.

Alana wasn't sure how to answer. He stood before the table that was beneath an open window, a tray of food there. Clearly, he had not eaten. She glanced at Angus, who nodded, indicating she was free to go inside.

As she did, Godfrey picked up his doublet and shrugged it on. His cheeks were flushed by the time he had buttoned the short coat up. "I asked you what you want," he said harshly.

"And I told you," she said. "Godfrey, I am not your enemy."

He faced her, fully dressed. "You paid homage to Robert Bruce. Iain of Islay is your liege lord now—and your lover. Pray tell, how could you not be the enemy?"

Alana trembled, hating the conflict challenging them. Had she come to care for Godfrey? Or had she always cared for him, without ever having realized it? They had been raised together. He had taunted her and bullied her through most of their childhood, but she had done the same back to him. Growing up, she had thought that she despised him; she had thought him her enemy. But she suspected she had been wrong. "I refuse to be your enemy," she said stiffly.

He made a harsh, derisive sound. "That is a refusal you cannot make! We are at war, you and I, and I am a prisoner here, while you have been made Brodie's mistress!"

She rubbed her chilled arms. "I do not think I am Brodie's mistress just yet."

"Why? Because Iain has learned that you are a witch?"

"Yes!" she cried, losing her temper, at last. "He has learned I am a witch, and while he is here, he is in command, and you know that."

Godfrey now stared closely at her. "Ha, so he doesn't like you very much now?"

"That is cruel," she whispered. But how right Godfrey was. And she felt like a harlot, not the lady of the keep.

"No, your treachery is cruel. Do you know how we

worried about you when you were found missing? Do you know how I worried?"

She was at a loss. "I am so sorry. I wish I could have been able to confide in you."

"Truly? Because now I know that you went all the way to Slioch Mountain to warn your lover of Buchan's planned attack. You saved Bruce and his army. You betrayed your uncle, your father, everyone!"

She flushed. "Do you finally, truly, hate me?"

"I have never hated you, not even on the day we met, when you poured a chamber pot over my head the moment I stepped out of my father's wagon."

Alana had forgotten how horrid she had been when Duncan had first come to Brodie as her guardian and its lord, his young son with him.

"You hated me then, and you have hated me ever since. It was a lie, our becoming friends, to defend Brodie from Bruce." He turned his back on her, trembling.

She reached out and touched his arm briefly. "It wasn't a lie. Godfrey? I will do everything I can to keep you comfortable and to make certain you are released as soon as possible."

He whirled. "My father won't pay a ransom. He will be furious with me for surrendering Brodie. He will think my capture just deserts."

Alana thought he was right. Duncan was selfish, ambitious and cruel. "I will see you freed," she said firmly, meaning it.

"That will not make you my friend. We will never be friends again. I trusted you. I wish I hadn't."

"Don't say that. I don't want to lose you."

"It's too late. What is wrong, Alana? Do you have

regrets? Oh, wait! Your lover isn't lusting after you anymore? He doesn't want to bed a witch?"

Alana felt sickened. Godfrey's words were close enough to the truth.

"So you have sacrificed your family for love? Was it worth it?" he taunted.

She was close to tears. "Maybe not," she managed to say.

"It's too late for regrets," he said. "And as I look at you now, I almost feel sorry for you. Did he turn away in horror, last night? Like everyone else? Everyone except me?"

"No. Yes." Despair consumed her. "I will come see you again, later." She turned to go, stumbling.

"Don't bother!" he shouted.

Alana tripped, and reached the open door. She had to glance back at him.

Tears filled his eyes. But he remained furious. "Alana, are you carrying his bastard yet?"

She froze.

"I mean, who would ever think that you, of all women, would bring a bastard into this world!"

She could think of nothing worse. "I am not with child."

"For how long?"

She stumbled away, as swiftly as she could.

ALANA REALIZED SHE was hiding from Iain. She had spent most of the day in the cellars, inspecting what was left of Brodie's provisions for the winter. She had then gone into the kitchens to supervise the supper being prepared. When she had seen Iain in the corridor, at noon, she had reversed course to avoid coming face-to-face with him—to avoid speaking to him.

She knew she could not continue to avoid him, as Brodie was too small a castle, and he had not indicated that he would soon leave. In fact, she had heard that he was going to spend the next few weeks improving Brodie's defenses. He had sent men into the forest to cut down trees, never mind the cold. They had only just returned with the onset of dusk.

And because it was finally growing dark, Iain and his men had gathered in the hall, and were waiting for their supper. It would be night soon. Then what would happen? Did he think to share her bed again?

What if she was with child?

What if she brought a bastard into this world?

Alana could barely stand upright. Years ago she had realized she would never marry, and she had stopped contemplating having a family. Now the thought of bearing a son or a daughter was a great joy.

But her child would be a bastard. She did not want her child to suffer from lack of legitimacy, as she had. She did not want her child to be an outcast or worse because he or she was lowborn, without lands or titles. Her child would have no power in this world. What kind of life could she give him?

Now she realized her blood flow was late. She had had her monthly before she had been imprisoned at Nairn. That had been in early December. There had been nothing since, and it was early January now.

She told herself she was late and that was all. Hadn't she just trekked across the Highlands and almost frozen to death?

A maid dropped a platter onto the floor, breaking

into Alana's thoughts. Fortunately it had been empty. She hurried forward to help the girl pick up the shards of pottery.

Boar and venison had been roasting slowly on spits in the kitchen hearths for most of the afternoon. Platters of meat filled up the entire table in the kitchen. Alana finished helping the young girl tidy up and straightened. She watched several kitchen maids carry the plates into the hall. One was Meg, who had ignored her since she had come down to help with supper.

Alana sighed. She did not want to go into the hall with everyone else. She took off her apron, sitting down on a stool at the table, which was empty now, except for a casket of wine.

Maybe Iain wouldn't bother with her tonight. She did not feel relief at the thought—she felt dismay and hurt.

"Iain is asking for ye," Meg said sharply.

Alana looked up. Meg scowled at her from the doorway, turned and left.

Alana got up grimly and left the kitchen. She walked slowly into the hall. As she did, the loud sound of conversation, laughter and ribaldry washed over her. The castle was, once again, in a very festive mood.

And why not? This time was a respite from blood and death.

Iain sat at the head of the table, eating. Every seat was taken. His men were eating ravenously, and there was a great deal of drinking. The maids and Meg were pouring wine almost as quickly as it was drunk.

Alana paused by one fireplace, not going any closer. Iain looked at her.

He wasn't smiling, and she did not smile, either.

Meg was suddenly beside him, pouring him wine, and leaning into him with her breast as she did so. Alana tensed, but did not move. Clearly, Meg was seizing an opportunity.

Iain spoke with her, smiling, his posture easing as he did. When she left, he looked at Alana and gestured for her to approach.

It was a summons, she thought, and she slowly walked over to where he sat. Dread warred with her high state of nervousness.

"Ye will not eat?" he asked.

"Every place is taken."

A brow lifted, as he knew what a pitiful excuse that was. "Did ye have a pleasant visit with Godfrey this morning?"

"Are you spying upon me?" she asked immediately. The moment she spoke she regretted it.

"Should I spy on ye, Alana? Have ye changed yer loyalties, again?"

Her fists clenched. "I thought I had proven myself at Slioch!"

"Ye did—fer a time. But yer a Comyn and yer a witch. Sit down."

It was a command, and the man next to Iain leaped up, glancing uncertainly at her as he did before hurrying away.

"He fears ye," Iain said with some surprise.

Alana slid onto the bench. Iain handed her his mug of wine, signaling Meg for another one. Alana gulped half of it down. "I told you yesterday. Men do not desire me—they fear me."

Iain's gaze narrowed. "If ye only have the sight, why would they fear ye?"

She faced him entirely, her temper rising. "For the same reason that you do not trust me—because they assume I have other powers!"

He stared at her for a moment, then sipped his wine. "What did Godfrey have to say?"

"Angus was there—did he not tell you what we spoke of?"

"He said Godfrey was in tears. He said ye cried, as well, and there was fighting and shouting."

"I betrayed our friendship. But you know that. Godfrey is angry with me. I do not blame him."

Iain studied her. "Ye still care for him."

"I have lost a friend, but yes, I do." She recovered some of her composure. "Will you send a ransom note, soon? I do not think it right that he is imprisoned because of me."

"I will send a ransom note by the end of the week. Of course, when I am gone, ye could free him."

"Is this a trap? He is your prisoner of war."

Iain swirled his wine, then looked right into her eyes. "Yer mistress here, and when I am gone, ye will answer to no one."

She flushed, looking back at him, thinking of his behavior toward her last night. She had awoken feeling like a common castle maid. She thought about what he had just said. She had not even considered freeing Godfrey when Iain left. "I do not feel as if I am the mistress of Brodie."

"Bruce gave ye Brodie in return fer yer fealty, after ye served him well. No one can change that—except fer the king. Ye'd have to commit treason, Alana."

She stared down at her wine. She could not lose Brodie now, not when it was all she had and it had only so recently been given to her. "I will not betray Robert Bruce."

"That is good to hear," he said.

"And when do you plan to leave?"

"In a month or so—after I make fortifications to the south wall. Are ye anxious fer me to go?"

Did she want him to leave? His being at Brodie now, with so much tension between them, was so painful. "I don't know." What she wanted to say was that she wanted their love back.

His stare was hard. "Ye have avoided me this entire day."

She started, unable to look away. She thought about the previous night and said, slowly, "Yes."

He shoved his plate and mug aside, folding his arms on the table. Leaning toward her, he asked, "Why?"

She did not dare accuse him of treating her like a common harlot, did she?

"Why, Alana?"

She wet her lips. "I was not pleased last night."

He sat back, arms crossed. "I recall last night quite differently."

His smirk ignited her as nothing else could. "I am not a harlot, to be used quickly and lightly, and left so easily the next day!"

His eyes remained surprised. Then he began to smile. "So ye needed more than what ye got?"

"Do not leer. You have never spent the night with me sleeping on your side, apart from me! You barely kissed me—we barely touched."

His smile vanished. His cheekbones were tinged with red. "I did not mean to go to ye last night." He spoke low, and leaned close. "But when the time came,

I could not help myself. How can ye blame me fer thinking ye have put a dark love spell on me?"

She gasped. He actually believed she had bewitched him!

He abruptly stood. "If ye dinna want me to come to ye tonight, remove the spell."

She could barely speak. "There is no spell!"

He gave her a dark look and walked over to the fireplace where some of his men stood. He kept his back to her as he was handed wine.

Alana could do nothing but stare, dismayed.

WINTER RETURNED TO the north with a fierce and savage intensity, the snow piling up outside the castle walls almost as high as the crenellations. Iain sent a ransom demand to Duncan, who remained at Elgin. News came that Bruce had fallen ill, and had retreated farther south, where he was Christina MacRuari's guest. Like Angus Og, she remained one of his most powerful allies, but now, rumor held that they were lovers.

Alana took over the management of Brodie with determination, sending men in good weather to Nairn for provisions from the east, while Iain's men spent any fair days hunting, bringing home more venison and boar. The fortifications to the south wall were postponed until the spring.

Alana spent every morning with Godfrey. He was cool, but grew less hateful, and she knew he began to look forward to her visits, no matter what he said. She gave him permission to write to his father, and Alana hoped Duncan would listen to his son's plea and pay the demanded ransom, so he could be freed.

Iain continued to share her chamber—and her bed.

And while their relationship had changed, there were times when Alana slept in his arms, and other times when there was an explosion of passion that neither could stop. On those occasions, she felt like the young girl he had first loved once again.

It was mid-February now. Alana began to worry that she was with child after all. And if she was, whose fault was it? She had not turned Iain away, not a single time.

"You are morose today," Godfrey said.

Alana smiled quickly at him. They were seated side by side in front of the fire in his chamber. "I do not know why we haven't had a reply from your father yet. Maybe you should write the earl."

"Buchan gives even less of a damn about me," Godfrey said harshly, and he stood. "It has been over a month since Brodie fell to Iain. Why haven't you received a communication from either Buchan or your father?"

Alana wet her lips, shifting in her chair so she could look at him. "I have heard Buchan is in the south, plotting the war against Bruce with his allies. My father might be with him."

"Alana, if you are suggesting that neither has heard of your treachery by now, you are mad."

If only their receiving such news was the greatest of her concerns, she thought.

"What is wrong?" Godfrey asked.

She touched her belly. "I'm afraid I am finally with child."

Godfrey paled.

Alana closed her eyes, instantly regretting telling Godfrey such a secret. She still felt terribly over taking Brodie from him, and that he was imprisoned because of her. She still cared about him as a friend, but she did not—and should not—trust him.

"So your lover doesn't know?"

"He doesn't know." She opened her eyes. "Will you tell him?"

"Why would I have to? He will realize it soon enough." Godfrey folded his arms across his chest. "Why won't he marry you, Alana? He is a fourth son, a Highlander, with no lands, no titles, nothing except what Bruce has given him. It is hardly as if he is above you."

She got to her feet. "Bruce wants him to have a great heiress."

"Well, if Bruce wins this war, he will have many great heiresses to choose from. If Bruce loses, and Iain keeps his head and evades capture, he will return to Islay with nothing."

Alana hesitated, feeling cold. "Bruce wants to give him Alice."

"Alice?" It took Godfrey a moment. "Your sister?" He seemed aghast.

"You do not think it rough justice?"

"No. I do not think it justice, not of any kind." Godfrey walked over to her. "Brodie is yours now. Perhaps this would be a good time to find a husband."

"I have been thinking about it, and you are right," Alana whispered. If she was with child, she should marry now and give her child the legitimacy she never had. Bruce had said he would find her a husband—perhaps she should send a letter to him.

Godfrey was staring at her. Alana realized he was saddened, for her—for them.

"Am I interrupting?"

Alana gasped, whirling. Iain stood in the doorway, his gaze sharp. How much had he heard?

He looked back and forth between the two of them, holding an untied but rolled-up parchment in his hand.

"I have heard from Duncan," he said.

Godfrey paled. Alana walked to him and took his hand. "What does he say?"

"He says he is impoverished from this war, and cannot afford the ransom," Iain said, handing him the vellum.

Godfrey realized Alana was holding his hand. He pulled away, taking the parchment, his expression twisted. He walked away from them both to read it.

Alana faced Iain. "You never come up here."

His gaze was hooded. She could not tell what he had heard. "I received the missive and thought Godfrey would wish to know immediately."

Last night, after he had made love to her, she had reached for him, instigating another bout of passion, this one wild and urgent. After he had fallen asleep, she had crept into his arms, sleeping that way for most of the night. "That was kind," she said.

He suddenly tilted up her chin. "Godfrey is right. If Bruce loses this war and I escape with my head, I will run to Islay, very much like a dog with its tail between his legs."

Her pulse pounded. He had clearly overheard the last part of their conversation—but had he heard them speaking of her possible pregnancy? "You would never turn tail and run."

"I beg to differ. Sometimes it is the most clever of actions." His smile faded. His gaze was searching.

Alana turned away. She did not want him looking into her eyes, not now.

Godfrey approached, distraught. "He said he can make payments. He said he will make a quarter payment in the spring. Will you accept that?"

Alana tensed, and Iain glanced at her briefly. "I have no use for ye otherwise, so yes, I will accept payments for yer ransom. But, Godfrey? I will not release ye until the entire ransom has been paid."

Godfrey trembled, handing him the vellum. "You ask a king's ransom."

"Not truly," Iain said. And then he turned to Alana, his expression serious. "Can ye come downstairs with me?"

She was alarmed, terribly so. He had heard that she was with child! "Is something amiss?" she asked with a slight smile.

Unsmiling, he said, "The messenger brought several letters, Alana, and one is from Sir Alexander."

February 11, 1308—Berwick
My Dear Daughter, Alana,
Terrible news has reached us here in the south. We have learned that Iain MacDonald has taken Brodie and commands it, and that he holds Duncan's son hostage. But there is more. Gossips claim that you have sworn fealty to the traitor, Robert Bruce, and have been rewarded with Brodie Castle. I cannot believe it.

My daughter, I know well that we are not close. But that does not mean that you are not in

my heart, always. I am concerned for your welfare now. My brother, Buchan, is furious. We
must put these rumors to rest.

It is said that Bruce is ill, and is the guest of
Christina of the Isles. There will be no war now
until the spring. As I write, Buchan has gone
to Dundee, and I am returning to Balvenie. My
daughter, I am inviting you to join me there, so
we can put an end to these vicious speculations.
As importantly, you can finally meet your sisters, Alice and Margaret, and at long last, we
can be father and daughter for a time, until the
war calls me back.
Sincerely,
Your Father, Sir Alexander Comyn

Alana's hands were shaking as she finished reading
her father's letter. She could not quite breathe, and she
hurried to a chair and sat down.

She was alone in the hall. Iain had left her there to
read the missive in privacy, ordering everyone away.

Sir Alexander had heard of her treachery, and he
did not believe it. But the news was true. And now, he
wanted her to join him at Balvenie. Her sisters would
be there. He would be there.

He wanted to become acquainted with her, finally,
that much was clear!

How could she go? She was a traitor to him, her
uncle and their cause!

"Alana?"

She turned to glimpse Iain standing on the threshold
of the hall. He was concerned. "I am not very well,"
she managed to say.

Iain strode to her. "Ye have finished reading it?"

She nodded and handed it to him. When he had given her the roll, the seal had not been broken. "You may read it if you wish."

He quickly held it open and read the brief missive. Grimacing, he rolled it up and handed it to her. "Ye cannot go. It is a trap."

She leaped to her feet. "What do you say?"

"Yer father entices ye to Balvenie, where ye'll be imprisoned fer treason." He was final.

"I don't believe that! You read the letter. He doesn't believe that I am a traitor and he wants me to meet my sisters!" She was breathless. "I think he wants to get to know me, at last!"

"Since when do ye play the fool?" He was cool. "Yer father is dancing to Buchan's tune. Can ye not see that the earl is behind this?"

Alana gasped, shocked by the suggestion that her father would be inviting her to Balvenie upon the earl's command so she could be seized and captured. It was impossible. "I do not believe that."

He clasped her shoulder. "Alana, why, after all these years, does he wish to see ye? Think!"

She pulled away. "People change, Iain."

"Ye want to go?" He was incredulous.

"I don't know! But I want to know my father better, before he dies! Have you forgotten about my vision? He will die in this war! I want to meet my sisters!"

"At what price, Alana? At the cost of being thrown in a cage like Buchan's wife, fer the rest of yer life?"

She knew Iain was trying to protect her from capture or even death, but she could not believe that if she went to her father, he would hand her over to the earl.

"You're wrong, Iain. My father is not trying to lure me into a trap."

"I forbid ye from going," Iain said. "And that is the end of it."

Alana choked.

"And, Alana?" Iain was now walking away, but he paused. "Yer a traitor. Ye have betrayed the Earl of Buchan and King Edward. So, no matter how yer father entices ye, no matter how ye feel, ye cannot go to yer father, not now, not ever." With that pronouncement, he strode from the hall.

Feeling sick, Alana collapsed upon her chair.

CHAPTER THIRTEEN

"It is very late," Alana said, sitting back against the pillows in the bed she shared with Iain. She held the covers up to her neck as he walked inside, holding aloft a taper. It was close to midnight and most of the castle had gone to sleep hours ago. Outside, an owl hooted.

He shut the door and set the taper down, smiling. "Are ye waiting up fer me?"

She smiled back, her body humming with desire. "I have never been asleep when you have come to bed," she said frankly.

He gave her a look, stoking the fire that continued to burn in the hearth. Then he turned and unbuckled his belt. "Bruce wants to march next month."

Alana stiffened as he tossed aside his belt. "The messenger brought word from Bruce?"

Iain pulled off one boot, then the other. "Aye."

It was the end of February—next month was but days away! "Where will you go? When will you be in battle again?"

He shrugged off his leine, and then stood—magnificently nude—before her. "Bruce has ordered me to march south on the seventh."

He was bathed in the firelight and she had to pause for one moment to admire him. Iain was a mass of hard muscle. "So soon," she said.

"John Mowbray must be brought to heel, once and for all—he is Buchan's best ally here in the north."

Mowbray was a formidable foe, she thought with a sinking sensation. Iain sat down beside her, tugging the furs from her hands. She was naked beneath the covers. "I thought ye'd be pleased," he said, nuzzling her breasts and then tasting a taut nipple.

Alana clasped his shoulders and fought not to close her eyes. "I thought I wanted you gone, as well, so I could have Brodie to myself," she said. He was distracting her to no end, so she reached down and seized him. "I am worried," she whispered.

His eyes gleamed. "Good. Show me how much ye worry, Alana."

She gave him a look and released him, but only to push his shoulders. He obediently went down on his back. Alana came down on top of him. "I will always worry about you," she breathed.

He caught a hank of her hair in his hand and tugged on it. "Witch."

She smiled slightly. "I could wait until you leave, but you must know, I am writing my father."

He groaned. "Fine. Write him if ye must."

Alana bent over him. Using her tongue she laved him; using her fingertips, she stroked him. He gasped and she took him slowly and fully into her mouth.

Within moments, he had flipped her over and was impaling her. "Maybe I'm wrong," he gasped, thrusting deep. "Maybe ye dinna need any spell to control me."

She seized his nape. "This is my spell."

THE NEXT DAY, Alana fanned a page of parchment with her hand, and then blew gently on the wet ink.

She laid the page down and reread what she had written.

February 23, 1308—Brodie Castle
My Dearest Father,
It is my greatest wish that we become closer, as a father and daughter should be, even after so many years of estrangement. And I am eager to meet my sisters. But unfortunately, I cannot come to Balvenie at this time. It is not safe for me to do so.

I pray you will understand, but Brodie Castle belonged to my mother, and it has always meant everything to me. When I was eight years old and Brodie was given to Duncan of Frendraught, it was a terrible blow, one I felt even as a small child. I have dreamed of Brodie being restored to me for my entire life.

I have had to make a terrible choice, and I have paid homage to Bruce. I am mistress of Brodie now.

Father, you have many things in this world. I have one. I am seeking your understanding and I beg your forgiveness. But you must know that as your daughter, I will always be loyal to you, no matter the oath I have taken. I will never raise arms against you.

I am also praying that this war will end soon, so it will not keep us apart.
Sincerely,
Your Daughter, Alana le Latimer, Mistress of Brodie Castle

Alana trembled as she stood up. She had no clue as to whether her father would forgive her or not, or if he would want to see her again. She could only hope the war would end soon, so they would not be on opposing sides—and that her vision of her father's death had been wrong.

Iain stepped into the chamber she was using, a small room behind the hall where Duncan and Godfrey kept their records and made their ledgers. "So ye have written to Sir Alexander." It was not a question.

She faced him, flushing. "I have no more secrets. Do you want to read it before I seal it?"

He eyed her. "'Tis a privy communication, Alana. No."

Alana was pleased. She rolled up the now dry vellum and used hot wax to seal it. She did not have her own seal, and she used the Fitzhugh one, which her mother had used. When she was done, she turned. Iain continued to regard her.

"I have confessed my treachery," she said.

His dark brows lifted.

"And I have asked him for his forgiveness."

His expression hardened. "Even if he forgives ye, Buchan never will. Buchan still wishes execution upon his wife."

"I know. I am afraid of my uncle, Iain, you may be certain." She walked over to him. "When will a messenger be leaving here?"

"I'll send a man today, Alana, because I ken how important this is to ye."

She started in surprise when she suddenly felt moisture between her thighs.

"What is it?" he asked quickly.

Could she be bleeding? Was it possible? As she turned her back on Iain, a terrible cramp seized her. She doubled over, crying out and clutching her abdomen.

Iain wrapped her in his arms as she fought her way through the terrible pain. And then it was gone. Alana did not need to look to know that her monthly had come, at last. But she had missed three entire months.

"What just happened?" Iain asked tersely.

Alana turned in his arms to look at him when another cramp knifed through her. She cried out more loudly, her knees buckling, hanging on to Iain to keep from falling. This pain was longer and stronger and she had to fight to survive it. Sweat poured down her body and more moisture trickled down her thighs.

"Yer bleeding!" Iain exclaimed.

The pain was receding and Alana looked down and saw a small puddle of blood on the floor. A new pain began—it was heartache. "I am losing our child," she said.

THE CRAMPING LASTED for the afternoon. When it finally ended, Alana closed her eyes against burning tears, hugging a pillow to her breasts, and she fell asleep in numb exhaustion.

She awoke because the chamber was too warm. Blinking, she saw a fire roaring in the hearth as Iain stood before it. Eleanor sat in a chair beside her bed. Her grandmother took her hand and squeezed it, asking, "How do you feel?"

Iain whipped around and strode over to them.

For one moment, Alana looked blankly at her, and then, with growing dread, at Iain. *She had lost their child.*

She knew she should not weep—she should be relieved. But she was heartbroken. Why? Why had this happened?

"You will be fine, Alana. You lost blood, but nothing unusual, considering this was your third month," Eleanor said, stroking her hair.

"I do not feel fine," Alana whispered.

"Why dinna ye tell me?" Iain cried.

"Bruce wishes for you to marry a great heiress!" she said.

"What does that have to do with my son?" he shouted back.

Alana leaned back into the pillows, crying. "Everything," she whispered.

He stared at her, in anger, in anguish. "At least ye will be fine," he said finally.

Alana shook her head. "No. I will not be fine."

ALANA AWOKE, the chamber in darkness. For one moment, she did not recall her miscarriage, and then when she did, misery and grief washed over her. She lay back against her pillows, tears filling her eyes.

She saw a tall shadow standing by the hearth. It was Iain, she realized, and his back was to her.

She felt more grief. She vaguely recalled his anger the other day—or had it been that same day, but earlier? She did not know how long she had been asleep. She did not know if hours had passed since her miscarriage, or if it had been days.

BRENDA JOYCE 303

Iain turned to face her. The fire was behind him, and his face was in shadow. "Are ye awake?"

She nodded, not having the strength or will to speak.

He slowly approached. As he came closer, she could finally see his grim expression. Their gazes met. "Are ye in any pain, Alana?"

"No."

A strange silence fell, broken only by the occasional hiss of the fire as a log fell apart. "Ye should have told me ye were with child," he finally said.

More tears burned her eyelids. "I am tired," she finally said.

"I cannot understand why ye dinna tell me."

Alana wanted to discuss what had happened, but she did not have the strength to do so. Besides, he might marry her sister Alice one day. Wasn't that the real reason she hadn't said anything? She did not have the desire to speak of her sister and his future marriage. Not now.

He grimaced, realizing she was not about to speak. "I'll tell Eleanor yer awake," he said. "She has been with ye all night, and she went to rest."

"Let her rest."

Briefly, the light illuminated his face and she could see anguish in his eyes. But then he was in shadow again, and she wasn't certain that she hadn't imagined his grief. "Someone needs to sit with ye."

"I am tired," Alana said again. Somehow, Iain had become a stranger. In the past, she had always welcomed his presence; now, she wished him gone.

She closed her eyes and rolled onto her side, hoping he would leave.

For a moment, there was no sound in the chamber, except for the fire. Then she heard his heavy footsteps as he walked away, followed by the sound of the door opening and closing.

She choked on a rising sob.

LARKS WERE SINGING madly from the pair of oak trees just outside the castle walls. A soft, pleasant breeze had taken the chill off the morning, as had the sun, which was trying to peek through the clouds, hinting at blue skies and the coming spring. But Alana did not feel any joy as she stared across the busy courtyard. She did not feel any warmth. The winter had been long and hard, and even devastating, but she remained numb and indifferent to the pleasant day now. She stood upon the front steps of the hall, a wool mantle about her shoulders, woodenly watching as Iain mounted his warhorse. His knights milled about him, already mounted and ready to ride out.

It March 7. Iain was returning to war.

Tears filled her eyes. She had lost their child two weeks ago. What if she lost him, too?

She had been crying at the oddest moments, quite suddenly, ever since the miscarriage. Alana knew she was grieving. She was suffering from melancholia. It was as if a heavy fog of pain weighed her down. She could not sleep at night, tormented by thoughts of her unborn child, or by dreams of a beautiful baby boy. It was so difficult getting up in the morning. Even the most mundane tasks and chores were hard to perform. She could barely lift her arm to brush her hair, and she had no appetite. She was becoming unattractively thin.

But now, for the first time since the miscarriage, she felt fear as she watched Iain astride his dark warhorse.

Iain was going back to war. She had almost seen him murdered once, at Boath Manor. And she had had that vision of her uncle preparing to deliver a blow with his sword from behind, a blow that appeared as if it would kill him. Her alarm increased.

"Iain?" she whispered.

It was as if she had lost her voice, her whisper was so low, so rough, and he could not have heard her, but he turned his mount sharply to face her.

She inhaled as, from across the courtyard, their eyes met.

Iain had barely spoken to her during the past two weeks. She did not know if he was angry because she had lost the child, or because she had not told him about her condition—another deception on her part. She had been relieved that he hadn't tried to share her bed—he had taken a different room—or tried to make love to her.

He had checked on her once or twice a day, politely asking how she was feeling each time. Her answers had always been the same. Short, brief—she did not want him to linger with her. So she had told him she was fine.

But she wasn't fine and they both knew it.

And now he was leaving to attack Sir John Mowbray.

Why hadn't they spoken of the lost child? Of his anger? Of her pain? Of Alice and the future?

Alana suddenly went down the steps. As she did, he rode over to her. She wanted to tell him that she was so sorry, for everything—she wanted to beg him to stay safe.

His face was set and grim. "I have left ye with twenty good men, and they have orders to keep ye safe."

"Thank you." Shouldn't they talk about what had happened now? "Iain?"

He had been lifting his reins to turn his mount back around. But he settled it, his stare hard and intense.

What should she say? "Are we in danger, here?"

Relief flitted through his eyes. "I dinna think Brodie is in danger, not when the fighting is to the south. Buchan and Duncan have gone to defend Mowbray, so they cannot attack ye here."

"My uncle doesn't care about Brodie."

"Buchan is a man who thirsts for revenge. He will want revenge, Alana, upon ye."

She grimaced. She did not want to discuss Buchan now! "Iain, I am so sorry. I should have told you about the child."

He stiffened. "Aye, ye should have. Ye kept another secret from me—that ye carried my child!"

"I am sorry...so sorry!"

His gaze was hard, anguish in its shadows. "It's finished now."

"I am so sorry I lost our child." Tears ran down her face.

"'Tis not yer fault, Alana. God has His ways." He was harsh. "I must go. Send word if there is danger."

He was leaving—and they were at such odds! "Iain, you must stay safe!" She laid her hands on his bare knee. "You must come home to me!" Pain stabbed through her. "I cannot lose you, too."

"I am a warrior, Alana, and one day, God willing, I

will die by the sword, with great courage and greater honor. But that day is not today."

She was not comforted. "Beware, Iain, always."

He studied her and lifted his reins. "Do not do anything foolish while I am gone." He whirled his horse and he and his men began trotting from the courtyard and through the entry tower, and out the castle gates.

Feeling so sick in her heart, so frightened, Alana stepped back, hugging the mantle she wore to her chest. "Go, Iain," she said hoarsely. "Go with God."

He gave her a last look, and cantered after his men.

Alana did not move, watching him vanish into the vault beneath the entry tower. She heard his horse's thundering hoofbeats as he galloped through the castle gates. The sound receded—and vanished.

He was gone.

Alana turned slowly and saw Eleanor upon the top step, her expression openly worried. She slowly went up.

Eleanor put her arm around her. "He will be fine, Alana. He is a very good warrior."

"He will not be fine if Buchan murders him." Choking on her words, Alana walked into the hall with Eleanor. "We have hardly spoken since I lost the child, and now he is gone."

"He loves you, Alana," Eleanor said.

"Does he?" She went to the fire and stood there, thinking about Iain, whom she still loved in spite of her grief over the loss of their child. "He is angry."

"He is grieving, Alana, as you are. It will pass."

"But I kept another secret, Gran."

Eleanor sighed. "Trust me, Alana. This is a difficult time. But the sun will shine again."

Alana hoped she was right.

Eleanor took her silence for acquiescence. "At least you have the will to be up and about. That is a good sign. Do you want to help me in the kitchens?"

Alana had spent the days since her miscarriage by herself, in her chamber, consumed with her grief. Her back hurt and she rubbed her spine. "How is Godfrey?"

"He has been asking for you. I have been visiting him in your stead. I told him what happened."

Alana straightened. "He hardly needs to remain locked up now." How firm she sounded!

Eleanor paled. "Alana, are you certain?"

"I am certain," she said. She was suddenly filled with purpose. Godfrey was not her prisoner—he was Iain's. And she had never approved of his being taken prisoner when Brodie had surrendered. She walked swiftly upstairs.

A tall, blond Highlander she recognized but did not know by name stood outside Godfrey's door. She forced a smile and he smiled in return, unbolting the door and opening it for her.

"Thank you," Alana said, inflecting her words to pose them as a question.

"Seoc, my lady."

Godfrey was standing at his window. He whirled and stared. "Are you all right?"

"I will manage," she said. She prayed she would not start crying now.

"I heard you lost the child," he said grimly. "When you did not come to see me, I demanded to know what had happened to you."

"I have been sick with grief," she said. She could

barely get the words out. "I know I should not be aggrieved. I know I have no right to bring a bastard into the world. But when the time came, I desperately wanted my child."

"Alana!" Godfrey hurried to her and took her arm. "I would have given that child a name."

Alana collapsed in his arms. He held her and did not speak, stroking her hair. "I am so sorry," he whispered. "I wanted to come see you. Iain would not hear of it."

She looked up at him. *Godfrey would have married her, for her child's sake. Godfrey had wanted to see her.* "I do not deserve your friendship."

He brushed hair from her cheek and eyes. "No, you do not." He stepped away from her.

She had betrayed him—returning to Brodie with an army, demanding he surrender, and never telling him that if he did, she would become Brodie's mistress.

"Will you forgive me, for all I have done?" She stepped away, aware now that the Highland lad outside the door was watching them closely.

"Do you mean for stealing Brodie from me and my father? How can I forgive you for that?" He glanced at Seoc.

Alana stared at his back. Then she turned. "Seoc, leave us."

"My lady, Iain has told me to keep a close eye on the prisoner."

She felt a sudden outrage. How welcome the feelings were. "I am mistress here."

He paled. "Aye, my lady."

"Iain is lord of Nairn—not of Brodie." She squared her shoulders, filled with sheer resolve. "Brodie belonged to my mother, it was her dowry. Now, it is my dowry—King Robert has said so. I swore fealty to him on bended knee, with no weapons in my hands, and for my oath, he has given me Brodie."

The Highlander was white.

"Leave us," Alana ordered.

He nodded and hurried away.

Godfrey began to smile. "Spoken like a true queen... well done."

She whirled. "Godfrey." Her mind raced, her thoughts jumbled, and the one thing she knew clearly was that Iain would disapprove if she simply released Godfrey. But she could not keep him as *her* prisoner, either. She crossed her arms as they stared at one another now. "You have been imprisoned in this room for almost two months," she finally said. "I never expected Iain to hold you prisoner. We had never discussed your fate, when we came to take Brodie. I will not keep you locked up in this chamber, now that he is gone. You have my permission to come and go as you please, as you used to do."

Godfrey started.

"You can hardly escape on foot, with no weapons and no supplies," Alana said. "In fact, it is such a pleasant day, why don't we walk together?"

Godfrey nodded, his face pale, his eyes wide. Alana took his fur-lined cloak from a wall peg and handed it to him; the nights were still cold. They left the chamber and saw that Seoc sat on a stool outside the door, sharpening his dagger. She assumed he had been eavesdropping. He did not look at them now.

Alana was angry. Was she in command or not? Did

Iain truly mean to spy on her? He did not trust her? They went downstairs and did not speak until they were outside.

"What do you think to do, Alana?" Godfrey asked, speaking low.

"You are free, Godfrey!"

"You are freeing me?"

"I am in your debt, many times over. And I have hated seeing you imprisoned here. This is your chance—take a horse from the stables and go!"

"You will let me run away?"

"Yes!"

He halted, reaching for her arm. "Will Iain forgive you for this?"

"I don't know if he will forgive me for not telling him about our child, Godfrey—I cannot worry about his reaction to your escape. But you cannot remain here, a prisoner because of my treachery, when I never agreed to taking you prisoner in the first place."

After a moment, he said, "If I am going to escape, I will need to plan it. I will need a dagger at the least."

"I can get you a dagger. If you leave now, Godfrey, you will be at Elgin by the late afternoon."

He hesitated. "I don't think I should leave you," he said. "If you mean to let me escape, then I have time."

THE DAYS PASSED slowly as they waited for news of the war. There were rumors that King Edward was sending an army to the north to aid Buchan, even as Buchan's allies were deserting him. There were whispers that Mortloch had been attacked. Spring finally came in full force, chasing the last of the patches of snow away. Wildflowers began to bloom, thistle came to life, the oaks turned green. And finally a messenger came with real news—Mowbray had concluded a truce with Bruce before any real fighting could begin. So Bruce had attacked Sir Roger Cheyne at Mortloch; those rumors were true. Mortloch had fallen in a day, and Bruce was marching toward Balvenie.

The messenger also carried a letter for Alana— from Iain.

She practically tore it open. But Iain only wished for her to know that the war was going well for Bruce, and that he was also well; he asked after her health, and promised to write again soon.

Alana was shocked to have received such a brief and impersonal missive. She was afraid that her worst fears had come true—that Iain no longer cared about her. She was ready to burn the letter in the hearth, not in anger, but out of despair. Godfrey restrained her.

"He does not seem like a man of letters, Alana…. Do you even know if he can write?" Godfrey asked.

"He can read."

"He may be able to read, a little, but that does not mean he can write. And even if he can, I cannot imagine him penning a love letter." Godfrey took the letter from her and scanned it. "I do not think he wrote this— I cannot even read the signature, which looks like an *I* and a *Y,* while the rest of the letter is perfectly penned."

Alana took the parchment back and stared at the beautiful cursive and the crude signature. Godfrey was right. Iain had dictated the letter, and only then had he signed it. She did not burn the letter.

The news brought a terrible pall to the castle. Iain would never express his personal feelings in a letter, she decided, but his failure to do so was hurtful, anyway. She feared that her miscarriage—and her deception—had ended their relationship. She wondered if he still cared about her at all.

And Alana was agonizingly aware that Sir Alexander remained at Balvenie, finalizing its defenses. Images kept returning to her now, of her vision of her father's bloody corpse. Iain had forbidden her from going to Balvenie, and he had been right. Only a fool would have walked into the jaws of the enemy. Going to Balvenie had been too dangerous then, and doing so now remained as dangerous. She was Bruce's vassal after all. But Alana was afraid she might not see her father again. She was tempted to go.

Were her sisters and Joan at Balvenie, even as Bruce prepared to besiege it?

She had told Godfrey of her vision, and he insisted she must not even think of going to Balvenie. Sir Alexander would need help to defend it from Bruce. Not only was Robert Bruce beginning to appear invincible, he was becoming popular. Every village he passed through was turning to take his side, and his army was growing by leaps and bounds. Buchan could show up at Balvenie at any time to aid his brother in its defense. And they both knew that if she was there when he returned, she would instantly be taken prisoner.

But Alana was torn, and she was not convinced. She felt an urgency to see Sir Alexander now.

Although he never spoke of it, Godfrey was restless and grim. She knew he was as torn as she was, but for different reasons. Duncan had left Elgin to see to Banf's defenses, and while Godfrey did not want to leave her at Brodie, so close to the war, it was his duty to join his father in the fight against Bruce. She knew he yearned to be at his father's side now.

On March 28 it snowed again, but the snow had melted by nightfall, when a second messenger was found hiding in the woods.

Alana was in the hall with Godfrey and Eleanor, about to sup, when Angus escorted a man inside. She instantly tensed, for the man wore English mail over a doublet and jerkin. As Angus dragged him toward her, she saw that his hands were manacled in front of his body. "My lady, we found this English dog in the woods, hiding. He claims he is not a spy, but a messenger." He shoved the man to his knees. "Show proper respect, dog."

"Angus!" She leaped up. Such a messenger had to come from her uncle or her father. "Who has sent you?" Alana hurried forward. "Or are you a spy, indeed?"

Still on his knees, the man looked up. He was grizzled and gray. "I come from Balvenie. I have a missive from Sir Alexander Comyn for his daughter, Mistress le Latimer."

"I am Mistress le Latimer," Alana cried.

"Rise," Angus said harshly, "and give the letter to my lady."

The man stood, clearly relieved that he still had his head, and handed Alana a rolled-up parchment. Alana felt her heart thundering. The image of her father as a bloody corpse flashed through her mind. She feared terrible news. "Is my father well?" she asked. "Is Balvenie under siege?"

"The castle is under siege, my lady, but when I left, your father was well."

She could barely breathe. "Are his daughters and his wife with him? Is Buchan there?"

"The earl has not yet returned to Balvenie, but yes, Lady Joan and her daughters are with Sir Alexander."

So the family had gathered at Balvenie. She suddenly imagined how the hall must appear, with the women of the castle cowering there in fear as the siege engines rammed the gates, as catapults rocked the castle walls. She could imagine Joan there, an elegant and well-dressed lady, comforting her frightened daughters.... She broke the seal and unrolled the parchment.

The message was brief.

March 27, 1308—Balvenie
My Daughter,
We are under siege. I await reinforcements and my brother's arrival, but fear the strength of Bruce's army. Even more, I fear for my wife and daughters. If we are defeated, I will be executed as a traitor, but they will become Bruce's hostages.

I was pleased to hear your vows of loyalty to me. I must send my wife and your sisters to Brodie, immediately. Can you hide them until I can arrange for their transport to the south or possibly to England? They must not fall into Bruce's hands.

I eagerly await your reply.
Your Father, Sir Alexander Comyn

Shaking, Alana sat down hard on the bench by her grandmother.

"Alana?" Godfrey asked.

She did not hear him, and looked instead at the messenger. "You are to return to Balvenie at once. Tell my father that I will do as he asks." She stood. "Lady Joan and my sisters will be safe here."

CHAPTER FOURTEEN

THE WOMEN ARRIVED at midnight.

Alana was expecting them. Her father's messenger had told her that Sir Alexander intended to send them to Brodie the moment he received word from her.

Alana held up a taper as the three women were escorted into the hall. Alana stared intently, but all three women wore their hoods.

Then she turned to Angus. She had sent him with six other soldiers to fetch the women. "Were there any problems?"

"No, my lady. We waited safely in the woods while Sir Percy took your answer to Sir Alexander. It took but an hour for the women to steal from the castle, using an underground tunnel. No one saw us."

"Thank you," Alana breathed, touching his arm. "Why don't you get some rest?"

As Angus and his men left, the smallest woman removed her hood. She was in her mid-thirties, strikingly fair, with very dark hair. Lady Joan stared at Alana. "I suppose I owe you a great debt." She did not smile and her blue eyes were hard and cold.

"You owe me nothing." Alana smiled, but as she spoke, she thought about how Joan had insisted her father have nothing to do with her when she was born. "I am Mistress Alana le Latimer."

"Even if we had met in different circumstances," Joan said, refusing to smile, "I would know who you are. You look exactly like my cousin Elisabeth."

Alana did not know if she was receiving a compliment, as clearly, Joan did not like her. Either that, or she was very angry. "This is Lady Fitzhugh," she said, gesturing to her grandmother, who came forward. "And Sir Godfrey, Duncan's son."

Joan nodded at Lady Fitzhugh and Godfrey.

Eleanor inclined her head. "You have hardly changed in the past twenty years, Lady Joan."

"Actually, I have changed a great deal," Joan said, glancing at Alana again.

Alana was now filled with tension. She realized she must be a constant reminder of her father's love for another woman during their betrothal. If Joan did not hate her, it was clear that she disliked her intensely.

"You could be mistaken for one of your daughters," Eleanor said with a smile.

Finally, Joan's expression eased. Her daughters were taking off their cloaks. Alana stared at the two young women, who stared as unwaveringly back.

Margaret was slender, blonde, not even sixteen and terribly beautiful. She was blushing as their gazes met, her eyes wide and curious. Alice stood beside her, holding her hand tightly, her expression frozen. She was fair-skinned, dark-haired and very attractive, as well. In fact, Alana felt a frisson of shock as she stared at Alice, for it was almost like gazing into a mirror. Their coloring and features were so similar—no one would ever mistake them for anything but sisters.

Dismay flooded her. Iain would find her very attractive, she thought. And she was Buchan's heir.

Godfrey touched her elbow as if to steady her. Alana was so grateful for his presence.

"As you know, these are Sir Alexander's daughters, Lady Alice and Lady Margaret," Joan said tersely.

Alana was acutely aware that Joan had referred to them as if they were Sir Alexander's only daughters, but it did not matter. They were her sisters. She did not know what to think or feel. Her sisters had been raised by her father in grand castles and fine halls, and they had had everything; she had been raised as an unwanted ward by a man who had molested her. Iain might marry Alice, who was a great heiress, when Alana loved him so—when she had nothing but Brodie. She was relieved that they were safe, but there was dismay in her heart, too, and even, perhaps, jealousy.

Why had Sir Alexander abandoned her?

She must not think of the differences in their lives now. "Welcome to Brodie," she said. "I am so relieved that you have escaped the siege at Balvenie." That much was true.

It was a moment before Alice spoke. "Thank you for giving us refuge," she said. Her gaze quickly moved over Alana from head to toe, before jerking back up. She flushed.

"I could not refuse," Alana said hoarsely. Alice was as interested in assessing her as Alana was. "We do not know one another, but we are sisters."

Alice seemed distraught, as well. Alana wondered if their expressions were as identical as their features. The tension between them felt impossible.

Margaret exclaimed, "Father only told us about you recently. What a surprise it was!" Margaret seemed excited by the fact that they were sisters, and Alana felt a moment of surprising warmth in her heart.

"He told us very recently," Alice said harshly.

The warm feeling vanished. "It must have been a shock." If Bruce lost the war, Alice would be the Countess of Buchan one day. And Alana would lose Brodie....

"Yes," Alice said tersely. "I had no notion that I had a half sister in the world."

"I know this is difficult."

"Do you?" Alice cried.

Alana felt like shouting back that this was as difficult for her, too. She had been abandoned by their father, she had been raised with nothing, and all she had was Brodie Castle and a lover who wished to marry her sister! "I am sorry," she said again.

Joan stepped between them. "My daughters are exhausted. It is very late, and they would like to go to their chamber. But I would like a private word with you."

Alana could not imagine what Joan wished to discuss with her. "Gran, could you show my sisters to their chamber?"

"Of course," Eleanor said. She smiled at the girls.

Margaret smiled back and turned to Alana. "I hope we can speak tomorrow, Alana."

She wondered if they would become friends. "I will make a point of it. Good night."

Margaret hesitated, then impulsively hugged Alana. Alice nodded, and Eleanor and the two girls left. Alana was stunned by Margaret's display of affection.

"Margaret is very young, and she is also naive,"

Joan said, clearly disapproving of her daughter's spon-
taneous outburst.

Godfrey glanced at her. Joan was clearly waiting
for him to leave, and Alana decided she did not want
to be alone with her father's wife. "Godfrey is privy
to all my secrets," she said.

"Really?" Joan was cool. "Was he privy to the secret that you pledged your fealty to Bruce? And that
you meant to take Brodie from him?"

Alana flushed. "Brodie belonged to my mother, as
you well know. It should have always been mine, and
I took back what belonged to me."

"You look exactly like Elisabeth, so why am I surprised by all that you have done? My cousin was ca-
pable of many things, so many things, to serve her own
self-interest, that she probably would have gone over
to the enemy, too."

Alana flinched. "My mother would not have had
to swear fealty to the enemy," she said tersely. "My
mother was mistress of Brodie Castle. She had lands,
a title, a husband. I did what I had to in order to get
my lands back."

Joan's eyes widened. "So you are too clever for your
own good. You think to speak back to me?"

"I beg your pardon," Alana instantly said. Joan was
her enemy, unfortunately, that much was clear. However, she was her father's wife and Alana had no wish
to fight openly with her. "I did not invite you to take
sanctuary here so we could argue. It is my wish to help
my father and my sisters, Lady Joan. It is my wish to
help you."

"Is it? I do not trust you, Mistress Alana. You betrayed us all—Alexander, myself, our daughters, Buchan and King Edward!"

"If you do not trust me, then why are you here?" She was beginning to regret having offered Joan and her sisters sanctuary.

"I did not want to come. I wanted to attempt to flee to England directly! But Balvenie is under siege, and such a journey was too difficult to quickly arrange. Alexander had no men to spare. He insisted we come here."

"If you wish to go to England immediately, I will attempt to arrange it."

"The sooner, the better." She turned and glanced at Godfrey. "You do not look like a prisoner."

Godfrey folded his arms, unperturbed. "I have known Alana since we were small children. I am not deserting her in a time of war."

Joan laughed with contempt. "Oh, God! Alexander was smitten with her mother, and you are smitten with her. And what of her lover?"

Alana froze, actually feeling the blood drain from her face. "What?"

Joan whirled. "The gossip is rampant, Alana. Everyone knows you are sleeping with Iain of Islay."

She swallowed hard. "And you believe the gossip?"

"Of course I do—not because he was at Brodie all winter long, but because you are your mother's daughter."

She felt as if she had been stabbed. "And my father?"

"He refuses to believe it—but he refused to believe that you had taken an oath of fealty to Bruce, too. Your confession sent him into his cups."

Alana walked away from her. She felt defeated. Joan had hated her mother and Joan hated her, but worse, Joan was making her feel ashamed.

"Will he come back here?" Joan demanded. "Are we in danger from Iain MacDonald? Will you protect us from him?"

Alana faced her. "I promised my father I would keep you safe, and I mean to do just that."

Joan stared searchingly now, with fear. "We must go to England as soon as possible," she finally said. "Before Iain learns we are here, before Bruce hears of it."

Alana nodded. Joan was afraid of being taken captive. In spite of her hostility, Alana felt sorry for her then.

"I am going to retire with my daughters," Joan said. "Good night."

Alana did not speak, watching her leave. Godfrey got up and walked over as she vanished from their sight. Alana began to shake.

"Well, she certainly hates your mother," Godfrey said.

"She hates me."

"Yes, that is obvious. Alana, what will you do if Iain appears here? I am fairly certain that, if he hears you are harboring Lady Joan and his daughters, he will attempt to take them all captive."

Alana stared in dismay. She did not want to add to the conflict between them, but she had promised her father that she would keep his wife and her sisters safe. "Let's hope they are gone before he finds out."

A MAID HAD stoked the fire in her hearth so it was roaring. Alana stood before it, clad for bed in a long linen shift, her hair in two braids. The sooner she sent Joan and her daughters to England, the better, she thought. Joan despised her and Alice was hostile, as well. At least Margaret was friendly.

A knock sounded on her door. Alana tensed. After the terrible interview with Joan, she did not know who or what to expect. She went apprehensively to the door and opened it.

Margaret stood there, clad in a sleeping gown, her long blond hair in a single braid. She smiled shyly. "I couldn't sleep. Can I come in?"

"Of course," Alana said, surprised. She stepped aside and Margaret hurried in. She sat down on the bed, tucking her legs beneath her.

"You are so beautiful!" Margaret exclaimed.

Alana sat down next to her. "So are you."

"You look so much like Alice, but you are the prettier one," Margaret exclaimed.

"I doubt that," Alana said, suddenly thinking again about the fact that Alice was a great heiress, and that Bruce was interested in marrying her to Iain. How the notion sickened her. "Alice is beautiful…and she is a great heiress."

"Yes. One day, she will be the Countess of Buchan. Even if Bruce fights this war for years, Father advised her to never give up her rights to the earldom."

Alana flinched. Did that mean that Alice would seek to claim the Buchan lands, even if Bruce defeated her uncle? Even if he defeated King Edward and remained King of Scotland? Slowly, she said, "She is his true and only heir."

"Yes." Margaret studied her frankly. "I was so excited to learn that we had a sister, Alana. Of course, I hate this war, and I am afraid for Father, being at Balvenie while it is besieged. But I was eager to meet you—and when he said we must come here, I was pleased."

Alana knew that neither Joan nor Alice had been pleased, and she remained silent.

Margaret took her hand. "I hope you can forgive my mother. She cannot accept that you are Father's daughter. She has said so. She told us that, once, she and your mother were friends. She felt betrayed when she learned that your mother loved the man she meant to marry."

Alana was grim. "It is hard to blame her. What about Alice? She doesn't like me, either."

"Alice did not want to come here. She did not want to meet you," Margaret said. Her blue eyes held Alana's. "She is still upset that our father was with another woman, even if it was before his marriage to Mother."

"I would probably be upset, too," Alana said.

"I'm not upset. It was so long ago. I think it's wonderful that I have another sister!" Margaret grinned. Then her smile faded. "Alice is a wonderful sister. Truly. I pray you will become friends soon. But...we are on opposite sides of this war."

Alana hesitated. "Margaret, maybe if you try, you could understand. My mother died when I was born, and I was raised by Lady Fitzhugh, who isn't even my blood grandmother. And because I am illegitimate, I had no status here, or anywhere else. Brodie was my mother's, but it was given to Duncan, who was also made my guardian. I have grown up a bastard with no means and no dowry; you have grown up with everything, including two parents who love you. We are on opposite sides of this war because I found a way to get

Brodie back. But you are my sister, and I will do everything in my power to keep you safe from my liege lord, and to get you to England."

"I am so glad we are sisters," Margaret said, squeezing her hand. She then yawned and stood up. "Mother doesn't trust you, but I do. And I hope we do not leave too soon!"

Alana stood, smiling. "I hope so, too. That way, we can become better acquainted."

Margaret hugged her impulsively. "I am suddenly tired. I had better go back to bed before I am discovered."

Alana walked her to the door, joy filling her heart. "Suddenly I am tired, too," she said, and hugged her youngest sister in return.

"How can we get them safely to England?" Alana asked tersely.

It was the next morning. The sun was high, but she was alone at the table in the hall with Godfrey. Her guests had yet to arrive, and Eleanor was sleeping late, as she had begun to do recently.

"You cannot spare any men." Godfrey was final.

Alana began shaking her head. "They are frightened. Having been a prisoner, I do not blame them. Bruce is at Balvenie—why can't I spare a dozen soldiers?"

Godfrey reached across the table and took her hand. "I am afraid that your uncle would seize the opportunity to attack you, Alana."

The Earl of Buchan might or might not be able to march on Brodie, and she did not want to take a chance that the former might happen. "They cannot wait out

this war here. Iain will learn of their presence—so
will Bruce. Alice would be a valuable hostage." And
it would be worse than that—she could then become
Iain's wife. If Bruce wished it, she would not be given
a choice.

"I would go to Banf and speak with my father but
he will not want to spare any men, either."

Alana's mind raced. "It would probably be too dangerous to send them with a guide, in disguise."

Godfrey gave her an incredulous look.

"So we will remain here—very much as if we are
prisoners?"

Alana leaped to her feet, whirling at the sound of
Alice's voice. Her sister stood on the threshold of the
room, her face starkly pale. Clearly, she had been
eavesdropping.

"You are not prisoners," Alana said.

"If there is a choice," Alice said, coming forward,
"then I would flee south in disguise as farm women
with a single guide."

"That would be terribly dangerous!"

Alice's eyes were wide. "And why would you care?
Because we are sisters?"

"I would care because we are sisters," Alana said.
"And I promised Sir Alexander to keep you safe."

"Even as you went over to the enemy—even as you
bed the enemy," Alice said harshly.

So her sister had heard the gossip, too. She squared
her shoulders. "Unlike you, I am a bastard, and had no
hopes of ever marrying."

Alice folded her arms across her chest. "And that
justifies your becoming Iain of Islay's lover? That justifies your treachery to our family?"

"Brodie was a part of my mother's dowry, Alice. It should have never been taken away from me."

"Of course it should—you are illegitimate, and you could not inherit Brodie!"

Alana trembled. "You will never understand—you have everything, Alice. But Brodie is mine, now."

"So you are pleased? So you wish for Bruce to triumph over our father?"

"I am in a terrible position," Alana cried.

"So you do wish for Bruce's victory—for Iain of Islay's victory!" Alice accused.

"I fell in love with him!" Alana said, feeling her own cheeks warm.

"The way your mother fell in love with my father?" Alice snapped. "Is that why you swore your fealty to Bruce? Out of love for the enemy?"

"No! I did it for Brodie."

They stared at one another. Alice's gaze was hard, but searching.

"Finally, I have a dowry, Alice," Alana said harshly.

Alice shook her head, her expression taut with disapproval. "So you will marry Iain MacDonald?"

Alana shook her head. If only Alice knew of Bruce's plans for her and Iain! "He will be awarded an heiress, one greater than me. But Bruce promised to find me a husband."

"Of course he did," Alice said. She paused a moment, then, "I cannot trust you." She turned abruptly and marched from the room.

Alana closed her eyes in dismay.

IT WAS DUSK the following day when the bell in the watchtower began ringing. Alana was in her chamber, braiding her hair, when she heard the alarm. She dropped her comb and ran into the corridor. As she did, Lady Joan appeared, her face white with fright, Alice and Margaret crowded behind her, everyone in their nightclothes.

Godfrey came racing up the stairs. "Iain has returned," he said.

Blanching, Joan gave Alana an incredulous look, while Alice stared in accusation. And then Joan and her two daughters fled into their chamber, slamming the door closed.

Alana was in shock. Her heart thundering, she gasped, "Are you certain?"

"Very," Godfrey said, his expression grim.

Alana ran past him, filled with disbelief—with excitement. Iain had returned! But as she ran barefoot downstairs, doubt began. She did not know how Iain felt about her now. Her first impulse was to believe he had come home to see her, but what if he had heard about Lady Joan and Alana's sisters? Had he come to take them prisoner?

Her steps slowed as she reached the ground floor. She remained thrilled that he had returned, in spite of her promise to protect Joan and her sisters. The front door flew open and Iain strode in. His hair was longer now, and disheveled, tangling about his shoulders. His face was hard, his jaw covered with a growth of beard. Their gazes instantly locked.

Alana halted, filled with apprehension; his eyes blazed. Very aggressively, he strode to her.

He pulled her hard into his embrace, his mouth covering hers. Alana went still, shocked by his fierce passion and the explosion of desire within her. His tongue thrust deep as his mouth claimed hers.

Alana finally flung her arms around his shoulders and kissed him wildly back.

And when he broke the kiss, he said, "I have missed ye."

Tears arose. Before she could respond, he lifted her into his arms and carried her upstairs. Alana clung to him and kissed his grizzled jaw. "I have missed you, too."

"Good." He strode into her room, kicked the door closed and laid her on the bed, coming down on top of her.

Alana reached for the hem of his leine. "Your swords," she said.

"To hell with them," he said harshly, spreading her legs with his knee. He jerked up her clothing, his mouth on hers, their tongues entwined. Alana became so hollow she felt faint. He drove hard into her.

And they mated as if it were the first time—blinded by desire, by lust. But unlike the first time, Alana was overcome with love.

When the pleasure and ecstasy had faded, when they were sated and exhausted, Alana lay in his arms, beyond relief. Iain kissed her shoulder, her temple, her hair.

She shifted so she could look up at him. "I am so sorry I lost our baby," she whispered.

"Shh," he said. "We will make another one soon enough."

It felt as if he meant that he wished to remain with her, and be a father to her child—but that was impossible, wasn't it? She wanted to cry. She clasped his rough cheek instead. "I wish I had told you about the child."

"I ken ye dinna keep yer secret to be malicious, Alana." He kissed her temple. "Ye should have told me, but yer too independent fer yer own good."

He had forgiven her for her deception! She clasped his jaw. "I also regret not sharing my heartache with you when we lost the child. We could have mourned him together."

"Ye were grieving. So was I. I could not think straight." He kissed her hand and studied her for a moment.

Alana was so relieved. Somehow, they had put this tragedy behind them.

Iain then grimaced, and rolled away from her, onto his back.

Alana adjusted her clothing, glancing at his face. He stared seriously up at the ceiling now. As he slowly turned to look at her, she thought, *He knows about Lady Joan and her sisters.*

He sat up. "Were ye planning to tell me about yer sisters and Lady Joan?"

Alana rose to sit as her heart sank. "I promised my father I would keep them safe," she said carefully. "It is my duty to keep them safe."

"Aye, but ye dinna answer me, Alana."

She shook her head. "No. I was not going to tell you."

He grimaced and stood, hands on his hips. "Yer a difficult woman," he said. "Yer too independent, Alana."

She stared up at him. "How angry are you?"

"I'm not angry. Yer family fights Bruce and yer position is perilous."

She hugged herself. She did not like the sound of that. "How perilous?"

"Bruce has heard they are here, Alana. I must take them prisoner."

She gasped.

"I am sorry," he said. He turned and started from the room.

For a moment, Alana stared after him, sick with dismay. She had to keep Joan and her sisters safe! But she could not fight the man she loved—and she dared not alienate Robert Bruce. If she did, she would have two enemies, Buchan and Bruce!

She leaped to her feet and ran after him.

Iain was in the hall, standing outside the chamber she had given to Joan and her daughters. Joan stood in the doorway tensely, as Iain said, "I have no choice, Lady Joan. But ye will be treated well, I can assure ye of that."

Joan's expression was ravaged. She glared at Alana, as if she blamed her for their capture.

Alana slowed. Iain was staring into the bedchamber. She had no doubt as to what had caught his attention— as to who had caught his attention. Oh, God. How could he look at Alice now? After they had just made love?

She walked up to him.

Alice stood with Margaret before the bed they shared, their hands clasped. She was terribly beautiful, her hair in one long dark braid, draped over her shoulder, her complexion perfect and pale, her lashes long and dark, as she stared fearfully at Iain.

Iain stared back and said, "Lady Alice, why dinna

ye and yer sister return to bed. I am sorry to have interrupted yer rest."

Alice trembled, unmoving. She did not release her sister's hand. Margaret stared at Iain, her eyes as huge as saucers. Then she looked at Alana.

Alana winced. Margaret had guessed that they were lovers. Either that, or she had been told.

"You will truly take us prisoner?" Alice asked harshly. She glanced at Alana now, fear in her eyes, as well as accusation.

"Aye. But ye will not suffer, I vow it. We will speak more on the morrow," Iain added. He then stepped aside so Joan could return to the room. "Good eve," he said politely.

"Good night," Joan managed to respond. She gave Alana another dark glance and shut the door abruptly.

Alana did not move. Iain had finally seen her sister, who was beautiful and powerful at once. He had seen the woman whom Bruce hoped to wed him to. She was shocked when Iain put his arm around her. "What are you doing?" she asked, attempting to push him away.

He gave her a puzzled look. "I dinna come all this way to sleep alone."

Alana was confused. "She is very beautiful."

His brows lifted. "Are ye speaking of yer sister?"

"Yes."

His stare was quizzical. "Margaret must be all of fifteen," he finally said. "And she is not as beautiful as ye."

Alana closed her eyes. "I was speaking of Alice and you know it."

"Alana." He pulled her into his arms. "I dinna want Alice, I want ye," he said.

Alana pushed against him, staring up into his smoldering blue eyes, shocked. "She is an heiress—the greatest heiress in the north of Scotland!"

"So?" He began to kiss her.

Alana pushed at him, stunned. Iain wanted her! She could not decide what that truly meant. Even if he desired her above her sister, he might still wish to marry Alice—or Bruce might insist he do so, and only a fool would object. Iain was no fool.

"Why do ye resist?" he murmured, taking her wrists and restraining her. Now he claimed her mouth with his.

Alana could not move, and as his lips plied hers, as his tongue sought hers, her frantic thoughts finally ceased. She moved into his arms, returning his kiss wildly.

IAIN HAD NO plans to linger. The siege at Balvenie was going well, so well they expected the castle to fall within days. Bruce had ordered him to march toward Elgin. Once Balvenie fell, they would attempt to retake Elgin another time.

Alana watched him eating ravenously the following morning. She was seated with him, as was Godfrey. Iain had not questioned her about him, and she knew he had somehow already known that Godfrey was free to come and go as he pleased. The men had greeted one another cordially, but warily, a moment ago.

Alana had thought herself as famished, until she had learned he must immediately leave, and that Balvenie would soon fall. Now she feared for her father's life again, but differently than she had from her visions.

"Will Bruce spare my father when Balvenie surrenders?" she asked.

He stopped eating abruptly, laying his knife down. "I will do my best, Alana, to see that he does."

She stared grimly at him. Prisoners caught by Buchan and King Edward were treated as traitors—they were executed, either by hanging or beheading. Her father could suffer the same fate, but he could also be exiled to one of Buchan's English estates. She was about to speak when she saw Alice and Margaret entering the room.

Iain glanced at them. "Good morning."

Neither woman spoke; both nodded hesitantly at him. Alana watched Alice closely now. She sat down as far from Iain as she could, at the other end of the table, near Godfrey, with Margaret beside her. Alana saw no sign of interest from her sister. She only saw fear and distrust—and tension.

But she was not relieved. Iain desired her over her sister, but in the end, that had nothing to do with a political marriage.

She could not worry about the future now. She had far more pressing concerns.

She faced Iain again. "If Balvenie falls, will you send word immediately?"

"Of course. And I'll send word about yer father."

She nodded, so frightened now, for Sir Alexander—and for herself. She glanced at Alice again.

She had been staring at Alana with intense dismay. Now, she ducked her head, and clasped a mug but did not drink from it.

Alana looked at Iain, expecting him to be observing her sister—but he was studying her, instead. "Walk with me," he said, suddenly standing. Clearly he meant to depart.

Alana stood, glancing across the hall. Joan had yet to come down, and she assumed that she had no intention of doing so, not while Iain was present. "I wish you could stay another day," she heard herself whisper.

"I wish I could, as well," he said. He suddenly tilted up her chin. "I will send word, and I will do my best to protect yer father."

He meant it, she thought, her heart swelling, but there was no predicting the revenge Bruce would wish to take upon any member of the Comyn family. Alana was about to walk with him from the hall when she heard racing footsteps. There was no mistaking the urgency in the sound.

Angus rushed inside, so intent that he did not close the front door. "We have just received this!" He handed Iain a sealed missive.

Iain broke the royal seal and unrolled the parchment. He read it quickly, his expression becoming troubled. Then he looked grimly at Alana.

Her heart turned over with alarm. "What is it?"

He glanced past her at her sisters. "Sir Alexander has been wounded."

Alana froze. The image from her vision, of her father as a bloody corpse, filled her mind. She fought to see Iain instead. "Oh, God." She realized she had seized his arm.

"He is alive, Alana, but he has been badly wounded, and he escaped Balvenie. He is at Elgin now."

Alana began to shake.

Her sisters ran up to them. "How badly?" Alice cried. "How badly is he hurt?"

Iain hesitated, his gaze on Alana. "He is dying," he said.

CHAPTER FIFTEEN

MARGARET WAS STARTING to cry, and Alice held her, her own eyes red. Alana felt the same terrible grief, or perhaps she felt even worse, for she knew that Sir Alexander would die. Her visions always came true, and now this one would, as well. She glanced at Godfrey. He was pale. But then, he knew about her vision of her father's death, too.

Suddenly Joan rushed into the hall with Eleanor. "What is happening? Why is Margaret crying? Who has come?"

Iain turned toward her. "I am sorry, Lady Joan, but Sir Alexander has been mortally wounded."

Joan cried out, her knees buckling, her face draining of all color. Alice left Margaret, rushing to her mother and putting her arm around her. "No," Joan whispered. "No."

Alana gazed at Joan and her daughters and felt a terrible pain. They loved Sir Alexander—far more than she, an abandoned child, ever could.

Godfrey came over and steadied her. Alana was grateful, but she saw that Iain was not. His eyes were wide and hard as he stared at them.

Alice suddenly turned to Iain. "We must go to him!"

Iain was forbidding as he spoke. "I am leading the

march on Elgin, Lady Alice. We will besiege it and this time, it will fall. It is not safe fer ye to go there."

"I don't care!" she cried. Tears began. She seized his arm. "I must see my father—he cannot die!"

Alana tensed, disliking the moment they were sharing. "It is not safe," he repeated. "And as much as I dinna wish to add to yer grief, yer prisoners here."

Alice cried, "He is our father! But you only care that we are your prisoners!"

Iain tensed with rising anger. "It is not safe—ye will wind up in the midst of a siege, and ye could die along with Sir Alexander."

Alice trembled with dismay, releasing him. "I will never marry you," she hissed.

Alana almost gasped. How had Alice learned of Bruce's interest in their union?

"I dinna realize there was to be a union betwixt us," Iain said coldly. "I am protecting ye, Alice, and I am protecting yer sister and yer mother, too."

"No. You are keeping us from Sir Alexander as he lays on his deathbed!"

Alana could not stand to hear any more. She left Godfrey's side, hurrying to Iain and touching his arm. "Iain. He is my father, too. I must see him. We all must go!"

Iain turned to her. "Alana, I cannot allow it."

Suddenly it was as if they were alone in the hall. She laid both her hands on his chest. "I am asking, no, begging. Take Joan and my sisters to our father. Delay the attack on Elgin. Take me to my father."

Iain inhaled, his gaze locked with hers, his expression grim. "They would take ye prisoner," he finally said. "Buchan would have ye locked away for the rest of yer life!"

"I don't care!" she cried, for in that moment, she was desperate.

"I care," he said. "No one goes to Elgin, except for me."

Margaret sank onto a bench and began to weep.

OUTSIDE, THE APRIL morning was sunny and bright, but Alana felt chilled to the bone as she stood beside Iain as he prepared to mount his steed and ride to war. The front gates were open, and she could see his Highland army, two hundred strong, milling about the ridge. His banner with its red dragon flew above it.

"Ye will forgive me," he said.

Alana could barely speak. She felt dazed. Her father was dying, Alice had heard about the marriage and Iain had denied them a visit to Sir Alexander. She found her voice. "I will probably forgive you, one day," she said hoarsely.

He seized her arm and pulled her close, kissing her roughly on the mouth. "I am going to war. I will think of ye every day, Alana."

"And I will think of you, every single day." His refusal to allow her to see her dying father did not affect her love. Nothing could affect her love for Iain, she thought. "And I will pray that God keeps you safe." She felt almost no emotion now—she felt nothing but the need to see her dying father one final time, even if it meant risking capture by her uncle.

She *had* to see Sir Alexander before he died. There was no choice. He was her father, and she loved him, in spite of everything.

"I am keeping ye safe, Alana," he said.

She could not smile at him. She knew what she must do. Part of her was afraid—of course she was. She had no wish to be captured by her uncle. Still cold, she hugged her light wool mantle closer to her chest.

He leaped astride his horse and galloped from the keep.

Alana did not wait to see him ride all the way through the entry tower; she whirled and ran into the hall, refusing to think, filled with determination. Joan sat at the table, weeping. Margaret held her hand tightly, red-eyed. Eleanor sat on her other side, offering comfort. Alice was standing with Godfrey, and they both whirled.

Alana halted. "We will ride to Elgin in an hour," she said. "Godfrey, you will guide us."

He paled.

No one spoke during the hard ride to Elgin. They kept to the main road, but were prepared to veer from it and into the woods at the first sign of any other travelers— or of any soldiers. At noon, Alana insisted that they pause briefly to rest, for it was clear to her that her sisters and Lady Joan were not up to the task of such a rapid and hard ride. And in the midafternoon, they heard thunder in the near distance.

Godfrey halted everyone abruptly. Thunder boomed again. Alana flinched, in that moment realizing that it wasn't thunder that they were hearing—it was the battering ram.

Iain had begun his siege.

The other women realized it, too, as they looked at one another with fright. "How will we get in during a siege?" Joan asked hoarsely. Her eyes were red from weeping. She had not been able to stop crying since they had left Brodie.

Now they could hear the frightened whinnies of horses, the shouts of men. They had not expected Iain to attack so swiftly. Alana rode up to Godfrey. "She is right. How will we get in?"

Godfrey gave her a look. "He will probably grant you anything."

"I already begged him to allow us to go to Sir Alexander!"

"I doubt you begged enough."

Alana began shaking her head. "We should tie the horses up in the woods and go on foot. Tonight, when the fighting stops, we can try to gain entry through a side door. You will be allowed in, Godfrey, surely, as will Lady Joan and the girls."

They dismounted and led their horses into the forest. As they walked along a deer path, the sounds of the battle growing louder, Godfrey said, "What if Buchan is there?"

Alana prayed that was not the case. "I have to see my father." She did not know what she would do if she learned Buchan was within Elgin.

Alice suddenly seized her arm from behind, causing her to whirl. "Why? You do not even know him! You cannot love him! You betrayed us and pledged to Bruce!" Tears streamed down her face for the first time since she had learned of Sir Alexander's wounds.

Alana cringed. "I do care. That is why I have risked Iain's wrath to bring us here!"

Alice released her horse and started running through the forest toward Elgin and the siege.

Alana was about to set chase, but Godfrey restrained her. "You cannot possibly reason with her now. And she will not go far."

He was right. She glanced at Joan and Margaret. To her surprise, Joan's eyes were not filled with hostility or hatred. They only mirrored grief, enough so, that suddenly Alana had the urge to comfort the other woman. But she did not dare do so.

They paused when they reached the edge of the woods, where Alice sat huddled beneath a pine tree. The hill beyond was bare; Elgin sat upon the adjacent ridge.

Iain's army was lined up there. Archers were firing upon Duncan's men on the ramparts, as they fired back. Other Highland warriors loaded and shot missiles from three catapults. A dozen men were working the battering ram upon Elgin's front gates. No one was yet attempting to climb the castle walls.

Joan and Margaret sat down with Alice under the pine tree. Alana now saw Iain upon his warhorse, riding back and forth along the ridge, directing his men. Some of the numbness within her faded. She watched a hail of arrows descend upon him and fear stabbed through her, but the arrows bounced off his shield.

Godfrey tied up their horses and turned to Alana. For a moment, he watched the battle, too. "He is right. You should not go within, Alana. You are a traitor. If my father is inside, if Buchan is, you will be seized the moment you are recognized."

Alana knew he was right. And for one moment, she thought of heeding Godfrey. But then she knew she must see her father one final time. She had to know why he had chosen Alice and Margaret over her; she had to know if he truly loved her at all.

She fought sudden tears. She had to know why!

"I have no choice," she said hoarsely.

"There is always a choice," Godfrey said.

TWO HOURS AFTER dark, the catapults ceased. The archers had already retired to their cook fires, and the battering ram had been parked with stone brakes. An eerie silence fell upon the night.

Godfrey led the women, all in hoods, from the woods and across the first hillside. By the time they reached the next ridge, Elgin a dark silhouette atop it, two more hours had passed. Unspeaking, they traversed a gulley in order to skirt Iain's entire army.

Margaret was the one who knew where the side door was. She had often used it as a small child, going outside to play with the dairymaid's children, in a time when the land was not at war, but at peace.

When they finally reached the door, Joan could barely stand, and both of her daughters held her up. Godfrey called out softly until the peephole was opened.

"Who goes there!" a soldier asked. Through the slit in the wood door, the whites of his eyes showed vividly in the dark night.

"It is Godfrey of Frendraught, and Lady Comyn and her daughters are with me."

The peephole was abruptly drawn closed. Alana trembled, and several minutes went by, but then the door was opened. "Godfrey?"

"Sir Edwain?" Godfrey asked.

"Good God, your father will be thrilled that you are

here." Sir Edwain pulled the door wide and the women rushed inside. He then shut it and bolted it behind them.

"Sir Alexander." Joan seized his arm. "Is he alive?"

"Yes, but barely, my lady," the knight said grimly. He glanced briefly—curiously—at Alana. "I will take you to him."

As they rushed across the bailey, Godfrey asked, "So my father is here, defending Elgin?"

"Yes, and we have been expecting the earl at any time."

Alana's heart leaped with relief. Her uncle wasn't at Elgin—not yet. She only had to fear discovery by Duncan. She tugged her hood up higher, until the brim fell across her forehead.

"My friend, let us take the ladies to Sir Alexander, and then I will seek out my father," Godfrey said, but in a tone of command. Alana knew he meant to protect her from Duncan.

They soon entered the castle. Inside, torches lit the walls, and weeping could be heard. As they hurried to the stairs, they passed a pile of dead soldiers. Amongst them was a very young, freckled boy, and Alana looked away, trembling.

When would men realize that no good ever came of war?

They raced up the narrow stone stairs and onto the second floor. The torchlight in the corridor was duller now.

Alana's heart turned over hard. Ahead, a door was open. Inside, the room was lit by candles and with firelight. And she knew exactly what she would next see....

Joan whimpered. Alice broke into a run, rushing inside ahead of them. She screamed.

Joan and Margaret followed, Alana staying behind them. They faltered upon the chamber's threshold. Alana looked past them.

Sir Alexander lay upon the bed, his clothes soaked with his blood. His face was so white and still, he looked like a corpse. His weapons lay in a pile on the floor.

Alice held his hand, but she dropped it and whirled, fury in her eyes, her tone. "How dare you come with us!" she screamed at Alana. "Traitor! Whore! Be gone! Leave us alone! Go back to your Highland lover!"

Alana flinched, but otherwise did not move. Joan ran to her husband and sank onto the bed, taking his hands in hers. "Alexander," she cried. "It is I, Joan. I love you! You cannot die!"

"Father!" Margaret dropped to her knees by his shoulder. "Please don't die. Please don't leave us."

Alice glanced from her sister and father to Alana again. "Go away," she said.

Alana hugged herself. "He is my father, too."

Choking on tears, Alice knelt beside Margaret. "Father? Can you hear us? Please, wake up!"

Godfrey touched Alana from behind. "You should speak with him now, and I will get you back outside, before I seek out Duncan."

"I can't," she whispered, stricken. "I have to say goodbye, too!"

Godfrey grimaced. "Then I will do my best to keep Duncan away from this room." Suddenly he seized her arm and their gazes locked.

Alana froze, for an instant thinking he meant to

kiss her. Instead, his gaze darkened and he turned and hurried away.

"Joan?"

Alana jerked as Sir Alexander whispered his wife's name. She saw his lashes fluttering as he attempted to open his eyes.

Joan stroked his forehead. "We are here, darling. I am here with the girls."

"Alice?" he gasped. "Margaret?"

"They are here," Joan whispered.

Alana felt dismay stabbing through her.

"We are here, Father," Margaret cried.

He turned his head slightly toward his daughters. He seemed to smile. "Alana?"

Alana started crying. She went forward. "I am here, also…Father."

He was still gazing at Alice and Margaret. "I love you so." He suddenly looked at Alana. "I love you. I always have."

The tears streamed down her cheeks. Alana somehow nodded. But his eyes were closed. "Oh, God," she gasped, terrified that he was dead.

Alice laid her ear upon his chest. She looked up. "He lives."

Still clasping both of his hands, Joan said, "Try to give him some water."

Alice took a mug from the side table. She sniffed it then tried to entice Sir Alexander to drink. But he lay unmoving and unconscious.

Alana realized they would keep vigil now, until he died.

She glanced around the small chamber for the first

time. She retrieved a small stool and brought it over for Alice to sit upon. As Alice sat, their gazes briefly met.

She then rolled up a rug and gave it to Margaret as a makeshift seat. Margaret smiled weakly at her, her blue eyes bright with tears.

Alana stood at the side of his bed, with Joan and her sisters, and she thought, *I do love you.* But she wished he would explain to her, so she could understand, why he had left her to be raised by Eleanor, why he had chosen his other daughters over her.

THE FIRE BEGAN to go out, some hours later. The room felt terribly cold. No one wept anymore. Outside, a dull light stained the night.

Alana got up and went to the fire and poked it with the iron. Flames hissed.

"Elisabeth."

Alana whirled at the sound of her father's voice. His eyes were wide-open and so very blue and he smiled, the smile of someone happy and surprised. She did not know who or what he was looking at.

And then the light was gone.

Joan cried out, collapsing upon him, weeping.

"No!" Alice and Margaret cried as one.

Alana stared at her father's sightless, lifeless eyes. He was gone.

She hugged herself, fighting not to cry, wondering if he had actually called out her mother's name with his last dying breath. And as she stood there, shaking and shaken, the night sky blushed pink. The shadows inside the chamber lightened.

The sun was about to rise, and when it did, Iain would renew his siege.

She wanted to hug her father as her two sisters and Joan were doing. But she was afraid to insert herself amongst them. And time was running out. She had to leave.

Alana wet her lips and managed to speak. "It is dawn. The siege will soon begin. Sir Alexander wanted you safely out of harm's way.... Joan? We should go."

Joan was sobbing softly, clasping her husband's lifeless hands to her breast. She could not respond, but Alice whirled, her arm around her weeping sister. "We cannot leave him!"

Alana blinked back tears. "I am afraid for you if you stay here."

"What difference will it make?" Alice said. "Iain took us prisoner, if we stay here, he will do so again."

She had never been in a siege, Alana thought. "Or you might suffer injury or death during this battle."

Alice's eyes widened.

There was a sound at the door, and Alana turned, expecting Godfrey.

The Earl of Buchan smiled coldly at her.

Her heart seemed to plummet through her entire body. She cried out, backing up into the bed.

"So the whore dared to enter my castle," her uncle snarled. His eyes were hard and cruel.

Her heart exploded with panic now. She could not move—she could barely draw a breath.

Joan stood up. "He is dead, John. Alexander is dead."

The earl barely glanced at his brother. "I was told he would not live." His burning gaze held Alana's. "But some good will come of this night. I punish treason with death, Alana," he said.

"No," Joan said instantly. Alana started. "She brought us here, risking her life to do so, and she is your niece. Alexander is—was—her father!"

Alana was shocked that Joan would defend her now.

"I do not care!" Buchan strode forward, hand raised. Alana ducked, but too late. His blow was severe, and it knocked her off of her feet, onto her father's lifeless body.

Alana cried out in pain as Joan gasped. Alice stared, horrified, while Margaret screamed, "Stop!"

Alana pushed herself up to stand, but then Buchan seized her hair and jerked her hard toward him. She gasped as she crashed face-first into his legs. He then kicked her hard in the ribs. Alana careened onto the floor, buckling over. Tears of pain blinded her.

"Ye will die for touching her," Iain roared.

Alana looked up as he moved past her, sword raised. On the floor, on her hands and knees, Alana realized that he was going to kill her uncle. She was shocked, as this was not the vision she had had!

But Buchan seized Alice, pulled her in front of him, and laid a dagger at her throat. "I have heard you bed one sister, but will wed the other," he said.

Iain froze, his sword in midair.

Buchan smiled. "Drop your sword, Iain. Or watch your bride die."

Joan cried out.

Iain dropped his sword, and did not reach for the other sword on his left hip.

"John! My God! Alice is your niece!" Joan begged.

Buchan moved toward the door, dragging Alice with him, using her as a shield. No one spoke, everyone watching him. Alana still crouched on the floor while

BRENDA JOYCE   351

Iain remained in the room's midst, as still as a statue, as watchful as a hawk.

Buchan went through the doorway with Alice, who was white with fright, her expression one of desperation. They turned right and disappeared from sight.

Iain knelt down beside Alana. "I will kill him," he said, reaching gently for her.

"I am fine," she told him. "What will he do to Alice?"

"When he loses this war, she will be a useful hostage to him," Iain said, helping Alana to stand. "And yer not fine." He tilted up her chin, his gaze on her jaw, which was surely turning black-and-blue, for it throbbed so badly. "Ye disobeyed me, Alana, damn it. I ordered ye to stay at Brodie. I forbade ye coming here!"

"I could not obey, Iain! Oh, God, he has Alice!" Alana cried, genuinely frightened for her sister. "We must help her!"

His glance flickered toward Sir Alexander, then Joan and Margaret, who held one another. "I am sorry, Lady Joan." He retrieved his sword.

"He has lost his mind!" Joan was crying again. "His brother is dead and he has abducted Alice! Why? To use her against Bruce one day?"

Iain's grim expression was answer enough. "Wait here." Iain turned and strode from the chamber.

Alana started. Images from her vision flashed in her mind—of Buchan, about to murder Iain. She hesitated. Then she took up her father's short sword and raced after Iain, who was at the end of the corridor. "I am coming with you!"

He whirled, incredulous. "Go back to the bedchamber, Alana," he ordered.

She ran up to him. "I can't let you hunt Buchan alone!"

"Ye defied me by coming to Elgin—and ye openly defy me now? To my own face?"

"I wish to help you, Iain!" she cried breathlessly. Alana ran past him. Where would Buchan take Alice? Would he take her up to a tower room, to imprison her as he had imprisoned Alana? She started up the stairs.

Iain quickly seized her arm, then rushed past her to lead the way. There were no torches lit in the stairwell, and it was almost as dark as the night. "Ye think he's gone to the closest tower." It was not a question.

"I do."

"We must be wary," he said softly. "Duncan is within, too. However, he is probably on the ramparts, wondering why I have yet to begin the siege."

Alice nodded, even though Iain could not see her action. He reached the landing and paused until she was beside him. They started down the hallway. On the farthest end, the Earl of Buchan stepped out of a chamber.

Buchan saw them and froze; Iain broke into a hard run, sword raised. Alana ran after him.

The earl withdrew his sword, backing into the room he had come from. He slammed the door closed.

Alana knew Alice was within, she was certain. Iain was ahead of her—she could not keep up with him—and he reached the chamber. Alana ran up to him, panting.

He gave her a terse look. "Ye stay here, in the hall, ye dinna come inside. This time, ye obey me."

Alana nodded.

"Vow it," he said.

She hesitated. "I can't."

He was disbelieving. Then he reached for the door's iron handle. To their surprise, it lifted in its latch— Buchan had not slid the bolt inside.

Iain gave her a sharp glance, nodded and pushed open the door. He did not move as the oak door swung open.

Alana glanced past him. There was no light inside the chamber. She saw nothing but dark shadows.

A few sconces boasted torches in the hallway, however, so they were in the light.

"Alice?" Iain spoke.

There was no answer. There was no sound at all now, except for Alana's heavy breathing.

Her heart raced. She imagined Buchan within, her sister in his grasp, his hand covering her mouth. She looked up at Iain. He gave her a warning glance, one she knew meant that she was to stay still. "Be careful," she mouthed silently.

He stepped back, away from the open doorway, closer to her. As he did, he pulled the chain and cross he wore from his neck. He tossed the necklace into the room.

The gold made a soft metallic sound as it hit the stone floor. And then they heard the scrape of leather soles on stone, just to the left of the doorway.

Buchan had dragged her sister farther away from the door, Alana thought. And as she had that notion, Iain charged within. "A Bruce!" he roared.

Alana raised her father's short sword, rushing inside after him.

Buchan stood to the left of the door, and he released Alice so he could raise his own sword and meet Iain's onslaught. Their swords clashed viciously and rang.

Alice stumbled. Alana lowered her sword to seize her hand and pull her toward the doorway. She glanced at Iain—he and her uncle were locked in battle, blade to blade, Iain savagely intent, Buchan appearing frightened.

"You came back for me?" Alice gasped.

It took Alana one second to make up her mind, as she watched the men disengage and then strike at one another again. This time, their swords shrieked so loudly, it was as if someone had pulled on the wrong strings of a harp or violin.

"Go! Go back to Joan and Margaret, then find Godfrey if you can and leave the castle!"

Alice's eyes went wide. Then she nodded and ran off.

Alana faced the two men inside and saw that Iain had backed her uncle into the far corner of the room, and he was smiling ruthlessly now. But before he could deliver a fatal blow, she heard the many booted footsteps racing toward her from the stairwell. Alana saw Duncan, Godfrey and another soldier rushing up the hall. She screamed in warning. "Iain!"

But he had heard them, too. And for the first time since finding the Earl of Buchan, Iain glanced at her—away from his enemy.

Fear seized her—Iain was engaged with Buchan, and Duncan would surely capture her. "It is Duncan, Godfrey, one more," she gasped, raising her sword to defend herself.

The Earl of Buchan snarled, "You're finished now, Highland dog."

But Iain did not hear him. Either that, or he did not care. He leaped away from Buchan, rushing toward

Alana at the door. Clearly his intention was to defend her now.

Buchan rushed after him, sword raised. His expression was vicious, his eyes murderous. It was déjà vu—it was her vision come true.

"Iain!" Alana screamed in warning.

Iain turned and met the blow with his own sword, so hard, that Buchan's sword was driven from his grasp, and it fell, clattering across the floor. Iain ran to her just as Duncan came into striking distance. Duncan snarled, the sound animal-like, thrusting his blade toward her. From behind, Iain roared, leaping in front of her and deflecting the blow. Their swords screamed.

Alana watched the two men strain against one another, and knew this was a different match entirely—Duncan was a seasoned soldier, unlike her uncle. But Duncan also had Buchan and the other men to help him bring Iain down.

She turned. Buchan had just staggered to the doorway, sword in hand. But Alana saw blood on his sleeves—he had been wounded in the earlier fight.

There was no time for any sense of relief. Godfrey suddenly turned and pushed his blade against the throat of the soldier behind him. "Alana, go, go now!" he shouted.

Alana froze, realizing what Godfrey was doing—he had trapped his father's soldier against the wall so she could flee. She looked back at Iain, as he and Duncan parried violently another time. Iain's blow was so powerful that Duncan was propelled back into the wall. Iain struck again and Duncan's sword arm shot back into the wall, and he released his sword, which tumbled away.

Iain turned to look at Buchan. Her uncle raised his sword, staring back.

Alana knew what he meant to do. "Iain!" she screamed. "We must flee!"

She knew Iain had heard her, and that he understood fleeing was the best course of action at this moment. But determined as he was, he reacted instantly, savagely striking at his enemy. Buchan was driven from his feet, but he managed to hold on to his sword. And there was no more time; they had to escape. Iain leaped past Duncan, took Alana's hand and they were flying as if on wings, past Godfrey, past the soldier and down the hall and stairs.

They fled through the downstairs, past awakening housemaids and soldiers, and through the hall. In the next corridor Alana saw her two sisters and Joan, slipping outside. They ran after them.

Alice cried out when they reached them. Iain took the lead and they hurried after him, across the back courtyard. Two boys with a wagon filled with wood gaped at them. And then someone shouted out in warning from the ramparts above.

Ahead, Alana saw the small side door that they had used last night to enter Elgin. A pair of Iain's Highland warriors stood there guarding it.

"Who goes there?" Someone shouted from the ramparts above them. "Identify yourselves!"

They were but strides away from that door. While Buchan's and Duncan's men were atop those walls, Iain's men were outside them.

"It is I, Lady Comyn, Sir Alexander's wife," Joan suddenly shouted, slowing down as she did so.

Alana did not know what to do, and did not have

to decide. Iain seized her and dragged her to the door and pushed her though it.

"Sir Alexander is dead," Joan cried loudly. "The Earl of Buchan is wounded. And Duncan has just been defeated.... We are fleeing Elgin, as you should!"

Alana heard her every word and gasped, as Iain shoved each of her sisters in turn through the small door. "Lady Joan!" he barked.

She came running to him then, while a commotion began on the castle walls. Dozens of soldiers appeared, staring down at them in confusion. And then Joan and Iain, followed by his two men, were safely outside. As they ran from the castle, a dozen of his mounted warriors galloped up to them to protect them from Elgin's archers. But no arrows were fired at them.

CHAPTER SIXTEEN

WHEN THEY WERE safely in the midst of Iain's men, dozens upon dozens of mounted soldiers between the women and the enemy soldiers atop Elgin's walls, Alana sank to the ground. She began to shake wildly.

Sir Alexander was dead. She would never see him again. But he had told her that he loved her, and that he always had.

Buchan had almost succeeded in abducting Alice, in her own stead. Alana and Iain were so very fortunate to have escaped Elgin with their lives. As she realized that, she heard the battering ram striking the castle's front gates. Iain had renewed the siege.

Swarms of arrows whizzed in the air as the archers upon the ramparts began firing back at Iain's army.

A man screamed as he was struck.

Alana looked away from the battle, deciding they were at a safe distance from it. Alice and then Margaret collapsed on the grassy ground beside her, breathing hard. Margaret gazed at her fearfully. Alana took her hand, which was trembling, thinking not about the war, but about their father. She would never know him now, not truly. They would never become close. She glanced at Alice.

"I am sorry," Alice whispered, her eyes filled with tears. "That I said those terrible things to you."

"It doesn't matter," Alana said hoarsely.

"It matters. It matters very much. You loved our father, too."

"I did." Alana trembled. "Why? Why did he love you and Margaret more than me? Why did he raise you, but not me?"

More tears filled Alice's eyes. "I don't know."

"It was because of my wishes." Joan stood above them, devoid of all color, her eyes bleak with grief, with hopelessness.

Alana wanted to hug herself, but Margaret would not release her hand. She squeezed it harder, instead.

"Elisabeth was more than my cousin, she was my friend. We both loved him, but he was my betrothed. When I found out, I hated her," Joan said. She dropped to her knees. "And I blamed her, not Alexander, for their affair." She shrugged. "Alexander had no choice. I gave him no choice. He was not allowed to bring you into our lives."

Alana realized she was crying.

"You sent Iain of Islay after Alice," Joan said unsteadily. "And you went with him. Why?"

Alana bit her lip, shaking her head. "She is my sister." She glanced at Alice and their gazes locked.

Surprised, Alice said, "You sent Iain to rescue me? After all the hateful things I said? After how I have treated you?"

"Yes," Alana whispered.

"But you love him," Alice cried. "And you sent him into the enemy's lair—and you went yourself—for me."

Alana nodded. "I could not leave you behind," she said.

A silence fell over the group, but the sounds of the

battle intensified around them. Joan sat down, seeming exhausted. Alice quickly put her arm around her. "I miss him," Joan whispered.

"We all do," Alice said unsteadily.

Margaret continued to grip Alana's hand. "Will we go back to Brodie?" she whispered.

Alana stared at her, certain she was thinking about the fact that they were Iain's prisoners once again. She recalled the promise she had made to her father—to keep her sisters and his wife safe. Grief flooded her. She closed her eyes, determined to keep her vow.

"Alana."

Iain's voice caused her to jerk and look upward. He sat astride his huge warhorse. "I am sending ye back to Brodie with six of my men."

She stood up slowly. Her limbs felt useless and weak. "Brodie is hours from here—we do not need such a large escort." She did not want to deplete his forces.

He suddenly slid down from his horse, took her arm and began walking her away from the other women. "I want ye safely home."

She trembled and clasped his cheek. "Thank you for going back for Alice."

His eyes darkened. "When I come to Brodie, ye will explain to me why ye defied my command."

She grimaced. He was referring to her taking her sisters to see Sir Alexander at Elgin, against his explicit orders. "I am too tired to argue."

He seized her chin and kissed her hard on the lips. "I will come when I can."

She tensed, sick with dismay, with dread. "Will Elgin fall? And after Elgin, then what?"

"Until Buchan surrenders, or is killed, we will war on the north." He was final.

She somehow nodded, knowing that if he had not had to get her out of harm's way, he would have killed Buchan when they were inside Elgin. She realized the sacrifice he had made for her sake.

For one moment, his stare held hers, and then he turned and leaped effortlessly astride his stallion. He galloped toward his soldiers and into the fray of shouting men, whistling arrows and frantic horses.

ANOTHER NIGHT HAD fallen, this one bright with stars and a crescent moon. Alana stood outside upon the ramparts of the watchtower, filled with grief over Sir Alexander's death.

They had arrived at Brodie in the early afternoon. Alana had gone into Eleanor's arms, finally allowing herself genuine tears. Joan, Alice and Margaret had retired to their bedchamber. They had not come out since.

Alana wiped her eyes. She had so many questions now, and not just about her father's choice to surrender to Joan's dictums, but about his life.

She wiped her eyes again, as a wolf howled, perhaps from a nearby ridge. And she thought of Iain, whom she already missed terribly.

He did not die by Buchan's sword, and she thanked God. She thought about her vision—it had been as accurate as all of the other ones she had had. In it, she had never seen Buchan murder Iain. He had merely been poised to do so. She could not help wondering if her vision had come so that she could warn Iain—saving his life for the second time.

But there was danger still. Buchan lived. He would

seek to destroy Iain again—just as Iain sought to destroy him.

She wanted to know how the battle for Elgin had gone that day. She hoped Iain would send her word, and soon. God, if only Buchan would surrender or die, so this terrible war could end, so they could pick up the pieces of their shattered lives.

But then what? She did not want to really consider the future—for in it, Iain might wed her sister, and Bruce had promised her another man as a husband.

The wolf howled again. It was a cool April evening, and Alana turned and went down the stairs, crossing the courtyard. Iain was probably inside his tent, drinking wine and planning the next day's siege. She wondered if he missed her as much as she did him.

She entered the hall. It was empty.

It was so strange, being home at Brodie without Godfrey. Somehow, he had become her best friend.

What would Duncan do to his own son for his treachery? Worse, what would Buchan do? She would never forgive herself if he came to serious harm, because of her.

Alana started upstairs. Everyone was asleep, and the castle was stunningly silent. In her chamber, she shed her mantle, closed the shutters and put on a sleeping gown. She was too tired to braid her hair, and she left it down. However, in spite of her exhaustion, she did not think she would sleep at all that night.

"Alana?"

She whirled at the sound of Alice's voice. Her sister stood in the doorway, dressed for bed, her eyes red from weeping. Alana had the urge to rush to her and take her into her arms. But she did not move.

Such an impulse was premature at best, rash at worst.

"May I come in?" Alice whispered.

"Of course." Surprised—and filled with hope—Alana turned and poured her sister a mug of wine. She handed it to her, taking one for herself. Alice hesitated and Alana sat on the bed, leaving room for Alice to join her.

But she did not. "I have come to thank you for everything that you have done for me, my sister and our mother."

"I do not need or want your thanks," Alana began.

"No!" Alice cried. "You defied Iain to get us to Father before he died, and then you had him rescue me, putting him at great peril. And you went with him—putting yourself in peril, too. You are brave and good and I was so mean to you."

They were forging a truce, Alana thought with excitement, with hope. "I am not brave, Alice, I was very frightened, but not as much for myself as for Iain."

"You love him, truly?"

Alana inhaled. "He is the only man I have ever loved." Alana felt herself begin to blush. She looked down. "He is the only man I have ever been with."

Alice sat down beside her. "Then you must truly love him."

"I do."

"But we hardly know one another. Why, Alana? Why risk his life for me?"

"You are my sister, even if we are strangers." How she wanted Alice to understand.

But Alice shook her head. "But you pledged your

fealty to Robert Bruce. How could you be so loyal to me and so disloyal to our family? I cannot understand."

Alana wet her lips, wondering how she could explain. She finally said, "Have you heard that I am a witch?"

Alice paled, her eyes widening. "Is this a jest?"

"No. I have visions of the future, Alice, and I have had them since I was a small child. Our father gave me some land for a dowry, but no man would have me, because of my visions."

Alice's eyes were as huge as saucers. "Did Father know?"

"Yes." She smiled, but it felt tight and odd. "I am a bastard and a witch. When I was eight, our uncle gave Brodie to Duncan, and made me his ward. I have grown up unwanted and unloved, as well as ostracized and shunned. The exception, of course, being my grandmother."

"But Lady Fitzhugh isn't really your grandmother."

"No, she is not. But she has always loved me as if we are flesh and blood."

Alice was shaken. "I grew up with two doting parents, with nurses and maids, with silks and velvet... always knowing that I would one day marry a fine nobleman with titles and lands."

"Yes," Alana said softly. "You are so fortunate. I did what I had to do in order to regain my mother's lands, Alice. It was a horrible decision to make, but now, I have no regrets—Brodie is all that I have."

"We have had such different lives," Alice mused. Her eyes darkened. "It isn't really fair. But you do not seem bitter."

"I have been bitter. At times, I have been jealous and resentful."

Alice suddenly laid her hand on her arm. "If you were truly resentful, you would not have defied Iain to take us to Elgin, and you would have let me suffer at Buchan's hands."

Alana shook her head. "I was his prisoner once. I was afraid for you—I could not bear it if you had suffered as I did."

"I am so sorry I was mean to you when we first met. Alana, I was the jealous one then."

"What could you have been jealous of?"

Alice shrugged helplessly. "Father told us about you. He told us he loved you. I was afraid of you—afraid Father loved you more."

Alana was in disbelief. Sir Alexander had told her sisters that he loved her! She realized that some small vulnerable part of her had been in doubt over his last words. But her father had genuinely loved her.

She gave in to impulse. She hugged her sister briefly. To her surprise, Alice hugged her back. Then she stood up. "Can we begin anew? As friends? As sisters?"

"Yes," Alana answered, feeling dazed. But didn't every coin have two sides? Didn't the phoenix rise from the ashes? For now, it seemed as if her father's death was giving her a family after all. "Alice? I made a promise to our father that I would keep you safe. I am going to do everything in my power to get you to England."

"That would be wonderful...but you will defy Iain yet again? For us?"

"I am a woman of my word," Alana said. "And I

believe he will find it in his heart to forgive me." She somehow knew her words to be true.

But what about Robert Bruce? He would not be pleased if she helped her sister, a valuable hostage, to escape. Alana feared Bruce's anger—but she must help her sisters and Lady Joan, anyway.

Alice was suddenly tearful. She smiled and put down her mug. "You are truly my sister!" she exclaimed, hugging her again. She stepped back. "It is late. I should return to my bed." She went to the door, and then paused. Very seriously, she faced her again. "Alana? I would never marry him, not when you love him so."

Alana exhaled in relief.

THE SPRING TURNED warm, the days lengthened and another week passed, but with agonizing slowness, ending with a terrible jolt. For Alana received a missive from Iain, one filled with ill tidings. Sir John Mowbray had violated his truce with Bruce, and had brought a great army to Elgin to relieve it from Iain's siege. Iain could not predict how long it would now take for Elgin to fall—or if Buchan's stronghold would actually capitulate.

Alana was despondent. She was sick and tired of the war. And while Margaret seemed oblivious to the news—she was still grieving over their father's death— Alice was pleased. They were becoming friends now, but nothing could change the fact that they remained on opposite sides of the war. Alice did not want Elgin to fall. She wanted Bruce's defeat, even if she never spoke openly about it.

Yet somehow, their new friendship blossomed. Long

walks outdoors turned into long conversations, mostly about Sir Alexander, and his virtues, his character and his life. Alana finally began to understand the man that her father had been—a man of honor, a man of courage, with great strengths, and some weaknesses. And she loved him more.

The sisters began to spend the evenings together before the fire in the great hall, sipping wine and hoping for the war's end. Alana learned that Alice was intrigued by a young nobleman she had met once, a few years ago—Henry de Beaumont. When she spoke of him, her blue eyes sparkled and lit up.

All the women plotted together, trying to find a course to help Joan and her daughters flee to England. Alana knew that it must appear as if she were innocent in this plot, as if her sisters and Joan had escaped her, as well as Iain, so that Bruce would not hold her to blame.

By week's end, Joan had written a dozen letters to English noblemen opposed to Bruce, begging for their assistance. She wrote the letters in private so no one could claim that Alana knew of them. Joan then bribed the two messengers with gold to deliver the missives for her—so it was as if Alana did not know of the conspiracy to escape.

Their best hope was John MacDougall, Lord of Lorn, who was related to the family. His mother was a Comyn, the daughter of John Comyn, Lord of Badenoch. John had been fighting Bruce for the past two years, and had decimated his army two summers ago at Dalrigh. He had a great many ships in the eastern seas and Joan thought him their best chance of escape.

The next week began with heavy rain. It was pouring out when Godfrey walked into the hall, shaking the water from his mantle.

Alana had been repairing one of Iain's leines. She threw it down with a glad cry and rushed into Godfrey's arms. "I have been so frightened for you!"

He enclosed her hard in his embrace. Alana suddenly realized their position and she tensed, but he immediately released her. "So you have a care for me after all," he teased.

"You know I do. We did not hear any word about your fate—what happened, Godfrey?" She took his arm and guided him to the table while ordering a maid to bring food and wine.

"Buchan accused me of being a traitor. But my father actually defended me. As it turns out, he cares because I am his only male heir." He was grim. "And then Buchan fled the siege in the middle of the night. I was encouraged to leave."

"Are you at odds with Duncan?"

"Terribly so, but I am his heir," Godfrey said flatly. "I suppose he will forgive me, in time."

Alana hoped so. "Where is Buchan now?"

"He is with John Mowbray, attacking Iain from his flank."

Alarm stabbed through her. "I am so glad you are unharmed. Is Iain in danger?"

"Every battle is dangerous, for every man." Godfrey turned to the women, greeting Lady Joan, Alice and Margaret. He then went to Eleanor and they briefly embraced.

When he sat down, Alana sat down beside him. "Will you stay long?"

"I cannot. I am joining Buchan and Mowbray,

Alana. I have sat out this war for entirely too long."
He withdrew a rolled and sealed parchment from beneath his mail.

She did not recognize the seal; Joan did. She cried
out. "That is the MacDougall crest!"

Alana glanced around—they were entirely alone in
the hall, with no servants to witness them. "How did
you get this?" she whispered.

"I met the messenger on the road, purely by chance.
I believe Sir John must be eager to help Lady Joan and
her daughters, for he is vehemently opposed to Bruce."
Godfrey took up a cup of wine and drained it.

Joan stood and took the parchment. Alana nodded
at her. Joan hurried away to read it privately. Alana
looked at her sisters and saw the excitement and hope
on their faces. Alice inhaled and held out her hand.
Alana took it and squeezed.

Godfrey glanced quizzically at her.

Alana whispered, "I must not be a part of this."

"Of course not," Godfrey said, smiling slightly.

Joan returned, without the missive. She sat down
next to Alana, and whispered, "Can we get to Dunstaffnage? If so, John's ships will take us to Carlisle."

Alice and Margaret trembled with excitement;
Alana looked at Godfrey. The stronghold was far to the
southeast of them, just across from the isle of Lismore.

"If you are not captured by Bruce's soldiers, the
journey is easy enough, directly down the great glen,"
Godfrey said.

"What will we do when we get to Carlisle?" Alice
asked, flushing. Her eyes were bright with hope.

"I will write Sir Henry Percy again," Joan said
swiftly. "Surely, if Sir John can deliver us to Carlisle,

Percy can arrange passage for us to one of King Edward's estates."

Alana faced Godfrey. "My soldiers are sworn to Iain," she said, low. "They will have to travel in disguise—I have two men I trust, to escort them."

"You have three," Godfrey said instantly.

Alana seized his hand. "You would do this for me?"

"Yes, Alana, I would." He turned to the three women. "There is every chance you will be discovered. Are you certain you wish to flee?"

"We must try!" Alice cried.

Alana trembled, thinking not of Bruce, but of Iain now. She would claim innocence to the king, but she would not deny her hand in this, not to Iain. "Lady Joan, please write to Sir Percy instantly, for as soon as we receive his vow of aid, we can reply to MacDougall, and accept his offer." She breathed hard.

Godfrey looked at her. "You are a courageous woman, Alana le Latimer."

She met his unyielding gaze. "I promised Sir Alexander I would see them safely to England."

Godfrey stood. "Iain will forgive you. He would forgive you anything, as long as he has your love."

He sounded envious, she thought. Alana hoped he was right.

ALANA POUNDED THE dough with her fists. They had not had a good loaf of bread in weeks, but yesterday she had gone to the market with a large escort of soldiers for more provisions, never mind that she and Eleanor hardly cared whether they had bread on the table or not.

Joan and her sisters had left three days earlier, and by now, they must be at Dunstaffnage—unless they had been captured. How she missed them, and how she missed Godfrey! Alana inhaled. Joan had promised to send word the moment they arrived at Sir John's fortress. She was praying for a messenger at any time.

She began to roll the dough, sorrow sweeping through her.

She had become so quickly attached to her sisters, and when they had hugged and said goodbye, everyone had been in tears. Alice and Margaret had promised to write. Then Alice had seized her hand.

"No matter what happens, we will always be sisters and friends," she had said hoarsely.

They had embraced, hard.

Alana sighed, shaping the dough into an oval. How she missed them all—even Joan.

"Alana?" Eleanor hurried into the kitchen. "There is smoke on the horizon."

Alana stared at her grim grandmother, then removed her apron and hurried from the kitchen, Eleanor behind her and unable to keep up. She ran from the hall and outside, realizing that several of Iain's soldiers had gathered atop the watchtower. She crossed the courtyard and rushed up the narrow stone steps.

"What is it?" she cried.

Angus faced her. "There is fighting close by," he said.

It was a beautiful May day. The sky was the bright blue of a robin's egg, with an occasional fluffy white cloud. The sun was high and strong. The hills bloomed with yellow wildflowers and purple thistle. But in the north, a dark pall hung over a distant ridge.

"Do we know who it is?" Alana asked. "Are we in danger?"

"I have sent a scout, my lady," Angus said.

Could Iain be there, just miles away, in the midst of battle? She had not heard from him since he had retreated from Elgin. Word was that Bruce's army was to the southwest, near Aberdeen, and that Buchan's army was in hiding. But such news was not confirmed, and Alana did not know if another battle was imminent or not.

That night, the scout returned. Alana was seated with Eleanor before the fire in the hall when Angus came striding inside. "There is nothing to fear," he said. "Kincorth has been razed to the ground. So has the village of Kinloss."

Alana nodded, reaching for Eleanor's hand. Those were Buchan lands. "Was it Iain?"

"We dinna ken, my lady," Angus said.

She trembled, recalling his ruthless devastation of Nairn. But this was war, and until it was over, the innocent would pay, as well as the enemy. There was nothing to be done now, Alana thought, except to wait for word from Joan, a missive from Iain and the end of the damned war. If only he would come to her.

She had never missed him more.

THE DAYS GREW warm. She received a letter from Joan— she and her daughters were safe at Percy's Carlisle estate, awaiting word from King Edward as to their disposition. Alice and Margaret enclosed letters, as well. They were relieved to be safely in England, and prayed for Alana's safety. Alice wished they could have a reunion in London one day. Alana read her words and felt close to tears.

Iain did not send word. He did not send a messenger, either.

"Why hasn't he sent me a letter?" Alana cried in frustration to Angus. She was worried, as well.

"It is gossip, my lady, but it is said that Bruce is hunting Buchan now, fer he has finally recovered from the illness that plagued him all winter. I have heard his army has been seen near Inverurie," Angus said. "Ye will hear from Iain soon, my lady, I am certain of it." He smiled encouragingly at her.

And finally, a messenger came from Iain.

Alana ran into the courtyard, as fast as her legs would carry her. Angus and a dozen Highlanders stood there, next to a beaming soldier with long blond hair. Her heart felt as if it might explode inside of her chest. Clearly, the news was good!

"My lady!" The tall blond Highlander turned, smiling. "I have word from Iain of Islay."

Alana halted, panting, hands clasped to her chest. "Is he well?"

"He is more than well, my lady! Bruce has defeated the Earl of Buchan—he has defeated the baron Mowbray—their army has been scattered to the four corners of this land!" the messenger cried.

Angus and his men began to cheer.

"What?" Alana gasped, in disbelief.

"Bruce has crushed the Earl of Buchan! And his army has been entirely dispersed. The earl has fled—he is in hiding—and we believe he will go to England."

Alana reeled. "Buchan's army is truly finished?"

Angus steadied her. "There is no army left, my lady," he said.

Oh, God, she thought. "The war here in the north? Is it over?"

"It is over." The messenger grinned. "And Iain wishes ye to know that he will come to ye here at Brodie as soon as he can."

Tears blinded her. Iain was safe. Her uncle had no army left, and he was running away to England. "Thank you," Alana whispered. "Thank you."

IT WAS A late June day. Alana galloped a gray mare across the countryside with an escort of soldiers behind her. Buchan had been defeated a month ago, and Iain had not returned. Alana could not stand the waiting. She had taken to riding every day, galloping hard and fast across the countryside, jumping fallen trees and streams.

If only Iain would return!

The signs of the war were everywhere, just beyond Brodie's walls. The ridges were scorched. Villages had been reduced to ashes, manors to rubble. Livestock wandered loose, seeking fodder. Beggars were on the roads. Forests that had been green were blackened and burned.

She wondered when the Harrying of Buchan would end, and if it ever would. Robert Bruce clearly meant to bring the defeated earldom to its knees. His vengeance knew no bounds. He would destroy every living thing, or so it seemed.

"Lady!" Angus cried.

Alana saw the banner on the horizon at the exact moment that he spoke. She pulled up her mare abruptly, her heart lurching with excitement. Oh, God! It was Iain!

A moment later he came galloping over the horizon

upon his dark warhorse, a dozen Highlanders behind him, his banner with its red dragon whipping in the wind above them.

Alana bit her lip, crying.

He thundered toward her, his long dark hair flying about his shoulders. And then he halted beside her, his mount rearing.

"Iain," she whispered, crying helplessly now.

He leaped from his stallion, reached her in two long strides and pulled her into his arms, embracing her as if there was no tomorrow. He kissed her deeply, for a long, long time.

And then she was smiling up at him and he down at her, while she remained wrapped in his arms. "You are home," she whispered.

"I am home," he said, pulling her even closer against his hard body. "I have missed ye terribly, Alana."

"I have missed you." She strained to kiss him again, and they kissed for a very long time.

When he pulled back his eyes were fierce with passion. Alana touched his rough cheek. "Is it over?" she whispered.

"Buchan is in England, Alana. He has no army now, and they say he is ill—very ill, perhaps dying."

She recalled Buchan's cruelty and shivered. She would not care if he died.

He stroked her hair. "Lady Joan has been openly claiming that Alice is the next Countess of Buchan. If Buchan dies, I believe there will be a great fight over the earldom."

"But Bruce controls the Buchan lands."

"Aye," Iain said, his gaze holding hers.

There would be another war, she thought, with dread. "There will always be another war, won't there?"

"'Tis the way of men," he said.

She took his face in her hands. "I have missed you so!"

"Alana." He was firm, attracting her entire attention. "I am home for a time, and I dinna wish to think about war."

She gasped. "You called Brodie home!"

He slowly smiled. "Aye, I did…if yer here, then I am home."

She clung to him in disbelief. "Iain—what are you saying?"

"I am saying that it is time we made another child. But not a bastard."

She began to shake. She could not breathe properly. The love in her heart took her breath away, while the desire in her body made her feel faint. "Not a bastard?" she echoed, dazed.

"Ye wish to marry me, do ye not?" he said, smiling wickedly.

She inhaled. "You will tease me now about such a thing?"

"Ye asked the Bruce fer my hand in marriage," he laughed.

"I did!" she cried, pounding a fist on his chest.

His smile faded. He caught her hand and raised it to his lips and kissed it. "I asked the Bruce fer yer hand in marriage, Alana," he said.

She reeled. "But I am not a great heiress…. What about Alice—the next Countess of Buchan?"

"No. Yer no great heiress, just a small one, and I dinna care that ye only bring me Brodie." He swept her hard against his aroused body. "I have loved ye fer a very long time, Alana le Latimer, and it's time I made ye my wife."

Tears of joy streamed down her face now. He swept her up and placed her atop his charger, and then leaped astride behind her. Clasping her firmly about the waist, he spurred his mount forward, toward Brodie—toward home.

* * * * *

Dear Readers,

I hope you have enjoyed Alana and Iain's story as much as I have. Once again, my muse led me to portray a small, brave woman fighting for her life and her love in a bygone and dangerous world dominated by men. As you know, this is a theme that I have returned to time and again, for nothing fascinates more than a woman confronted by male power—and triumphing over it in the end by bringing that man to his very knees out of pure love and raw passion.

While Alana is a fictional character, her family is not. Joan le Latimer was married to Sir Alexander Comyn, the sheriff of Aberdeen, and the Earl of Buchan's second brother. She did have a cousin, Elisabeth. However, I have entirely fabricated the story of their lives. If Elisabeth fell in love with her cousin's fiancé, much less had a love child with him, it would be a great coincidence—and so very cool!

Donald of Islay was the cousin of both Alexander and Angus MacDonald. Angus Og gave him command of a Highland army, and he was sent to fight for Bruce. Donald was one of four brothers, the youngest being Iain. I found no mentions of Iain in history otherwise, and chose to use him as this story's hero. Obviously I have entirely fictionalized his life.

The other major historical characters that I have attempted to portray are the Earl of Buchan and Robert Bruce. I have characterized them for my own ends—portraying them in a manner that is the most dramatic possible, to best enhance Alana and Iain's love story.

This is the third story I have written that is set during Bruce's bloody quest for Scotland's throne. In 1307, Bruce began his campaign to destroy the Earl of Buchan and the entire Comyn family, once and for all. By the summer of 1308, Buchan's armies were decimated and scattered to the four winds, with Buchan having fled to England, where he would soon die. Bruce then began his infamous and merciless Harrying of the North.

Alice Comyn was the Earl of Buchan's heir. She married Henry de Beaumont sometime before July 1310, and the couple put forth their claim to the Buchan earldom, resulting in a long struggle that was one of the causes of the Second War of Scottish Independence.

This novel is a work of fiction. This period in Scotland's history is filled with conflicting accounts and huge gaps in information, allowing me to pick and choose what I want to write, how I want to write it, while permitting me to fill in any blanks any way I wish. I have put Alana and Iain's love story ahead of historical accuracy. While most of the battles, incidents, events and characters are a part of history, I have exercised poetic license throughout. Any errors in fact are mine.

Happy Reading,
Brenda Joyce

New York Times bestselling author

RaeAnne Thayne

Lucy Drake and Brendan Caine have only one thing in common...

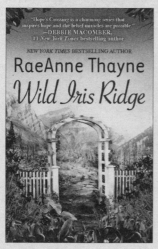

And it's likely to tear them apart. Because it was Brendan's late wife, Jessie—and Lucy's best friend—who'd brought them together in the first place. And since Jessie's passing, Brendan's been distracted by his two little ones…and the memory of an explosive kiss with Lucy years before his marriage. Still, he'll steer clear of her. She's always been trouble with a capital *T*.

Lucy couldn't wait to shed her small-town roots for the big city. But now that she's back in Hope's Crossing to take care of the Queen Anne home her late aunt has left her, she figures seeing Brendan Caine again is no big deal. After all, she'd managed to resist the handsome fire chief once before, but clearly the embers of their attraction are still smoldering….

Available now wherever books are sold!

Be sure to connect with us at:

Harlequin.com/Newsletters

Facebook.com/HarlequinBooks

Twitter.com/HarlequinBooks

www.Harlequin.com

REQUEST YOUR FREE BOOKS!

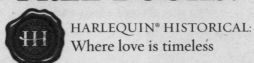

HARLEQUIN® HISTORICAL:
Where love is timeless

2 FREE NOVELS PLUS 2 FREE GIFTS!

YES! Please send me 2 FREE Harlequin® Historical novels and my 2 FREE gifts (gifts are worth about $10). After receiving them, if I don't wish to receive any more books, I can return the shipping statement marked "cancel." If I don't cancel, I will receive 6 brand-new novels every month and be billed just $5.44 per book in the U.S. or $5.74 per book in Canada. That's a savings of at least 16% off the cover price! It's quite a bargain! Shipping and handling is just 50¢ per book in the U.S. and 75¢ per book in Canada.* I understand that accepting the 2 free books and gifts places me under no obligation to buy anything. I can always return a shipment and cancel at any time. Even if I never buy another book, the two free books and gifts are mine to keep forever.

246/349 HDN F4ZY

Name _____ (PLEASE PRINT) _____

Address _____ Apt. # _____

City _____ State/Prov. _____ Zip/Postal Code _____

Signature (if under 18, a parent or guardian must sign)

Mail to the **Harlequin® Reader Service:**
IN U.S.A.: P.O. Box 1867, Buffalo, NY 14240-1867
IN CANADA: P.O. Box 609, Fort Erie, Ontario L2A 5X3

Want to try two free books from another line?
Call 1-800-873-8635 or visit www.ReaderService.com.

* Terms and prices subject to change without notice. Prices do not include applicable taxes. Sales tax applicable in N.Y. Canadian residents will be charged applicable taxes. Offer not valid in Quebec. This offer is limited to one order per household. Not valid for current subscribers to Harlequin Historical books. All orders subject to credit approval. Credit or debit balances in a customer's account(s) may be offset by any other outstanding balance owed by or to the customer. Please allow 4 to 6 weeks for delivery. Offer available while quantities last.

Your Privacy—The Harlequin® Reader Service is committed to protecting your privacy. Our Privacy Policy is available online at www.ReaderService.com or upon request from the Harlequin Reader Service.

We make a portion of our mailing list available to reputable third parties that offer products we believe may interest you. If you prefer that we not exchange your name with third parties, or if you wish to clarify or modify your communication preferences, please visit us at www.ReaderService.com/consumerschoice or write to us at Harlequin Reader Service Preference Service, P.O. Box 9062, Buffalo, NY 14269. Include your complete name and address.

HH13R